Where Love Is Found

Tiya Rayne

Where Love Is Found: -- 1st ed.

ISBN-978-1-093529-53-1

DEDICATION
TO HARRIETT, MY REAL LIFE GRAMS. AND TO THE REAL DUCK, I HOPE YOU FIND YOUR JACKSON.

CONTENT

ONE

"Ooh, baby! This pussy is so good," Cliff moaned as he buried his face back between my legs.

He wasn't telling me something that I didn't already know. My pussy was damn good. And I'm not being cocky or conceited when I say that. Every woman should feel the same way. If you don't, you're not living at your full potential.

Between every woman's thighs is the source of all power. It brings life into the world. Every person you have ever met has gone through a pussy at some point in their life, either through ejaculation, artificial insemination, or birth. Hell, men have started wars for what's between a woman's legs. They murder, go broke, and leave their wife and kids for the right pussy.

So, I didn't feel like a bitch when I replied, "It sure is."

I ran my hands over Cliff's low-cut waves.

Damn, he could clean a coochie out. Cliff's tongue game was top rated, which was why I kept him in my rotation.

Another life tip: every woman should have three types of men in her rotation. Number one, a good coochie eater. I'm talking about a man that will go down on you at the drop of a dime. He will feast on your goodness like it is the bread of life. You need someone that can suck your soul out, have your toes curled, and have you speaking in foreign languages. There is nothing better than some good head.

The second type of man you need on your call list, is a king dick. A man that's hung like a horse. One that can relocate your damn ovaries while he's up in you. Sometimes you need that dick that leaves you paralyzed for a few days. It will have you walking like

1

you've been riding a race horse. You should be drooling while he's knocking your walls loose.

The last man you need in your rotation, is the sex scholar. Someone that can read your body like a well written book. A man that knows what he's doing. This guy doesn't necessarily have a big dick, but can work you over with what he has. He's just the right type of nasty, and knows when you need it fast and rough or slow and deep. He can play your body like Stevie Wonder can play a damn harmonica. He's usually the first one you call when you need some. He was born to fuck.

If you have these three diverse types of men in your arsenal, you're on the right track. And if you find a man that can do all three, then wake your ass up because you're probably dreaming.

I'm brought back to the moment with a moan when Cliff added two fingers into my tight heat hitting that bundle of nerves perfectly. That's all I needed. I came on a loud moan and a gush of sticky liquid. Like a pro, Cliff slurped up every bit of me like he was drinking through a straw. Damn right he should.

If a man can't finish the job by drinking down every ounce of your juices, leaving not even a drop to run down your thighs, then he has no idea what the fuck he is doing, and you need someone more qualified.

Cliff climbed up from between my legs, placed a kiss above my navel, and then laid on his back beside me. I glanced at the clock on my night stand. 9:45 a.m. Nothing like starting your day off with an orgasm. I rolled out of my California king bed and pulled my robe off the bottom of the bed before slipping it over my body.

I took a minute to admire Cliff. Smooth chocolate skin stretched over a well-toned athletic body. High cheek bones and a face chiseled by the gods. His eyes are the color of honey shaded by thick curly lashes. Thick full lips and a full beard. The man was gorgeous. Too bad his dick was severely average. His tongue was the only reason this brother got a call from me.

"I'm heading to take a shower, you can relax as long as needed. Just long as you're ready to leave when I am."

He looked over to me with a cocky smile on his face. The smile a man gave when he thought he'd laid pipe in bed. His arms were behind his head. His dick was sticking straight up beneath his gray jogging pants.

Some men should be banned from wearing jogging pants.

"Damn, you ain't even gone get your boy off?"

I rolled my eyes at his request. "When I sent you the text to come over, did it not entail that this was for me and me only? You could have said no."

I had no shame in telling him this.

How many booty calls had a man made where he got his, and the woman was sent home with an over worked pussy, messed up hair, and nothing else to show for it? At least I let him know upfront what to expect.

Cliff chuckled. He still thought my brutal honesty was my way of being funny. If he only knew.

"I know, baby! But damn, you got a brother hard as shit with that tasty wet pussy."

I didn't comment, instead I headed for my attached bathroom.

"Aye, Charli, wait!"

I stopped in my tracks and watched him lean up from the bed. His brown skin looked delicious against my creamy white Egyptian cotton sheets. He better be glad he's fine as hell, lord knows he had shit else going for him.

"So ummm, next week my mama's having a cook out, and I thought maybe you would like to go?"

I lifted one of my professionally threaded eyebrows at him. My hands crossed over my chest lifting my . c-cup breasts higher underneath the silk robe.

"And why the fuck would I do that?"

Cliff ran a hand down his face. He's trying me again. For the last few weeks, Cliff had been trying to upgrade himself in my life. First, he started giving me sob stories about needing money in order to spend more time with me— that shit was never going to work. Then he started to mention things about "our" future. Now he wanted me to meet his mama. Hell No!

"I'm saying, we been together for 6 months. I think it's time we take our relationship to the next level."

What fucking relationship? I called him only when I needed my pussy ate and every so often I will grace him by riding his dick to the heavens, however that does not make a relationship. I didn't do relationships. Ever.

"We have not been together six months."

"Five and a half, then. Does that really matter?"

Yes, muthafucker, it did, because at the six month mark was when I usually served men their exit papers. Which you will obviously be receiving today.

"Cliff, you know my rules." My hands slid from under my breasts to my hips. "You said you were fine with them."

"Yea! I was, but I'm not with my girl any more. I called it off last night."

"Are you out of your fucking mind?" I shouted!

"Damn, Charli," He stood to his feet and snatched his shirt off my floor, roughly pulling it over his head. "I thought you would be happy that you don't have to be my side chick anymore. I'm trying to upgrade you to my main girl."

At this I laughed.

"Honey, first of all, I was never your side chick. The term side chick implies that we have a relationship, and we damn sure don't have that. Plus, how the fuck would me being with you be an upgrade?"

"What is that supposed to mean?" He squared his shoulders and folded his arms over his chest. His attempt to intimidate me would have made me laugh if I wasn't so pissed off.

"Cliff, you work the grill at Waffle House. Now don't get me wrong, there is nothing wrong with honest work, but you've only had that job for three weeks. Before that, you were unemployed and living off the girl you just dumped. Now, let's do the math, you just ate my pussy on thousand-dollar sheets. Your crusty-ass feet are rubbing against a Persian rug that cost more than everything you own, combined. Not to mention you pulled your busted-up Cutlass through my gated community, into my marble driveway and parked it in one of my six car garages. Now tell me again, how does me upgrading to your main chick benefit me?"

I could see the egg and anger all over his face. This fool had clearly lost his mind.

I never brought up money around the men I fucked. You could take one look at me and tell I wasn't hurting for it. So when I chose a man to take to bed, he didn't have to make the same bank as me. I never felt like a man had to match my check, few will. The fact that Cliff didn't have shit was never an issue for me, but today, he needed to be checked.

"Oh! You're so quick to throw your money up in my face, but I'm the guy you call when you want some dick. I'm the one laying pipe. If I walk out that door, you won't ever find another man that can lay it down like me."

I laughed so hard tears came to my eyes. It made it even funnier that he was deadass serious.

"Boy, Bye! You should really leave before you say something that will get your feelings hurt." I turned towards my bathroom, done with this dude.

"Don't fucking walk away from me, bitch!"

My head snapped around so fast I could've needed an exorcism.

"You did not just call me a bitch?" Now he was about to get the truth. "You actually think you're the only man I have on speed dial for dick? Baby, you aren't even on my favorites list. The only reason you got called this morning, is because your bum ass was the only one that could get here fast enough. And if it wasn't for your tongue game, you wouldn't have even gotten a call back with that basic ass dick. Don't get mad at me because you thought you were going to use me to make a come up. Thought I didn't know about the holes in your condoms? You're a dumb ass if you thought I would be foolish enough to get pregnant by you. I told you not to let your girl go. You thought I was joking?"

"Yo, fuck you, Charli!"

"Trust me, you've tried and failed."

He took a step towards me like he had the notion to put his hands on me. I knew he wasn't that dumb. When he raised his hand and brought it across my cheek, it only took the few seconds after I hit the bed for the impact to register. This muthafucker just hit me. My hand slipped in between my head board and mattress and retrieved the little .38 I have stashed back there. My papa didn't raise a fool. I aimed the gun at his head, and he had the right mind to step back.

"Aye yo, put that shit up, Charli. You don't know what you're doing with that."

"My granddaddy is from the back woods of Alabama. I was learning to shoot a gun while you were still shitting in your diapers. I can hit a mark from fifteen yards away. Trust me, I know what I'm doing."

I clicked off the safety causing the sound to echo in the quiet room.

"Right now, that should be the least of your concerns. See, you let this big house and bougie attitude fool you. I'm from the West end, born and raised. I still have family there. Hell, I could shoot you and have my cousin and his boys dispose of your body without anyone ever finding out. Or maybe, I'll call my connection at the police department and have him do it for me. Luckily for you, I have shit to do today. So, I'm going to give you a choice. You can either walk out my door and never come back, or your mama will be planning a funeral instead of a cook out. The choice is yours."

I watched the sweat drop from his brow and run down the center of his nose. I couldn't believe this worthless man had the audacity to put his hands on me. I should've shot his dick off for that alone.

He wisely backed away from me, grabbed his shoes off the floor, and continued out of my bedroom. I followed him with the gun still aimed at his head. When he got to my front door and stepped on the other side, I could see some of his courage came back.

"You will never find another man like me, Charlice."

"That's the point." I kicked my front door shut in his face.

Well, that's the end of Cliff. I slipped the safety back on my gun and headed back to my shower. It's Sunday, and I can't be late to Grams'.

TWO

Every Sunday, rain or shine, my family met at my Grams' house for dinner after church. This tradition had gone on for as long as I could remember. Of course, the family had grown over the years.

Charlie and Sadie Jeffries had five children. Their oldest was a son, Ellis Sr. I don't remember much about him. He died in 1991 during Desert Storm. His flag and pictures are displayed on the wall in Grams' house. Uncle Ellis only had one child, Ellis Jr, or Eli.

Eli was one of my two favorite cousins. He's a few years older than me, and he's been in trouble with the law a few times, but not since I got him a job working security for my office. He and I were raised in the same house after his father died. We're like siblings. Eli understands me more than anyone else in my family.

Josephine—or Aunt Joe as I know her—is the second oldest of Grams and Papa's kids. Josephine has been with Uncle Kenny for forty years. They have three children together, seven grandkids, and still aren't any closer to getting married. From Aunt Jo, I have my cousins: Kenny Jr—the basketball coach, Keva—the deacon's wife, and Keisha—the professional baby mama.

The family thought for the longest that Kenny Jr. would be their claim to fame. He was an outstanding basketball player in high school and even went off to college to play for free. However, his lack of control and inability to take responsibility for his actions got him kicked out. He was lost for a while, until about three years ago when

I got him the job at my old high school coaching boys' basketball. It's amazing what you can get approved when you're fucking the district superintendent.

The next child in the Jefferies household was Aunt Vivica. She's married to Uncle Walter— who never comes around. Rumor has it, he and Papa got into a huge argument the day Uncle Walter and Aunt Vivica got married, and he was no longer welcomed in Papa's house. Even so, I still had a better relationship with Uncle Walter than I did with my aunt.

Between my two aunts, Vivica and I have the rockiest relationship. For some reason, she has never liked me.

Aunt Vivica and Uncle Walter have two daughters; Chante is the oldest and married to Quincy, the lawyer. Grams likes to say Chante and her husband have champagne taste with a beer budget. Quincy makes good money, but he out spends his means. Always wanting to keep up with me and the partners at his law firm. He's a long way from matching my pocket.

Devin is Aunt Vivca's youngest daughter. She's not only my second favorite cousin, but also my best friend. The girl has a talent for doing hair. I've been trying to convince her to go back to school and get her cosmetology license so I can buy her her own shop. Unfortunately for Devin, she let that four-letter disease drag her down. Love. Her senior year in high school she fell in love with some no-good deadbeat named Miles that got her pregnant. Now she's stuck with two kids, another on the way, and a man that doesn't want her to better herself. I think he doesn't want her to do anything with her life because he enjoys the perks of living off the state. Hard to get food stamps when your meal ticket owns her own business. She's blindly in love, and he's a controlling fuck up. Despite how much I push, she won't go against his request.

The youngest and only living son of my grandparents, is Martin. He and his wife live in California with their three sons. They don't visit.

The last Jefferies child is my mother, Bernita, or Nita as my family calls her. I'm Nita's only child. To say my mother and I have an estranged relationship, would be an understatement. I haven't talked to my mother since she dropped me off at my grandparents' doorstep when I was sixteen. She packed up and moved on with her then boyfriend, Ricky, the stock broker.

There are only three things Nita loves: herself, men, and money. There is no room for anything else in her life. Not family, and damn sure not a child she never wanted. She rarely ever comes home to visit. The only time any one hears from Nita is when she's between men and in need of money. Last time Grams mentioned her, she was down in Florida somewhere working as a bartender.

The speaker in my Audi A6 cut off and was replaced with the ringing of my cell phone. I hit the hands-free option on my steering wheel. I smiled because I already knew who it was.

"Hey, Grams! How do you like it?... And before you object, it's already paid for."

Since I was a little girl, I've had a knack for business. I've been making my own money since elementary school when I was selling shitty handmade bracelets at top price. The love of business traveled throughout my life. I graduated at the top of my class at Emory University, and came out the gate making $80,000 a year at Piers Consulting firm as one of their consulting associates. After getting my Masters in Marketing at Harvard, I realized my full potential and started my own consulting firm.

The Partners and Senior Partners at Piers thought I was insane for passing up the type of money they were paying to branch out on my own. But my Papa once told me that if you want to be successful in the world, you have to follow your passion, not a paycheck. I knew I could do it on my own.

Eight years later, I'm the queen of Consulting. Charlice Rose consulting is the most successful consulting firm in the South East. My people and I travel all over the world fixing companies. I specialize in marketing, but I have people under me that can fix anything from management, to leadership, to training. My business has afforded me lots of amenities, and one of the things I like to do with my money, is spoil the woman on the other end of this phone.

"Charlice-Rose Jefferies, you are a mess. I knew when Eli came over this morning before church something was going on. This is too much."

For the last few months Grams had been complaining about her stove. I've offered to buy her a new one a hundred times, just like I've wanted to buy her a bigger house—she refuses every time. So instead of buying her a bigger house, I paid off the one she has, and a few years ago, had it remolded by adding an extra bathroom and enlarging their master suit.

Today she came home from church to a brand-new stove and refrigerator. It's all Subzero brand. The stainless-steel gas stove had six gas burners and built in double ovens. The refrigerator has French doors with a touch screen computer system on the front that can help you track your grocery list and everything else. It's probably all too much for Sadie Jefferies, but she deserved it and so much more.

"Grams, I want you to have the best. Plus, if it wasn't for all your good food, I would probably starve to death." I joked only slightly.

Her boisterous laugh came through my speakers. "You're right about that. You need to be over here learning how to cook. One day you're going to settle down and find a man that you will need to cook for. Not to mention when you have me some great-grandbabies."

I flinched at the mention of kids.

"Now, Sadie," I said, using her real name jokingly, "you know I'm never getting married."

"Duck." I rolled my eyes at the nickname I received as a child. "You need to settle down and start a family and stop spending your money on us old folks. We don't want you wasting your hard-earned money on us."

"Speak for yourself, woman." I heard my grandfather's voice in the background.

I laughed at his outburst.

I never had a chance to be a daddy's girl. I wouldn't know my biological father if the man was standing in front of me. Knowing Nita, she probably doesn't know him either. My Papa has always been the man in my life, and I am truly a Grand-daddy's girl.

I could imagine him climbing in his recliner in nothing but his tank top, worn jeans, and white knee socks. All my life, Papa has been the same. The moment he was home for the day, he changed out of his clothes and climbed in his recliner to watch TV. He worked all his life, never getting higher than a fourth-grade education. He retired from the Brick House when he was still in his late twenties, and later retired from working for the highway department when he was in his late fifties. Now he spends his days fishing, working around the house, and in that recliner—like I want him to.

"Hey, Papa!" I said loud enough for him to hear me.

"Hey, little Duck! You on your way?"

"Yeah, I'm stopping to pick up my contribution to dinner first."

"Is it one of those strawberry cheesecakes from that factory?"

I chuckled. "It can be."

"You spoil him." Grams' voice finally cut back in on the phone. "The new pastor couldn't even go pray for Sarah Hurst today, because your grandfather kept going on and on about his new fishing boat you got him. He even invited the man and his wife to the house for dinner today, just so he could show it off."

"Sarah Hurst is always needing prayer. Pastor will have plenty of chances to pray for her."

"Charles Howard Jefferies, you know you ain't right." My grandma tried to scold her husband, but her voice told me she wasn't really mad.

I laughed through the phone at their antics.

If I could find a man like Charles Jefferies, I would probably settle down, but I was positive my grandmother had found the only man worth loving.

"You still there?" Grams asked.

The sound of the TV faded in the background which let me know she was walking away from my grandfather.

"Yeah, I'm here."

Grams sighed. "Your mother called me today."

Now I know why she walked away from Papa. Not only are my grandfather and I a lot alike, we both have the same dislike for Nita. Grams was the only one in the family that still spoke to her.

"Grams, you know I don't care…"

"I don't know what happened between you and your mother. Lord knows neither of you will tell me, but it's time for ya'll to bury this."

This was a conversation I hated to have with Grams. She still believed there was a chance for Nita and I to make amends, but our relationship was irreparable. Nothing could ever fix it.

"Now, I know Nita has her ways, but I really believe she's changing. She's been talking like she has more sense lately. She even asked about you and mentioned coming home for a visit soon. She also been goin' to church a lot."

I knew Nita better than anyone. When I was seven, she dated a Muslim named Rasheed. She had both of us cutting off meat and wearing head wraps. At nine, she dated Daniel who was Rastafarian. She started smoking weed, growing her own herbs, and even tried to

11

dread her hair. So I knew my next question was valid.

"Let me guess, is the new man a deacon or a minister?"

Grams sighed again on the other end of the phone. "A bishop."

I laughed so hard tears formed in my eyes.

"Grams, the only person Nita is fooling is herself. As soon as this man's money runs out, or he gets hip to the type of woman she really is, she will be back to her old ways."

"I don't think he has any money. I had to send her...." She trailed off knowing she'd said too much.

"Tell me you aren't sending that woman the money I give you."

"You watch your tone, young lady. Now I have my own money aside from what you give me. And if you have a problem with how I spend the money you give me, then you don't need to give me any more money."

I pulled up to a red light behind a huge Dodge truck that looked like it was in dire need of a wash. I ran my hands through my wavy chin length asymmetrical bob.

I loved Grams, but she has a weak spot for her kids. Nita being her biggest weakness.

"I'm sorry, Grams. I just don't want you to spend your money on someone that will never appreciate you."

That was Nita's biggest problem. She believed everyone owed her something, and Grams and Papa were horrible about letting her have her way. Not even my other aunts could get away with the shit she did. It wasn't until I was in undergrad that Papa finally changed his opinion. However, Sadie was still blind to Nita.

"A mother's job is always thankless, Duck. You will learn that when you have your own kids one day." There's that word again.

The cars in front of me started to move, so I removed my foot off the brakes to roll forward.

"Your Uncle Martin called me too..."

I lost focus. I didn't notice the dirty truck in front of me had slammed on brakes. My reaction was too slow, and I hit the back of the truck.

"FUCK!" I shouted.

"Charlice, what was that noise? And why are you cursing? Are you alright?"

"Grams, I have to go. I'll see you in a few."

I clicked the button on the steering wheel to disconnect the call, then followed the truck into the median and cut my car off.

Shit, this wasn't how I wanted to spend my Sunday. First that asshole Cliff, and now a damn car wreck.

A burly white man stepped down out of the truck. A large black dog stuck its head out of the driver's side door, but the man said something, and the dog backed away. The white guy turned towards me. He was huge, what I would call husky, but in that still hot way. He's also tall, maybe 6' 6". His black v-neck t-shirt fit snugly around his huge biceps and outlined the definition in his pecks. His thighs looked like tree trunks in his dark wash denim pants and that dick print was lovely.

Damn! I could only imagine if it was that big in denim, what it would look like in some sweatpants. He folded his arms across his broad chest impatiently when it took me too long to climb out of my car.

I couldn't believe I'd been sitting in this car checking this man out. I'm a connoisseur of fine men. It doesn't matter the race, I just enjoy the sight of them. However, my legs would only spread for a brother. I was once with a Hispanic guy, but that was the furthest I've strayed from black men. So even though I have taken the time to check out this man's body, there won't be any hanky panky with him.

I opened my car door and climbed out.

"I'm so sorry!" I apologized right away. "No matter the damages, I'll pay for it."

The burly man's eyes dropped down from my face to my feet then back up again in slow motion.

Was he checking me out?

His arms lowered down to his sides as his eyes, they were stunning hazel by the way, met mine again.

"No worries, ma'am. It was just an accident." A sexy southern accent fell from his mouth. His tongue then ran over his bottom lip—a plump lip that's slightly bigger than his top and stood out amongst his dark blonde full facial beard.

"Besides, there isn't much damage to my truck. Although your hood may need to be touched up."

I looked at both cars. I didn't realize how much trouble it would be to take my eyes off the man. Those deep-set eyes and thick bushy eyebrows was causing a sister to be distracted.

He was right though, his truck looked untouched, and other than a little bit of paint transfer and scratches, my Audi was fine.

"Still, you could be hurt. Do you need me to call an ambulance?"

He smiled, and fuck me, my pussy got wet. That smile was sexy as hell. Even under all that facial hair, I could tell he had deep dimples the way his cheeks dipped.

"It will take a little more than a little tap on my fender to hurt me. If you haven't noticed, I'm a big man."

I tried to fight it, but I couldn't. At his words, my eyes dipped down to that lovely dick print in his pants. When my eyes looked back up at him, I could tell he knew exactly what I was thinking about. He smirked, and my brown skin flamed with embarrassment.

"I guess you're right. At least let me follow you to a mechanic so I can make sure there are no damages."

Despite the usual protocol where I would try to deny all fault and get out of paying this guy anything, I knew I was in the wrong, and this could have ended a lot worse than a little paint transfer.

"It's all good, gorgeous. But if you want to make it up to me, how about coffee?"

Ok, white boy! I recognized him trying to take his shot. I admired his confidence, but I wasn't interested.

"Nice try, but I'm actually headed somewhere. I will leave you my card though."

I headed back to my car where I searched out a card. When I turned around to hand him the card, he was right up on me, and his eyes were obviously staring at my ass. I smiled, I thought white men liked their women small in the hips and larger up top. The way his eyes stared at me, led me to believe he was an ass man. Lord knows I have enough of it. I was average in the tits department, but I have ass and hips for days.

I handed over my card, and he read it. I waited for that spark to appear in his eyes like it does every man that read my card and realized I'm THAT Charlice Rose. However, his eyes didn't spark, and he didn't even look at the card long enough to read anything but my name.

"Well, it's nice to meet you, Charlice Jefferies. I'm Jackson Keller and just because we can't get that coffee today doesn't mean it can't still happen. There is no expiration date to my offer."

His persistence and charm made me smile. I liked him, I If he were black, I might've even made a detour to my dinner plans and fucked him in the back of his pickup.

"Tell me something, Jackson Keller, do you always hit on the women that you've run into?"

That gorgeous smile lit up his face again as he folded his arms over his chest. "Not always. And remember, you ran into the back of me, so maybe this is your M.O. Do you always run into the back of an unsuspecting man, then climb out of your little car looking beautiful just to turn down his coffee date?"

I laughed and placed my hands on my hips.

"You've discovered my plot," I said jokingly. "Now you'll tell everyone, and it won't work again."

The smile remained on his face as he continued to stare at me. Those stunning hazel eyes crinkled around the edges as he took me in. From the spark in those hazel eyes, I could tell he liked what he saw.

I dressed down today in a plaid button-down Rails Hunter Shirt, AG brand skinny jeans, and Christian Louboutin pointy toe pumps. I didn't even do a full make-up, just a little foundation to cover up the mark that asshole left, some eye liner, and mascara. It was empowering to know that he'd been checking for me and I wasn't even at my best.

When he took longer than expected to respond, I lifted a curious brow at him.

"You sure you're ok?" I asked with a smirk.

"I'd be much better if you took me up on my offer."

Was he really still trying this?

I liked him, I'll admit, but it didn't change anything.

"Call me if you find any problems with your truck, Jackson Keller," I announced as I backed away from him and climbed into my car.

"I'm a very persistent man, Ms. Jefferies, especially when I see something I like." He hit me with that smile and wink. I was definitely going to have to change these damp panties.

"I can appreciate a little game of cat and mouse. Maybe I'll see you around, Mr. Keller."

I had no business encouraging this man. Especially when I had no intentions on anything coming from it, but he's been the first guy since high school to catch and hold my attention on a level more than just the carnal. Don't get me wrong, the lust was definitely there.

A big country white guy had actually hit on me. That was different.

THREE

After stopping by the Cheesecake Factory for my Papa's favorite dessert, I arrived at 4200 Oak Moore Drive—my childhood home.

After my fender bender with Jackson, I was running a little behind. I noticed that most of my family was already there.

As soon as I climbed out of my car with the cheesecake, a black Chevy Impala pulled up behind me. Its music blasted out the car even with all the windows up. I watched as Eli got out the passenger side of the car, tugging up his pants. He gave the driver a quick handshake before closing the door. The car didn't drive off, instead the driver window rolled down.

"Heyyyyy, Duck?" Douglas, my cousin's home boy, called out the window to me, dragging out the word hey.

I smiled as I waved. "Hey, Dougie!"

"When you gon' marry me, girl? You know I'm saving myself for you."

"Boy, Bye!"

I laughed as Eli threw up his middle finger to his friend. Dougie waved one last time before reminding Eli to bring him a plate and drove off. I was still laughing when Eli approached me. He reached out for my face with a scowl on his. It wasn't until his finger glided over the bruise on my cheek that I realized what he was doing.

"Do I need to handle a muthafucker?" he asked, and he was all serious now.

I wasn't lying when I told Cliff that I had a cousin that would help me dispose of his body. Hell, if I told him to, Eli would finish the job I started, but my cousin had come a long way from his troubled past, and I was determined to make sure he never went back.

"No worry, cousin. You know Papa taught me well. That .38 helped him see the error of his ways." I cracked a smile.

It took a minute for the smile to appear on his face, but eventually, it did. He dropped his hand away from my cheek.

"As long as you handled it."

"I did. Now, let's talk about why you got Dougie dropping you off. Where is your car?"

He rubbed the back of his neck. "The hooptie finally put me down. It needs a new transmission, I don't think it's worth putting the money into it to get it fixed."

"Come on, Eli. Why didn't you tell me? I told you I would get you a new car."

He shook his head before I could finish my sentence. "I don't need you spending any more money on me. You gave me a job and helped me get an apartment, I don't want to be in further debt with you."

"I don't have a ledger where I'm keeping track. You know I got your back. I don't do this shit for you to pay me back, Eli."

"You do enough, little cousin. You don't need to buy me a new car. I'll figure it out, but as of right now, I have a way to and from work. Ok?"

I smiled, placing my hand on his shoulder. "Ok, I won't buy you a new car."

He nodded.

"I'll just give you one of mine," I said before strolling off.

He couldn't refute me if I wasn't there to listen.

"Damn it, Duck!" Eli shouted behind me.

I ignored him as I walked through the door to my grandparents' house. The smell of soul food hit me almost as hard as the sound of a house full of hollering kids.

The front door opened to the wide foyer. Hardwood floors ran through most of the house with the exception of the carpeted bedrooms. Off from the long foyer on the right was the formal living room.

Even at the age of thirty-three, I could count on one hand how many times I'd been in that room. Grams didn't play about her formal living room. All the furniture was encased in plastic that had turned from clear to brown. That room was only used for special occasions, like if the pastor came to visit, or when Eli's parole officer used to come over.

The stairs to the upstairs were straight ahead. To the immediate left of the stairs was the entrance to the huge kitchen. And just as you entered the house, on the left was the living room where my papa sat watching a basketball game in his Lazy Boy recliner. Uncle Kenny and Kenny Jr., were sitting on the long couch near the windows. Royce, my cousin Keva's husband, was sitting on the love seat near the door. His wide hips took up over half the couch.

"Papa, I brought your favorite," I said, walking into the living room with Eli on my heels.

"There goes my girl!" Papa let the legs down on his chair as he climbed out of his seat to give me a hug. I hugged him with one arm as I held the pie in the other hand.

"What took you so long?" he asked, pulling back to look me over.

His mahogany brown skin and almond shaped eyes were mirror images of mine.

As far as looks went, I mostly favored my Papa and Nita. I shared the same high cheek bones and button nose as my mother. However, my full bow-shaped lips, diamond-shaped face, freckles and one dimple were all my own. Or they could be my biological fathers, hell if I know.

"I had a little wreck." I shrugged off the incident, but just thinking about Jackson brought a smile to my face.

I was only smiling because he was funny.

"A wreck?" my Papa shouted.

"Duck, you didn't mention a wreck?" Eli turned me around eyeing me all over like I was hiding a broken limb.

"I'm fine," I said to both men. "I ran into the back of someone. My car barely has a scratch, and the guy and I walked away fine."

Papa sighed. "Maybe you should talk to Quincy about some legal advice. I don't want this man trying to sue you with false claims."

I thought about that, honestly I did. I do run a business, so I'm not naïve. That's why I made sure to take pictures of Jackson's car and mine before I left the scene, however, I didn't think Jackson was that type of man. I'd only just met him, but he didn't seem to be thinking of ways to cash in on me. He seemed to have had only one thing on his mind, and it damn sure wasn't money.

"Papa, I have lawyers I can seek council from. Plus, I wouldn't ask Quincy's non-client having ass to help me with my laundry."

Eli started laughing behind me. Papa only gave me that warning look about using curse words, but even that wasn't as severe as he wanted it to be.

"I heard that, Duck!" Quincy appeared in the doorway connecting the formal dining room to the living room.

"Good!" I replied. "Let me go say hey to Grams and put this pie away."

"Hand me your keys so I can check out your car," Eli stated.

I handed over my keys as I headed in the direction towards the dining room.

Approaching the door, Quincy stood in my way. His snake eyes watched me with too much interest to already be married to my cousin, Chante.

I had an insatiable appetite for sex, and I had no qualms about fucking men in relationships. I honestly preferred you had a girlfriend, that way I knew your ass wouldn't get attached and I could send you right back to her when I was done, but I drew the line at married men, and I would never dabble in my family.

Quincy had his eyes on me from the moment Chante brought him home. Even after three years of marriage and a newborn, he still watched me. I ignored all his flirtatious smiles and unnecessary touches. I knew that all I had to do was give him a time and a place and he'd be waiting for me.

Quincy wasn't my type. It wasn't because of his looks, trust me, the brother is fine. Tall, light-brown skin, low cut fade and just the right amount of facial hair with chestnut brown eyes, and the man could do damage to a damn suit. He was almost an uncanny twin to the actor Laz Alonso, but Quincy was trifling, and more importantly, he was married to my cousin.

"Do you mind moving out of my way?" I asked when he still refused to let me pass.

His whiskey colored eyes raked up and down my body, and it didn't feel remotely as good as when Jackson did it earlier.

That sleeze-ball smile hit his face, and he turned to the side to let me pass. I went to walk by him and he brushed his erection against my side with a smirk.

"All you have to do is ask, Duck! And all of that could be yours."

I turned to him with a sneer. "From the feel of it, I'll be short changed."

I didn't give him time to reply as I strolled passed him through the dining room and into the kitchen.

"Grams, I'm here!" I announced as I entered the kitchen.

Both of my aunts and most of my cousins were already here helping Grams' cook.

"Uh-oh! She's here, we better hide our men," my unnecessarily loud cousin, Keisha, said with a sneer.

I despised women like Keisha. She's one of those females that thinks because she tries to have a relationship with the men she fucks, it makes her better than me. Every few months she has a new man sitting at Grams' dinner table introducing him as her boyfriend. She's a year younger than me with four kids and three baby daddies, but I'm the hoe. I had no problem admitting what I was, but how dare she pretend that she isn't the same. I never brought men around my family. The only person they've ever met was Sean, but that was under dire circumstances. They had no idea who or how many men I'd actually slept with.

"Trust me, Keisha, you have nothing to worry about. I wouldn't touch anything you had between your legs, not even your jeans. Remember, I had to give you the money for that last prescription."

Keisha's dark skin flushed as she stared at me. She swung her long lace-front off her shoulders and turned back to the macaroni she was boiling.

That's right, bitch, don't come for me. I placed my cheese cake in the brand-new refrigerator and planted a kiss on Grams' cheek.

Sadie Rose was still a classic beauty, even at the ripe age of seventy-three. She was what black folks called "red bone". In her younger years, she looked like Dorothy Dandridge—at least in my opinion. She's a little heavier now, but still just as beautiful.

"Is that a new wig?" I asked Grams as I grabbed a glass and poured some of her homemade lemonade.

Grams touched her shoulder length curls. "No, Devin came over last Tuesday and put this in. I don't know how I feel about it yet. You know I love my wigs."

I laughed. Nothing would keep Sadie Jefferies from her wigs.

She's worn wigs since I was in my teens.

"I think it looks good, and I know Papa loves it. He don't have to worry about it falling off when he's pulling on it," I said with a wink towards her.

Grams laughed, and her face turned bright red.

I don't know why people think that once you got a certain age, you no longer enjoyed fucking. No matter how old I got, I would never stop spreading my legs. An orgasm still remained the best stress reliever. I got at least one every single day, two most days, either by my own hands or someone from my list. Like I said, my appetite was insatiable.

"Hush your mouth, Duck!" Grams lightly scolded.

"That was very rude and disrespectful, Charlice. I swear Nita didn't teach you any manners."

As always, my Aunt Viv was ready to find any way she could to argue with me. Just the sound of me breathing irked that woman.

"Does talking about sex bother you, Aunt Viv? Maybe if Uncle Walter was putting it down more, you wouldn't be so uptight."

The kitchen was a mix of gasp and chuckles. They all knew I was right.

"That's enough, Duck!" Grams warned. "And Vivica, leave the girl alone. I wasn't offended, and neither should you be. Your father and I still have a very healthy sex life."

"Ugh. Mama!" Vivica grimaced.

Again, the kitchen filled with groans and laughter. I only smiled and gave Grams a high-five.

"Still, Grams?" My cousin, Keva, started while placing the dressing in the oven. "You are a woman of God, you shouldn't be discussing so freely what happens in your married bed, and especially to someone like Duck. I pray for your salvation every night, cousin."

"That's sweet, Keva, but maybe you should stop worrying about my salvation and ask the Lord to bring your edges back instead."

Grams tried to hold her laughter in as long as possible, but it only came out in bursts through her nose. Her reaction triggered everyone—except Keva and Aunt Viv.

I didn't know what caused my horrible relationship with my aunt, so I didn't know how to fix it. Even if I did know how to salvage it, I doubt that I would. Why would I make amends with someone that held a grudge with a child?

WHERE LOVE IS FOUND

The food was nearly done by the time my favorite female cousin walked in the door.

"Hey everybody!" Devin's cheerful voice called out as she walked into the kitchen. Her three-year-old daughter, Naya, on her hip.

Of all of Sadie and Charles' grandkids, Devin and Eli were the only ones to inherit Grams' light-brown eyes. Devin was beautiful inside and out. She had Grams' light-brown skin, doe-shaped eyes, and the biggest heart ever. I've never met a more caring and loving person. She always went out of her way for others, and rarely was that same kindness ever returned to her.

For instance, everyone in the family went to Devin to get their hair done, and I'm the only one, along with Grams, that actually paid her. I guarantee Keisha took her big watermelon head over there to get that custom-made lace front she had on, but I bet she didn't pay Devin for her time and services. It made me angry that Devin allowed people to walk all over her. Whenever I was around, I made sure no one took advantage of her. Unfortunately, the biggest leech of her kindness, was her boyfriend, Miles.

"Give me my God child," I said, taking a sleeping Naya off her hip. "Should you be carrying her when you're four months pregnant?"

"Oh, stop worrying, Duck," Grams said with a chuckle. "Your Uncle Ellis wasn't even walking when I was pregnant with Joe. You'll see when you have your first one."

Once again, my body did that subtle flinch at the mention of kids.

"Please, Grams. You know Duck ain't having kids." Keva laughed, and Keisha joined in.

"Right, it's hard to hoe with a baby on her hips."

"And you would know." I directed my insult to Keisha.

She had four kids, and it definitely didn't stop her from sleeping around.

"I'm not a hoe. I know who all my baby daddies are."

"Thanks to DNA."

Devin tried to hide her laughter behind her hand.

"You always bringing up old stuff, Duck. I only got one DNA test, and he was--"

"Ya'll stop all that bickering." Grams cut off the argument she knew was coming. "Duck, go on out there and tell them menfolk it's time to eat."

23

I cut my grandmother some slack and headed towards the living room, leaving a fuming Keisha behind. Devin followed behind me.

"Hey, Duck, I just want to say thanks again for the gift certificate for Miles Jr." She rubbed her barely-there belly with pride.

I hated that if this baby was a boy she was naming him after that asshole, but I didn't say anything. I knew how badly she wanted this one to be a boy, I was hoping for another girl just so she couldn't give her that dumbass name.

"All my girls are saying how I don't even need a baby shower with the amount you gave me. They think you gave me more this time than you did with Kylie and Naya."

I did. I always went all out for my God kids.

"Don't worry about it. You know I always got you. Although, if you would let me open that shop up for you like I want to, you could afford to do stuff like that yourself."

Devin looked down, and that sad look appeared. I knew she hated this subject. Part of Devin wanted that shop as much as I wanted it for her, but the other part wanted to keep her man happy.

"Maybe one day," she said, and her response brought me a little hope.

The first time I offered to buy her shop and pay for cosmetology school, she was excited. She couldn't even contain herself. Then she found out she was pregnant with Kylie, and after talking to limp dick, she turned it down every time I asked. Until today. Maybe my baby cousin was coming around.

"You know my offer never expires, Dee." I smiled as I repeated the words Jackson said earlier.

I'm a little surprised my interest in him hasn't worn off yet. It will soon. It always does.

With one last encouraging smile to Devin, I headed into the living room to announce supper was ready.

Fifteen minutes later, we were all sitting at the large dinner table surrounding Grams' Sunday spread. Ham, fried chicken, green beans, macaroni and cheese, rice and gravy, homemade biscuits and dressing. The food trays were being passed around, and conversation was flowing. I was sitting between Devin and Eli like usual. Across from me was Kenny Jr. and on one side of him was Keisha's new boyfriend of the month. Some gold tooth, baggy clothes, skinny dude with ashy knuckles. Seated at the head of the table in Grams' usual spot was Pastor Murphy.

The new pastor looked to be in his early forties. He was tall with a bald head and goatee, nice-looking with his cinnamon brown skin and white teeth. His wife looked about as homely as my cousin, Keva. She was an attractive woman. With a better wig and clothes to fit her full figure, she would be turning heads left and right.

"Mr. Jefferies, I want to thank you for inviting us to your beautiful house for supper. It makes me so proud to have a man like you on the deacon board. I look down over that pulpit every Sunday I've been at the church and see you and your lovely family in the pews. You sure are bringing up your house in the right way," Pastor Murphy praised as he scooped more green beans on his plate.

My grandfather nodded proudly. He was proud of us, and it didn't have anything to do with all of us going to church.

Papa worked hard for his family. He was always a laid-back man. Grams was the disciplinarian of the house. However, when Papa spoke, you knew to listen. Even before I came to stay with them permanently at sixteen, I was always here. The first twelve years of my life were spent in this house before Nita finally got tired of sneaking out and moved into a place with Russell— the fireman.

Pastor Murphy went on to say, "And how is Martin doing up there in California? It's a hard road saving souls in a place so full of sin."

The biscuit I'd just bit into got lodged in my throat, and I started to choke. Eli pounded on my back like a damn drummer, and I was finally able to get the biscuit down.

"You alright, Duck?" Eli asked

"Mmhmm, it just went down wrong," I said, taking a sip of my water.

"You should be a pro at choking on things." Keisha quipped.

A few chuckles went around the table. The new boyfriend looked at me with a new spark of interest in his eyes while he ran his tongue over his lips like he might be LL Cool J. Homeboy was a far cry from LL.

"At this point, her throat should be used to it," Chante chimed in lowly.

Keisha burst out laughing giving Chante a fist bump across the table. Quincy gave Chante a disapproving look, and she dropped her head like the submissive bitch that she was.

"Hey! Ain't nobody gone be talking about my cousin." Eli jumped in like he always did.

He and I both knew I could handle these chicks.

I opened my mouth to put them both in their place, but Grams stopped me.

"Girls, not in front of company."

Yeah, she knew I was about to shame them. I smiled at Grams before taking another sip of my drink. I looked over at Keisha and tipped my glass to her, she had the right mind to look nervous. I could destroy her ass in one sentence, and bring shame to her and her new boyfriend.

And Chante was really showing out. She hardly ever opened her mouth, let alone came for me. Usually Aunt Viv stepped in for her, but I wasn't worried about Chante. If I told her how bad her husband wanted to taste my pussy, she would be having a meltdown in a corner somewhere. With a simple yes, I had the ability to fuck up her little world.

"Now, Charles," Pastor Murphy said looking directly at me, "I don't think I've ever seen that one at church?"

I've said this before—I knew men. I knew men as well as I knew business, and I'm a fucking beast when it comes to business. So don't think I'm being cocky or full of myself when I tell you, I knew the new pastor at Mt. Sinai Missionary Baptist church, wanted to fuck me. The way his eyes crinkled around the edges when he stared back at me. From the way his lips slightly parted, even the way his pupils were now dilated, and it wasn't from the taste of Grams' buttermilk biscuits. His eyes dropped momentarily to the open buttons of my shirt before running back up to my face. I bet right now he had a hard-on in his tighty-whities

"No, Pastor Murphy, you wouldn't see Duck in church. She would probably catch fire," Royce said jokingly.

Despite me calling him a fat-ass and hand-pecked, I liked Royce— or Roy as we called him. He was the youth minister at the church, and that's how Keva met him. He was as black as tires and had an ass fatter than mine. He liked to take cracks at me every now and again, but I always felt like his jokes were harmless. Besides, I couldn't take him seriously. He married Keva and watched Keisha like her pussy hung the stars in the sky, and I knew for a fact, Keisha had sucked his dick before. I walked in on it, not something you ever wanted to witness.

Neither had any idea I'd caught them, and the bitch had the nerve to call me a hoe, at least I didn't fuck men that were married into the family.

"The day Duck goes to church, is the day I know Jesus is on his way back," Eli said and nudged me with his elbow into my side.

I stuck out my tongue at him. Eli always got a pass with me. Besides, everyone knew I didn't do organized religion.

I did believe there was a higher being. Some one that deserved my prayers and to thank for the creations that we see around us. I definitely didn't believe in that science bull shit, like some star shitted in outer space and suddenly mankind was created.

I just didn't do church and living by some made up rules some man created and wrote in a book Centuries after the shit happened. To me, church was something I was forced to do as a child. It all seemed like some big fashion show that people did just to prove that they were more Christian than the next person.

If you didn't go to Sunday school, regular service, prayer night, bible study, and choir rehearsal, then you weren't as saved as the person that did. I refused to be forced to do something that I wasn't sincere about. And don't get me started on those so-called pastors.

"Pastor Murphy, I'm afraid you won't get Duck to go to church. Some people just don't want to be saved," Keva said in her usual holier than thou tone. "Lord knows if I've been praying for her soul and it hadn't happened, it never will." Keva giggled.

"What makes your prayers so special, Keva?"

Her eyes flashed to me, and she smiled smugly. "The way I live my life, Duck. I've been saved since I was nine years old, and I've never strayed from the Lord's word."

"Amen, Baby!" Aunt Jo praised.

Aunt Jo was always proud that she had at least one child that she could brag about to the church folks. For a while, it was Kenny Jr., but after he didn't make it to the pros and got hooked on painkillers and alcohol, she had to let that go, and we all knew Keisha ain't got shit going for her. So I understood why her pride and joy was in believing her saintly daughter had the blessings of God himself.

I cocked my head to the side and smiled at Keva. "You sure about that?"

The entire table went completely silent. I took a slow sip of my glass of water as Keva studied me with a nervous smile. She had no idea I knew the things I knew.

"Yes, I'm sure, Duck! I'm not like you. My husband has the honor in knowing he was my first and last."

I laughed at how easily I could have called her out. But, like with Chante and Keisha, I bit my tongue.

And the family said I was heartless.

"Ignore Duck, Keva. She just wants someone to feel as low as she does," Aunt Viv stated. "You are a gifted woman of God."

Keva smiled proudly, and Aunt Jo nodded her head in agreement.

"Well, according to who you ask, so am I," I stated with a wink.

Keva gasped in disgust along with a few others. Devin laughed beside me and gave me a fist bump. Eli shook his head and mumbled 'TMI' under his breath.

Pastor Murphy cleared his throat getting everyone's attention again.

"Well, I would like to extend an invitation for you, Ms. Duck, to come out and hear one of my sermons."

I leaned back in my chair, giving the good pastor my full attention. I took in his full lips and perfect teeth. His eyes lit up at my interest in him.

"Thanks, Pastor, but I'll pass."

Again a few grunts of disapproval went around the table.

"Well, I have private hours. You are welcome to come and seek council. It is my desire….. that no soul go unsaved if I can help it."

"Amen!" Aunt Jo agreed.

She had no idea this pastor could give a shit about my soul. He wanted to touch and agree with something, but it wasn't my salvation.

I glanced over at the pastor's wife, and her eyes locked onto me with an angry glare. My mouth went up in a smirk.

Relax sister, I don't want your man.

"Pastor Murphy, I fear you may be wasting your time," Papa said. "I don't force my little Duck to the Lord. I figure, she will come when the Lord calls for her."

"He gone have to break through Satan's phone call first," Keisha mumbled.

The entire table laughed, and another conversation picked up. Thankfully, not about my soul.

However, I could tell by the heated look coming from Pastor Murphy that he was still thinking about some alone time with me.

CHAPTER FOUR

The rest of my Sunday went as planned. I went home with a plate of leftovers from Grams, which I ate while I caught up on some of my shows, and I ended my night with a bubble bath, a glass of wine, and an orgasm from my favorite vibrator.

Mondays were always my late days. I had nothing on my agenda until the afternoons when my team and I went over new contracts and discussed our current client's concerns.

As soon as I walked into the building, my assistant, Troy, greeted me at the door. Troy started going over my schedule for today. Most of it I already knew, but his job was to remind me and to make sure I stayed on schedule.

"…..And Mr. Yakamura called again today. He's really hoping you take on his company," Troy said, finishing his debriefing.

"Thanks, Troy! I'll return his call today."

I walked into my large glass office, and I got the same feeling I always did when I came to work— happiness.

I loved what I did, and I wanted my office to show my love for my job. I couldn't imagine sitting in a dark box all day looking at the walls. My office was huge, probably the size of two regular size offices. It had its own bathroom with a closet and walk in shower for those days my job kept me late. A wall with a built-in wet bar and mini fridge. On the opposite side of the bar was a sitting area with a couch and two chairs.

My entire office was made up of sound proof glass. The back wall gave you a view of downtown Atlanta. The other walls viewed out into my employees. The best part was with a touch of a remote, the glass became tinted, and no one could see inside.

"Oh, last thing," Troy said, standing at the front of my desk with his tablet clutched to his chest. "This came for you today." He picked up a rectangular shaped Manila envelope and handed it to me.

I looked down at the envelope and noticed there was no return address.

"Did they say who it's from?" I asked, turning the letter over in my hands.

Troy shrugged. "Nope, some guy just dropped it off this morning."

"Ok! Thanks, Troy. That will be all."

He smiled and nodded before leaving my office. I stared at the envelope a little longer before picking up my gold plated letter opener and ripped it open. Inside were two paper objects. The first one was a letter hurriedly written out on note pad paper. From the messy slant of the letters, I assumed a man wrote it.

Dear, Ms. Jefferies.
I saw this yesterday, and I immediately thought of you.

I placed the letter down to look at the other paper. It was a bumper sticker. Big white letters written on a black background read, Bad Driver. In smaller letters beneath bad driver were the words: Seriously, I fucking suck.

I burst into laughter as I stared down at the bumper sticker, I immediately knew who the letter was from. I picked up the letter and continued to read.

I'm afraid I have some bad news. It appears my dog, Lady, is very distraught about the wreck. She's even thinking of filing charges. I've talked to her, told her you seemed like a nice person, maybe a little heavy-footed on the gas pedal, but nice. I was able to convince Lady to come to an agreement. She agrees to reconsider her lawsuit if you agree to have coffee with me today. I've included my number at the bottom of this letter; call me if you would like to discuss any further actions. As a fair warning, Lady is known to be quite the beast in the court room, I would take this offer if I were you.
Signed
Jackson Keller (unsuspecting victim in a diabolical car crash

scheme.)

By the time I'd finish reading the letter I'd laughed so much my cheeks hurt. I couldn't believe how funny he was and still persistent. I checked the clock on my desk and noticed that I had ten minutes before my staff meeting. Even though I had no intentions of going on a coffee date, or seeing Jackson again, my phone was in my hand and dialing the number scribbled at the bottom of the paper.

The phone rung three times. Before I could talk myself into hanging up, a gruff voice came over the speaker.

"Keller landscaping, this is Jackson Keller speaking?"

"Tell your dog she doesn't frighten me."

His chuckle through the phone was just as sexy as seeing it on his face in person. I could envision those hazel eyes crinkled around the edges. That thick beard accenting that sexy full bottom lip. And those dimples. Damn, I just ruined my thong. What was Mr. Keller doing to my body?

"Hello to you too, Ms. Jefferies."

"And unsuspecting victim? I think you're pushing it there. I'm still not convinced the wreck wasn't your plan to get my attention."

"Well, if it turns out to be successful, I'll definitely add it to the repertoire."

I chuckled.

"I will say this, Mr. Keller, you are nothing if not persistent."

"I did warn you."

"You did. I thought you were joking."

"Nope..... So, does this call mean you are taking me up on my offer?"

I spun my chair around, turning to admire my view of Atlanta. I sighed into the phone.

"A sigh," Jackson said before I could speak. "I'm hoping that is a sign of surrender. Have I finally chased you down?"

"Jackson, I don't think...."

"Don't think, Charlice. Just do. Why are you so scared to take my offer? Are you one of those weird people that don't drink coffee? I mean, if you are, we can work around it. Get you some help. Maybe take you to get some type of counseling or something."

Another chuckle. Damn, he had me acting like some little teenager.

"I like coffee, Jackson."

"Good, because I was already trying to think of ways to hide that fact from my friends and family."

I laughed out loud.

"If it isn't the coffee, what is it? Is it my beard?"

"You're......not my type," I admitted.

I was met with silence on the other end of the phone. For a moment, I feared that I might have finally turned him away. That thought bothered me in ways I didn't care to study right now.

Jackson's voice came through the phone cutting off my concerns.

"So, you're one of those people. I never took you for the narrow-minded type."

"Excuse me?" his comment had me sitting up in my chair.

"To each its own, Ms. Jefferies. I just thought you were the type of woman that didn't fit into a small box. Not like the people that think they can only find love and happiness with someone that looks like them. It's absurd. It's like they're saying, 'I love sweets, but I only eat one type of cake.' There are billions of men out there, Ms. Jeffries, and you're only limiting yourself to less than a third of that number."

I found myself speechless. Jackson made a valid point. Though I found all men attractive, I'd only ever dated—and I use the word dated for lack of a better word—black men. And though I'd had my share of duds, like Cliff, I'd also been with some outstanding, hardworking, intelligent, and loving brothers. However, I had been limiting myself. Truthfully, I was attracted to Jackson. He was funny, charming, and sexy. If he were black, I would have agreed to his coffee the first time he asked. Probably would have already fucked him and added him to my list.

"Ok, Mr. Keller. Since you are such an equal opportunist dater, tell me, how many black women have you dated?"

A chuckle. "None."

"What?!?!"

"But it's not from lack of trying. It seems every woman of color I've come across and tried to date, has the same mindset as you. I keep running into your type."

"First off, stop saying my type. I'm not a type." I huffed.

"Then prove me wrong, Charlice." His voice dropped lower into a sexy bedroom growl, and I had to clench my thighs together to stop the ache. It seemed like I would have to pull out one of my vibrators and head to the bathroom after this call.

Jackson had talent. We hadn't even done anything yet, and I was already dripping for him.

I glanced at the clock on my laptop and realized I only had about five more minutes before my meeting.

"Look, Jackson, race issue aside…."

"It's not an issue…"

"….Anyway, with that aside, you still aren't my type."

"Again, is it the beard? Because, I've been told there are benefits to this beard."

That damn voice again. Another clenching of the thighs.

"It's not the beard." I sighed, finally time for me to let Mr. Jackson go. "You say you know my type, well I know yours. You want a relationship. I don't do relationships, Jackson. I don't date. Ever."

Another long pause from him. I had a feeling he was letting my words fully register.

"So you're telling me you're only interested in sex?"

"Yes!"

"And you've done this before? With other men?"

"Obviously." Many times.

"And men are ok with this? They are ok with being with you knowing you're only into sex?"

"What are you trying to say?"

I did nothing to hide the irritation in my tone.

"Don't get me wrong, I'm all for a woman's right to her own sexual freedom. Women should have the same liberties to enjoy their sexuality as men without all the ugly labels they receive. I just find it hard to believe that any man could settle with having you for just a short roll in the hay."

For the second time, I was rendered speechless by this man. For a woman that loved to talk and always had something to say, that was a remarkable feat. Jackson Keller had shut me up twice in one conversation.

Look, I knew I was beautiful. I wasn't a woman with low self-esteem. Did I think I was the most beautiful woman to ever grace this earth? Hell no! But I had enough confidence to know I wasn't a troll. So men telling me I was beautiful or sexy or whatever term they used to explain my looks, was nothing to me. However, having a man tell you how much value he saw in you did make me a little weak in the knees. Yet, it still didn't change anything.

"Despite how you feel, Mr. Keller, the truth still remains. You want something I'm incapable of giving. Which is why once again, I have to turn down your coffee offer."

"I love a challenge, Ms. Jefferies."

Oh, my God, this man was determined. His resilience made me smile, despite my exasperation.

"This is not a challenge."

"Hmmm, how about we discuss what is or isn't a challenge over coffee? We can go as friends."

"Friends?" I playfully scoffed as Troy entered right on time ready to usher me out of my office and into my boardroom. I held up one finger to hold him off.

"Why not, everyone needs a friend, right? Just think about it."

"I have to go, Mr. Keller. But, I will think about your offer. Only as friends."

His chuckle greeted me. "That's all I ask. I'll be expecting your call. Good day, Charlice."

"Goodbye, Jackson."

I switched off my phone with the biggest grin on my face. There was something about that man. I shook my head, ready to start my work week.

"Whoever that was on the phone must be special," Troy said, following me out of my office. "I've never seen you smile like that."

"What are you talking about? I smile all the time."

I did. I was generally a happy person, at least I thought so.

"There is a difference between your generally happy smile and the smile you have now. Your smile now is the smile of a woman that has just spent a few minutes talking to the man of her dreams." Troy nudged my shoulder with his own.

I looked over to my well-dressed assistant that had been with me since I left Piers and started my own business and smiled even bigger. If I were another person, in another time, Jackson Keller might have been the man of my dreams, but I don't dream about men. If I did, they either had their face buried between my legs or my heels over their shoulders. I was not falling for a man I'd only met once and talked to on the phone for ten minutes.

I ignored Troy's words and the thoughts they inspired. I pushed open

the doors to my conference room, and I was met by my team. I was
in   all   business   mode   now   .

☐ *FIVE*

Three days. Three fucking days had passed, and the only thing I'd been thinking about more than sex, was Jackson Keller.

What the hell? Not only did he scrounge around my brain during the day, but he popped into my dreams at night. Usually something like this would require a little scroll through my contact list. I just needed to get my fix, a little sexual distraction. Yet, every time I looked through that damn list, nothing jumped out at me. It's like being hungry, but every time someone suggests a restaurant, you turn your nose up at it. At this moment, a sistah was starving, but it seemed like if your name wasn't Jackson Keller, the coochie didn't want anything to do with you.

I pulled my silver BMW X7 into the driveway of Devin's small rental. Already the neighbors had congregated outside on their porches to see who was pulling up into their neighborhood with this car. On this side of town, only people that drove my car were drug dealers or folks that were lost. You'd think they would be used to seeing me by now considering I was here every two weeks to get my hair done.

I stepped out of the car and grabbed my black hair store bags along with my work suitcase. My phone went off in my pocket, and I pulled it out to look at the screen. Another text from Cliff. I'd blocked his cell phone and the landline he'd tried to call me on. I guess he had a new number or was using a friend's phone. Not to worry, it would get blocked too. I didn't even read the message before I deleted it. I could guarantee it was the same as the others.

"I'm sorry."

"Please forgive me."

"Can we just talk it out?"

Hell No! Once I cut a dude off, it was for good. There was no dick in this world worth a second chance after they'd wronged me. And putting his hands on me, was beyond wrong.

The door to the house opened before I made it up the steps. Kylie rushed out the door to give me a hug. She looked just like her mother did at this age.

"Hey, Little Bit!" I said, giving my God daughter a hug and kiss.

"Hey, Aunt Duck. Guess what, my teacher wants to have a conference with Mommy. She says it's a good conference though."

I smiled down at her, her hair was in neat braids with clear beads on the ends.

"Oh, that sounds great. Are you still coming over tomorrow?" I asked as I allowed her to hold my hand and guide me up on the porch.

"Yep! Can we order pizza and watch Netflix again?"

Man, I loved this kid.

"Sure can."

I walked into the house, and immediately, the smell of weed and cigarette smoke greeted me.

I had to fight to keep from rolling my eyes at the sight of Miles and his dumbass friends sitting in the living room. Miles had more sense than to smoke in the house with Devin and the kids, but he had no idea how that smell lingered on their clothes after hitting one.

I'd learned my lesson over the years about cussing his ass out. He only took it out on Devin by ignoring her or not coming home at night. That shit ate her up. I had to give it to him, he'd never put his hands on her. Myself and Eli both warned him about that upfront. I didn't think he wanted to call either of our bluffs. He knew Eli would whoop his ass, but he didn't know if I would really shoot him in the nuts.

I would.

"Ky, where's your mama?" I asked without taking my eyes away from Miles.

He squirmed in his seat. That's right, asshole, I made you nervous.

"In the kitchen," she sung before disappearing back down the hall.

"Damn, beautiful! Why you lookin' so mad?" one of Miles' boys said to me.

My eyes rolled to the back of my head. I hated that damn line. I wished they would erase it from whatever fuck boy pick up line book it was written in.

"How can I make you smile?" Homeboy tried again to get my attention.

"By playing in traffic."

Most of Miles' friends knew not to play these games with me. I had no problem with a man shooting his shot. I was independent as fuck, but I still liked a man to come on to me. I usually put them down gently, if not efficiently, but today wasn't that day. I was horny and irritable.

Resounding oohs went around the room as I headed out of the living room and into the kitchen.

"Stuck up bitch!" the guy called after me. "Now I see what you mean, Miles."

I ignored him and greeted my cousin.

"Hey, love!" I called out as Devin put her cellphone down.

I took Naya off her hip, and my God daughter came to me happily. She immediately started playing with my necklace.

"Hey, girl! Guess what?"

"You sound just like your daughter," I teased.

Miles walked into the kitchen at that exact moment. He did this anytime Devin and I were alone together. He was probably making sure that if I slipped Devin some money, he didn't miss it. He'd want to ask for it later. Miles grabbed a beer out of the fridge and popped the top staring at us.

Devin's excitement grabbed my attention back.

"They have an early opening in Pepperdine, and Naya just got in."

My excitement was sudden.

"Oh, my God! Are you kidding! Way to go, Auntie's smart baby." I planted happy kisses all over Naya's face. She giggled and squirmed in my arms.

"I'm smart, Auntie Duck. I'm going to school with Ky."

"You sure are. When does she start?" I directed my question to Devin.

"Monday."

"Great, I'll write up the check before I go. I can get her supplies too if you want?"

"We can buy damn school supplies," Miles said with a grunt.

I didn't acknowledge him. I knew that's what he wanted.

"Thanks again, Duck! We really appreciate all you do for the girls." Devin tried to drown out Miles' attitude.

Before I could reply and tell her how much her thanks wasn't needed, Miles spoke up again.

"I don't understand why they need to go to that bougie ass school. I mean, Kylie is one thing because she's in school, but Naya got two parents at home all day. She don't need a fucking daycare."

For Devin's sake, I continued to bite my tongue. Be calm, Duck. Don't go in on his dumbass, I reminded myself.

"Miles, baby, don't be like that. I told you this three-year-old program is one of the top programs in the state. Naya will roll right from head start into their elementary school."

"Nobody listens to me. I guess I'm the stupid one. We barely got them folks off our backs when Kylie started at that damn school, what you think they gon' say when Naya starts? They cut your food stamps, what you gon' do then?"

It took Jesus himself to keep me from cussing his ass out. I so badly wanted to tell his deadbeat ass that if they cut the food stamps, he could get a goddamn job, or I'd just continue to supply Devin with money like I always did.

"Baby, this is a fantastic opportunity. Don't you want to give our daughters the best education we can?"

"We ain't the ones givin' them the education." Miles cut his eyes to me as he took another swig of his beer.

I smiled and winked at him.

Yeah, dumbass, I'm taking care of your kids, do something about it.

It's not my fault Miles was feeling like less a man. If he was trying to take care of his family, I would never overstep the way I do. In fact, I would always go through him if I wanted to do something special for the girls, but since he wanted to lay on his ass all day, he got no respect from me. There was no reason Miles didn't work. Hell, I would even accept him selling drugs, at least he would be bringing in some money.

Devin, always the peace maker, spoke up. "Duck wants the same thing we want."

"Duck need to have her own Goddamn kids instead of trying to make our kids like her."

"And what's wrong with them being like me?" I asked, still keeping my cool.

I deserved a damn reward for the amount of patience I'd shown today.

"You're a fucking hoe with money. Why would I want my daughters to be like you?" Miles shouted, causing Naya to cover her ears and bury her face in my shoulder.

I had reached my limit. I was doing well thus far, but it seemed little Miles needed to be checked.

"Better to be a hoe with money, than a hoe without it, like your bald-headed-ass mama."

"What the fuck did you just say about my mama?" Miles pushed away from the fridge and took a step towards me.

"First of all, take a step back. Then take that bass out of your voice when you speak to me, little man. We both know you're not about to do shit."

"Little Man!?!"

I placed my God-daughter on the floor. I wasn't scared of Miles, but if I needed to put my foot in his ass, I didn't want to have Naya in my arms.

"Yeah! I didn't stutter."

"Ok! …..Ok guys! Calm down. Not in front of the baby."

Devin picked up Naya, and immediately, Naya reached back for me. I took her from her mother, and she buried her face back in my neck.

"Man, fuck this! I'm leaving. A man can't even find peace in his own damn home."

"He could if he had one."

"Duck!" Devin pleaded. "Miles, when will you be back?"

"I don't know!" he shouted. "I'm not driving."

"Well, take my car."

Which was what he wanted to do in the first place. I didn't say anything this time. I buried my face in Naya's hair taking in the smell of her natural hair products.

Devin grabbed her car keys out of her purse on the small kitchen table and handed them to Miles. Miles kissed her forehead, and she beamed up at him like a puppy dog getting a pat on the head.

UGH!!!!

"You uh, you got twenty dollars I can borrow?"

I snorted. "Borrow implies you're going to pay it back."

I didn't feel bad for starting back up with him. He started with me first. I was doing well until the kids comment.

"Fuck you, Duck!"

"Better men than you have tried."

"No, you mean a lot more men than me have tried."

It always made me laugh when someone tried to make me feel bad about my life decisions. Like I should be ashamed. I learned a long time ago, never do anything that you would be ashamed to admit. This was my body, and I got to decide what I wanted to do with it. Who I spread my legs to, and how frequently I spread them was nobody's business.

I watched Devin hand Miles a twenty-dollar bill out of her purse. I didn't miss the way his eyes quickly counted the rest of the money in her wallet before she closed it. He glared at me one last time before squeezing by me to head out the door.

"I don't know why y'all can't get along?" Devin said while heading out to the back room she'd transformed into her very own beauty salon.

A stylist chair sat in front of a vanity with a large mirror. Every hair accessory and product any one could ever need crowded the space around the vanity. In the corner of the room were two dryers. On a tall shelf was a television along with a stereo, and on the opposite side of the room were shelves stuffed with even more hair needs and accessories. Devin had everything she needed to be a full-time operational beautician, except her own building and a license.

"It's because I have bigger balls than him," I stated, finally answering her earlier question.

Devin laughed as she wiped down her salon chair. "You are so wrong, Duck!" She shook her head. "And just so you know, my man has big balls, and a big ass dick to go along with them."

"Ewww! Girl, do not make me throw up the sushi I had for lunch."

I placed my God child down on the floor in front of me and took a seat in the chair. Devin pulled my neatly tied silk scarf off my head.

"I don't know why you won't just wear your natural hair." Devin remarked for the hundredth time. "It's so pretty. It's soft and curly like my daddy's. You know you're the only one in the family to follow Grams' rules about no relaxers."

Grams was never a fan of relaxers. Not after she nearly lost all her hair in her youth because of one.

In its natural form, my springy curls fell well past my shoulders. However, I never wore my own hair. I always braided it down and got a weave sewn on top.

My hair was another one of my traits I couldn't pin on Nita and Papa. Just like my freckles and one dimple, my hair must have come from my biological father. It was a mixture of loose corkscrew curls and waves. Devin was right, my curls were a lot like Uncle Walter's. My hair was more like his than his own kids who took after Aunt Vivica's tighter curls.

"You know I'm too lazy to style my own hair."

Devin chuckled behind me as she tugged on my mid-back length strands.

"So a deep condition and a full sew-in? Are you going short or long this time?"

I pulled the bundles from the black plastic bag.

"To the shoulders. And skip the deep condition, I already did it."

"Look at you coming in prepared." Devin joked.

"Hey! Hey, family!" Keisha sung as she walked into the room.

Her four kids followed behind her.

"Mama! I'm hungry," Quisha, Keisha's ten year old daughter said as she walked in.

Keran, Keisha's oldest, gave me a hug with his little brother on his hip. Despite being raised by Keisha's ignorant ass, all her kids were respectful and well-behaved.

Even though Keisha ran my damn nerves up, I still did for her kids. Like now, Keran was wearing a brand new pair of Jordan's I bought him for making the honor roll again.

"Girl, don't start that shit. You should have ate before we got over here. Damn, I can't do nothin' without ya'll chaps beggin'."

"There was nothing to eat at the house," Dontae mumbled under his breath.

He was six-years-old and one of the nicest kids I knew.

I didn't miss the new outfit Keisha was wearing or the fact that her nails looked freshly done. It wasn't uncommon for Keisha to forget about her kids needs while she catered to her own.

"Get out my face," Keisha fussed at little Kareem as he reached for her out of his big brother's arms. "Ya'll should have went with y'all daddy today."

"Which one? Their real daddies or the new boyfriend?"

Keisha's eyes narrowed at me. Every time she got a new boyfriend, she had her kids call him daddy.

"Don't start with me, Duck!" Keisha warned.

I ignored her and instead used my phone to place an order online.

"Don't worry, guys, I just ordered some pizzas. They should be here in thirty-five minutes."

The kids cheered and told me thank you.

"Keran, make sure Ky and Naya gets some pizza when it comes."

"Yes, ma'am, Aunt Devin." Keran picked up his three-year-old brother and headed back out to the front to wait for the pizza with the other kids.

"I swear, my kids can have just ate, and they will still beg for food."

I shook my head at my cousin's denial. I was pretty sure those babies hadn't eaten.

"So anyway," Keisha went on to say, "my boo is taking me out of town this weekend, and I want something sexy and long."

Devin laughed. "I got you, cousin. I got a new lace front in I bet you will like. I just got it in the mail yesterday. It's over there in one of those boxes."

Keisha went to search the boxes for her new wig.

"Oh, and Devin, you need to do something about your sister," Keisha commented nonchalantly. "She called me this morning asking to borrow some money. She said the baby needed pampers. I told her, I need my money. I can't be loaning her money. Besides, she the one with the man that's a lawyer."

"I just gave that girl money last week," Devin argued. "What is she doing with it?"

I kept my mouth closed. Some things weren't my business to tell. I didn't have the best relationship with all my family. However, they all knew that if they asked, I would help them in any way that I could.

I know where all Chante's money was going. I knew a lot of shit that I didn't tell. It was something I picked up when I was younger. I was really good at reading people and situations, and I was also really good with making friends in the right places. I knew at least one secret on every person in my family. Some of the secrets were small, but some of them, were life changing.

"Well, it's your sister," Keisha argued. "Plus, you can afford to loan her money. Everybody knows you'll just get it back from Duck."

"Don't play that bullshit, Keisha. I've given to everybody in the family, including you."

Keisha held up her hands. "I'm not complaining. I'm just saying, some of us don't have it like that to give her. I don't know why she won't just come and ask you."

She knew damn well Chante would never ask me for money. Too much pride. She would die if she found out they were even telling me this.

All my life, for some reason, Chante had been in competition with me. If I got a Barbie, she had to get two. If I got a new dress, she got three new dresses. Aunt Vivica helped feed the feud. She always pitted her daughter against me, even with stupid shit. Chante was a few months older than me. When I got my period early, her mother was mad. Told everyone that Chante had already had her period even though she didn't. When Chante got her boobs first, Aunt Vivica made a huge announcement over Sunday dinner about Chante needing bras and how other little girls her age were still flat chested. It was then she cut her eyes to my still flat chest. She was sitting all high and mighty until my mom finally told her that she and Chante could probably share the same bra considering Aunt Viv's breasts were so small. Aunt Vivica got so mad she stormed out of Grams' house slamming the door.

Now my cousin was in some serious trouble, and she wouldn't even ask me for help. It's sad. Even if I offered to help her she would still refuse.

We heard a loud commotion coming from the front of the house.

"Oh, Lord! Keva is here with that badass boy of hers," Keisha stated as she took the new blonde wig back to her seat on the dryer.

"He still carrying that bottle around?"

"Isn't he three?" I asked.

Both Keisha and Devin replied yes.

Keva came through the door carrying two grocery bags. RJ ran into the room behind his mother screaming at the top of his lungs while climbing up on the dryer beside Keisha.

"Keva, you need to tell him to get down!" Keisha shouted over the yelling toddler.

"We don't like to tell RJ what he can and can't do. We want him to discover the world in his own way."

"Well, if he tears up Devin's dryer, you and Roy will be discovering a way to buy her a new one."

Keva narrowed her eyes at me but turned to her son and spoke in a soft voice.

"RJ, wouldn't you like to play in the living room with your other cousins?"

"NOOOOOO!!!!" he shouted and started to beat on the dryer louder.

"RJ, the Lord is watching you. Do you think he would be happy with your behavior?"

RJ only shouted louder. Keisha looked like she wanted to beat the kid over the head. I didn't blame her, he was annoying.

"Alright RJ, I'm going to pray and ask the Lord to change your mind. Heavenly Father....."

"Oh, for fuck's sake!" I shouted. "Royce Jr., if you scream and hit that dryer one more time, I'm going to lock you in a closet and wait for the monster inside of it to eat your toes."

"DUCK!?!" Keva shouted.

RJ immediately quieted down and sat on his bottom. His eyes were as wide as saucers.

"RJ, there is no such thing as monsters," Keva tried to explain.

"Yes, there are," I argued. "And I know a lot of them that like misbehaving little boys. If you go in the living room and play quietly with your cousins, I'll put in a good word for you."

The little wide-eyed boy nodded silently at me. He climbed off the dryer chair and walked, quietly, out of the room.

"Charlice Rose Jefferies, you have overstepped. You know nothing about raising kids."

"Clearly, I'm not the one in the room that has a problem with raising kids. That boy is spoiled. And usually that isn't a bad thing, but he is also horrible."

"What do you know about kids? You don't have any."

"I know adults," I explained. "And your son will grow up to be an adult one day. What you do now will determine what kind of adult. Not calling him out on his shit while he's a kid will make him a shitty adult when he gets older."

"No offense, sis," Keisha spoke up. "But Duck is right. That boy is bad. Why you think Grams refuse to watch him?"

"If my child is a problem, then he and I will just...."

"Girl, sit down. Nobody said you had to leave, you know that boy bad." Devin joked, and Keisha and I both laughed.

Keva stood in the door awkwardly.

"I just wanted to bring these towels by. Mama said you could use them. The church only wants the dark colored ones." Keva sat two bags down on the closest surface. She took a seat in the other dryer chair.

"Tell Aunt Jo thank you," Devin said. "You know, Keva, you should let me do something to your hair. Don't you and Roy have an anniversary coming up?"

I watched the uncomfortable look that spread across Keisha's face.

Eventually, the two sisters were going to butt heads. Keva had no idea how bad her sister wanted her husband and vice versa. But, knowing what I knew about Keva, I doubt she cared.

"Yeah, we have an anniversary coming up, but I don't want all those chemicals and that fake hair in my head. You know I'm all natural now. Just like the Lord intended me to be."

"Trust me, honey! There is nothing natural about that dry ass afro."

Devin and Keisha erupted into laughter.

"For your information, Duck, natural hair is very pretty. More women are giving up the relaxers and going natural."

"Correction, natural hair isn't pretty, it's fucking gorgeous. However, that uncombed and untouched wool's ass on your head is just laziness. Going natural is not an excuse to not care, Keva."

"Preach!" Keisha encouraged, barely looking up from the magazine she was reading.

I wanted to go in on her and tell her that if she wasn't so focused on sleeping with her sister's man, she would have told her this already. However, once again, I bit my tongue. My phone went off in my pocket, and I pulled it out. I assumed it would be another call or message from Cliff.

A huge smile took over my face when I noticed it was a text from Jackson. He'd started sending me text messages after we spoke on the phone. He called them, 101 reasons I should go out with him. Usually they were silly and had nothing to do with real life issues. The numbers were random and never in order.

Jackson: #77 My dog says I give really good belly rubs. She's hard to please, so I'm sure I must be excellent. Hate for you to miss out on this.

"Now who got you smiling like that?"

I allowed Jackson to distract me, and I forgot where I was. I quickly placed my phone back down in my pocket without replying.

"I smile all the time."

"Oh no, cousin," Keisha said, sitting up from her chair with a huge smile on her face, the magazine forgotten. Nothing got her this riled up except new dick, and gossip.

"Only thing that makes someone smile like that is a man."

Devin chuckled over my head. "She has a point, Duck."

I rolled my eyes playfully at them both.

"Why does everything have to deal with sex with y'all?"

"Exactly."

For once, I was agreeing with Keva. I had many reasons to smile, and it had nothing to do with a man.

"The Lord makes me smile like that."

I should have known Keva would say some shit like that and ruin the moment.

"Girl, if the Lord got you smiling like that, you must be on your knees for something other than prayer." Keisha joked, and we all laughed.

"He must be blowing that back out," Devin added through her laughter.

Keva stared at us with disgust written all over her face.

"Y'all all going to hell," she scolded us.

"We ain't talking about you and the Lord's relationship, Keva," Keisha stated. "We're talking about the man that has Duck's nose wide open."

"I think our little Duck has met someone." Devin sang from over my head.

My phone chimed again, and I rushed to check it. It was a picture of a huge black dog rolled on her back with her belly exposed, and a large male hand rubbing her pink belly. This time, I could feel the smile on my face. I noticed how quiet the room had become. When I looked up, all eyes were on me.

"Why are you guys looking at me like that?"

"Oh. My. Goodness! Duck, I was just joking at first," Devin sung as she came around to stand in front of me.

Keisha was damn near out of her seat as she waited for any gossip she could take back to anyone that would listen. Even Keva was staring at me interested.

"Usually, I don't get involved in these sinful conversations, but now, even I want to know. Who is this man?"

"I bet he fine, and probably rolling in money," Keisha said, dreamily twisting the blonde tips of her wig around her manicured fingers.

Although I'd been with men that were well established and successful in their own right, I'd also been with men that were like Cliff. I guess to Keisha, a dream man would have to be rich.

"If he has Duck smiling, he has to be special. Probably kind and supportive." Devin sighed dreamily.

"How about y'all calm down. Jackson is just…..a friend."

"Jackson? Is that his last name?"

I could already see the vulture look in Keisha's eyes. She was going down her list of known people hoping she would know who Jackson was. Like I would ever fuck anyone that ran in the same circles as her. I do have some standards.

"No, Jackson is his first name."

Keisha scrunched up her face like what I said had a funny smell.

"I know he got clowned a lot. His name sounds white as fuck." She laughed at her own ignorant joke, but I didn't laugh.

"Wait--" Leave it to Devin to pick up on my mood. "He's white, isn't he?"

Keisha gasped, and Keva shoot to her feet.

"He's…… a little…. Melanin deficient."

"Duck, I've never known for you to be into white men?" Devin queried.

Keva shook her head and looked away. I knew she wouldn't have anything to say about Jackson's race. If anyone understood me, I knew she did. Even though, she had no idea I knew her deepest, darkest secret.

"Ewwww, Duck. I can't be with no white man." Keisha fell back in her seat. Her earlier excitement waned.

"And why not?"

"Because I like my men with a little extra sausage, if you know what I mean?"

"Oh come on, Keish. Tell me you don't believe in stereotypes?" Devin asked.

"You can't be that small minded," I said, taking offense to my cousin's comment. "I know for a fact not all brothers are packing." I also knew that Jackson was more than equipped. With that huge print I saw in his pants, there was no way he's fitting anyone's stereotype.

"You would know, you've seen enough of them," Keisha stated, and Keva laughed.

I ignored her remark.

"I also know for a fact that you've had at least one dick in your mouth that supports my point." I quirked a brow at her.

Roy's dick was the size of a Jimmy Dean sausage link, but she was sucking it like that shit was a Roger Wood smoked sausage. Obviously, a little extra is not a requirement for my dear cousin.

Keisha's brow lifted towards her hairline, I could tell she was trying to decipher exactly what I knew.

A lot, bitch!

"So, you like this guy? Have you been out with him?" Devin brought the conversation back around.

"Like I said, Jackson is nice, but he's just a friend. He wants a relationship, and I don't do relationships."

"Seriously, Duck? You're still doing that no dating thing?"

"Why are you so against relationships?" Keisha asked, her attention was back in the conversation.

I knew she was looking for a broken heart story, but my aversion to love had nothing to do with unrequited love.

"I don't do relationships, because I don't believe in love. Love is a made up word to give people a reason to do dumb shit."

The girls gasped. Keisha looked as if she didn't believe my reason, and Devin looked hurt.

"You want to know what I think?" Keva asked.

"Not really," I replied, but apparently it was a rhetorical question because she answered anyway.

"I think you say you don't believe in relationships because you know that no man will ever want you or marry you with your past."

This was why I didn't share with my family. No matter how good their intentions were, they would always become judgmental assholes. They pretended their sins and crimes were better than anyone else's.

"Like the old folks used to say," Keva continued, "why buy the cow when you can get the milk for free? No man is going to want your cow."

"First of all, my cow isn't for fucking sale, and even if it was, most men couldn't afford it."

"All I'm saying...."

"Shut up, Keva! Duck is beautiful, funny, successful, and independent. Any man would be honored to make her his wife. If a man has a problem with her past, then screw him. He doesn't deserve her," Devin stated, stepping back in front of me.

Though her words were kind, they weren't needed. I didn't care what Keva thought about me. At least I was true to myself, which was more than I could say about her.

Devin continued, turning back to me, "I don't know what your issue is with love, but if a man can make you light up the way you do every time you look down at that phone, he is worth getting to know. Even if it doesn't go anywhere or ends badly, you should chase happiness no matter what."

Usually I would have disregarded Devin's words. She's as bad as Grams with wanting me to settle down, but today was different. I didn't know if it was because of Jackson Keller, or the sadness buried behind Devin's eyes. Either way, her words made me think.

"Dee, I don't know why you're wasting your breath." Keisha sat back in her seat, finding her magazine interesting again. "Duck ain't gone change. You know what they say, you can't turn a hoe into a house wife."

"No, but you can make her a baby mama."

Keva and Devin laughed as Keisha looked at me with her mouth hanging open.

"You asked for that one," Keva admitted through her laughter.

SIX

I stared down at my phone again. The message I'd typed up over five minutes ago was still waiting for me to hit send. The simple words stared back at me.

ME: Still want that coffee?

I had no idea why I hadn't sent it off. I mean, having coffee with Jackson didn't mean I was looking for a future with him. It would just be two people out enjoying an overpriced beverage. What harm could it do? In fact, I was sure that it would be a smart choice. After this date, Jackson would more than likely prove just as uninteresting as all the other guys. If I lost interest, I could focus on other things. Maybe even get my appetite back and finally get that dick down that I needed. Or, maybe, I could convert Jackson into my way of thinking. He would stop trying to have a relationship with me and finally put me out of my drought.

See, sending the message was the best option.

I quickly hit send on my phone and watched as my message went from sent to delivered. I exhaled and placed the phone down on my coffee table. I refused to be one of those females that waited by her phone for a man to respond. I may be acting out of character by agreeing to this date, but I wasn't that damn far gone. I lifted my glass of Merlot to my lips and took a sip. The taste calmed my rattled nerves even more.

When the doorbell went off, I was startled enough to spill some of my wine on my blouse.

"Who the fuck is at my house at this time of night?" I asked my empty home.

Immediately following my question came the sound of knocking. Whoever it was seemed urgent to get my attention. Most people knew I didn't do company unless you called first. However, whoever it was had to have been here before, because the guards at the front entrance know not to let just anybody in here.

I headed to the door. I glanced out the peephole and rolled my eyes at the sight. I swung the door open with a growl.

"What the fuck are you doing here, Cliff?"

He looked just as good as he did the last time I saw him. All that smooth chocolate skin stretched over defined muscles. His goatee was trimmed to perfection and dark low fade shaped up expertly. His Braves baseball cap pulled low casting his eyes in shadows. Cliff looked good enough to eat, I just wasn't hungry. Especially not for him.

He gave me that slow panty melting smile. It used to get my pussy wet when I remembered exactly what his mouth could do. However, now it just made me want to kick his ass off my doorstep.

"Hey, baby! I came to see you. I missed you." He stepped up towards me, and I held up a hand to keep him back.

"Are you on drugs?" It was clear he'd been drinking, I could smell the alcohol on his breath, but he must be on crack in order to show up at my door like this.

"What?! No, you know I don't do that shit." He looked at me confused before shaking his head.

"Well, are you suffering from some form of psychosis, had a brain injury due to an accident, or maybe struck with some rare case of amnesia?"

Cliff shook his head. That crease in his brow deepened. "No! I have none of those issues. Why do you ask?"

"Because I'm trying to figure out why the hell you would show up to my house uninvited."

He smiled and chuckled. "Damn, baby! You still mad at daddy?"

At this point I really did believe he had lost his grip with reality. This wasn't just the alcohol. When the fuck had I ever called him daddy? I may not have had a daddy, but I sure as fuck knew his basic dick having ass wouldn't be called one.

"Cliff, it's late. I'm tired, and I have work to do tomorrow. I'm going to tell you this one last time. It's over between us. Don't call my phone or come by my house anymore."

I went to shut the door, but his Timberland boot stuck out and stopped the process.

Gone was that happy smile that first greeted me. Right now a hardened scowl was etched across his features.

"We aren't over until I fucking say we over," he threatened. "Especially when I know you're pregnant."

Despite the insanity I saw dancing behind his eyes, I laughed in his face.

"Boy, I am not pregnant."

"Naw, not yet anyway."

The meaning of his words wiped the smile off my face. Did he really just threaten to rape me to get me pregnant? He had truly lost his damn mind.

Cliff pushed at the door, almost getting it open. I shoved against it trapping his foot between the door and the door sill.

"Cliff, go back to your girl. There is nothing here for you."

"I'm not letting you go. You're mine, Charli. Only mine!" he shouted as he shoved against the door, sending me flying back into the foyer.

He stood in the doorway, his chest heaving up and down in his dark shirt. He slammed the door shut nearly shaking it off the hinges. I fought the fear that was trying to take over me. Fear that wanted to push me into that place. A place I didn't want to be. This was my body, no one got to take from me ever again.

"Cliff, I'm going to warn you one last time to get the hell out of my house."

Cliff yanked his shirt from over his head and tossed it to the floor.

"I've been thinking about that pussy day and night. We were good together, Charli. Let me make you feel good, baby."

He went for his belt, and I leapt to my feet. He grabbed for me, but I dodged out of his way and smacked the wall alarm, setting off my alarm system. The blaring sound went off, and Cliff froze.

"Fuck! Turn it off!" he shouted as he grabbed for me again, and I kicked at his stomach, causing him to bend at the waist from the pain.

"You have only a few minutes before the police show up at my house. Their response time is incredible when you live in a neighborhood like mine."

In the distance, the sound of sirens could be heard. Damn! That was faster than even I expected. Cliff turned towards the door.

"Fuck!" he shouted before turning back to me. "This ain't over, Charli. You're mine, baby."

"Get the fuck out, you psycho," I demanded.

Cliff turned and rushed out the front door. I hurried to the door and slammed it shut. Even with the sirens nearly two seconds away, I still wanted the barrier between he and I. I slid down my front door until I was sitting on my ass. The adrenaline started to wear off, and my body began to shake.

I fought back my demons as they tried to take over me.

"You're ok, Duck. You're safe. This is your body," I repeated those three sentences until the police were on my doorstep.

***

Nearly two hours later, the last cop finally left my house after taking my report fifty times. They made sure we talked to the people at the front gate and took Cliff's name off the list of approved guests. They also repeated more than a few times how I should go down to the station, file a report, and get a restraining order. In the end, there wasn't much they could do without the restraining order. I was just glad they came so fast and chased him away. Never again will I make a joke about how fast the cops show up in white neighborhoods.

I closed the door after the last officer left.

"I want to know who the fuck he is, and where he hangs out."

I called Eli not long after the cops came. I was still pretty shaken up by the whole ordeal, and one of the policemen asked if I had someone I could call to come stay with me. Eli was the first person I thought of besides Sean. For only a fraction of a second, I thought about Jackson, but I quickly dismissed that idea.

"Eli, I don't want you getting in trouble. Let the cops handle it. Besides, I'll be getting a restraining order in the morning."

I walked past him into the kitchen to grab another glass of wine. I thought the situation called for it.

Eli was on my heels.

"Duck, I'm not going to ask you again. Where does this muthafucker stay? Is he the same dude that put his hands on you the other day?"

I knew if I told Eli yes, I would be signing away Cliff's life. Although I didn't give a shit about what happened to that asshole, I did care about my cousin. So instead of answering, I just looked up at Eli, letting him know I wasn't telling him anything.

Eli slammed his hand down on my marble countertop. He knew it was a lost cause. I loved my cousin too much to risk him over this.

"I'm going to bed. You can have anything in the fridge you want," I said, tossing the empty bottle of wine in the trash.

"Like I would eat your left over take out and condiments." He smirked.

I breathed a sigh of relief at his joke. I didn't cook, so I never really had food in my house. I survived off of wine, takeout, and leftovers from Grams' house.

I stopped by Eli on my way out the kitchen.

"Thanks for staying with me."

He looked over at me, and smiled. "Anything for you."

I bumped his shoulder as I made my way up the stairs to my bedroom. I climbed in my massive bed and placed my wine glass beside me. I noticed I had a text message notification on my phone. I almost forgot about the message I sent Jackson. I slid my finger across the screen to read the message.

Jackson: Anytime. Anywhere.

The message was sent thirty minutes ago. Some of my enthusiasm about the date had started to disappear. I was no longer so sure in my plan. I had a crazy stalker I was dealing with, should I really get Jackson involved in this drama? Before the thought could form in my head and talk me out of it, my fingers were already flying across my keypad.

Me: Tomorrow. Noon. Starbucks on the corner of S. 28th street.

Jackson: See you there.

I placed my phone back on my nightstand, feeling skeptical about tomorrow. Was this really a good idea? By the time I reached the bottom of my wine glass, I was feeling confident in my plan, and sleep greeted me like the arms of a familiar lover.

SEVEN

At exactly twelve o'clock, I pulled into the parking lot of Starbucks. I took a deep breath before pulling the visor down and glancing at myself in the mirror. You would never be able to tell I had a rough night last night. Concealer covered the circles under my eyes. If only I had a quick fix to cover up my cousin's suspicion.

Our conversation came back to me from this morning.

"How was your night?" Eli asked as soon as I walked into the kitchen.

He was eating a bowl of cereal. It was the overly sweet kind I kept for whenever my God-kids came over.

I placed a K-cup of coffee into the Keurig while grabbing a mug.

"Good, how about you?"

I turned to look at him when he didn't immediately reply to my question. Those light-brown curious eyes were on me.

"You had another dream last night."

My entire body froze. It was only for a second, but it was long enough to make a difference to my cousin.

"I......don't remember it."

"Funny, that's the same shit you use to say when we were kids." The lack of inflection in his tone told me he was angry.

"It's not uncommon for people to have bad dreams and not remember them."

"Don't play with my intelligence, Charlice."

Damn! He must really be mad if he's using my real name.

When we were kids growing up in Grams' house, Eli and I often shared a

57

room. Not because we didn't have our own room, but because I often would play in his room at night so that I could fall asleep and sleep in his bed. He never woke me up and sent me to my own room. He would just put me in his bunk bed or throw a blanket over me on the floor and let me sleep. It's why he knew I was often plagued with nightmares.

I turned to him with my coffee in hand. "Look, Eli, I had a really rough night last night. It was probably just a dream about last night."

Eli's eyes watched me closely. He stood from his seat at the bar and walked over to the sink beside me running his empty bowl under the water. He placed the bowl in the dish drain and turned to me.

"The name you called out in your sleep had nothing to do with last night."

This time when my body froze, it was for a lot longer.

"What……what name did I call?" I questioned with a shaky voice.

Again, Eli's eyes studied me. "Same one you called when you were a kid. You called for Aunt Nita."

I shook my head and placed a fake smile on my lips. "No wonder I can't remember those dreams. They are clearly filled with delusions."

"Yeah," he agreed. "Delusions." Eli walked away from me, leaving me stranded in the kitchen.

The memory broke, and I was once again at Starbucks. I climbed out of my car, yanking down on my pencil skirt. I grabbed my purse and headed towards the door. I spotted Jackson right away. It was incredible how easily I found myself smiling at him.

His wide shoulders filled out a dark blue Polo with the name Keller Landscaping printed on the right side of his chest. Those hazel eyes swallowed me up. I forgot how fine this man was. My memory did not do him justice. He stood to his feet, and my head lifted with his height. He smiled at me, and those barely hidden dimples greeted me.

"Good afternoon, beautiful." That deep voice made my heart beat just a little faster.

"Good afternoon, Mr. Keller." I tried to say it as normal as possible, but I could hear the hint of a purr in my voice. I couldn't help it, fine men made more than just my pussy purr.

Jackson smirked at me as if he knew the affect he had on me. "I waited until you came to order." He said directing me towards the line.

I didn't care what time you came to this place there was ALWAYS a line. However, I didn't mind. The way Jackson's thick thighs looked in his khaki pants distracted me from the wait. Whoever thought Khakis could look so damn good.

We placed our order at the counter, and after receiving our coffee, we headed to a table.

Jackson pulled out my seat, and I sat down with a smile plastered on my face. He sat in front of me, and for a moment, he just stared at me.

"So, you mean to tell me, you went through all that work to get this date with me, and this is how you would like to spend your time?" I teased.

Jackson chuckled, and it was a sexy sound.

"You know, for a moment I thought I was going to have to make a deal with the devil to get you on this date. Thank you for relenting and saving my soul."

"Don't thank me yet, the date isn't over. You may still need his help."

He laughed again as he took a sip of his coffee. "Then I'll be sure to keep that appointment I made with him."

I laughed. "I'm flattered, Mr. Keller. I've never had a man give up his soul for me."

"It wouldn't be the first time I've questioned your choice in men."

I smiled again at him. I liked how easy he was to talk to. His witty comebacks were entertaining.

Again we did that weird thing where we just stared at each other with big cheesy smiles. I'd never been one of those people that made kissy faces in public. The ones that held hands as if they might get lost without the guidance of their significant other, or gazed into each other's eyes passionately like star crossed lovers. The people you wanted to murder with a dull spoon for being nauseously cute. Yes, today I was that person.

I cleared my throat and looked away from those hazel eyes that I was convinced had placed a spell on me.

"So, tell me a little about yourself."

I took a sip of my coffee before I answered. "There isn't much to tell."

"Sure there is. All I know about you so far is that you're beautiful, have an aversion to nice guys, and have shitty taste in coffee."

My laugh came out so boisterous and loud everyone at the coffee shop turned to look at me. I covered my mouth as I tried to contain my laughter. I watched the mirth dance in Jackson's eyes.

"For your information," I said once I got my laughter under control, "this coffee is delicious. It's a whole lot better than that tar you're drinking."

"There are seventeen ingredients on the label of that cup, I'm not even sure coffee is in it. At this point, you're drinking hot sugar."

Another laugh from me. When my laughter died down again, Jackson took a sip and lifted a brow at me.

"I did notice you didn't argue your aversion of nice men?"

I shook my head at him.

"Who said you were a nice guy?"

"Touché, Ms. Jefferies." He winked and then dragged his pointed pink tongue along his full bottom lip. I ignored the fluttery feeling in my belly that let me know the seat of my panties were probably drenched right now. "I still want to know more about you," Jackson added.

I had to clear my throat before I spoke again. "What do you want to know?"

"Let's start out with the easy stuff. Do you have any siblings?"

I gave a short dry laugh. "Please, Bernita Jefferies didn't want the one child she had. She would never dream of having another."

I didn't mean to go that far into detail. I was a very private person. My family didn't even know the details of my life. The only reason they think they knew about my sexual escapades was because I went to high school with Chante and Keisha, who were eager to bring back any news they could on me. Most of the shit that was spread in high school were lies. I didn't care enough about what people thought of me, so I didn't dispute the lies, and I felt in order to correct my family on their thoughts about me, I would have to let them in on all of my life, and I wasn't having that.

So it threw me for a loop that in just a few minutes of this date, I had told him something personal about me.

"I'm guessing your mom isn't winning any mother of the year awards from you?"

His calm demeanor and non-judgmental gaze lured me and made me continue to talk. It's like there was truth serum in this damn coffee.

"No! I haven't talked to my mother since I was sixteen, and even before then, our relationship was strained. Having a child wasn't very conducive to her ultimate dreams."

"And what was that?"

"To marry a rich man and never have to work."

He tilted his head slightly to look at me. "Did she ever fulfill that dream?"

I scoffed. "Hard to find a man to marry you when you're a selfish manipulative bitch."

He only nodded his head. Again, I admired how he seemed to keep his face blank of any thoughts or judgment.

"Well, the only thing worse than being an only child, is being the middle child," he said with a laugh. "My brother is three years older than me, and my sister is four years younger than me."

"Are you guys close?"

"My sister and I are close. Even more so since she's had the twins." I loved the way his eyes lit up when he mentioned his sister's kids.

"What about your brother?"

Jackson ran a hand down the back of his neck.

"Uh...... Jeff and I are......" His face scrunched as he tried to find the right words to say. "Still trying to find our common ground," he simply explained.

I offered him the same respect he gave me about my mother—I didn't judge.

I took another sip of my coffee, just to break up the seriousness of the conversation.

"So," I cleared my throat and began. "Tell me about Keller Landscaping. What made you go into the field of Ornamental Horticulture?"

Jackson laughed, and I took a few moments to admire the effect it had on his face. How the lines around his eyes appeared when he laughed. The way his gorgeous lips turned upward exposing straight teeth. It made his hardened and tough exterior look younger when he smiled.

"My dad," he answered. "Every Saturday, my dad would drag my brother and I out of the house early in the morning to cut the grass, trim bushes, cut back trees, or tend the many flower gardens my mother kept around the house. We grew up in a lower middle class neighborhood. My father bought his house by years of saving up for it. He taught us to take pride in the things that you have. Hence forth, making sure the outside of our house was as well- kept as the inside. Initially, working in the yard was a punishment, but at some point, I started to love it. After I left the military, I needed something to do with my down time. So I started my company. I'm not rolling in the money like you." He chuckled, and I laughed along with him. "But it keeps the bills paid, and I love what I do."

"Well, that's all that matters, right, loving what you do?"

He nodded and cracked his knuckles before leaning back in his seat. I loved the way that Polo shirt stretched across his chest and hugged his biceps.

"So why consulting?"

I smiled as I answered the question. "I love it, and I'm damn good at it."

For the next hour, Jackson and I talked about everything and anything. I learned that he loved to cook but hated to clean up after himself. He's allergic to mushrooms and used them to get out of a test one time in tenth grade. He loved finding new adventures and spending time with his nephews.

When the hour was up, and we both had to get back to work, I was kind of sad it was time to say bye to him.

Just as Jackson was about to say something else, I heard my name called.

I looked up to find Detective Sean Myers and his girlfriend, Rochelle, standing over our table.

"Charli, I thought that was you."

Sean and I went way back. He was four years younger than me. I was a senior in high school when I first met the shy freshman. Some asshole grabbed my ass in the hallway. Sean saw it and beat the shit out of the guy. I thanked him by popping his cherry in the back seat of my car. He was tall for his age with wide shoulders, milk chocolate skin, and dark-brown soulful eyes. He was gorgeous, and ever since that first time, he and I have always kept in contact.

I liked Sean because he understood me. He never tried to make us more than what we were. We got together every now and again just to fuck, and boy could he fuck. I taught him everything he knew. He's always been working with a cobra sized dick, but that first time he had no idea how to use it. Now he's slanging that thing like a pro. I understood why his longtime girlfriend always wraps herself around him whenever another female is around. She's welcome.

"Well hello, Detective. It's nice to see you two out."

I glance over at the girlfriend. She's a beautiful girl, half black and Korean. Her long jet black hair was pulled up in a top-knot. She's petite and on the slim side, a complete opposite from me.

Her brown cat shaped eyes narrowed down at me. Despite how friendly I was to Rochelle, she absolutely hated me. I don't blame her, I do fuck her man whenever they are on a break.

Sean smiled wide, showcasing those perfectly straight white teeth. Always oblivious to his girls hatred towards me.

"I'm sorry to interrupt your...." He cut his eyes over to Jackson, leaving the tail end of his sentence open for one of us to fill in.

Jackson looked at me with a smirk on his face. He sat back in his chair and took a sip of his coffee leaving the ball in my court.

Funny, Mr. Keller, but two can play that game. I looked up to Sean without saying a word, allowing the moment to become awkward so that he would be forced to speak.

It worked.

"Uhhhh. I...uh...just wanted to come by and check in on you. I heard about the situation last night at your house. You should have called me."

Ugh! Why did he have to bring this up now?

I knew when the cops showed up, that it would get back to Sean. He's friends with a lot of beat cops, and apparently, cops gossip more than women at a beauty salon. The moment my address came up, Sean would've started asking questions.

"What happened at your house?" Jackson asked

The playful smirk from just a few minutes ago had been replaced with a furrowed brow.

"Nothing. Just a little pest problem," I said to Jackson then turned back to Sean. "And the police handled it for me. They actually responded pretty fast. So, no need to worry. Besides, isn't pest control beneath you, Mr. Homicide Detective?" I joked with Sean.

About two years ago, he got promoted to detective. I helped him celebrate by fucking him to exhaustion all night long.

"Beneath me or not," Sean said with a smile, "you're my best friend. You know I always got your back."

Rochelle's eyes nearly rolled out of her head. Even without all the fucking Sean and I do, we were actually good friends.

I nodded my head. "Thanks," I said, dismissing them.

"Well, y'all have a good day, and um… Give me a call, Charli." Sean gave me a conspiring wink as he lead Rochelle away.

One of my rules for the men I sleep with, was that you didn't call me, I called you. I could give a shit if you're in the mood. I called the shots. When I wanted to fuck, I'll notify you. If you're not available or not in the mood, fine, I'll find someone else.

It had been about a week since I last gave Sean a call. I never called him when he and Rochelle were together. We've gone long stretches of time without being physical because of their relationship. He was the only guy I'd fucked that I actually remained friends with.

The moment Sean and Rochelle disappeared out the glass doors of the coffee shop, Jackson spoke.

"Let me guess, the cop is one of your exes?"

I grabbed my purse off the chair beside me and went to stand the same time Jackson got to his feet.

"I don't have exes. Remember, I don't have relationships."

"Ok! Then is he one of your fuck toys?"

At this, I laughed. I loved the little jealousy I detected in his voice. I've never been into jealous lovers, but something about Jackson being a little jealous had me turned on.

"Why, is that a problem for you?" I asked as he walked me out to my car.

He chuckled. "I'm a confident man, Charlice. I'm not easily intimidated by some guy that fucked my girl."

"Your girl?" I questioned, hiding the fact that I kind of liked that coming from his lips.

Another one of those confident smirks from Jackson. "What's that saying, ask and you shall receive? Well, I'm claiming what's going to be mine. What you did before we met has nothing to do with me, I'm only concerned with what happens after."

I crossed my arms over my chest. Despite how hard I tried, the smile I was fighting refused to give up its spot on my face.

"And what happens after?"

Jackson took my hand and rubbed his roughened thumb against the smooth skin on the back of my hand. I couldn't help but think about the fact that he was rubbing his thumb in the exact way he would rub my clit.

"What are you doing this weekend?"

I blushed. Damn him, I blushed like a weak little girl.

"Baby sitting, but I thought we were keeping things friendly? Shouldn't this be our goodbye?"

That's right, Duck, cut this off now. You have no need to see him again.

He took a step closer, towering over me. His large body didn't intimidate me as I looked up into those hooded hazel eyes. I loved the way he smelled, like man and sawdust. An odd combination, but it worked on him. He smelled like a man.

"I'm asking as a friend," his deep voice admitted.

"Do you always ask your friends out on the weekend?" I cocked an eyebrow up at him.

He smiled that panty melting smile. "Only the really attractive ones." There goes that damn tongue rolling over that plump bottom lip again. "Besides, it's clear you have no problems with friends." He smirked, hinting back to Sean.

I laughed and rolled my eyes.

"I thought you understood, Mr. Keller. I don't date." Even I could hear how weak that argument was.

"And as I said, Ms. Jeffries, this isn't a date. Just two friends hanging out. Just like today."

I looked away from those stunning eyes, giving myself time to at least look as if I was holding out. When I turned back to Jackson, he had the biggest grin on his face. He knew I was going to cave.

"When?" I simply asked with a playful eye roll.

"Next Saturday at nine a.m. I'll pick you up from home. Wear something comfortable," he stated before letting go of my hand. I felt the absence of his touch immediately.

"Who the hell goes on a date at nine o'clock in the morning?" I demanded with my hands on my hips as Jackson backed away from me with a sly smile.

"Remember, it's not a date." He winked. "Text me your address before then." And then, he jogged back to his dirty truck before I could argue anymore. That damn white boy.

EIGHT

Two days before my not—a—date with Jackson, I was speeding into my Grams' driveway. Just fifteen minutes ago, I got an urgent message from her telling me to come home immediately. I was in the middle of a meeting with a potential client when my assistant delivered the message. I quickly apologized and had my assistant take over the meeting.

I was already on edge because of Cliff's crazy ass. Last week after the coffee date with Jackson, I got a message from a private number. It was a picture of Jackson holding my hand, right before he asked me out this weekend. The picture captured everything. I could tell in Jackson's eyes that he wanted me, not just to fuck, that was evident too, but he wanted me. The woman with major attitude issues. Looking at me in the picture made a few things obvious too, I may want Jackson a little more than I let on.

Although the picture was creepy enough, the text that went along with it was worse. "I'll never share you." Who the fuck does something like that? I've been a little paranoid ever since. I'm not too worried though, I can still handle Cliff.

My biggest fear as I broke the speed limit to get to my grandma's house was my Papa. A year and a half ago, Papa had a massive heart attack that scared us shitless. He'd been taking it easy and managing his diet ever since, but as I made the twenty-minute drive to my grandma's house in a record breaking ten, I couldn't help but think the worst.

I parked my car in the driveway and ran as fast as my Louboutins would take me. I used my key to rush in the house and immediately started calling Grams' name.

"Grams! Grams!"

"In here, Duck." Her voice called back from the kitchen.

She didn't sound in pain or sad, but that didn't mean anything. I rushed into the kitchen to find her standing at the stove humming a tune. She was stirring something in a pot. I looked around the room to make sure I wasn't missing anything. My heart still kicked up in my chest. Everything seemed in place. Kareem, Keisha's three-year-old son was sitting in his high chair at the island.

"Um, Grams, is everything ok?" She turned towards me with a smile.

"Of course. Go on and sit down so I can fix you a plate."

Without thinking, I did as she instructed. My brain still stunned by the urgency of her earlier phone call.

Grams placed a plate of spaghetti, homemade rolls, and sweet carrots down in front of me, and a smaller plate in front of Kareem. I looked to Kareem who smiled at me before digging into his food.

"Why did you call me?"

Sadie Jefferies wiped her hands on her apron before leaning against her sink to stare back at me.

"So, what's this I hear about you dating a white boy?"

Gotdamn Keisha! That bitch can't keep nothing closed, not her legs or her mouth. I had no intentions of telling my family about Jackson.

"I'm not dating anyone, and why would you call me over here like something was wrong? I thought something happened to Papa."

"This is an emergency. I had to talk to you before you did something foolish, like run that boy off. Now, I don't know why you couldn't come to me about this white boy. You know your Papa and I don't care who any of y'all date, as long as they treat you right. Does he treat you right?"

My mouth was still hanging open. Too much was going on at once. She called me out of an important meeting to talk to me about Jackson, and now she's wondering if he treats me right.

"Grams, you've been misinformed, Jackson and I…"

"Jackson? That's his name? Who his people? I wonder do he know them Parker people that own Parker Furniture store."

I took a breath, this was why I didn't tell my family anything.

"You wouldn't know his people, Grams. And not all white people are related."

"You don't know who I know. What's his last name?"

"Anonymous," I said, then pushed my plate of untouched food away as I climbed to my feet.

I walked over to the pantry where Grams keeps her aluminum foil. Now that I knew this wasn't an emergency, I was going to take my food and head back to work.

"When are you going to bring him to Sunday dinner?"

"Never. I told you, I'm not dating anyone." I found the aluminum foil amongst the wax paper, cupcake holders, Ziploc bags, and plastic wrap.

"What happened to you that has you so scared to fall in love?" My body froze momentarily at her question.

I turned back to my grandma with a practiced smile.

"Nothing happened."

"I think you're scared you're going to end up like your mother. Always searching for love in the next man."

"You and I both know Bernita is not looking for love in these men."

Grams could deny it all she wanted, the only thing my mother was looking for was a man to take care of her, she could give a shit if he loved her or not. Bernita Jefferies had no idea what love was.

"Look, Grams, I don't do relationships because I don't believe in love. It has nothing to do with Bernita."

She looked at me and gave me one of those smiles. The one she used to give me when I was a little girl and hurt myself, but I would try not to cry in front of Papa and Eli. That same sad knowing smile spread across her full face.

"Sometimes I look at you and I think you're a grown woman, then you say things, and I remember you're still a child. You have a world of secrets hidden behind your eyes, Duck. No need to deny it," she said, cutting off what was surely about to be my denial.

"A mother knows her children. It doesn't matter if she's your own or your grandchild. I see it in your eyes. You can't lie to me."

Even though everything on my body stiffened at her words, I

WHERE LOVE IS FOUND

placed a smile on my face.

"There is nothing to hide, Sadie Rose." I wrapped my plate up in the aluminum foil I found.

"Mhhmmm," Grams said. "So, nothing happened up at your house last week?"

Jesus! Can none of my family keep a damn secret?

I didn't care how rattled that last picture and message made me, I wasn't going to tell her about it. I would never allow my problems to become hers.

"It's not a big issue. The situation was handled."

"Duck, I have told you about that fast-tailed lifestyle you live. It's going to catch up to you. Men can become scorned lovers too. I don't want to see you get hurt, baby." Grams placed a hand on my cheek.

I turned and placed a kiss on her withered palm and then backed away.

"I'll stay safe. Now, can I please go back to work so I can try to salvage this meeting I almost ruined?" I laughed.

I could tell that my reply wasn't suitable for my grandmother, but she knew there was no getting through to me. She placed a kiss on my forehead.

"Go on. I'm expecting to see Mr. Jackson 'No last name' at Sunday dinner this week."

I didn't reply. There was no need. Sadie would never meet Jackson because we weren't dating. I placed a kiss on little Kareem's head and walked out the door.

****

The day of the not-a-date, my nerves were all over the place. Just that morning, I had to call the police to the house again. That fucker came to the house beating on my door again. He begged me to let him in and help him. He ran off right before the cops came. I called Sean too. He showed up raging mad before the police came. He couldn't believe that the cops had yet to catch Cliff. I thought the same thing.

Cliff wasn't the brightest bulb in the box. There was no way he could evade the cops this long. I told them to check with the girlfriend after that first time he showed up at the house, but she told the cops she hadn't seen him since she turned him away that morning. Seemed like all the women in Cliff's life was giving him the boot.

I hated these sick games Cliff was playing, but I refused to let him keep me held up in my house. No man would have that type of power over me. I made sure to keep a piece with me at all times. I even told Sean about my weapons. He took his time looking them all over to make sure they were properly working. He told me if Cliff showed up again to put a bullet right in between his eyes, and then call him. I promised him I would.

Sean hated to leave, but he had plans that night with Rochelle. I figured he was going to pop the question soon. She'd been begging him for it. Even though I'd hate to lose that dick permanently, I wasn't selfish, and I wanted Sean happy. So if that moody bitch made him happy, then what could I say?

By the time eight-forty-five rolled around, I had changed clothes three times. Jackson said dress comfortable, but comfortable could mean anything. I ended up with a pair of 7 For All Mankind distressed skinny-jeans, a BeBe one shoulder silk top, and my Chanel sandals.

My doorbell rang at exactly eight-fifty. I already knew who it was because the security at the front gate notified me of his arrival. I opened the door to a smiling Jackson. He looked sexy as hell with the sun shining through his hair. His golden skin glistened underneath his black UnderArmour t-shirt and baller shorts.

"Why the hell are you dressed like you're going to the gym?"

A smile from Jackson. "Are you going to invite me in before criticizing what I'm wearing?"

I rolled my eyes and opened my door wider before stepping back to give him access.

His eyes scanned the interior of my house, taking in the open floor plan, hard wood floors, tray ceilings and floor to ceiling glass windows. "Nice, but your front yard could use some flowers." He gave me that playful smirk.

I made sure I had a company that came over to cut my grass and keep my grass green, but that was all that went into my yard. With the exception of a few shrubs that lined the short walk way to the front door, I didn't have any flowers.

"Are you here for a job or a date?" I teased Jackson.

"So this is a date?"

I quickly shook my head! Damn, I fell into that trap.

"No, not a date. Just two new friends hanging out….. at a gym apparently. Or a frat party," I said, looking down at his outfit.

He laughed. "Just go get changed. You'll like where I'm taking you."

I doubted it. However, I didn't argue, I just went and changed into a pair of yoga pants and old Emory university tee with my Nike running shoes. I was telling myself to give this a chance. If it turned out to be a huge bust, I could finally write Jackson off and be over this little infatuation I had with him. When I came back down the stairs and walked into my living room, Jackson's eyes grew large. He took in my tight fit yoga pants, and his mouth dropped open. My last outfit cost a total of eighteen-thousand dollars, and his mouth fell open for a thirty-dollar pair of Yoga pants? Why the hell did that turn me on?

"Are we going to go, or are we finally going to do this thing my way?" I teased as I spun around and showed him my ass.

Part of me wished we could just bypass all this date stuff and fuck already, but another NEW part of me kind of wanted to see how this date went.

Jackson cleared his throat and stood to his feet. I almost choked on what was being barely contained behind those shorts. Forget this damn date, I wanted the pole in his shorts.

"Point me to the restroom, and then we can go."

I didn't even attempt to take my eyes away from what his hand was trying to block. I just threw up my hand and pointed to the hall bath. Jackson escaped around the corner and out of sight.

Damn! Jackson was packing. I practiced a few Kegel exercises to calm the ache in my clit. I hoped we could make it through this not-a-date without yanking each other's clothes off.

By the time Jackson appeared back in the living room, he seemed to have charmed his snake into behaving.

"You ready?" he asked, those hazel eyes staring back at me.

I nodded, and he led us out the door. I locked up and followed him to his truck.

"Do you ever wash this thing?" I asked jokingly as he opened my door.

"Why would I? I think the dirt on a vehicle tells its story."

"The only story this thing is telling is that it's neglected."

Jackson laughed as he closed my door. In spite of the truck being a dirty mess on the outside, it was spotless on the inside. Not even a piece of paper in the cup holder. And the bonus, it smelled just like Jackson.

I was startled when a black wet nose landed on my shoulder. I forgot about the dog. He brought another female on our date? I turned to face the dog. I wasn't a pet person. I didn't have anything against them, but I don't understand the passion in cleaning up behind an animal that doesn't even appreciate you. It's like marriage without the added bonus of sex. The dog stared at me, her brown eyes seemed to take me in. If I didn't know any better, I would think she was really trying to size me up. See if I was worthy of her human.

"This isn't a date, and I'm not trying to take your place." I found myself saying to the dog.

She continued to look at me, then tilted her head to the side as if she didn't believe me. When Jackson opened the door on his side, we both turned to see him, me with a smile and her with a happy wag of her tail. He rubbed her head then sat in his seat.

"You girls get to know each other?" he asked.

The dog turned to me one last time then turned around on the back seat to lay down.

"She likes you. That's a good thing. Lady is usually very possessive of me."

"And you thought to stick me in the truck alone with a vicious dog that gets jealous of females around her man?"

He laughed. "She's not vicious."

"That's what all dog owners say until they are on the news trying to explain why Spot chewed the neighbor's kid's face off."

A shake of his head. "Your pessimism is adorable." He started the engine, then glanced over to me.

"Are you ready?"

"I guess."

He laughed as he backed out of my driveway.

The moment we pulled onto the highway, Jackson started to talk.

"So, tell me something about you that no one else knows." He said, glancing over to me.

"My secrets are a very pricey commodity. I don't just give them away."

Another chuckle. He took one hand off the steering wheel to rub his thumb along his bottom lip.

"Ok, how about an even trade. I'll give you a secret of mine, and you can give me one of yours?"

"I won't make any promises," I said, looking out the passenger window as the busy Atlantic traffic came to a standstill.

"I'll take my chances. Let me see......" He paused, running a hand through his hair.

I loved the way his wide arms flexed and the muscles bunched whenever he moved his hands.

"Ok, I got one. My dad had this big shed behind our house. He kept all of his tools and things in it. Well, when I was about thirteen, I picked up the nasty habit of smoking. One day after school, I was dying for a smoke, so I went into the shed and fired one up. I thought I heard someone coming, so I quickly tossed the cigarette to the floor and walked out of the shed. I had planned to go back and get it, because hey, they were hard to come by at that age. Two hours later, the entire shed was burning to the ground. I'd completely gotten sidetracked and forgot about the cigarette. To this day, my father thinks some neighborhood kid burnt down that shed."

I laughed, I couldn't help it. Jackson glanced to the passenger seat with a smile on his face.

"Damn," he stated. "You're gorgeous when you laugh. I can watch you do it all day."

My laughter immediately died down. My stomach fluttered, and for the first time, it had nothing to do with a sexual urge. Again, I wasn't new to compliments, but it was something about the way Jackson talked to me. There was a sincerity in his voice that I'd never heard before.

"Whatever. Don't think just because you told me about your short stint as a juvenile delinquent that I'm going to tell you any of my secrets." I turned from him and looked out of the window. The traffic was starting to move again.

"I know you have secrets. You don't have to tell me where the bodies are," he said with a chuckle.

I faced him. "Are you suggesting that I've possibly killed someone?" I gave him an innocent look.

He glanced at me before turning back to the road.

"Knowing you, it's probably more than just one."

At this, I laughed again.

"I'm not that bad."

I chuckled at his incredulous look.

"You're a fine one to talk, little arsonist." He roared with laughter. "Fine, you want one of my secrets?"

He nodded his head.

"Ok." I took a deep breath as I got serious. "I went on a date with this guy one time. He was really sweet, and I thought he was the perfect guy. He picked me up in his nice new car looking so good." I cut my eyes over to Jackson, and even though his eyes were on the road, I knew I had his full attention. I continued on. "Then it happened. Jackson, it was awful."

"What? What happened, Charlice?" His hands tightened around the steering wheel causing his knuckles to whiten.

"He…He…He wouldn't tell me where he was taking me on our date, so I shot him in the foot." I started to laugh at the face he gave me. He was so invested in my story.

Finally, that cute smile broke across his face. "Not funny, woman. I thought I was going to have to go whoop some dude's ass."

I shook my head. "Seriously, where are we going? And I swear if you're taking me to a gym, that story is going to be true."

His laughter rung out in the car. "I'm not taking you to the gym. Can't you just sit back, relax, and enjoy the suspense?"

"Fuck no!"

Another one of his loud rowdy laughs. "Tell me, what else would you be doing on a Saturday morning at nine a.m?"

Before I could answer, he seemed to think about his question.

"You know what, I don't want to know the answer to that."

I playfully punched him in the arm. "Despite what you think, Mr. Keller, my Saturday mornings would usually be spent running errands for my grandparents or hanging with my God-children."

"You have God-children?"

"Yes, two and a half. They are actually my little cousins, but their mom and I are really close, so she named me God-mother."

"Tell me about them."

I smiled thinking about my sassy babies. "Well, Kylie is the oldest, and she is hilarious. She's super smart and independent. She loves being helpful and thinks she's a fashionista. Naya is three, and she wants to be just like me. She copies everything I do. I haven't met the youngest yet, but I'm super excited to spend time with them."

I turned to look at Jackson, and he was just staring at me with a smile on his face.

"What?"

He shook his head and chuckled. "The way your face lights up when you talk about your God-children, it's adorable."

I blushed. Damnit!

"Yeah well, my God-children are great kids."

"I can tell."

"So, what about you? Any God-children...or children?"

He chuckled. "Very subtle."

"Hey, a woman has to ask these things."

He ran his hands through his hair before looking over to switch lanes. "No, no God-children or children, but I do have two really great nephews."

"Yeah, you mentioned them before. Your sister's kids, right? So are you the fun uncle?"

"Are you kidding? I'm the world's greatest uncle. I have a shirt and a mug to prove it. I've held that title for five years straight now."

I laughed. "Oh, we're cocky about it."

"Damn right."

We both laughed until it slowly faded away.

"I love being an uncle," Jackson admitted. "And I know one day, I will love even more being a dad. What about you, you want kids one day?"

I continued to look out of the window as I allowed his question to run its usual course around my body.

"Don't think you can distract me with this talk about kids. I still need to know where the hell you're taking me."

"You will see." He laughed while taking an exit to the right.

NINE

Not long after taking the exit, we pulled up to a sign that read, Sweetwater Creek. Jackson pulled his large truck into the nearly empty parking lot. There were only three other cars around us. A large forest was in front of us.

Jackson stopped the car and hopped out. His dog eagerly waited for him to let her out. I watched in bewilderment as he came around to my side and opened the door.

"Have you lost your mind?"

"What?" If this wasn't the craziest situation ever, his confused look would be adorable.

"I'm not going in there."

"Why not? It will be fun. They have tons of beautiful sights, one of them is a pretty amazing view of the Atlanta city skyline. Plus, I packed a picnic for us."

Ok a picnic was cute, but still. "If you haven't noticed, I'm black. Black folks don't go into woods voluntarily, Jackson."

"Don't do that. There are tons of African Americans that enjoy hiking."

I crossed my arms over my chest. "I'm pretty sure I know more than you, and the ones I know, don't."

Jackson sighed and ran his hands through his hair again.

"Ok! Can you just give it a try? I know this isn't usual for you, Charlice, but I wanted to do something with you that you've never done before. Look, I can't afford the things you're used to, but what I can do, is give you experiences that you've never had. I just need you to trust me. And I promise, if you hate it, I will bring you back to the truck and take you to some fancy restaurant that you have probably eaten at a million times."

Well, what was I supposed to say to that? The idea of a private picnic sounded sweet, and he was right, I'd never been hiking. Hell, I didn't even know they had places to hike in Atlanta. Besides, I had been to every decent restaurant in Atlanta, and doing something like sitting in a crowded fancy restaurant didn't appeal to me with Jackson. I'd much rather have him all to myself.

I sighed. "Fine," I grudgingly admitted. "But, if this is one of those crazy white people things where you drag me into the woods to rape and kill me, I'm coming back to haunt your ass."

Jackson laughed. "How is being a serial rapist a white thing?"

"Because that's the shit y'all do."

He shook his head. "You have nothing to fear but snakes and mountain lions."

I paused before climbing out the car.

"What?"

"I'm kidding. I'm kidding. Come on."

Jackson helped me down and then went to the bed of his truck to retrieve a large green hiking bag with an attached picnic basket. He grabbed a leash for the dog and turned to me. "Ready?"

"No! But I guess it doesn't matter."

He laughed and grabbed my hand to lead the way.

***

I was a slow walker. I knew that I was slowing Jackson down tremendously, but not once did he complain. The dog definitely found me utterly annoying and useless. And despite the run-ins with the spider webs, the near death falls, the cluster of gnats that attacked us, and the scorching heat, I really did have a wonderful time.

Jackson kept me laughing and entertained. He showed me things I never knew. Apparently, one of the Civil War forts on the trail was used in some Hunger movie. The picnic was just as romantic as I thought it would be. I had a really great time. So much fun that we decided to do a few of the smaller trails and some more sightseeing.

By the time Jackson pulled up in my driveway, the sun was going down. I'd just spent all day with this man, and I still wasn't ready for him to leave.

Jackson opened the passenger side door—I hadn't had to touch a car handle all day—and walked me up to my front door. He lingered, and so did I.

"I had fun on my not date," I said jokingly.

"I'm glad." He stepped closer to me.

I had to look up just to see his eyes.

His height and body heat didn't scare me off, if anything, it had reawakened that other side of me. I'd been on my best behavior today. I was so busy enjoying myself, I didn't focus so much on sex. However, now, having him right at my door with his bulky body fitted in that t-shirt, I was focused. His smell of sweat and musk permeating the air, had me wanting to explore something else right now.

"How about you come in for some…..coffee." I gave him a naughty smile.

There was no mistaking the real reason I wanted Jackson to come into my home. Just to prove my point, I took an extra step towards him brushing my breasts against his chest.

He bit down on his bottom lip, and damn if the action didn't encourage my desire. I could already feel his large body grinding between my thighs.

"Actually, I think I better head home."

My brain made the sound of a record scratching. What the fuck?

"Very funny, Jackson! You almost had me." I chuckled.

Jackson stepped back. "No really, I'm going to go home."

Ok, this was not what I had planned for tonight. What was his problem? I knew he was attracted to me, he worked too hard to get a date with me, and plus, I knew his dick worked because I'd seen it hard. So what was the problem?

"Ok, what are you trying to do? I mean, I just invited you into my house."

"I know, and I'm going to leave because I want to see you again."

"Which is why I'm trying to get you to come inside."

"I told you, Charlice. This isn't some one-time thing for me. I like you, and I want to see how far this goes."

"Jackson, I don't date. I don't have boyfriends. I told you this, this is what I do." I pointed towards my front door.

"I won't be just another guy you fuck, Charlice. If that means I'll never get to sleep with you, then whatever. I want more. I want to be different from all those other dudes."

"You are different...."

".....Only because I'm white."

Silence surrounded us. Jackson just wanted way more than I could give him. I could admit that I liked Jackson. I liked him a lot. And maybe if things were different, if I were different we could really have something, but I can't give him what he wanted.

"Jackson, I....."

"Don't say anything. Tomorrow morning, I'm going to send you a text that says good morning, you can reply if you want to. I'll continue to text you throughout the day as I think about you, again, reply is optional. Next Saturday, only if you aren't busy with your God-children, I will pick you up around seven where we will hang out again." He stepped a little closer to me, but not as close as before. "I never said I needed a label right now. If it makes you feel better, we can continue to call this a friendship. I just want to be in your life. And don't think for a moment, me turning down your offer was easy, beautiful. I just know what I want, and it's not one night with you."

I was speechless again. How was this man capable of rendering me without thought? I never knew what to expect from him.

"Alright!" I finally said. "I guess this is goodnight."

"Goodnight, Charlice!"

The moment my hand touched my front door, it opened. I paused, and immediately, Jackson had me tucked behind him.

"Did you lock your door before we left?"

"Yes! And I turned on the alarm."

"Go back to the truck and call 911. Do not get out," he said with his back towards me.

"I'm not sitting in your truck. I can handle myself."

Jackson spun around to face me. "Take your little ass back to the truck and call 911."

Wow! I thought sweet Jackson was sexy but alpha—do—as— I—say—Jackson was fucking HOT.

I didn't argue, I just went straight to his truck. Jackson gave three quick whistles, and Lady was out of the truck and at his side. He gave me a stern look before entering the house.

I was so nervous I almost forgot to call the cops. After getting off the phone with the 911 operator, I realized Jackson had been gone too long. I prayed nothing happened to him. It was those worries that made me climb out of the truck.

I made my way quietly inside the house. Unlike those dumb chicks in horror movies, I wasn't going to call out his name and bring attention to myself. I followed the sound of movement towards my bedroom. I stopped at the linen closet on the way to my room and pulled out one of my hidden .45s.

I crept closer to my bedroom, stopping when one of my floorboards gave. Once enough time had passed and nothing happened, I crept closer. Before I could walk in my room, my arm was pulled and shoved down, nearly twisting my hand until I dropped the gun to the floor. Then I was grabbed by the neck and shoved into the wall. At the exact same time, we both recognized each other.

"Damnit, Char! I told you to stay in the truck." Jackson let me go immediately. His eyes examined me making sure I was ok. "Fuck, babe, I could have killed you." He rubbed my neck.

"I'm the one with the gun," I said in a strained voice.

Jackson lifted a thick eyebrow at me. "You mean the one lying on the floor? Trust me, I was safe."

"Hey! I know how to use that gun. You just caught me off guard."

He gave me a smirk that said 'Sure you do'. I ignored his jibe.

"Did you find anything?" I asked, stepping around him.

My eyes went directly to the mess on my bed.

What the hell? All of my sex paraphernalia was lying destroyed in the middle of my bed. Underwear, condoms, handcuffs, lubricants, and even my collection of vibrators were all broken up in little pieces.

"Why would he do this?" I asked no one in particular.

Jackson and Lady came to stand beside me. He placed a comforting hand on my shoulder.

"Come on, let's go downstairs and wait for the cops."

I let him guide me back down the stairs and into the living room where we waited for the cops.

***

Once again it didn't take the cops long to get to us. They asked us a hundred questions and did a thorough search of the house, even taking the destroyed paraphernalia in order to search for fingerprints. I was relieved when Sean showed up. I sent him a text not long after the cops came.

"What time did you leave the house?" the young-faced cop asked me.

I felt like I was the one under investigation. They had asked me so many questions, most of them pointless.

"I left about nine something this morning," I admitted, rubbing the throbbing out of the center of my forehead. Jackson placed a hand on my back. Just having him here had been a comfort.

"And where did you say you went?" Again, the cop asked.

I'd answered that same damn question about ten times. Could they not just compare notes?

"Like I've said for the hundredth time, I went out on a date."

He scribbled that on his notepad, apparently in invisible ink just like all the others before him.

"And what time did you get back home and realize the door was open?"

"About six, right before she called the station," Jackson answered sensing my irritation.

"Sir, I need her to answer these questions," the baby-faced cop stated.

Jackson did that half chuckle thing he did whenever he was trying to stay calm. I first noticed it the day he met Sean. Was it odd that I was paying attention to his mannerisms?

"Like he said, around six."

Another second to write my reply in his notepad. "So, you were gone on a date for nine hours? Where did you go on this date?"

"None of your gotdamn business. What does this have to do with my house being broken into? You're asking me questions like I'm the suspect."

Sean appeared out of nowhere. He said something to the young cop that had him walking away with a glare towards me.

Jackson took me in his arms and hugged me. I needed his warmth and comfort right now.

"Aye, Charli, I'm sorry about that," Sean said, getting my attention.

Jackson released me and I turned back towards Sean.

"I know these questions seem intrusive, but they are protocol."

I waved Sean off. I knew the officer was just doing his job, but I was tired and angry. I couldn't believe I was still dealing with Cliff's bullshit.

"I know, Sean. I just don't understand why they haven't found this guy yet."

"Trust me, it's frustrating me too, baby, and I got every guy I know on this case."

Only because I wasn't in my right mind did I not correct him on the endearment he just used. It wasn't the first time he called me baby, it's usually followed up with how good my pussy tasted. However, he had never said it so freely outside the bedroom. It didn't bother me, but I did notice how Jackson's body tensed at the word. I still let it pass, Sean clearly wasn't in his right mind either.

Sean liked to be able to solve problems. He's one of those people that liked to be needed. So I knew that being unable to solve this case for me was driving him crazy.

"I know you're doing all you can, Sean." I reached out and touched his arm lightly.

"Did anyone check the alarm?" Jackson asked, crossing his arms across his wide chest.

Sean cut his eyes over to Jackson giving him a suspicious look. "Why?"

"Hmmmm, I mean, it didn't seem strange to you that the alarm wasn't cut or triggered. The guy obviously punched in the alarm code. Did you give this guy your code, or did he ever see you putting that code in?" Jackson directed his last question to me.

"No. Neither," I replied. "I don't think he even knew I had it until the night he showed up at my door."

Sean stared at Jackson curiously for a moment. "Thank you for bringing that to our attention, Mr....."

"Keller. Jackson Keller."

"I see. Well, Mr. Keller, I had already thought of that, seeing as I've been a cop for eleven years. In fact, I've already dusted the device for fingerprints. And from my many years in this line of work, I can confidently say those fingerprints belong to Charli, but by all means, you're welcome to double check."

"Sean," I warned.

Sean looked to me and held up his hands in apology. "Sorry!" he said to Jackson. "I'm a little on edge." He turns to me. "He brings up a good point, you should change your code," he said to me.

Oh trust, I had already planned to do that.

"You know, Charli, it isn't safe to stay here alone tonight. I have some guys that are going to watch the house, but if you want, I can camp out in the guest bed. Make sure that asshole doesn't come back."

"Oh, Sean, you……"

"Thanks for the offer, but I'm going to stay." Jackson cut into my reply, staring Sean down. "Wouldn't want to interfere with your job."

I ignored the pissing contest the two had going on and focused on Jackson's words. This was the first I had heard of him spending the night. I wasn't mad though. I wanted someone to stay, and maybe I could get Jackson to climb in bed with me—especially since that dumbass destroyed my vibrator. This seemed like a win/win.

Sean looked to me, waiting for me to confirm or deny Jackson's statement. I stared blankly back at him.

"Well, alright then," Sean finally said. "You two have a good night, and don't forget to call me if you need me, Charli." He wrapped his arms around me giving me a quick hug.

Jackson shut the door on the last officer and turned to face me. Though the idea of having Jackson here was comforting, I didn't want him to feel obligated to stay.

"You know you can go home, right? I'll be fine here by myself."

"I'm good. Just show me to your guest bedroom."

I gave Jackson a quick tour of the house. He let the dog back inside, he put her outside when the cops came so she would be out of the way.

"And you're sure she's not going to eat my walls or anything, right?"

Jackson laughed. I was standing in the doorway to his room across the hall from mine. He was in nothing but a pair of dark grey jogging pants. Thankfully, he kept a change of clothes in his gym bag in his truck. Somewhere that bitch karma was laughing her ass off at me. I had a man this damn fine in my house with a dick print like a fucking arm hanging between his legs, and he wouldn't even give me any.

Jackson wasn't one of those lean guys you see all over television. He had thick muscles, a wide chest, and a slight gut. He was thick as hell. Not fat, but damn sure not skinny. His body was amazing. A few tattoos on his arms and chest. A dark blonde happy trail that started slightly above his navel and disappeared into the low waistband of those joggers.

"Lady isn't going to destroy your house. She's well trained, and I'll keep her locked behind the bedroom door so you don't have to worry about her waking you up with dog kisses."

I made a face, and Jackson laughed.

"If that beds not comfortable, you can always climb into bed with me. I don't mind."

Yes, I gave it one last try.

Jackson's hazel eyes dilated as he pulled that plump bottom lip into his mouth.

"I've slept on the ground before, I can sleep anywhere. Besides, if I crawl into your bed, Char, I'm crawling between those legs, and when I do, you better be ready to admit to being mine and only mine. Are you ready to commit to me?"

Fuck! Just to have him between my legs I was ready to commit to anything, but I knew that Jackson was serious, and I didn't want to give him false hope. I would never be ready for what Jackson offered. No matter how tempting that body was, I cannot give him that commitment.

I smiled. "Goodnight, Mr. Keller."

I turned around and sashayed my ass back to my room. I could hear his growl behind me. I purposely wore my red satin and lace chemise from Frederick's of Hollywood. It was just short enough to show the bottom of my rounded ass. And since fuckboy destroyed all my underwear, I had nothing covering up my globes.

I walked into the room and closed the door behind me. Finally, the day caught up to me. I collapsed down on my bed and fell asleep to thoughts of Jackson burying his face between my legs.

TEN

I woke the next morning to the sound of cabinets banging in my kitchen. For a split second I panicked, until I remembered Jackson staying over last night. I jumped out of the bed and did my morning routine. I snatched the silk bonnet off my head and fluffed up my wavy bob before pulling on a robe and heading down stairs.

I found Jackson bent over in my fridge.

"I had planned to make you breakfast, but I must have caught you before you went grocery shopping." I didn't know how he recognized me without even turning around.

I tried not to pout at the disappointment of him having on a shirt this morning.

"I just went to the grocery store last week. Did that asshole take my groceries?"

I rushed to the fridge. Jackson stepped back allowing me to have a look. I scanned all the shelves checking for the groceries I just bought.

"Everything is still here."

Jackson looked at me with a raised eye. "There is only condiments, water, and a bag of apples in there."

"Yeah! I told you I just went to the grocery store."

He shook his head. "No wonder you're so damn grumpy. You're hungry." He shut the refrigerator door. "I checked all your cabinets and your pantry. Other than a shit ton of wine and coffee, you have no food in this house. What do you eat?"

I walked over to the long drawer in my kitchen and pulled out my large white organized binder of takeout menus. I opened it up and handed it to him.

"They are separated in category. You have the pizza up front. Chinese is after that." I headed towards my coffee machine and popped in a k-cup to start a brew.

"So, you don't cook? At all?" He seemed startled by this question.

Maybe this was a deal breaker for him.

"No! I never learned to cook. I can pop popcorn. I'm pretty good at that."

Jackson chuckled and shook his head. He closed my white binder and placed it down on the island.

"Don't tell me you're one of those men that thinks a woman has to be able to cook and clean, are you? Because let me say, I can't cook, but I can run the hell out of a business. And a lot of men can't do that. So, I'm sorry if my lack of knowledge around a stove has turned you off."

Jackson took two steps and was on me so close, I had to strain my head to look up at his eyes.

"Before you start labeling me, maybe you should give me time to answer. I don't give a shit if you can cook or not. I can cook just fine. I was only asking because I was going to offer to cook you a meal. A real meal, and not this take out junk." He pointed to my binder.

I was feeling rightfully chastised, but I would never let him know it.

"There is nothing wrong with my take-out."

He hummed and stepped away from me grabbing another coffee cup out of the cabinet over my head.

"Let me cook for you. I can take you back to my place, and we can hangout all day eating and watching TV."

Why did that sound so fun? It was almost hard for me to turn him down, but I did. We were not ready for that.

"I can't. Today is Sunday," I said, adding my cream and sugar to my coffee. "Sundays are reserved for Sadie Rose. I've never missed a Sunday meal in all my thirty-three years, and I won't start. Besides, her Sunday meals supply me with enough leftovers to last another day."

He laughed and handed me his coffee mug. I changed out the k-cup and brewed him a cup. He leaned his back against the cabinet in front of me and crossed his arms over his chest. I got a memory flash of what that chest looked like shirtless. My bottom lip found its way between my teeth.

"What are you thinking about?" Jackson's deep voice dropped another octave.

He knew damn well what I was thinking about. I glanced down to his crotch. Hell yeah he knew what I was thinking about.

"I'm trying to figure out why you're being so stingy with that pole in your pants."

A sexy chuckle from Jackson. The coffee maker finished brewing his coffee, I turned and grabbed it, then handed it to him. I watched those full lips spread as he placed the mug between his lips and sipped. How did he make every damn thing he did feel so sexual?

"I'm not being stingy. I'm being selective."

"Really?" I let a beat of silence bounce between us before I asked the next question. I allowed him to let his guard down. "So, when's the last time you fucked?"

My question caused him to choke on his sip of coffee. I watched him as he coughed. I wanted my question answered. When he finally composed himself, he wiped his hands on a napkin he grabbed.

He eyed me. "I'll answer your question, but just know that whatever question you ask me, you also have to answer."

I shrugged one shoulder. I didn't have a problem with that.

"Alright, I last had sex a month ago….."

"Who was it with?"

He looked at me and smiled. "My ex –girlfriend, Vanessa. I had a moment of weakness and fell back into bed with her. Not my proudest moment."

"How long had you and Vanessa been dating?"

He rubbed his beard. That was a new thing. I'd never seen him do this before.

He sighed before saying. "On and off for about three years."

My eyes widened.

"It's not what you think." He tried to clarify, but I was pretty sure it was what I thought it was.

There was no way I was a serious thing for Jackson. If this woman, Vanessa, had been in and out of his life for three years, she meant something to him. And I don't have a problem with that. I liked Jackson, but he's not my man. However, why pretend that he wants something with me if I was just something to do between his ex.

"I can tell by that look in your eyes that you are definitely thinking the wrong thing. But hear me out, Vanessa is my sister-in-law's best friend. When we initially dated, I did it more for her and my brother. Vanessa is beautiful and all, but we lack a true connection."

"And it's taken you three years to come to that fucking conclusion."

Another tug of his beard. "No! Initially I liked her, and I thought she was great, but then, all the marriage hints started being dropped, and I realized that I didn't love her enough to marry her. After a year, I called it off. She and I have both dated other people since then, but it seems that if we are both single at the same time, we usually hook back up for a few months before I realize why we broke up to begin with. I'm not caught up or in love with my ex, Char."

"So, if this ex comes to your house tonight for a repeat of last month, you would turn her down?"

"Yes!" he admitted without hesitation.

I sucked my teeth in disbelief and rolled my eyes. Grams would knock my teeth out for this if she saw me.

"Oh, please."

"Why are you trying to make this into something it isn't?"

"I'm just trying to get you to see that you're going back to her for a reason. Now either she has the greatest snatch in the world, or you're in love with her."

He growled in frustration. "It's neither of those, Char. She was familiar, that's it."

I placed my coffee cup down and cross my arms over my chest. "Well, Sean and I have been fucking since I was in high school. I don't love him, but his dick is superb. If he came to my door right now and asked me to ride it, I would say yes."

Jackson's jaw ticked. I watched as those sexy bedroom eyes clouded over with anger.

"That explains a lot," he said. "But I'm not you. Sex doesn't drive me. Vanessa and I are over."

I laughed and walked away from him. He caught me before I walked out of the kitchen, grabbing my elbow and gently turned me back around.

"Why are you getting so upset?"

"I'm not upset!" I yelled before bringing my tone back down. "I just don't like these bullshit games. Every man I meet, I tell them from the start what I want….."

"And I'm doing the same thing with you."

"Are you really?" I yelled my question. "You're telling me that the woman that you've been back in forth in a relationship with for the past three years mean nothing to you? That if for some reason, we happen to get serious, she won't be a problem for us?"

"No! I'm telling you the truth. I don't want Vanessa."

I stared into those hazel eyes trying to find the truth. I wanted to believe him. For a moment, I wanted to put all my common sense to the back burner and believe that there was no way that he could still have feelings for the woman that he's been with for three years. And it was for that reason that I said the next words out of my mouth.

"I need you to leave."

Jackson reared back, his eyes widening as he watched me. I didn't have time for this. I was already doing shit I didn't usually do. Jackson staying over last night was way beyond my comfort zone, and I damn sure wasn't going to start making excuses for liars.

For a second, those gorgeous eyes just stared at me. Finally, he sighed.

"Fine, Char." He turned and headed up the stairs. He called for his dog, and she followed behind him, but not before looking me up and down.

I waited for him to come back down the stairs with my arms folded over my chest. He had his duffel bag in his hand. I opened the door and stood patiently waiting for him to leave.

He stopped in front of me. That damn smile plastered on his face.

"I'll play your little game today, but don't think for a second I'm letting you get away that easy."

He bent down and placed a kiss on my cheek. I could have turned away from him. I had plenty of time to turn my head or tell him to stop, but I allowed that brief moment for his lips to touch my cheek.

"Call me when you're ready to be a big girl."

He left me with that little nugget and walked out of my house. I closed the door and slid down to my bottom.

I did the right thing. Jackson wanted something with me he already had. I didn't believe in love or relationships, but I damn sure wasn't going to invest my time and energy in something that he would eventually abandon and go back to his ex. Ain't nobody got time for that.

***

"Ooh, Grams, this potato salad is so good," Keisha said cheerfully around her second helping of potato salad.

I made it to my Grams' house on time, but without my usual dinner contribution. I was surprised I even made it at all. My mind was still back at my house this morning.

"You sure are likinig that potato salad real good, Keisha," Chante said with a wide grin on her face. "You wouldn't happen to be expecting, would you?"

For fuck sakes, I hope not. I mean damn, does she not know what the fuck a condom is?

Keisha started smiling and nodding her head. Everyone cheered and congratulated her and her new boyfriend. My family always celebrated new life, didn't matter if it was the first baby of a new married couple, or the fifth from a single mother. A child was always a blessing, and even though Keisha was a bitch sometimes, I was still excited for her.

Once all the congratulations had died down, Grams turned to me. "I knew when I dreamed about fish a while ago someone was pregnant. I was hoping it would be Duck."

I nearly choked on the sweet tea I was drinking.

"Now, Mrs. Sadie, you know Duck isn't really the mothering type." A few chuckles went around the table at Quincy's joke.

"And you don't know enough about my cousin or my family to be making stupid ass jokes," Eli said, coming to my defense.

Eli stared at Quincy, challenging him to say anything else.

"He was just joking, Eli. Calm down." Chante tried to speak out in defense of her man.

Tension cut through the table. Eli was never a fan of Quincy. If he knew some of the things I knew, he would probably readily whoop his ass.

"I heard from Martin last night."

"Shit!" I announced as I tried to mop up the sweet tea I just spilled.

"Mouth, Duck," my grandfather chided politely.

"Dang girl, you all over the place this morning." Eli chuckled as he helped me wipe up the tea I just spilled.

Devin handed me a handful more napkins to wipe up the rest of the tea.

"It must have something to do with yesterday." Devin chuckled. "The girls and I came by twice to surprise you. Where were you?"

"I went hiking," I answered without thinking.

The moment the words were are out my mouth, I closed my eyes and scolded myself. This was not the information you gave out to my family. They would either make a bigger deal out of it, or start making assumptions.

"Hiking? What're you doing hiking? That's some white folks shit." Eli laughed.

Devin gasped beside me. I turned to her quickly shaking my head, but she was already talking.

"Oh, my God! You went on a date with Jackson!"

"Who is Jackson?" Eli asked.

"Duck, you dating now?" Papa questioned. He was no longer eating, his attention was fully on me.

"No, Papa! I'm not dating."

"Jackson is Duck's white boyfriend," Keisha admitted happily.

She got a full thrill at being able to announce that.

"You have a boyfriend?" Quincy asked it disgustedly.

No one noticed the scorned lover scowl on his face.

"When did you start dating white guys?" Eli questioned beside me.

"When she ran through the entire black male population in Atlanta," Aunt Vivica stated.

I ignored her comment. It wasn't the first shot I had ignored today. My mind just wasn't focused enough to retort.

"I would like to meet this Mr. Jackson," Papa announced with a smile.

"Well, tell us, how was the date?" Grams asked.

Her face was lit with excitement. I hated to disappoint her.

"It wasn't a date, Grams."

"I don't know, Duck. You guys were gone all day."

I turned to Devin praying that she would shut the hell up. Could she not read my body language right now?

"How long were they gone?" Aunt Joe asked.

"At least four hours."

"Oh, my God, Devin, stop talking!" I finally lost my cool.

The table went quiet again.

"Look, it wasn't a date. It was just two people and a dog on a hike, with a picnic."

"Sounds like a date to me," Keisha mumbled.

"WELL I DIDN'T ASK YOU!" I shouted the words completely losing my shit.

The entire family was looking at me like I'm the crazy one. And maybe they were right. I felt a little crazy right now. I slid my chair back from the table and stood up.

"I'm sorry, Grams. I had a really long night last night, and I woke with a terrible headache, I'm just going to head home."

"Baby, don't leave. At least take some food home."

I held up my hand to stop her.

"I'm not really hungry. It's fine."

I walked away from the table with mumbled allegations of drug use and hard partying. I made it outside to my car, and since I spilled my tea across the table, I could finally breathe again. I stopped at my car door and placed my hands on the roof of my car and took a few soothing breaths.

"Hey!" Eli called out to me.

I lifted from the car and went to get in.

"Not now, Eli."

He grabbed my arm before I could sit down and turned me back to him.

"What's up with you? You've been out of it since you came."

"It's nothing….." I tried to pull away, but he wouldn't let me.

"Hey! Talk to me," he demanded.

There was no getting out of this. I couldn't lie to Eli. He was like my brother, he knew me more than anyone else in my family.

I sighed and looked to my left. "I'm still having problems with Cliff." Admittedly, this was only half of my problem, but it was the only one Eli could help me with.

"What happened?"

"He broke in last night and destroyed some of my personal items."

Eli's jaw tensed up. That flair of anger sparked up in his eyes.

Grams always said that Eli took his father's temper. I've seen Eli at his angriest. When I was in third grade some fifth grade dude cornered me after school and groped me. I was crying in my bedroom when Eli found me. He made me tell him what happened, that same spark ignited in his eyes that day. The next day, he beat that guy so bad an ambulance had to take the young boy from the school. Eli got expelled. I wanted to tell Grams and Papa what happened, but Eli told me to keep it to myself. He didn't want me to have to relive it.

If he only knew.

When I saw that look in his eyes now, I knew that if he found Cliff, the guy was going to be in for a hurting.

"Alright, Duck! I'm done. I want his name and address."

"Eli,"

"I DON'T WANT TO HEAR IT!" He cut me off with a shout. "I'm done playing this game. If I have to find it myself, it's only going to make it worse."

Another sigh. I might as well give him the information. If the police couldn't find him, surely Eli wouldn't be able to find him either.

"Clifford Hall."

"Where is he from?"

"I don't know...."

"...Don't lie to me."

"I don't know. You know I don't get all that information from the men I sleep with." I sighed and took another breath to calm the tension down. "All I know is that he worked at the Waffle House over off Brush Street."

"Gotdman it, Duck!" Eli ran a hand over his short cut. "What the fuck are you doing messing with these lowlife dudes?"

"I didn't know he was this crazy."

Again, we both allowed for the tension to die down. I watched the house making sure nobody else would follow Eli out.

"What are the police saying? Have you called Sean?" Eli asked, after he'd calmed down a little more.

Everyone in the family knew that Sean and I were friends. I had to call Sean that last time Eli was arrested. Sean pulled some strings and got Eli off. I thanked him very thoroughly for weeks after that.

"Yes, Sean knows, but the police don't know where he is. Apparently, he wasn't living up to his potential, because who knew he was capable of breaking into homes without setting off the alarm and disappearing without a trace?"

"Alright, it may take me a while since the cops are asking questions too, but me and the boys will look into it."

"Eli, I don't want you doing anything that will get you in trouble. Promise me if you find him, you will turn him in to the police. I don't want you going back to jail."

"Relax, Duck," he said, placing his hands on my shoulders and looking me straight in the eyes. It's how he used to calm me down when I was a kid and on the brink of a panic attack. "I got you. I don't want you stressing about this anymore. And next time something happens, you call me. You hear me?"

"Yes," I lied easily. "Promise you won't tell Grams?"

"Duck," he started.

"I'm serious. I don't want her worrying about me."

He blew out a breath and stood up straight. "I'll hide it as much as I can. But you know how she is. She starts asking questions and won't stop."

I laughed, that's exactly how my Grams was.

Eli chuckled and grabbed my door for me to climb into the car.

"You need to head home and get some rest. I don't like seeing you like this." He shut my door when I was inside.

"Oh, and good luck with your new white boyfriend." He smiled, and I stuck my tongue out at him.

I pulled out of the driveway of my grandparents' house and headed straight home.

ELEVEN

"I told you, it's alright, Devin."

For the last hour, I had been on the phone reassuring my cousin that I wasn't mad at her for ratting me out to the family. She had apologized entirely too many times.

"I just hope I didn't ruin it between you and Jackson," she said, sniffling again.

I took another sip of my wine. I didn't want to talk about Jackson. In fact, I would rather talk about anything else besides him.

"There is no me and Jackson. Jackson already has everything he is looking for."

"What do you mean?"

I sighed and tossed my head back onto the couch. I can't believe I'm about to do this. I'm actually about to talk about my personal life to my family. I must have a gas leak in this house.

"Jackson has an on again off again relationship with his ex." Fine, I put it out there. Now she could tell me I did the right thing and I could move on.

"What type of relationship, and did you ask him about this?"

Not exactly the end result I was looking for.

"Yes, I talked to him, and he tried to say that it was nothing serious between them. He said he only fell back in bed with her when he was in-between girlfriends. I wasn't trying to hear those lies. Obviously he cares about this chick."

Silence from the other end of the phone.

"Did you hear what I said?"

"I heard you, just wondering when you became so judgmental."

"Excuse you?" I said lifting from the couch.

Devin chuckled. "I'm just saying. You have meaningless sex all the time, and you swear they mean nothing to you."

"They don't."

"Then why is it when he says the same thing you don't believe him?"

I paused. I couldn't believe she wasn't understanding how different those situations were.

"It's not the same, Devin. I wasn't back and forth with the same guy."

"Oh, really?"

"Really!"

"So I guess you haven't been seeing a certain cop for the last thirteen years."

I was left completely caught off guard. I had no response for that. Not only did she just slightly prove a point, but how did she know I'd been seeing Sean for that long?

Devin chuckled on the other line. "I bet you're wondering how I knew. Well, I went to school with his sister, and she used to tell me how obsessed he was with you. Then I caught him sneaking out of your car one day when you were home from college, and then I knew why he was obsessed. The way those windows were fogged up, I can only imagine what y'all were doing." She laughed at her own joke. "When he helped Eli out with that last arrest, I saw him looking at you that day in court. He had that same look on his face that he did the day he climbed out your car. It's like he knew he was going to get him some booty." Another laugh from her.

Ok, she had me. I couldn't get around that point. Sean and I have been fucking for that long—longer actually—but there was no love involved. We just both liked having sex, and we knew the other so well that it was simple for us.

"Ok, yes, Sean Myers and I have been having a thing going on for a while." Devin chuckled. "But, it is only carnal. I don't want a relationship with Sean, and he doesn't want one with me."

"And that's my point, Duck. Just because Jackson and his Ex keep finding themselves back in the bed together, doesn't mean that he's in love with her. Some people just like familiarity."

The exact word Jackson used. Familiarity. Did I over think his response? Thankfully the doorbell rang, and I didn't have to respond to her.

"Hold on, Dev, someone is at my door."

I peeked out of the glass inserts in my front door to find who was standing at my door. Speak of the devil.

"Dev, I have to go. I'll call you tomorrow, and kiss my babies for me." We said our goodbyes, and I hung up my landline.

I opened the door to a smiling Sean.

"Detective Myers. It's awfully late for you to be knocking at my door."

Sean gave me that blinding white small.

I stepped back and let him enter the house before closing the door behind him. He was in a button down dress shirt and dark gray slacks, his tie was hanging loose around his neck—he must be just getting off work.

"Hey, Charli. I just wanted to come by and check on you before I called it a night. I talked to the guys that watched over you last night. They had nothing to report, but I admit, I was worried about you."

"Thanks for checking on me."

Sean took a step towards me, he placed a hand on my shoulder. "I know you're tough, but I still would rather you have someone here with you every night if you could. You could ask your cousin, or even that guy from last night, and if you can't find someone, you can call me. You know I'm back with Rochelle so you don't have to worry about it turning into something it's not."

This was why I liked Sean. He just got me. He knew I didn't do sleepovers with guys that I was fucking. The latest you could stay was maybe until the early morning, but there will be no sleeping. Once you got too tired to fuck, you should take your ass back home.

Sean had never tried to stay the night. He knew to give me at least three rounds and then leave.

"Thanks for offering, but I think I'm ok for tonight."

Sean paused for a moment, but I could tell he wanted to say something. Finally, he raked a hand down his face and said, "Ok, it's none of my business, so you can tell me to fuck off if you want, but are you sure that guy from last night is ok?"

I laughed.

Every now and again, Sean would ask this question about who I was fucking. He'd never been good about leaving his profession at the door.

"Jackson is harmless."

He smiled down at me and threw up his hands. "Alright, if you say. Just know if he messes up, I'll kick his ass, nobody messes with my home girl."

We both laughed at the playfulness.

"I'm just glad to see you dating someone."

"Hold on." I held up one hand. "We are not dating. We're just friends."

My words and the smile on my face told two different stories. Sean must have picked up on it because he just shook his head and laughed.

"Whatever you say, Charli. Have you told him about your…"

"NO!"

He watched me carefully and nodded.

I thought back to what Devin said, why did I continue to keep Sean around? He was the only person I'd slept with that I kept in contact with even when we weren't fucking. I mean, he had a monster size dick and could eat coochie fairly well—thanks to my coaching—but that didn't explain why I kept going back to it. I didn't love him, that's for damn sure. He was just a friend that I genuinely cared about.

I walked him towards the door. He stopped in the doorway before he headed out and turned to face me.

"I want you to lock up all the doors and windows before you go to bed, and set that alarm. Did you change the code?"

I nodded, and he smiled.

"Good! Goodnight, Charli."

"Night."

I gave him a quick hug before shutting the door on him.

I'd had a long day and decided to call it a night early. I made sure to check the doors and windows just like Sean suggested before I climbed into bed. I fell asleep quickly.

TWELVE

I yawned again as I sat behind my desk. It'd been three days since that Sunday I kicked Jackson out of my house. I hadn't spoken to him or seen him since, and I couldn't believe I was about to admit this, but I missed him. How the hell did you miss someone you'd only been out with one time? I mean yeah, even before the hiking trip he would send me funny and thoughtful text messages.

Somehow, Jackson Keller was able to plant himself in my life without me noticing. He was like a goddamn tick. I found myself checking my phone constantly, hoping to have a missed text from him. Even when it did chime, I was breaking my neck to check it. His lack of communication had me irritable and short tempered.

Unfortunately, I was still getting calls and text messages from Cliff's crazy ass. He actually thought I was going to meet him somewhere. No matter how many times I blocked his numbers, he found a way around it.

It also didn't help that I hadn't been sleeping well at night. I kept waking up out of my sleep in cold sweats feeling like I was not alone. Whenever I checked, there was never anyone there. It was all starting to affect my ability to do my job.

"Boss lady, are you sure you're ok?" Troy asked the moment he walked into my office.

"I'm good, Troy." I yawned. "Why do you ask?"

"Because you've sent me the same email like three times."

I sighed heavily and rolled my eyes. See! This was outrageous.

"I'm sorry."

He chuckled. "No problem. You know, I looked at your schedule, and you really don't have to be here today. You only have to look over the report for the Connor firm, and you can do that at home."

This was why I had the world's best assistant. Not only did he know what I needed, but he was great about spacing out my schedule.

"I think you are on to something. I'm definitely going to get out of here." I grabbed my Armani blazer off the back of my chair and stood to my feet. I placed my jacket over my arm and grabbed my laptop bag.

"I don't know what's bothering you," Troy started. "But you seemed a lot calmer last week." He shrugged. "I'm just saying." He gave me a knowing smile before heading out of my office.

I headed to my car thinking about his words. I doubted my mood was in anyway affected by Jackson. I was always a happy person, but ever since that conversation with Devin I'd been uneasy. Maybe I did blow up at Jackson for no reason. Maybe I misjudged what he meant. Maybe that was why my car speaker was ringing.

"Keller Landscaping, this is Jackson Keller speaking."

Just the sound of his voice had slightly lessoned the knots in my stomach. What the hell does that mean? Shit, now I had to have a reason for calling him. I couldn't just call without a reason, that made me look desperate and I was damn sure not desperate.

"Hello, Mr. Keller," I said as casual as possible. "Did you erase my number? Is that why you're so formal now?" I gave a light chuckle.

He didn't take the bait. "I knew who you were. What do you want, Charlice?"

Damn, he sounded a little cold.

"Did I catch you at a bad time?"

He sighed. "Maybe not if you had called me three days ago."

Ok, he was pissed.

"If it's a problem, I can call you back another time."

"What do you want, Char?"

I felt a little relieved when he used the nickname he gave me. Lord knew I had more than enough damn nicknames, but I really liked the one Jackson gave me. No one had ever called me that.

"I found some socks at my place, and I was wondering if you were missing any." I cringed, but that was the only thing I could think of off the top of my head. It wasn't like this was a planned call.

"They aren't mine. And if they were, I have others. Is that all you wanted to say?"

He wasn't going to make this easy. Ok, fine! I was a big girl, I could admit when I was wrong.

"Look, I just wanted to apologize for slightly over reacting the other day. But, if you are too busy I can…."

"I don't do apologies over the phone. You want to apologize, I need to see you face to face."

If not for the humor in his tone, I would have cursed him out.

"You are really demanding right now."

"Hey, I'm not the one that needs to grovel."

"Who the hell said I was groveling? I called to simply apologize."

"I'm not accepting it over the phone."

I took a calming breath and came to a complete stop at the red light. "Ok, can we meet today?"

Another long pause from him. "I can't leave the office today, but you can come to me."

"To your office?"

"Yep!"

It was on the tip of my tongue to tell him where he could stick an apology, but the way my stomach was fluttering at just the thought of seeing him, I sucked it up. I wasn't doing it for Jackson. Hell, I hadn't had sex in over two weeks, this was a record for me, I was horny and frustrated, and it was probably another reason I wasn't sleeping well. Maybe showing up to his office with my tight pencil skirt and sleeveless silk blouse wasn't a bad idea. I might be able to finally end this dry spell.

"Fine! Send me the address."

I said goodbye to Jackson, and seconds after I hung up, my phone chimed with a text message. I had just enough time to plug it in before the light turned green.

***

I pulled up to a small rectangular building. A very well-manicured front entrance met me. The words Keller Landscaping painted on a white sign in black letters with a large tree. A large porch sat on the front of the building with rocking chairs welcoming you. It had a very cozy feeling. I spotted Jackson's truck along with a few other cars. And one white pickup with the same tree symbol that's on the sign. I stopped my car in front of the building, but before I got out, I slid my panties down my thighs, to my ankles then pulled them off. I stuck them in my purse then stepped out of the car.

The inside of the building was cool and brightly lit. Lots of windows gave off tons of natural light. The walls were an eggshell white with large mat framed pictures of well landscaped yards. A desk sat off to the left as you entered with a smiling brunette. Her hair was in a messy bun at the top of her head and her blue eyes were round shaped and stunning.

"Can I help you?" the female asked.

I walked over to her, dodging the few chairs and dark blue couch in the waiting room.

"Yes, I'm here to see Jackson Keller."

She looked me over, I didn't see any sign of judgment on her face. Something I'd grown used to by living in the south. Instead, she looked at me like I was a celebrity.

"Is that a Hermes Constance Bag?"

I looked down at my red bag with the large gold H shaped buckle. "Yes, it is." I smiled.

She knew her purses.

"OMG!" Her southern accent made her sound a bit like Ellie Mae Clampert. "I've seen those on TV and in the ads, but I didn't think I'd ever see one in person. Can I touch it?"

Ok! That was an odd request, but sure. I lifted up the bag, and she ran her hands over the leather.

"It even feels expensive." She giggled, and I couldn't help but laugh at her enthusiasm. "It goes well with those red bottom pumps you have on."

"You know a lot about fashion. You seem like my type of girl."

She blushed a deep shade of red. "I've always been into fashion. Never could afford the stuff, but I sure do like looking at it."

I liked this girl. She was sweet. I dug through my bag and pulled out my Hermes Constance long wallet that matched my bag. I got the wallet on sale when I purchased the bag. I took my few belongings out of the wallet and handed it to the girl. She looked confused at first.

"I have two of these. You can have this one."

Her eyes went so wide for a moment, I thought they were going to pop out of her head. I usually gave my old purses to my family—except for Grams, I buy her new. The other ones go up for auction with the proceeds going to the local boys and girls club. I wouldn't lose sleep giving this young girl a wallet.

The girl nearly leapt over the counter to give me a tight hug. I laughed as she screamed over and over, "Thank You."

"You're welcome."

"Is everything alright?" I knew that voice.

Was it common for a man's voice to be able to melt you like butter even when he wasn't saying anything remotely sexual?

The girl let me go and turned to Jackson with tears in her eyes. I took my time turning to face him. When I did I almost wanted to run and jump in his arms. He was in a red collared shirt with the company logo written on it. It was the same one the girl was wearing, but hers looked nothing like Jackson's. The arms fit tightly over his muscles while the chest stretched over those large pectorals. His husky size looked good in those black slacks. My eyes went directly to his crotch, still thick and hanging to the left as always.

"Jackson, look what she gave me," the girl squealed in the background.

Jackson didn't even acknowledge the brunette, his eyes were planted solely on me. He had that hungry look in his eyes that had my sex weeping. I tightened my slippery thighs.

"That's good, Jess. I'm going to have a talk with Ms. Jefferies in my office. Hold all my calls."

"Ummm, ok!" Jess agreed.

I walked over to Jackson, and his eyes followed me the entire journey.

"Hello, Mr. Keller." I purred towards him.

He gave me that damn smile I liked.

"So, Jackson, what do you want me to do about Mr. Russell?" The guy beside Jackson asked.

I was so focused on Jackson that I didn't even see this guy until now. I turned towards the tall, skinny, brown-skinned brother and smiled.

"Tell him we will be there Friday as scheduled," Jackson stated, then took my hand, dragging me away from the guy. I didn't even get a chance to say hello.

We walked into a room in the back. It was a simple office with one window, a file cabinet, a messy metal desk, a couch and three chairs.

Jackson shut the door and locked it as I looked around his office. It was such a man's office. A large picture over the desk chair of a manicured lawn. Plain eggshell walls and nothing covering the window but vertical blinds. It was basic yet cozy. Jackson walked up behind me, brushing his erection onto my ass before walking away. He just wanted me to feel him. He took a seat behind his desk chair.

"You had something to say to me, right?" Those hazel eyes lit up with amusement.

I dropped my purse onto the gray sofa and walked around to Jackson. Sitting down on the end of his desk, facing him, I crossed my legs.

"I'm sorry for over reacting the other day."

"And?"

I stared at him, not sure of what else I was supposed to be sorry for.

He rolled his eyes. "You're sorry for kicking me out of your house, right?"

Ugh, seriously?

"I'm sorry for kicking you out of my house," I admitted with an eye roll. "Am I forgiven now?"

"I'll think about it." He chuckled, and I gave him the middle finger.

Jackson leaned back in his seat, his legs were spread wide, and I could tell he was getting happier and happier to see me.

"You look tired, Char," he announced suddenly. "Have you been sleeping?"

I didn't want to talk about my lack of sleep or anything else with Jackson. I wanted Jackson. No, I needed Jackson. I just needed to tame the thirst, then I could go back to my regular schedule.

"I'm fine," I said, stepping down from the desk. I walked over and stood between his legs. "I didn't come over to talk about sleep."

I slowly slid the zipper down the side of my skirt. Jackson followed the movement with his eyes. His pointed tongue running over his full bottom lip. Once the zipper was fully down, I shimmied out of the tight fabric, taking a few wiggles to get it over my hips and ass. Jackson continued to watch me.

When the skirt dropped to my feet and my bare pussy was only slightly covered by the hem of my silk blouse, Jackson bit down on his bottom lip. I stepped out of the skirt and pushed it to the side with my heels. I sat back down on the desk in front of him and spread my legs wide. My soaking wet center on full display. Jackson only stared at it. His hands were resting on the arm of his office chair in tight fist.

"Aren't you going to touch it?" I purred.

I was done playing Jackson's game. I needed a release, and I needed it bad. He looked up at me briefly then back down at the view, but he didn't make a move. Apparently, Jackson needed a little more motivation, so I decided to get started without him. I placed my manicured fingers to my soaked slit. I hiked one leg up propping my heel up on his desk. My tangy and sweet scent coated his office. I slipped my fingers over my hardened nub and down between my pussy lips, the action made a loud slopping sound like someone mixing wet ingredients. Jackson tensed again, the vein in his neck throbbed as he watched me.

Jesus! Would he please get up and do something?

Finally, he stood to his feet. I almost tumbled off the desk when I saw the real outline of Jackson's erection. I'd been misled. My pussy tightened around my fingers in anticipation, and more of my essence oozed out. I could feel it run down my butt crack and onto Jackson's desk. He must have seen it too, because he grunted under his breath.

He stood between my open legs. I continued to stare into his eyes as I worked my center, my hips danced around my thin fingers. How I wished he would replace them with his thick ones. He was so close now I could feel his body heat and the brush of the monster between his legs. He watched my hand move in and out of me then slip up to work my swollen clit. Very slowly, he lifted his hands, and I dropped my head back and closed my eyes in anticipation of finally feeling his fingers dance over my clit.

One of his hands rested on my knee, and I moaned at the simple connection, the other hand landed on top of mine that was working my clit. However, he didn't take over, he just stilled my movements. When I lifted my head and looked into those hooded bedroom eyes, I saw desire, but also determination.

"I asked you, have you been sleeping?"

"What?"

I heard his question, I was just wondering why the fuck did it matter? Why was he asking about sleeping when I knew he could feel the heat and wetness from my pussy?

"You heard me. I asked you a question, you won't distract me with your body."

Ok, this was getting old. I leaned up from the desk trying to push him back, but he didn't budge. Instead of moving, he grabbed the hand I had placed on his chest to push him back, and knocked it away. He moved my hand from between my legs and gently and insanely slow, he started to rub circles over my nub.

Fuck! It felt so good.

"Answer my question, Char," he whispered the demand against my parted lips.

I was so sexually frustrated that I couldn't put my brain into two places, and right now it was stuck down between my thighs. So I answered his question without thought.

"No, I haven't. I've been missing you," I moaned. "Please, Jackson don't stop." I tossed my head back and laid flat on the top of his desk.

My back arched off the desk while my head hung slightly off the other end. Jackson applied a little more pressure and picked up the pace just a smidgen. It was just enough for me to get distracted, but not enough for me to get off. My hips lifted from the desk trying to get him to work faster, he wouldn't be swayed.

"I missed you too, Char. Is that the only thing that's been keeping you up, baby?"

Again, my distracted brain answered without thought. "I'm scared Cliff will come back." This admission got two fingers inside my soaking wet entrance. I whimpered at the intrusion, and Jackson growled. He moved his two fingers in and out of me as his thumb continued to work my nub with perfect precision.

"Has he done anything else since Sunday?" The words were growled out.

I think even Jackson was becoming distracted with the way my tight channel was clenching his fingers. This is going to be an embarrassingly quick nut for me. But what can you expect, it's been awhile.

"No!" I admitted on a long moan.

At this admission, Jackson's fingers were working me so well, I could feel my body tightening and the flutter in my stomach as my orgasm started to build.

"Jackson, please! Right there," I started to mumble random

106

commands.

Someone knocked at the door, and I almost cried at the intrusion. I went to sit up, but Jackson nudged me back down.

"Finish," he commanded in a gravelly voice.

I couldn't say no to that.

Jackson played my body like a pianist plays a keyboard. His fingers worked in wonderful synchronization. My body shook while someone jiggled the door knob and started knocking again. I heard voices outside the door, but I couldn't make anything out as I continued to dance on his thick fingers.

Then it hit me like a wrecking ball. My orgasm had me rising up off the desk like a demon was inside me. I moaned loudly as my body started to squirt my release. Jackson growled and cursed as he continued to work me over.

I slowly started to come down, my body quivering in little aftershocks. Jackson finally pulled his fingers out of me, and then helped me to sit up and stand to my feet. We both drowned out the noise outside as we stared at each other.

I thought finding a release would stop this craving for Jackson. It didn't exactly do what I wanted. My body was even more high strung. I wanted to say fuck who was at that door and ride him on top of his desk.

Instead, I said, "I should get you a towel for your desk and hands." Admittedly, I made a bit of a mess.

He smiled at me as he brought his soaking wet fingers up to his face. He smelled his fingers then stuck them in his mouth and sucked them clean.

Fuck it, I'm definitely about to ride him.

"Get dressed," he commanded, cutting off my attack.

I pouted, but I did as he said, sliding my skirt back up my legs and tucking my blouse in before zipping up. Jackson handed me a small clean white towel, and I used it to clean between my legs. He then took it from me and wiped up the wet spot on his desk. He tossed the towel in his bottom drawer, then grabbed my arm and pulled me to him. His lips were on mine, and I willingly opened them for him. His kiss was demanding and scorching, but too brief.

"I didn't want to know how your pussy felt and not your lips," he whispered.

Finally our attention was brought back to the door when we heard shouting on the other end.

"I don't care, Jessica. You get him on the fucking phone."

Jackson sighed and let me go.

"Who is that?"

"My brother."

"Why the hell is he yelling at my friend Jessica?" I asked annoyed.

Jackson turned to me with an amused smile. "When did you and my little sister become friends?"

Wait! That's Jackson's sister? I had no idea. I still like the girl.

"Since she recognized my bag."

We both headed to the door. Jackson stopped and handed me my purse off the couch.

"Come over tonight. I want to cook you dinner."

The thought of going over to Jackson's for dinner was not as unappealing as I wanted it to be. In fact, the thought of hanging out with him tonight sent butterflies dancing in my stomach. However, there was no way I was going to let him know that.

I gave him a cunning smile. "I'll think about it," I said then opened the door.

Standing in front of me was a red faced Jessica, a tall, dark-blonde haired guy that looked like the skinny knock off version of Jackson, and a brown-haired girl with brown eyes that were rimmed in red. The guy gave me one of those looks I'd come to expect from southern white men. The girl glanced at me and frowned. Her eyes took in everything on me, from my slightly crumpled shirt, to my disheveled hair, to the glowing smile on my face. She burst into tears and took off down the hall.

"Vanessa, come back!" the guy shouted after her.

He turned back to me and scowled. "You can leave now," he demanded.

I opened my mouth to put the asshole in his place, but Jackson stepped in.

"Don't ever fucking talk to her like that."

Jackson's voice was so hard and cutting, even I was a little scared.

The other guy looked to Jackson, and in one look, I could see years of dislike and issues. He looked at Jackson how I imagine my Aunt Vivica looked at me.

"We need to talk," the brother demanded and brushed between Jackson and I to enter the office. On the way in, he clipped Jackson's shoulder.

"I guess I'll go. You seem to have your hands full with your ex and your brother here to visit," I said the words playfully.

I wanted him to know I wasn't bothered by his mousy looking ex. Besides, while she was sitting in his office, it was my pussy she would be smelling.

Yes, bitch! That sweet and tangy scent was all me.

Jackson followed me out towards the front of the building.

"You're still coming over tonight, right?"

I stopped at the door and turned to him. He had his hands in his pockets, no doubt trying to hide the erection I left him with.

"You may not even need me by then." I waved bye to Jessica and headed out the door.

I   heard   his   laughter   on   my   way   out.

THIRTEEN

Despite what I told myself in the car after leaving Jackson's office, I found myself parked in front of the address he sent me.

"What the hell are you doing here, Duck?" I asked myself this question once again.

I should be distancing myself from Jackson, but yet again, I found myself spending more time with him.

I climbed out of my car, my contribution to tonight's dinner in my hand. As soon as I walked up to the porch I could hear the dog barking.

Jackson's home was nice from the outside. I could tell the ranch style home was older, maybe built in the 1950's. The brick exterior was painted a metal gray and the trim and railings were done in white. It was one level with a single car garage and a short walk way to the front door.

The most beautiful thing about the house was the gorgeous yard. Neatly trimmed shrubs, beautiful grass, and cut out flower beds ran along the walk way and along the front of the house. It was obvious Jackson took good care of his home.

The moment I stepped in front of the door it opened. Two things stood out, how good Jackson looked in his gray t-shirt, and the smell that was wafting out of his door. I didn't know what he was cooking, but it smelled delicious.

"I brought wine," I said, holding up the fifty-dollar bottle of

Cabernet.

Jackson chuckled and stepped aside for me to enter the house. The inside of the house was just as cared for as the outside. Dark walnut hardwood floors ran throughout the house. Beige paint coated most of the walls. To my left was a living room with a fire place. A short hallway led straight back to the kitchen.

Jackson took my purse, hanging it up on the coat rack by the front door, and then he grabbed the bottle of wine.

"Come on," he said, turning towards the kitchen.

His kitchen was slightly smaller than mine, but it was still very well kept for a man. Shaped like a short narrow hallway, a stainless steel refrigerator was to my left as I walked in. The wall to my right must have been recently removed to open the kitchen to the dining room. Recess lighting in the ceilings helped give the kitchen a cleaner look. The white cabinets up top that blended well with the white walls, and the cabinets from the waist down were done in a grayish blue, all smartly thought out to give the kitchen a bigger and lighter feel to it. It was gorgeous.

"Your home is beautiful, Jackson."

His face turned a deep red. "Thank you. Although, I can't take all the credit for it. Jessica picked the colors and the design, I just did the work."

"So, little sister is good with fashion and home interior."

I watched as Jackson dug through his drawers to find a wine opener. He finally found one that looked completely unused and twisted the cork out of the bottle of wine.

"Jess has always loved fashion and designing. She wasn't always good at it though. When she was in middle school, she got a sewing machine for Christmas one year. She made everyone matching shirts. My parents even took a picture with all of us wearing it. It was a disaster." He laughed as he poured me a glass of wine. "You ever saw that episode of the Cosby show when Denise made Theo the shirt?"

I burst into laughter. "The Gordan Gartrell episode?"

"Yep. It was like that but much worse. Thankfully, she got better over the years, but I'll never forget that first shirt."

I chuckled as I took a sip of the smooth full-bodied tasting wine.

"I bet it wasn't that bad, you guys just couldn't pull it off."

He smiled then leaned up against the counter facing me. For a moment, we watched each other. My eyes danced with his as I remembered the feel of his hands between my legs. From the way he was smiling at me, I knew he was remembering it too.

"So," I started the conversation back up, "what's for dinner?"

"I thought I'd do something simple today. Porterhouse steaks, sautéed vegetables, and baked potatoes."

Damn! And he called that simple. "That sounds delicious."

He just smiled as he pushed away from the counter. "Come on out back, I was just about to put the steaks on the grill. How do you take yours by the way?"

"Medium rare."

He turned to me and smiled. "My type of girl." I chuckled as I continued to follow him to his back porch.

The front yard was gorgeous, the inside was beautiful, but the back yard was downright breathtaking. I'd never seen anything so beautiful. As soon as you walk out the back door, a short covered walk way led you down three steps into a dug out pit that was turned into a fully furnished outside lounge area. Beautiful stone pavers surrounded the area. A large free standing wall held a fire place and flat screen television. On the other side of the drop down sitting area are four steps that led up to a covered outdoor kitchen. Planters with beautiful green plants ran along the back wall of the sitting area. It was gorgeous.

"Here, have a seat."

Jackson took my hand to help me down the three steps. I took a seat on the long curved couch. Jackson walked over to the kitchen area. He opened the mini fridge and pulled out a covered tray I imagine contained the steaks.

"Did you design this?"

Jackson turned to me briefly then turned back to his job of preparing the steaks.

"I did. I bought this home for an amazing price. It was a foreclosure, and it needed a lot of work, but I bought it for this back yard. I took one look at it and saw all the potential."

I was starting to have a lot more respect for his gift. I knew Jackson had to be good at his job, he did own his company after all, but I was never into yards. I just thought he cut grass for a living and planted a few flowers, but he was truly talented.

"I really love your place," I admitted.

Jackson chuckled as he joined me on the couch with a beer in his hands.

"Well, thank you. It doesn't have the class or the square footage of your place, but I like it."

I laughed and then took a sip of my drink. Jackson smiled at me before turning his beer bottle up.

"So, how was the family gathering?"

He snorted. "I knew you were going to ask about that."

I shrugged and waited patiently for him to tell me.

Jackson sighed and leaned back on the couch, his legs spread and beer rested at his side.

"At the time I thought that dating someone my brother knew would be a good idea. I was still trying to bond with him. I still wanted to have that big brother/ little brother relationship, but with age and time, I've come to realize, some relationships just aren't meant to be."

I stared at the side of his face. I tried not to get lost at how gorgeous he was. Most people are attractive head on, but their side view made them look like a cartoon character. Jackson was perfect both ways.

"So, I'm guessing big brother wasn't too happy about your last roll in the sheets with the ex?"

"No! He wants me to commit to Vanessa and stop using her. He puts all the blame on me, like she doesn't come willingly to my bed. And of course, she runs to him with every single problem thinking he will make me take her back." I could hear the annoyance in his voice. "She acts as if she's some type of victim in this. I've never forced her to my bed." He ran a hand through his hair and then took a sip of his drink. "He falls for it every time. I guess it's always easy to make me out to be the bad guy, like I'm incapable of changing."

I felt there was more to this story than what I was getting, but I wasn't going to pry.

I sipped my wine again. "Well, she's pretty. In a basic, plain kind of way, but if that's your type…"

Jackson tossed his head back and laughed. "Very subtle, Char," he teased before placing his beer down on the table in front of us and headed back to the grill.

"What? They say you can tell a lot about a person by their ex?"

Jackson cuts his eyes over to me while he flipped the steaks.

"And what does my ex say about me?"

I placed my glass of wine down and turned in my seat to face him. "She says you like quiet submissive women. Ones that do as told and is always ready to please her man. It also says you like vanilla sex."

Jackson stood at the grill crossing his arms over his chest.

"I have no problem with quiet or as you call them, submissive, women. I also don't have a problem with independent outspoken women that sometimes read people badly."

I laughed at his little diss.

"I love women, Char. Simple as that. I don't have a type. And I won't even comment on that sex crack. There is nothing vanilla about my sex except my ass."

I threw my head back and laughed.

***

Dinner was fantastic. Jackson was a great cook and host. We ended up on the couch laughing and talking.

My phone going off in my purse woke me with a start. For the first time in forever, I felt well rested. I didn't wake up at all last night. I felt invigorated. I rolled over on my bed and nearly hit the floor, if not for the tight grip around me.

"You better be glad my reflexes are good. You were about to eat that floor up."

I lifted up off my big comfortable bed to find Jackson lying underneath me.

"Why are you in my bed?"

Even this early in the morning, his gorgeous smile affected me.

"Not in your bed. You're on my couch."

I jumped from my spot and climbed to my feet looking around. Indeed I was still at Jackson's house. My shoes were off, and my purse was on the coffee table. I quickly grabbed my phone out and turned off the alarm.

I just spent the night with Jackson. Technically, this was the second time we've slept in the same house, but this time, I actually fell asleep in his arms. I ran a hand through my hair and immediately cringed at the tangled tracks on my head.

"You're cute when you're sleep. You snore."

"First of all, I don't snore. Secondly, why were you watching me sleep?"

Jackson sat up on the couch and placed his hands at his lower back pushing out his chest. An unmistakable cracking sound was heard.

"You absolutely snore, and I watched you sleep because I didn't get much last night."

He stood up and the action was accompanied by another cracking sound.

"Are you alright? Why didn't you wake me up to go home?"

He smiled at me as he pulled me by my waist into his chest. "And miss a chance to sleep with you in my arms? I'd take a sore back for that any day."

Damn it, I blushed.

"Still, you could have at least put me in the bed." I play pouted. "I feel bad about your back."

Jackson placed a kiss on my lips. It was quick and not lingering, but just enough to wake my senses and leave me wanting. He pulled away and walked off.

"Did you sleep well?"

I followed him into the kitchen. "Yes, I slept really well actually."

"Good," he said washing his hands in the sink. "Then that's all that matters. How about some breakfast?"

I looked down at my watch. "Actually, I have to go. I need to shower and get dressed for work."

Jackson pulled out a frying pan and put it on the stove. "Aren't you the boss?"

I nodded.

"Ok, then. You can afford to be late today. Besides, I'm not letting you leave without getting a sufficient meal in your belly. I've been in your kitchen. You need to eat."

I rolled my eyes playfully at him.

"Whatever! Let me call my assistant and tell him I will be late."

I turned to leave, but he grabbed me by the waist again pulling me back to him. He palmed my ass bringing me snug into him. I placed both hands on his chest. Jackson leaned down and placed a slow kiss to my lips that turned hot and steamy when his tongue dipped into my mouth and danced with mine.

I'm not much of a kisser. Never really had a reason for it, but I lost myself in his kiss. I got so caught up in how good it was, I didn't even think about the fact that neither of us had brushed our teeth.

Instead of that, I thought about how good his hands felt on my ass, and how good his lips felt on mine. Finally, Jackson pulled back slowly, placing soft kisses on my lips. He smiled down at me and patted my ass releasing me.

"You're getting a bit too comfortable with all the kissing," I said, heading towards my phone back in the living room.

Jackson chuckled behind me. "You like my kisses, woman."

I didn't answer. Only because the answer, damn right, was on the tip of my tongue. I wasn't trying to lead Jackson on. Nothing had changed between us. We were still just friends.

FOURTEEN

I was still able to make it to work at a reasonable time. And since all this bullshit with Cliff started, I was actually in a good mood today. My belly was full and a permanent smile was on my face. I wasn't in denial. I knew that my good mood and smile was from Jackson. He had this way of making me laugh and relax, unlike anyone else I'd ever been around. Even still, I knew that all this was temporary. Eventually, Jackson would lose my interest, and he'd be just like all the other guys I've slept with. However, I was determined to ride this out for the time being.

"Charlice, a Detective Myers is here to see you." My secretary came through my intercom.

"Send him in, Patricia."

I stood to my feet and hit the button to frost my office glass. It was a habit whenever I had visitors in my office.

I wasn't sure what brought Sean to my office. Hopefully he had news about Cliff.

My office door opened, and Sean walked in. He was wearing a black button up shirt, dark gray slacks and a gray tie. He was looking exceptionally edible today. Damn, he knew what those fitted pants did to me.

I gave him a one arm hug, and he wrapped both arms around me. We broke free, and I offered him a seat.

"What brings you to my office?" I said, leaning on my desk.

"I can't just come and see you?" He gave me his beautiful white smile.

I raised an eyebrow and placed a hand on my hip. He didn't need me to answer that question. I didn't do pop ups, especially not at my job.

Sean started to laugh. "I'm just kidding with you." He waved me off. "I went by your house last night to give you some news, but you weren't there."

He once again left the end of his sentence open for me to answer.

"Yeah?" I said, encouraging him to go on with his story.

Sean chuckled and shook his head. "Well I thought you would want to know that the detectives assigned to your case spoke to Cliff's family. They said that Cliff went up North to stay with relatives. The detectives believe he ran because he knew we were looking for him. We're still going to keep an eye out for him, but you can finally relax. You're safe."

I felt the weight of the world lift from my shoulders. This Cliff stuff was really stressing me out.

"That's great news. Thank you, Sean!"

We both stood so I could give him another hug. We released quickly, and I headed towards the door to see him out.

"I'm glad I was able to help you, Charli. You know I will always have your back."

I stopped at the door and held it open for him. He stood in front of me.

"What's wrong?" I asked when he didn't leave.

"I...um... Rochelle left."

"Sean, I'm sorry to hear that." I shut the door to my office for more privacy.

As I said, this wasn't new. Rochelle did this at least every few months. Whenever she couldn't get her way, she would walk out on Sean just so he could grovel at her feet to get her back. She was a whiney and needy bitch that often used Sean's love for her against him. No doubt she would be back in a few weeks once Sean finished jumping through all the hoops she required. That's why I usually fucked his brains out while he waited on her to come back. It was my little way of supporting my friend.

"I think it's for good this time, Charli," he said, shaking his head.

My heart went out to the broken look on his face.

"Are you kidding? Just a few months ago we were ring shopping?"

I picked out a damn good ring for that bitch.

Sean laughed. "I know, I know. But I'm kind of tired of playing this game, you know?"

I wasn't commenting. This was Sean's thing. One moment he was over her and in my bed, then two or three months later he would be telling me they made up. No matter how bat shit crazy she was, Sean loved her.

"I'm sure it will all work out," I told him. "If not, you will find a nice girl that isn't a bipolar bitch."

Sean threw his head back and laughed. "You really didn't like her."

I shrugged and rolled my eyes.

"Well," he said stepping towards me, "until then, I'm free." He grabbed me around the waist and pulled me into him. I went with ease. The familiarity of his arms comforted me. His lips found my neck. This definitely wouldn't be the first time I'd fucked him in my office. He hit that shit so good against my glass walls one time that it took three cleanings to get my ass print off the glass.

His hands dropped down to the hem of my skirt and lifted it up my thighs while he sucked on the sensitive skin where my neck met my collar bone. That's my spot. Just one nibble there, and my legs would spread wide open.

Just not that time.

I stepped away from Sean's soft lips, and he quirked an eyebrow at me.

What the hell, Duck? the words screamed in my head.

"You should go."

Sean looked shocked, not nearly as shocked as me at the words coming out of mouth. There had never been a time where Sean was available, that we weren't fucking. Except today, there was still no urge to retract my statement.

"O..K..!" Sean held his hands up in surrender. "Call me if you need me." He planted a quick kiss on my lips, then slipped out of my office.

I stared at his back, wondering why the fuck did I just let him walk out. Any other time we would have fucked all over this office, maybe even went back to my place and spent most of the day rolling in my bed. Yet, the thought of it didn't feel appeasing at the moment.

My phone went off on my desk, and I walked over and picked it up.

Jackson: We're going out Saturday.

My face lit up, and my heart started to race.

I sent him a text back.

Me: Pretty presumptuous of you to assume I don't have plans already.

Jackson: LOL! Saturday @ 12. Wear something comfortable, again.

I bit my bottom lip wondering if I should give in so easily, or make him sweat it out a little.

Me: Ok. I better like this date.

Jackson: You'll love it. And don't think I didn't notice you called it a date. Have a great day, beautiful.

I laughed at my slip up. He was never going to let me live that down.

***

"Grams!" I called out as I walked into my grandparents' house.

It had been three weeks since that day in my office. Since then, Jackson and I have gone on three official dates, and two unofficial dates. I'd been rock climbing, biking, and white water rafting. Every date I was tempted to curse his ass out once we arrived, but Jackson always managed to make me try it. And just like that first date, I actually enjoyed myself. I was always completely sore the next day, but it was worth it to hang out with Jackson.

Unfortunately, there had been no repeat of his office. The most he and I had done was make out like two virgin twelve-year-olds. Trust me, I'd tried to go further with him. That man had the patience and restraint of a monk. After the first two weeks, I finally gave up trying.

"In the kitchen, Duck!"

I followed her voice into the kitchen. She was at the stove stirring something in a pot that smelled delicious.

"Hey, my Duck. You look stunning today." I placed a kiss on her cheek and then went to the fridge to grab a bottle water.

"Thank you, I got this top from Macy's last fall." I turned back to Grams.

She was staring at me with a smile on her face.

"Duck, you are always beautiful, but I'm not talking about your clothes. You're glowing, honey."

I chuckled. "Good highlighter, that's all."

"You mean a good man. I know that look, I've been wearing it for fifty-six years."

I fought the blush that wanted to take over my face. I had no idea what Grams was talking about. I looked absolutely the same as I always did.

"I told you, Jackson and I are just friends."

"Mmhmmm. You just keep telling yourself that. Love has a way of catching up to you. You can run from it all you want, but sooner or later, it comes for you. The more you fight it, the harder it takes over you."

I rolled my eyes and folded my arms over my chest. "There is no such thing as love. It's just a word people use to justify their need to sleep with each other."

Gram's eyes widened. "What on earth are you talking about? Who put that foolishness in your head? I know not your mother."

I sighed. This was an argument I didn't want to have. Grams would never understand that I knew the truth about that four letter word. It wasn't real. It couldn't be.

"Don't worry about it," I said waving it away.

"No, Charlice." Grams dropped her hand towel and stepped closer to me. Her eyes watched me closely. It unnerved me the way she was looking at me. I felt naked, as if she could read all my secrets.

"What are you hiding from me?"

I laughed off her concern. "What? Nothing." I shrugged.

She continued to stare at me. Those light-brown eyes reading me so clearly. The look in her eyes changed from interest to sympathy before she looked away from me.

She saw something. I didn't know what it was, but I knew my Grams' might have read one of my secrets.

"What happened between you and Bernita?"

That was definitely not a conversation for today.

"Grams, it's nothing."

"It's not nothing, Duck! You got more secrets than a shady politician hidden behind your eyes. I know something happened. Every time I ask Nita, she changes the subject, and you just say nothing." Grams stared at me for a moment longer, her eyes squinted like she was trying to read something in the distance. I squirmed slightly under her gaze.

"Did she tell you something about your father?"

"My father?" Now I was confused. "How can she tell me about someone she probably doesn't even know?"

Grams grunted and turned her back to me.

Hold up!

"Wait a minute," I squealed. "Sadie Rose, do you know who my father is?"

"Blessed assurance, Jesus is mine."

"Oh no, you don't," I said, stepping back in front of my Grams. "Don't try to sing your way out of this. Who is my father?"

"Now, Duck, don't you go digging up old wounds. Some secrets need to stay buried. Never mention this again."

I flinched at her words, but she didn't notice. Never mention it again. Those words swarmed my head. I had to close my eyes and focus hard to make them disappear.

When I finally locked the gates on my unwanted memories, I opened my eyes, and Grams was watching me. I smiled charmingly.

Despite how this visit had turned out, I actually had a reason for it.

"I came by to ask you a favor," I said as gleefully as possible trying to chase away the somber mood in the room. "I wanted to see if you could teach me how to cook."

Again Grams' eyes widened, this time from shock and joy.

"You?" she teased, placing a hand to her hips. "Charlice Rose Jeffries wants to learn how to cook?"

"Yeah, I mean I'm thirty- three, I should be cooking my own meals and not always eating out. I'm trying to be healthier."

Grams threw her head back and laughed. "Healthy my ass."

I choked on my laughter.

"Grams!!" I chastised her jokingly.

"Don't Grams me. You're learning to cook for Mr. Jackson."

"He may benefit from it." I shrugged.

"Girl, come on over here. I'll show you how I won your grandfather over. My famous fried chicken and cornbread had your grandpa ready to marry me after our third date. I'll have your Mr. Jackson asking for your hand in marriage in no time."

I snorted. "Maybe we should stay away from the fried chicken, then."

Grams' laughter brought a smile to my face. I'd much rather see her smiling like this than the way she was earlier. I'd do anything to keep my grandparents happy and spare them from my truths.

FIFTEEN

It only took Grams three days to teach me how to cook a basic Cajun chicken and rice casserole. Most of the time was spent with me arguing with her that I didn't need the fried chicken and cornbread recipes. Poor Papa and Eli had to stomach through three days of my casserole for dinner until I felt comfortable enough to make it on my own.

Tonight I was going to surprise Jackson with a home cooked meal. The casserole was in the oven. The beers were in the fridge and the store bought cake was on the table. I finally had a chance to use all those nice dishes I bought when I got my house.

I once again fixed my hair in the mirror. I'd gone to Devin and decided on long auburn layers cut to the shoulder. It was a bold look for me, but I wanted something different. Something special. I felt silly for going through all this trouble. I was jumping through a lot of hoops just to get laid.

The doorbell rung breaking me out of my downward spiral of thoughts. I gave my appearance one last look. A bohemian inspired maxi dress with a deep V and front split, and strappy Giuseppe flats was the outfit I decided on.

I stopped at the door and took a breath, for some reason my heart was racing. I opened the door to find Jackson holding a bottle of wine and flowers. He was dressed casual today in a blue plaid

124

button up shirt. The sleeves rolled to right below his elbow. His dark wash jeans were loosely fitting his thick thighs. Jackson looked fucking fantastic in casual wear.

"Oh my God! Jackson those are beautiful." I said after noticing the combination of blue and purple flowers.

I was not a flower person. Other than a rose I didn't know what any of them were called. But I knew I loved this arrangement.

I stepped back and allowed him and Lady to walk in. I was so used to the dog I didn't even second guess if she was coming with him anymore.

He handed me the flowers, but his eyes were glued to my outfit. "You look stunning, Char."

I blush, "Thank you! I'm going to put these in water."

I closed the door and headed into the kitchen, Jackson and Lady were right behind me. I grabbed a vase I got one year for my birthday from my godchildren and filled it with water at the sink.

"I noticed that a lot of your things are purple and blue, I assumed you liked those colors."

I looked up at him and smiled. He's right, those are my favorite colors. I didn't think anyone knew that about me. Well, maybe Naya, she's always asking me what my favorite things were.

"Oh and I brought you wine." He held up the bottle for me to see. "I…uh…. Don't know much about wine, but the lady at the store said it was good. It's also pretty cheap." He rubbed the back of his neck.

"Trust me, I'm not picky about my wine. This is good." I took the bottle from him after placing my flowers in the center of my island. I placed the bottle of wine in my refrigerator and grabbed a beer out for Jackson. I handed him his beer and he smiled.

"I already got my beer in the fridge? Sooner or later I'll have my toothbrush at your sink."

I laughed out loud. "I doubt it."

"So what's on the menu tonight? It smells amazing in here."

At his compliment I lifted my head a little higher.

"Cajun chicken and rice casserole."

"MMMMmmmm, that sounds right nice. A woman that is beautiful and can cook." Jackson teased.

"Look, don't start giving out compliments until you've actually tasted the food."

Jackson placed his beer down on the counter and sauntered over to me. I watched his wide shoulders and that dimpled smile that drove me crazy. Damn he's sexy. His heat and delicious scent hits me before he did. My back was pressed up against the kitchen sink. He placed both his hands on the counter behind me trapping me in.

"What do you think you're doing?"

Those hazel heavy lidded eyes stared down at me.

"I haven't got my kiss yet."

"And you feel that you are entitled to it?" I crossed my arms over my chest, and cocked one eyebrow up at him.

That smirk lit up his face.

"The moment you came to the door in this thin ass dress I was entitled to everything. You're making it hard for me to behave myself." One of his big heavy hands landed on my hip and he pulled me closer to him.

My bottom lip slipped in between my teeth. I knew just how hard I was making him. His difficulty was brushing against my stomach demanding my attention.

"Who said I wanted you to behave yourself."

His lips landed on mine before the words were fully out of my mouth.

Jesus! Jackson's kisses could start a forest fire. His tongue danced along mine while his hand tightened on my hips. I didn't even remember my arms going around his neck. When his hand grabbed a handful of my ass and squeezed, I was ready to say fuck this food and let's take this to the room. I moaned into Jackson's mouth and he slowly started to gather the material of my dress, causing it to rise up my legs.

The stove beeped letting me know the food was done. Jackson started to pull away, but I was not having it. My fingers tangled in his thick hair as I pulled him closer. I could feel his smile against my greedy lips. He finally broke away from me.

"Your food is going to burn."

"Who the fuck cares." I grabbed for him again and he chuckled as he dodged me.

"Get the food, Char."

I groaned as I turned around to get to the food. His hand smacked my ass. I looked over my shoulder and caught him staring at my butt with a look of amazement. Yeah, I opted out of panties for tonight.

**

We were sitting at my never before used dining room table. The table was made of dark walnut with baluster turned legs. It set six people in high back gray fabric dining room chairs. The entire set was almost six thousand dollars. And none of that mattered at the moment as I watched Jackson take the first bite of the meal I'd prepared for him. I wasn't this damn scared when I opened up my firm. I had sweat pouring down my back towards my ass. I watched Jackson wrap his lips around the prongs of his fork. Keeping my eyes on his face carefully. When he didn't immediately spit it back out, I actually started to breathe again.

"Not bad." He said.

I finally picked up my fork and took a bite. The first bite was alright, it definitely wasn't like the one Grams' cooked. The second bite was too salty and the rice was still a little hard. After the third bite, I was done.

Well, that was a bust.

"You don't have to keep eating it, Jackson. I know it's bad."

Jackson laughed as he puts down his fork.

"You're right, it's bad baby. But you went through all the trouble to make it, so I'm going to eat it." He took another bite and chewed. "It's like crunching on small pebbles."

That's it, I was done.

I stood from the table and grabbed my plate. "Don't force yourself. We'll just order something." I took my plate into the kitchen and raked the disaster meal down the garbage disposal.

I didn't realize how badly I wanted to make a good meal until now. I'd never cared to learn how to cook, because I never needed to. However, right now I felt like a failure, and I haven't felt this way in a long time.

I didn't hear him come into the kitchen, I just felt his body behind mine and his arm wrap around me.

"I'm sorry I ruined dinner."

"Hey!" Jackson turned me around to face him.

My back was pressed against the kitchen sink.

"I told you I didn't care if you could cook. The fact that you went out of your comfort zone to cook me a meal, is more important than the food itself. Besides, Lady loves it."

I looked behind him to find lady liking her mouth while starring longingly at the tray of casserole sitting on the counter. I laughed, feeling the disappointment over the meal ebb away.

Jackson's thumb ran over my bottom lip. His eyes stared at the trail his finger made.

"I can watch you laugh all day." He said it as if he was thinking out loud.

The mood in the room shifted. The horrible dinner was forgotten. The heat from his body pressed against mine had my body tingling all over. I was hyper aware of everywhere his body touched mine. I ached from the simple connections. I wanted more. I think Jackson must have read my desire in my eyes. Those hazel eyes watched me closely as he tilted my chin up, bringing my lips closer to his. His kiss was gentle, soft, and even tentative.

Not what I wanted.

Jackson was sweet, but I knew deep down inside, a beast stirred. I wanted the beast. I sunk my teeth into his bottom lip gently and sucked it into my mouth. Jackson growled, but he continued with his gentle kisses. There was no denying that Jackson was a big man, and I imagined when he was with his Ex he had to be gentle. But I wasn't his Ex. I needed rough.

"Fuck me, Jackson. Please!"

Apparently I wasn't above begging.

My plea worked. I could feel the change in his body. His hand found its way into my hair. He fisted it and pulled my head back. It wasn't painful, just enough force to let me know the kid gloves were off.

His kiss deepened, causing me to whimper into his mouth. I was so turned on I could have climbed his fucking body like a spider monkey. I hiked one leg up, anything to get him closer to where I needed him. I grabbed for his belt buckle. I made short work of his belt, snatching it out of his pants loops and dropping it to the floor— all done with my eyes closed and my lips glued to his.

Jackson removed his hand from my hair to yank my dress over my head. He tossed it somewhere, and then we came back together like magnets. I grabbed his button up and yanked the fabric apart. Buttons flew everywhere, pinging off of appliances. Jackson lifted me effortlessly and I wrapped my legs around him. He turned us around, trading places with me, then placed me on the island in the center of my kitchen. The cold granite was a shock to my bare ass. Jackson yanked off his shirt and dropped it to the ground to join with my dress somewhere. He then grabbed my legs, pulling me to the edge of the counter top, my ass hung off the side. He dropped to his knees, pushed mine to my chest, and feasted on my pussy as if it was the prepared meal for tonight.

I collapsed back on the counter. My eyes rolled to the back of my head. Jackson ate my pussy like a pro. He spread my lower lips apart exposing my pink center, his tongue danced over my nub before slipping inside. I was screaming and moaning like I was being murdered. When he pulled the hood of my clit back to suck the exposed nub, I came so hard I went cross eyed.

Jackson sucked and licked me clean until I was crying for him to stop. He stood to his feet and ran a hand down his wet nose to his chin. I sat up and he pulled me to him for a scorching kiss.

Damn I loved the taste of my pussy on his tongue.

We both fumbled over his pants button. Finally getting it open and pushing it down his thighs just low enough to release this throbbing dick. It was thick, long, and heavy in my hand. Jackson broke our kiss to dig into his pants pocket and pulled out a string of gold wrapper condoms. He pulled off one from the top of the line and tossed the others to the counter. I watched in anticipation as he stuck the gold wrapper into his mouth and tore off the edge of the foil. He took out the condom and placed the foil on the counter. Once he was fully sheath in the prophylactic, he spun me around, facing away from him. I bent over the island and he entered me so fast and hard I didn't have time to brace for it. My hips slammed into the kitchen island. I cried out at his abrupt entrance, not from pain, but from the pleasure at being stretched so damn good.

"Don't run now, Char. You asked for this, remember?" He taunted as he slid in so hard I had to lift on my toes.

Curse words flew from my mouth as he broke my pussy in. When he smacked my ass I moaned so loud I could put a porn star to shame.

"Gotdamn, I love your ass." He announced before smacking it again.

It took a moment to adjust to Jackson's size and drive, but I was no punk, so I started to back it up on him. I slammed my hips back as he thrusted forward. Just when I got accustomed to him, he pulled out of me with a wet sucking sound. He spun me around, attacking my lips with a hungry kiss.

He started to lead me out of the kitchen all while still kissing me. At some point he must had come out of his jeans. We walked through the house like two drunk lovers, smashing into walls and furniture. I even heard glass shatter, but I didn't give a shit. I'd worry about it tomorrow.

After finally making it to the bedroom, Jackson lifted me off my feet and tossed me onto the bed. I bounced once before he was on top of me. His heavy body comforting. He used one hand to hold himself up and the other to direct his dick into me. It was a new angle and that delicious painful bite was back. Jackson's hips moved between my legs like they were possessed by the devil. He was fucking me so good my bed knocked against the wall, making its own rap beat.

He slid out, flipped me on my side, straddled one leg while holding the other against his chest. I screamed in pleasure at the new angle.

"That's right, Char. Take all this dick, baby, because you're mine now."

My second orgasm hit me and I was speaking in some gibberish language that had never been heard of.

Jackson fucked me for hours, flipping my body around like a damn ragdoll. I came so many times I lost count and he only came twice. He had amazing stamina. He rode my body like a fucking racehorse until I fell asleep in an exhausted heap with my body hanging off the side of the bed.

I was thoroughly fucked.

SIXTEEN

I woke up the next morning to an empty bed, a sore body and the smell of bacon floating through the air. For just a second I laid in the bed and remembered the night I'd just had. Never in my life had I had sex so damn good. I've slept with plenty of men, my numbers weren't astronomical or anything, but they were up there and I wasn't ashamed of it, but of all the men that had graced my bed no one had put it down like Jackson.

There was something different about being with him. I mean, yes his dick was big, I was talking long and fat. However, I'd had a few bigger than him. His tongue game was fantastic, I thought I would be permanently cross eyed for a moment, and his stamina—that man was like the energizer bunny. I thought my pussy was going to get up and leave at one point last night, yet, there was still something else about last night that made sex with Jackson so much better. I couldn't quite put my finger on it.

I grabbed the pillow on the other side of the bed and brought it to my face taking in his scent. I closed my eyes as his smell made my heart beat faster. "Get your shit together, Duck. You're in here smelling his pillow." This wasn't normal, plus I let him sleep over last night. Not in another room like before, but in my bed. But, in my defense, my body was too exhausted to kick someone out. Shit, I was too tired to even roll out of the wet spot. I had no idea he was here all night.

I finally rolled out of bed and headed to the bathroom to shower and brush my teeth. I almost screamed when I saw the mess of my hair. I had just got it done and already it was time for a redo. Jackson was definitely a hair puller, I would have to explain to him what being with a black woman that wore weaves was all about. There was no salvaging my hair. After my shower I tied a silk Chanel scarf over it and went down stairs.

On my way down the stairs I noticed that the mess Jackson and I made last night was all cleaned up. The pictures on the wall had been straightened. The clothes that made a trail from the kitchen to the bedroom were picked up and even the picture we broke was swept away.

I found Jackson in my kitchen without a shirt and in nothing but his boxer briefs. His body was incredible. He was definitely not sporting any six or eight packs, but his thick muscles and wide shoulders looked delicious. Those thick muscled thighs stretching the elastic of those briefs. I felt my body softening again for another round. I was turning into a Jackson fiend.

"You going to come over here and tell me good morning, or just stare at me from the doorway?"

Those hypnotizing eyes turned to me. His eyes raked down my short night shorts and tank top underneath my silk robe.

"Come here, baby." He demanded turning off my stove and taking a pan off the burner.

I didn't even pretend like in his arms wasn't where I wanted to be. I marched over to his open arms and allowed him to swallow me up. His lips are on mine instantly and I easily opened for him. Our kiss took another turn when Jackson's hand went under my robe to grip my ass. It was still tender from Jackson smacking the shit out of it all night, but I wasn't complaining. I wanted him again.

I moaned around his tongue and Jackson pulled me closer allowing my belly to brush against the hard pole barely contained behind his shorts. He pulled away when my hand dropped in between us to find the hem of his boxers.

"Eat first." he demanded.

I groaned. Despite how horny I was, I knew Jackson would not relent until I actually ate something. The man had incredible will power.

I turned to the stove to find puffy scrambled eggs, and perfectly crispy bacon.

"There is some fruit in the fridge." Jackson said from behind me.

"Where did you get all this food?" I knew it didn't come from my house.

"I went to the grocery store this morning after I grabbed a few things from my house."

My hand stopped midway, the piece of bacon I was about to eat forgotten.

"What time is it?"

"A little after ten, why?"

Just as he answered the doorbell rang.

"You expecting company?" Jackson looked down at his still hard dick barely being contained behind his underwear. I laughed at the sight. I had plans for it later.

"Don't worry big guy, I'm breaking you out of there later."

I headed out of the kitchen, I knew exactly who was there. It's Saturday, and my weekend with the girls.

"It's my cousin," I called over my shoulder. "I forgot I was supposed to get the girls this weekend. I'll try to take them in the living room and you can find some bottoms."

The bell rang again and this time someone knocked at the door like they were here with a search warrant. Even Lady got annoyed. She let out a quick bark.

Without taking the time to look through the glass, I swung the door open to stop the damn knocking.

"Now is not a good time, Devin…." The words trailed off at the end as Devin, Keva, Keisha, and both my god children stood on the other side of the door.

I should have looked first.

"Damn, Duck! What took you so long to answer the door?" Keisha said as she walked into the house before I could stop her. She was closely followed by Devin, Keva and the girls.

"And why does your house smell like food?" Devin said as she placed Naya down on the ground.

Lady came out of the kitchen to inspect the noise.

Kylie squealed as she rushed to lady.

"Kylie don't!" Devin tried to warn her daughter from getting too close to the dog, but Lady was already excitedly licking Kylie's face.

"Mommy, Aunt Duck has a dog." Naya said as she headed towards a happy Kylie and Lady.

"And a white man." Keisha stated.

I looked up to find Jackson standing in the kitchen door.

All eyes were on him now. Thankfully he was able to locate some gray workout shorts to cover up what I knew was under those boxers.

"Good morning, ladies." Jackson said when no one else could find the words to speak.

"Damn!" Keisha mumbled under her breath.

"Hi, I'm Duck's cousin, Devin. The two little one's are mine." Devin held out a hand to shake Jackson's. He stepped forward to shake her hand.

"Duck?" he smirked looking over Devin's head to find my inflamed face.

"Oh! Ummmm I meant, Charlice." Devin looked to me and turned her lips down briefly.

"My childhood nickname is Duck." I said by way of explanation.

The mirth danced in Jackson's eyes before turning his attention back to Devin.

"Well it's nice to finally meet you, Devin. I've heard a lot about you and these two beautiful little princesses." He turned to my god daughters who both seemed just as infatuated with Jackson as they were the dog.

"Are you Aunt Duck's boyfriend?" Naya asked and I could feel the embarrassing blush fill my cheeks.

Keisha busts out laughing as Keva looked at me expectantly— probably ready to take this back to the family.

"Don't be silly, Naya! Aunt Duck doesn't have boyfriends. Right mommy?"

Devin's eyes nearly popped out of her head as she stumbled over the right words.

"Don't call me silly, Ky." Naya's innocent voice replied angrily. "Can he be your boyfriend, Aunt Duck so we can keep the dog?"

"Ok, Girls. How about you two go in the living room and watch TV."

Anything to make this situation less awkward.

"Told you he isn't her boyfriend." Kylie mumbled to her little sister as they walked side by side into the living room.

I looked back up at Jackson and the laughter that was in his eyes earlier was gone.

"Hi, I'm Keisha. Duck's younger cousin." Keisha offered Jackson her hand.

"Younger by four months." Devin stated. Keisha rolled her eyes at Devin.

Jackson briefly shook Keisha's hand.

"I'm Keva. The only married one in the room." Keva cut her judgmental eyes to me before turning back to Jackson.

"Well, it was nice to meet you ladies. There is food in the kitchen. I'm going to get out of your way." He headed for the stairs and I cut him off.

"You guys can head into the kitchen I'll be there in a minute." I said to my cousins who were entirely too interested in what Jackson and I were doing.

Devin had to drag Keisha into the kitchen. The moment they were out of sight I turned back to Jackson to find that hurt look in his eyes.

"Stay!" I pleaded.

"No! I should go. I don't want to confuse anyone of who I am." He went to walk around me and I placed my hand on his chest to stop him.

"What did you want me to say? They are just kids, they won't understand when you disappear in a few months."

His eyes narrowed down at me. I knew immediately I had said the wrong thing.

"That's all I am to you, right? Someone to fill in space in your bed until you dismiss me for the next? I mean damn, Charlice did last night mean nothing to you?"

Damnit he's using my full name again.

"Jackson, you knew how I felt. I don't date and I definitely don't do labels."

He chuckled, but there was no humor in it. "I understand you very clearly now." He removed my hand from his chest and heads up the stairs.

"Jackson! Jackson!" I called out to his retreating back.

How did our morning go from promising to this? I had planned to ride Jackson about three more times today. I turned to the kitchen to catch all three cousins rushing away from the door. I rolled my eyes as I headed towards them.

I placed my hands on my hips. "Ya'll couldn't have called first?"

"We tried, but clearly you were occupied?" Keisha said with a smirk as she chewed on a piece of bacon.

"Shut up, Keish!" Devin barked. "I'm so sorry, Duck. And I'm sorry about the girls. I'll talk to them about that."

"It's not their fault. Children speak the truth. If you have a man in your house this early in the morning and he's shirtless, he should be your husband or at the least your boyfriend."

"Keva, I'm not in the mood for your bullshit. I just woke up twenty minutes ago."

"Damn! He had you sleeping like that?" Keisha asked around a mouth full of eggs.

"Will you get your greedy ass away from my breakfast?" I marched over to her to take the spoon out of her hand.

"I can't help it. This baby got me hungry."

I sighed as I felt a pressure headache coming. "Can we postpone this get together? I'll pick up the girls later today. I have some business to handle."

"You sure do. You were wrong for leaving him hanging like that. The man dicked you down good and cooked you breakfast, and you couldn't even lie to your godchildren about him being your boyfriend. That was a real bitch move." Again Keisha said sneaking another piece of bacon.

"How do you assume I was dicked down?"

"That Aunt Jemima scarf over that tangled weave."

I touched my tangled hair and frowned.

"As crude as Keisha is," Devin cut her eyes to Keisha then back to me. "She's right, Duck. You like Jackson. It's obvious by the fact that he is here this morning. Plus you've been glowing since he's been around. I think he deserves some kind of title. You could have said he was your friend or something."

"If the title isn't husband he shouldn't be here."

"Shut up, Keva!" Devin, Keisha, and I said at the same time.

They left me with something to think about. I guess they were right about how I treated Jackson. I mean he definitely meant more to me than someone I should brush off when I was asked about him.

I really needed to make it up to him. Which brought me back to this impromptu family gathering.

"So tell me again, why did all of you need to be here just to drop off the girls?" The sooner I could figure that out the faster I could get them out.

"Oh!" Devin shrugged. "Intervention."

"For who?" I placed my hands on my hips.

"Not for you." Keva said waving me off. "I've been trying to get the family to have a prayer intervention for you for years, but they won't listen. This is for Chante."

Devin rolled her eyes at Keva. "I think something is wrong with my sister. Like seriously wrong." Devin rubbed her rounding belly. "Gram's said that she let Chante borrow some money two days ago when she was at the house, and when she left, Grams noticed some money was missing from her purse. She isn't saying Chante took it, but she said it was there before Chante came over. Then I went over there yesterday and Amari was soaking wet and screaming at the top of his lungs while she was passed out on the couch. I think Chante is going through postpartum depression and money issues."

No, she was not depressed, she was on drugs. Her poison of choice were opioids. Like I said, I knew secrets.

For about two months I was sleeping with a Pharmaceutical rep that had a certain side hustle. Guess who I discovered was one of his most dedicated customers? Chante. Quincy had an issue with keeping his dick in his pants and his hands to himself when he was mad. Chante dealt with her problems by zoning out. In the end, the baby suffered the most.

"Well, good luck with that." I say heading back to the foyer to see my cousins out.

"Maybe you should come." Devin asked. "The more people the better, plus she will respect it more coming from you."

I stopped and spun around. "Are you kidding? Have you been blind the last 23 years? Your sister barely even talks to me without it being a shitty insult. She is not going to listen to me. She's just going to get angry and we will end up arguing or fighting."

"Duck is right, Dev. Chante will not listen to her." Keisha stated.

Exactly!

"Besides, Duck has some making up to do."

I rolled my eyes at Keisha.

"Fine! I guess you're right."

I felt bad for Devin. Her and Chante's relationship has always suffered due to Devin's close relationship with me. It wasn't from Devin's lack of trying.

Unfortunately, this intervention wasn't going to help. Chante needed rehab. She was too far gone for a friendly intervention.

I opened the door to see my family out.

Devin stopped at the open door. "You really do need to make it up to him. I'll just take the girls with me and you can pick them up later."

"Let them stay." I told Devin.

No need to ruin anyone else's day.

"I think I need me a white man." Keisha whispered beside me.

I followed her eyes to the top of the stairs where a fully dressed Jackson was coming down. He was wearing one of his t-shirts and dark wash jeans.

"We're going to go." Devin announced.

"Why? It's starting to get good." Keisha whined.

Devin grabbed Keisha and called out a good bye to the girls before all three cousins walked out the door.

When Jackson got to the bottom of the steps he placed his bag down at his feet and whistled for Lady to come. The dog rushed into the foyer with my goddaughters hot on her trail.

"Are you leaving?" Naya asked Jackson.

Jackson squatted down to get eye level with Naya. "Yeah, I have to go. It was nice meeting you. And thank you for watching my dog while I was busy."

He really was good with children. My stomach tightened at the sight.

"Awww, I thought you were going to stay and play with us."

Jackson looked up at me and that hurt from earlier was still there.

"Sorry, Beautiful, but I think it's best I go."

"Actually." I said cutting in as Jackson stood to his feet. "It would really be great if you could stay and hang out with us."

"Yay! Please stay, Mr. Jackson? We always have fun at Aunt Duck's." Naya was really trying to work her magic to get Jackson to stay.

I owed that girl a new toy.

"Yes, Mr. Jackson." I said teasingly. "I would love for my god daughters to get to know my new …..boyfriend."

Kylie gasped beside me and Naya squealed with delight. They were more excited than I was about the announcement.

The smile that spread over Jackson's face had me wanting to send the girls away so that I could finish my morning the way I had planned. It was very much worth the lie.

"I guess I could hang out for a little while." Jackson replied with his eyes glued to me.

"Yay! Let's go play, Uncle Jackson." Naya squeals placing her small hand in Jackson's and dragging him towards the living room. "I told you he was her boyfriend." Naya loudly whispers to her sister as they walk back to the living room.

I didn't follow right away. I took a second to inhale. My heart was racing. I was taking large leaps out of my comfort zone today. First Jackson spending the night, and not like the other times but actually sleeping over in my bed. Then me calling him my boyfriend, even though it was just for my nieces. My world was moving too fast, but I wasn't necessarily panicking like I thought I would.

"Hurry up and get dressed, Aunt Duck. Uncle Jackson is going to take us to a lake." Kylie demanded as she came around the corner with a huge smile on her face.

"Alright, alright. I'm moving." I headed upstairs to get dressed for our day.

SEVENTEEN

By the time we took the girls home that night, Jackson and I were exhausted. When Jackson's truck pulled back up to my house I couldn't even muster the energy to climb out.

"I never thought two people that small could have that much energy."

I laughed tiredly, barely putting in the energy to make the sound come out.

"They had extra energy for Uncle Jackson."

Jackson chuckled. "I was waiting on you to correct them on that."

I started to a few times, but Naya just took to it so easily. Even Kylie eventually started saying it. I figured it was no need to stop them. Even when Jackson and I eventually call it off, it's not like they will meet anymore men in my life to call uncle so I should give them this one time.

I shrugged. "Didn't feel the need."

The truck was quiet after my statement.

I looked back at lady in the back seat and even she was exhausted. I had to hand it to the dog, she'd been hugged and kissed within an inch of her life today, but not once did she complain about it. She ran with the girls and did every trick that they asked her to do.

"Come on, I'll walk you to the door." Jackson said bringing me out of my thoughts.

He opened his door and stepped out before walking around to the passenger side to let me out.

"You're not staying?" my questions caused Jackson and I to pause.

Where the hell did that come from? It just spilled from my lips without me thinking about it.

Jackson took my hand and helped me down.

"I'm going to be honest with you, Char. I want to stay another night with you. I promise I do, but I think I should go home."

Was he kidding? We just had a long day, and I didn't get my three more rounds like I wanted. Hell, even my butt wasn't as sore as earlier.

"Jackson, aren't we pass that stage in our relationship where you pretend to be a gentlemen."

"No!"

"Come on, Jackson!"

He laughed at my whining.

"Relax, Char. A lot happened today. Things that I don't think you've had time to register. Plus, what I said to you last night, about you being mine, was real. Before I come back to your bed, you have to be sure that's what you are ready for."

"And what is it I'm supposed to be ready for?"

Jackson watched me closely, those sexy eyes studying me.

"For us. For a real relationship. Which means no more of your bullshit rules. No more looking at this with an expiration date, and definitely no more men. I will be the only man that touches you. If you need something, anything, you call me. Also, no more pulling away when things get too deep."

Damn! Jackson wanted a lot. I wasn't sure I could give it to him. I was already feeling panicky and claustrophobic just hearing him talk about what he wanted from me.

Clearly he could see the panic on my face because Jackson sighed.

"Yeah, that's exactly why I'm going home. Come on."

He grabbed my hand and helped me down out of his truck. We walked side by side in complete silence to my front door. Jackson turned to me and placed a kiss on my cheek.

"Call me when you have an answer."

He headed back to his truck. I watched him climb inside and shut the door before I walked into the house.

That night I slept fretfully. Twice I woke in a cold sweat, that feeling of being watched keeping me up all night.

***

The next day I showed up to family dinner tired and with a lot on my mind.

The thought of tying myself down to Jackson freaked me out. It didn't matter that for the last month that's exactly what I'd been doing. Other than that incident with Sean in my office, I hadn't touched or thought about another man. In all honestly, I'd been in a relationship with Jackson all along. It was just the idea of making it official, and what all it entailed felt a lot like being tied down. And I couldn't be tied down.

"So, Duck! How did your dinner turn out for your fella?" Papa asked drawing my attention out.

"I hope it was better than what you fed me and Pops." I shoved Eli in the shoulder.

I wouldn't dare admit that it was in fact not better at all.

"Wait! Duck cooked?"

"Don't say it with that face, Devin. Yes, I cooked."

Devin laughed.

"Well, it looked like he ate well when we saw him."

I cut my eyes to Keisha and she winked at me.

"Hold on now," Grams said and everyone turned to her. "Keisha got to meet him?"

"I did too, Grams, shirtless." Keva just had to add.

"Well that settles it, if everybody else have met your boyfriend then it's only right I get to meet him."

"It's not like I planned to introduce them, they just popped up at my house."

The table went completely quiet as everyone stared back at me like I started speaking in Latin.

"What?"

"You didn't deny him."

"What are you talking about, Devin?"

"She means, I just called him your boyfriend and you didn't correct me." From the smile on my Grandmother's face you would have thought I told her I was getting married tomorrow.

"Is he your boyfriend, Duck?" Even Papa was caught up in the moment.

Everyone was staring at me expectantly. Did I really want to do this? Did I really want to commit to Jackson? It was one thing telling my god daughters. Not even admitting it to Jackson would be as official as admitting it to my family. If I weighed the options, I guess being with him with that label, was a lot more alluring than not having him at all. And from my understanding, those are my options.

"I guess," I started squirming in my seat. "If you were going to give him a label that would be the most accurate."

My Grams squealed in excitement while Devin hugged me at the table. Even Keisha cheered for me. Eli patted me on the back. There were a few faces around the table that didn't share in my excitement. Aunt Vivica was looking at me like she smelled something rotten. Quincy looked pissed and Chante was still looking like she lost her best friend. I assumed the intervention didn't go well yesterday since Chante hadn't spoken to anyone in the house yet.

Once the excitement died down, everyone started asking questions about Jackson. What does he do? How did we meet? Are we going to get married? I gave vague answers to most except that last one, that was a definite hell no. I drew the line at marriage.

When the conversation finally turned to something else I was relieved.

"The doctor said everything was going well, and I'll find out next month if it's a boy or another girl." Devin announced rubbing her belly proudly.

I was just as excited an anxious to find out what my new god child would be.

"Well, it won't be long before Duck will be bringing us some grandbabies too."

I choked on my tea and the table laughed.

"Just what the world needs, more sell outs." Quincy mumbled.

The table grew quiet.

"I'm sorry," I said. "Can you repeat that?"

He watched me for a moment, looking like a jealous bitch. He leaned back in his seat placing a hand on the back of Chante's chair.

"I just never took you for one of those people."

"One of what people, Quincy?"

I knew what he was trying to say, I just wanted his punk ass to say it out loud.

He looked uncomfortable for a moment. He should. But he continued on. "A sell-out."

Aunt Vivica hummed in agreement.

"With all the good hard working brothers out here you decide to settle down with a white man? I mean, most likely he's going through a phase. It's that slave master/ slave thing. He's no different from his ancestors just wanting to sample our women. He'll taint you and then toss you to the side like trash for one of his wholesome white women. And you fell for it." He shrugged.

I watched him closely, deciding just how I wanted to tackle this. Should I mention how he'd been fucking his white paralegal for the last two years? Russel down in the mailroom of his law firm gave me that bit of info, and I didn't even have to fuck him for it. Or maybe I should mention how riding the partners' dicks at his law firm for a promotion made him just as much of a sell out? Then again, maybe I should just dismiss him all together because I didn't have shit to prove to Quincy.

"Dating outside of your race doesn't make you a sell-out, Quincy." Devin argued.

Quincy shrugged and took a sip from his cup of tea with a smug grin.

"I beg to differ, baby sis." He placed his cup down. "Duck has officially given up her blackness."

I laughed and leaned back in my chair. "Tell me, Quincy, how does one lose their blackness? Because the last time I checked, I'm still as black as I was the day I was born."

He kissed his teeth. "Your blackness has nothing to do with the color of your skin." He argued.

This was something I wasn't going to tolerate. I wasn't blind to what was going on in the world. I knew that the moment I first agreed to coffee with Jackson that this type of conversation would come up. I couldn't control how the world viewed us, but I could damn sure put a stop to it in my own family.

"My blackness isn't something I get to remove or drop when I want to. It's not a checklist of things I need to accomplish or prove in order to keep. I prove my blackness every day I walk my black ass out my house. I'm reminded of it every time I'm in a business meeting and the clients speak to my assistant instead of me like I'm not the President and CEO. It shows when I take my cars to get serviced and the mechanic ask me what my boyfriend does for a living. They watch with that smug smile on their face as if they just know he's a drug dealer. My blackness is thrown in my face every time I walk into a boutique and someone second guesses me about if I really want to try on a fucking skirt, like I can't read a price tag.

Having a black man on my arm does not define my blackness. Just like having a black woman on your arm doesn't make you a good man. I prove my blackness every damn day of my life, so who I let lay beside me in my bed has nothing to do with who I am. It also does not stop me from giving back to my community. Every year I invest in black owned business, I donate to inner city schools, I help build playgrounds and fund libraries all right here in the community I grew up in. I donate to them just as much I donate to all the other large well known non-profits. And you know what, none of that's going to change just because my man isn't the same race as me."

Again the table falls silent. I watched Quincy. He had nothing to say at this point. I could have called him out on few things. Maybe brought to life his affair, or the many times he have turned down people of color as clients. However, just as my actions didn't prove my blackness, his didn't either. Because regardless of who he's with or how he acts, he was still a black man. So I didn't expose him.

"I think Duck has proved her point." Papa said. "And if anyone don't think so, they don't have to sit at my table." Papa turned to me letting it be known the matter was dropped. "Whenever you are ready, I want you to bring your young man to dinner. I would like to meet him."

I smiled and nodded at Papa. Other conversation started to pick up around the table. I still wasn't ready to bring Jackson to meet my family, and I doubt if I ever would be.

**

That night, while I lied in bed alone, I thought about Jackson. I thought about the way he made me feel and how much I enjoyed his company. It was a no brainer that my phone was in my hand.

ME: Ok!

Those were the only two letters I sent him, but I figured he knew what I meant. It only took a few seconds before he replied.

JACKSON: Dinner at my house tomorrow. Bring a change of

clothes.

And just like that, I was officially in a relationship.

EIGHTEEN

"I'm feeling lucky right now. It's hard to get time with you lately." Devin said as she took a sip of her strawberry lemonade.

We were sitting outside at Beverly's, an upscale bistro that served incredible soup.

"What are you talking about, I see you every Sunday at Gram's house." I placed the paper menu back down on the table and gave my cousin my full attention. I'd been to this restaurant a hundred times, I already knew what I wanted.

"Yeah, but you're always the first out the door now. Gram's said you don't even take leftovers home. You must be eating somewhere,"

Devin raised an eyebrow at me with that familiar smirk on her face. I ignored her apparent fish for information. It's been six weeks since Devin and my cousins met Jackson that Saturday morning. Since the announcement of Jackson being my boyfriend, the entire family had been trying to get more information on him. Sunday dinners had become the ask Duck a million questions time. Gram's had even started to make comments about little mixed great grands. And I didn't know how many different ways I could say that Jackson would not be coming to Sunday dinner.

Even though Jackson was my boyfriend—I was still getting used to using that word—we were not quite there in our relationship. He did have a spare toothbrush and clothing at my house. I did give him a spare key for convenience, but only because I didn't always feel like getting up to open the door when he was coming over. And yes, in my spare time I was either at his place or he was at mine, but it's required because we fuck a lot. Although I would admit, some of that time was our regular routine of a home cooked meal on Sunday nights as we cuddled up on his couch and watched television.

I guess, if you looked at all that, you would think we were ready to take the next step. However, the thought of introducing him to my family made me nauseas.

I lifted up my mimosa and poured the orange juice concoction down my throat,

Devin giggled. "Someone is in love." She sung the last word.

I placed the glass back down and wiped my mouth with my napkin before shaking my head.

"Not love, Devin. I like Jackson. I also like spending time with him, but it isn't love. It's great sex. Eventually, I'll grow tired of it and I'll move on."

My words came out assuredly, but I wasn't as convinced. The sex was phenomenal. I've never been fucked so good in all my life. Jackson had stamina, size, and ability. I was calling out to God, Buddha, and any other religious deities that there were. He put in work. Yet, even on the days where we were just lying around doing nothing, were fine with me. He made me laugh just as much as he made me cum. I wasn't so sure that I would get enough of Jackson any time soon, and for some reason, that made me uncomfortable.

"Forget about me," I said waving off the topic of my relationship, "I want to hear this big news you have?"

A wide smile broke out over Devin's face as she leaned up in the chair. "So, I've been thinking about going back to school and getting my license."

My mouth opened so wide you could drive a truck through it. I squealed with excitement and clapped like a circus seal.

"Are you serious?"

"Yes! I've been thinking about it for a while and I'm ready to do it. I just wanted to make sure your offer still stands?"

"Are you kidding me, of course it does. What made you change your mind?"

Devin sighed. "You! And the girls." She rubbed her rounded belly. "Naya's been talking about how much she wants to be just like you, and I'm happy. I would love for her to be like you, but I guess I want to be someone my kids can admire too."

"Devin, the girls love you. They are proud of you."

"Duck, I do hair out of the house I'm renting. I barely have a high school diploma. I'm not smart or sophisticated like you. I'm nothing to be proud of." She laughed nervously.

I didn't like this self-doubt. Devin may not have had a wall of degrees or living in a mansion, but that didn't mean she wasn't worth looking up to.

"First off, whoever is telling you you aren't smart, is a fucking asshole. Despite not having your license or a building, you still successfully run a business. It doesn't matter if it's out of your house. You keep your own books, and maintain you inventory, alongside raising two incredible daughters. You're a fucking superhero. Plus, you're kind, giving, hardworking, talented, and you're honest. Never allow anyone to belittle who you are. Not even yourself."

Devin's light brown eyes glistened before she looked down at her hands twisted in her lap.

"Thank you!" she said as she looked across the table at me.

I gave her an encouraging smile and a brief squeeze of the hand on top of the table.

"So, when do you start?" I changed the subject.

Devin wiped under her eyes to clear the tears that threatened to fall and chuckled.

"I haven't even enrolled. I wanted to ask you first, but I plan to enroll this week."

"Good. When will you tell Miles?" I knew this would be the real test. Devin did nothing without that fuck boy's approval.

She took a sip of her lemonade and then placed the cup back on the table. "I know he's going to be pissed, so not until after I'm enrolled. I don't want him to talk me out of it. He doesn't think I have what it takes."

"Look, Devin, I'm no expert when it comes to relationships. I think we both know that."

Devin laughed.

"But, I do know this, if your man isn't in your corner, if he can't support your dreams and encourage you to achieve greatness, then he isn't worth your time. Life is about growth. Anything that doesn't support that, doesn't belong. And, if you want, I'll be there when you tell him. Hell, I'll even tell him for you."

"No!" Devin laughed while shaking her head. "Oh no! You will only make it worse."

Damn right I would. I'd tell his bum ass to kick rocks while I was at it.

I took a minute to look at my baby cousin. She'd come a long way. Everyone assumed she would never do anything with her life when she got pregnant with Kylie in high school and dropped out. I knew Devin had more in her. That's why I encouraged her to get her GED and it's why I made the offer to her in the first place. She was destined for greatness.

"I'm happy for you, Dev, and I'm proud of you. I always have been."

"I know. You've always had my back. Thank you!"

The waitress came to the table and Devin and I dug into our food. I was half way through my broccoli and cheese bread bowl when Devin got my attention.

"Umm, Duck, do you owe someone?"

"What? No! Why?"

"Don't look now, but to your right over your shoulder, there are two angry white women staring over here… Duck don't look."

Before the sentence was out of her mouth I was already turning in my seat to see who was checking for me.

Well look what we have here. Its Jackson's little mousy ex. I would know her basic looking ass anywhere. She and her little blonde headed friend was in fact giving me the evil eye. I smiled at both of them and waved. They scoffed and turned away like I was the one being rude.

"Damn, did you spit in their drinks?" Devin chuckled when I turned back around.

"Nope! I just took her man."

Another laugh from Devin. "I haven't seen any one look at you like that since you were in high school."

I shook my head, there was always some bitter girlfriend in high school. It wasn't like I was trying to be with their men, trust, they could have had them back.

"Oh no! They're coming over here. Duck, behave." Devin warned.

I wasn't worried about Jackson's Ex trying anything. She didn't seem like the type. Plus, she didn't want this smoke. But I still moved my plate and drink to the side just in case a bitch got bold.

"You should be ashamed of yourself. How do you even sleep at night?" The blonde friend shouted drawing a little attention to my table.

Ok! So friend was going to run this show. Just like back in Jackson's office, mouse was going to let someone else fight her battle. That's fine with me.

I planted a smile on my face and leaned back in my chair to answer her question.

"Usually on my side after fucking Jackson to sleep."

Both women scoffed as Devin choked on her lemonade.

"You are a despicable and classless woman." Again blonde said after she recovered.

"And yet you are the one at my table causing a scene."

The blonde friend looked around as if she'd just now noticed that we were in a public place.

She nervously pushed her long blonde tresses behind her ear, her demeanor calming.

"Karma is a bitch. If you think it's okay to take a man away from his unborn child you are truly..."

"Hold the fuck up," I held up my hand. "What unborn child?"

"I'm pregnant." Mousy ass Vanessa finally found her voice. She placed her hand over her flat belly. "And now Jackson doesn't want to be with me because of you. He told me to get an abortion." Mouse got choked up and her friend placed a comforting hand on her shoulder.

Was my heart pounding in my chest? Yes! Did my head feel like it was going to explode and the temperature suddenly rise to a thousand? Yes! But I was not letting either of these chicks know. I was pissed beyond reason and as soon as I got out of here, I was going to have some words with Mr. Keller.

"Look, I have nothing to do with you and Jackson."

The blonde scoffed and turned her nose up. I really didn't like her.

"Anyway," I said stretching out the word. "Whatever shit you two has going on, need to be dealt with, and you both need to leave me out of it."

"You need to back off and allow them to be together." Blonde lost her cool and pointed a finger at me.

I took a deep breath. I needed to count to ten or pray or something. This chick was about to make me act real hood. I was five seconds away from being on the 5 o'clock news.

"Rather I leave Jackson alone or not has shit to do with him being in his child's life. Just because you are pregnant, doesn't mean he has to be with you."

"I don't know how you people do it," Blonde looked over at Devin and rolled her eyes.

I heard Devin mumble, "No she didn't," under her breath.

"But we aren't like that. Jackson needs to be a man for once in his life and own up to his responsibilities."

Ok! I was done with Blondie. I pushed my chair back, causing both women to take a step back. At least they had enough sense to do that.

"Only because I was in a good mood, did I allow you your five minutes of my time. However, my mood has changed and your time is up. Now you've been speaking to Charli, but in a few minutes I'm going to introduce you to Duck, and trust me you don't want to meet her."

Blondie stared me down for a moment as if she had it in her mind to say something else. However, my eyes told her she wasn't ready for me. I was pissed and I had no qualms with dragging this bitch around this café. Even if Blondie didn't catch on, Mouse did.

"Come on, Chelsea. She's not worth it." Mouse said with her hand still over her flat stomach.

Just the sight of that hand covering her non-existent belly made me furious all over again for more reasons than I wanted to admit.

Blondie, or Chelsea, squinted her eyes at me, she finally sensed the danger she was in because she backed away.

Once both females were gone, I turned back to my cousin and snatched my purse off the table in order to pay the bill.

"Duck," Devin whined. "Don't overreact. Give him time to explain himself."

I was too pissed to hear her logic. I dropped more than enough money down on the table to cover the bill and a healthy tip. I didn't even recall saying goodbye to Devin or making it to my car. I couldn't even tell you what the traffic was like as I made it over to Jackson's job. I was in a furious haze.

My Audi pulled up to a stop in front of Jackson's company. I climbed out of the car and marched inside.

Jessica greeted me as I walked in.

"Hey, Charlice! You look amazing today, as always."

I forced a smile on my face. I was pissed at her brother, but it didn't mean I had to take it out on Jessica.

"Thank You, Jessica. Is Jackson in his office?"

"Ummm yeah, but he's...."

I didn't stick around to hear what else she had to stay. I was down the hall standing in front of his door before she could warn me. I opened his office door and walked in. The reasonable side of me told me to wait. It reminded me that this was his place of business and I had to respect that. However, damn all that. I needed answers and I wanted them now.

Jackson was sitting behind his desk talking to five men that all wore the red t-shirts with his company logo on it. The moment I walked in all men turned to look at me. Jackson's eyes sparked when he saw me, that gorgeous smile sliding over his face, but when he noticed the look on my face his smile dropped.

"Char, what's wrong?" He was on his feet instantly.

"We need to talk." I demanded sauntering into the room.

I dropped my purse on his desk.

"Um, baby, I'm in the middle of something. Can we talk later?"

Again, a reasonable question.

"I just came from lunch with my cousin where I was verbally attacked by your ex and her bitchy blond friend."

Jackson paused. His body going rigged. He knew that I knew the truth now. I watched him closely, I needed him to give me a sign, anything that told me that what I believed wasn't true.

Without taking his eyes off me, Jackson said, "Fellas, can we finish this up a little later."

Part of me crumbled. The only reason he would send them out was if he needed to grovel or lie, neither of which I was interested in. I hated this shit. I hated myself more for wanting Jackson to be different from what I knew men to be. I almost fell in that trap. I should have known better. I let my guard down, trying to believe I could trust a man. Damn, I knew better than this.

"You know what," I stopped his guys from getting up. "Don't worry about it. It isn't worth it."

I turned to leave and before I made it to the door, Jackson was standing in front of it blocking it with his body.

"We're going to talk."

"No- the fuck- we aren't."

"Guys, give me the room." Jackson demanded of his crew.

"Ya'll sit your asses back down." I shouted.

The crew members were all standing around confused as if they had no idea who to listen to.

"I sign your gotdamn checks. Now get the hell out of here." Jackson roared.

Each man scurried to the door and eased pass Jackson like he was a snarling guard dog. Once the last man left Jackson approached me with his hands out, I stepped away from him. His face fell and I could see how my actions hurt him, but who the fuck cares.

"Is it true?"

That's all I wanted to know.

Did he get this chick pregnant and then refuse to be in the baby's life because of me? I wasn't even going to think about the abortion thing. Even the thought of him suggesting that to her turned my stomach.

"I can explain."

At those words the back of my throat burned and my eyes watered. I didn't need to hear anything else. I was done and nothing else he said mattered. I went to walk around him to leave and he grabbed my arm.

"DON'T TOUCH ME!"

Jackson let my arm go and held his hands up in a surrender posture, yet he didn't move from in front of the door.

"Char, baby! Please listen to me."

"The only thing I wanted to hear from you was that she was lying, if that isn't what comes out of your mouth then you have nothing to say to me."

"She is lying. Will you please just listen?"

I didn't want to.

My old self was telling me to walk out of this door and be done with Jackson, good sex or not. However, it was this new me that had me crossing my arms over my chest to hear what he had to say. I hated this new bitch.

"Vanessa is pregnant." He said and again I went to leave but he blocked me. "But not by me."

Damn I hated that little elation I got with that sentence.

"How can you be sure?"

"I've been fucking since I was fourteen, I know how to not get a chick pregnant. This is just the shit she does."

Jackson walked away from the door and sat on his desk. He ran a hand through his hair. For the first time, I could tell he was exhausted. This had obviously been something he'd been dealing with for a while.

"When she and my brother showed up at my office that day, he wanted me to finally make an honest woman out of Vanessa. I told him I wasn't and that I had moved on with you, that's when she started talking about being pregnant. I didn't take it serious at first, but apparently she has proven it to my sister in law and I am supposed to be the only man she's been with." He sighed. "Vanessa likes people to believe she's this sweet helpless innocent girl. Her father is a pastor and she grew up in a strict religious household. On the outside she's quiet and timid, but that is not who she is. Despite what she tells everyone, I was not her first. Instead of embracing the fact that she loves sex, she likes to play the innocent role. The only reason she is putting this baby on me, is because I'm the only guy her family has met. Plus, I'm the only one that she has been in a long term relationship with."

"You admitted to going back and forth with your ex, how can you be so sure this baby isn't yours?"

"Look at me, Char." He demanded while pointing to himself. "As much as I love kids, you think I would deny a child if I thought it was mine? Besides I've never fucked without a condom and I always provide my own."

Said every man ever.

"But you can't be sure. There is no full proof plan to prevent pregnancy. Condoms break, Jackson. Birth control fails. If you fucked her any time in the time frame of her getting pregnant, you could be the father. So to tell her to get an abortion so you could be with me is disgusting."

"What?" Jackson got to his feet. "What the hell are you talking about?"

I couldn't do this with him. I was so not myself that I was starting to believe him. I wanted what he said to be true. All my alarm bells were going off in my head. They were telling me to run, to abort. I was losing my mind with Jackson, I couldn't have that.

This was just the eye opener I needed. Better to do it now than when I've invested more of my time and energy to this charade.

I grabbed my purse off the side of his desk. He watched me carefully.

"This is why I don't do relationships, Jackson. You need to handle your responsibilities. Lose my number." I stated before swinging the office door open and walking out.

I heard a loud roar and what sounded like something heavy hitting a wall behind me, but I didn't stop or turn around. That weak part of me wanted to turn. It was the part of me I buried a long time ago. It wanted me to go back in that room and hold him close to my chest and believe him. Yet, the strong part of me, the part I created one afternoon as I recovered in a hospital bed, knew that I had to cut ties. I was going down a rabbit hole with Jackson and it wasn't safe for me. Nothing good could come from my involvement with him, this was for the better.

I wiped at my eyes as I backed out of his parking lot and headed back to my office.

☐

NINETEEN

"Charli, come on baby. What are you doing in there?"

Howard's voice called out from the other side of my bathroom door.

It had only been a few hours since that big blow up in Jackson's office. However, I didn't have time to waste mourning over something that never should have been. Despite my body and my mind telling me that fucking Howard was a bad idea, I was determined to get Jackson out of my system.

Howard was on my list for his stamina. He wasn't exactly big in size, but he could go all night, and that's what I needed tonight. I needed someone that could take my mind off earlier for a long time. And since Howard was a pilot, I lucked up with being able to get this time with him.

So why the hell was I still in this goddamn bathroom?

My hands were shaking at the thought of even going out there. When did this shit start happening? I looked in the mirror at myself, my make-up was flawless, my curls were bouncy, I was even looking delicious in this red Frederick's eyelash lace bra set. Everything was set, but my nerves were all over the place and my heart was beating so fast, I might need some of Pop's pills. Not even my body wanted this. I was as dry as a Popeye's biscuit, no lower belly flutters or pebbled nipples. I could just as well be heading to a gynecologist I was so not in the mood. This shit never happened to me. I was always ready.

"What the hell is wrong with you?" I said to the reflection in the bathroom mirror.

She had no answers for me.

"Fuck it!" I pushed up from the sink where my hands were just resting. I straightened the underwire to my bra and stepped back. I took a deep breath and exhaled, before placing my hand on the bathroom doorknob.

"Char!!!" A booming voice came from downstairs.

Fuck!

I forgot to take Jackson's key back. I'd been ignoring his text and calls all day, I should have known he would make an appearance.

I walked into the room and Howard was sitting up in the bed staring with wide eyes at my open bedroom door. He turned to me the moment I walked out and soon as his eyes landed on me, he forgot about the man in my house calling my name. That sexy smile came across his face, the one that got my attention the first time we met and fucked in the bathroom at the airport bar. Now that same smile made my stomach turn.

We were both so distracted, we didn't hear Jackson's heavy feet climbing up my stairs. I only noticed him when I could feel his presence at my door. He was wearing a t-shirt and his regular dark wash jeans. Nobody wore a pair of jeans like Jackson Keller. He looked the sexiest to me in just a simple shirt and jeans. That had been proven when for the first time tonight, my body woke up.

Jackson's hazel eyes seared into me. I could see the desire, the anger, and the disappointment staring back at me. I wanted to cover up, but my robe was all the way on the other side of the room. Instead of covering I stated the obvious.

"Jackson, what the hell are you doing here?"

He completely ignored me and turned to Howard, still lying in my bed.

"I'll give you to the count of three to get the fuck up and get out of here."

"JACKSON!"

"One!" He announced without turning to me.

"Charli, who the fuck is this guy?" Howard demanded.

"Howard, I'm sorry, just let me talk to him."

"Two!" Jackson continued to count ignoring us completely.

"Jackson, you can't do this. You can't just come in my house and demand that my company leaves. You and I are over."

"You heard her, dude! Now get out." Howard added.

"Three!" Jackson gave two short whistles and Lady ran into the room.

I'd been around that dog for over two months and not one time had I ever seen her like this. Even I was frightened. She was snarling at Howard like she was ready to rip him from limb to limb.

"What the Hell? Charli, get this gotdamn dog." Howard was nearly pushing through my head board he was trying so hard to get away from the dog. His knees was to his chest and his voice was as high as mine.

"Jackson, stop this."

Jackson cut his eyes over to me, his arms folded over his chest.

I could tell from that look in his eyes, he was not going to stop. Since I'd met Jackson he'd been sweet and kind and nothing but a gentleman, but the look in his eyes told me that Jackson also had a dark side, and I'd just provoked it.

"I'm going to count to three again." This time when Jackson spoke he was looking only at me, but his words were meant for Howard. "If you're not out of this house by the time I get to three, it won't be my dog you have to worry about. One!"

"You are INSANE!"

"Charli, you need to do something about this big ass white dude!"

"Two!"

"You don't get to walk up in my motherfucking house making demands like you own something in here. You need to worry about yourself and that bitch of an Ex."

Jackson did not react to my shouting or my words. His hazel eyes stared only at me as the word, "Three." Came out of his mouth.

Jackson turned back to Howard and took one step towards him. Howard scurried off my bed and fell face first onto the floor as his legs became tangled in the bed sheets. He finally broke free of my sheets and got to his feet butt ass naked. He scooped his clothes off the floor, placed them over his now severely soft erection as he rushed to the door.

Lady snapped at him and chased Howard out of my room

followed by the sounds of his high pitched screams. The entire scene was hilarious and I guarantee one day I was going to look back and laugh at this, however, at the moment I was furious.

"Are you out of your goddamn mind?" I asked the moment I heard my front door slam.

I angrily walked over to the other side of the room to retrieve my robe.

"See, this is some white folks shit."

I fought with the silk sleeves of my robe trying to get my arm in.

"I should have known better. This is all my fault. This is what I get for trying to be different, now I'm caught up in some mess."

I turned around and Jackson was standing right up on me. I had to take a step back he was so close. I had no idea he had moved from his spot. I didn't even hear him. His hazel eyes continued to stare at me, nowhere in those eyes did I see the sweet Jackson I'd been getting to know. What I saw, was doing to my body, what Howard wasn't able to do. It was why I was hiding out in my bathroom. I should be scared of the look in his eyes, but I was so turned on I couldn't focus.

"Did you fuck him?" Jackson's voice was deeper than usual, his nostrils were flared and his jaw tensed. He looked even larger than his usual self.

I placed my hands on my hips, my full attitude was out to play now. "It doesn't matter...."

Jackson took a step forward and I took one back before he caught himself. He closed his eyes and inhaled before opening them again.

"Answer my goddamn question, Charlice."

"No! I didn't." The words came out obediently.

Jackson exhaled and placed his hands on top of his head. He turned away from me as if he was gathering his thoughts, or calming down. I didn't know what to think of the situation. We both remained silent for a moment.

"I want you, Char." He said before turning back to me.

I finally saw a little of the old Jackson back in his eyes, but not nearly enough to hide that craziness from before.

"I've made that clear from day one. And I'm a grown man so when I want something I go after it. When you sent me that text saying OK, you became all mine. This shit you pulled tonight, can never happen again."

I finally woke up from the spell he put on me earlier.

"Jackson, when I left your office, I made it very clear that we were done. What I decide to do with my body at this point has nothing to do with you."

He shook his head in disagreement. "It doesn't work that way, Charlice!"

"What the hell are you talking about?"

"I'M TALKING ABOUT YOU RUNNING." His shouted words caused me to take a step back. "You don't get to do that. You don't get to quit on us because you're scared. Damn it, Char, I'm scared too. I'm putting my all in this with you. I know the stuff with Vanessa is messed up, but it doesn't change us. You have to believe me when I say, Vanessa's baby is not mine. If I thought for a second that it was, I would have come to you and told you."

He shook his head and looked down before back up at me. "I know you have walls built around your heart, and baby, I have no problem breaking down every single one of them. I'm a big man, so I can handle that no matter how long it takes."

That got a smile from me.

"But, you have to let me know if I'm wasting my time. If I am, I'll walk out your front door and I'll leave you alone. So you have to tell me now, do you feel anything for me, Char?"

There was nothing but silence in the room. My head was swimming with Jackson's question. He put it all out there and left the ball in my court.

"I'm flawed Jackson."

"I know that."

I shook my head fighting that burning feeling in the back of my throat. My eyes were blurring with tears. He didn't know. He would never know just how flawed I was.

"I have ugly scars from dark secrets."

"I know that too."

When the first tear fell from my eyes, Jackson walked up to me. His hooded eyes peered down at me. He placed a hand to my cheek and ran his thumb over the tears that fell.

"I'm not asking you to be perfect, Char. I don't care about the hurdles or the battle to win your heart, I just need to know that at the end of the journey it will belong to me. Answer the question, do you have feelings for me?"

I closed my eyes and dropped my shoulders. My body surrendered to the truth. "Yes!"

His lips were on mine instantly. My salty tears mixed in with his delicious taste. His hands grabbed the sash of my robe and yanked it lose. I could feel his warm palms rubbing against my side and circling around to my lower back as he pulled me closer to him. His tongue danced across mine. My fingers played in the soft hair at the back of his head. I loved running my fingers through his hair. Jackson bit at my bottom lip, and pulled a moan from me. His hands found my ass, a cheek in each palm as he squeezed with a firm grip before lifting me off my feet. His strength always made sex with him an adventure.

I wrapped my legs around his waist as I ground my center on the pole that was poking me through his jeans. He walked us to the bed and slowly placed me down, his heavy warm body covered mine. When he lifted away from our kiss, I whimpered. I loved the smile it brought to his face.

I lied on my back, one leg hung off the side of the bed and the other bent at the knee. I watched Jackson as he pulled his shirt up over his head exposing his thick muscled body. His few tattoos decorated his chest in beautiful artwork. He watched me the entire time he undressed. He dropped his shirt on the floor at his feet, and then popped the button on his pants. Already the head of his dick was sticking up from the waist band of his boxers. I licked my lips at the sight of it.

Jackson crawled back onto the bed, he grabbed the foot that's barely touching the floor and placed the heel of my foot to the center of his chest. His roughened palm stroked my inner thigh slowly. Usually when Jackson and I were together, we were wild in bed. Ripping clothes, hard kissing, hair pulling, and rough grabbing, but tonight it seemed Jackson had other plans.

His light touches ran all the way from my knee up to my thigh to where it dipped into my pelvis bone, but it never went closer to where I ached for him. I squirmed with need and impatience.

"Jackson." I moaned his name in impatience, but he ignored my plea.

He removed his hand from my skin all together, I would have cried out in frustration if the next action wouldn't have had me whimper and arch off the bed. Jackson swirled his tongue around my toes, allowing his hot wet tongue to brush the pad of all five toes. Jesus, be a fence! I'd never thought this could feel so good. When he sucked my big toe into his mouth I cried out. He took his time lavishing my toes, running his tongue over each one and wrapping his lips around them. I squirmed around on the bed, closing my eyes I relished in this newly discovered erogenous zone. He placed a kiss at the arch of my foot and gently bit before kissing it again. I giggled. My feet were ticklish.

I loved the smile that spread over his face. Jackson planted kisses from my foot all the way up to my inner thigh where he sucked the thin skin into his mouth. I growled at the pleasure and buried my fingers in the longer hair at the top of his head. I could feel his smile against my thigh, he knew what he was doing to me. He released my skin and if I were lighter skinned I was sure I would have a bruise there.

His lips traced a trail up to my pelvis. He kissed all around my panty covered pussy before planting his nose right at the center of my drenched underwear and inhaled. I gushed for him even more as he enjoyed the smell of my arousal. I wanted him to push those panties to the side and dive in so bad, but Jackson had other plans. He planted one simple kiss at my center before moving on to the other leg working his way back down to my toes. I was dripping wet and so turned on, I would probably cum the moment he even touched my pussy.

"Please," I gasped as his tongue twirled around my toes. "I can't take anymore." If he didn't fill me soon, I was going to combust from the heat swirling in my belly.

Thankfully he understood my need, because he let go of my feet and lifted from the bed just long enough to slip off his bottoms and put on a condom. He crawled up my body, placing kisses at every bit of skin he came into contact with. He sat up on his knees between my legs staring down at me. Both hands cupped my swollen breasts and squeezed. My moan turned into a squeal when he ripped the sexy lace number straight down the middle. I went to protest, but the look on his face shut me up.

I would never be able to wear this lingerie for Jackson again, because it would always be a reminder of what he walked in on. I didn't flinch when the panties were ripped next. The lace material lay in shambles underneath me.

Jackson stroked his covered hardened dick and I was jealous of his hands. I wanted to touch him, but I had no time to protest, as one fat finger slowly slid into me. My eyes closed and my head pushed back into the mattress. He slowly slid his finger out and grunted at the sound my wet sex made. I was soaking wet for him. Jackson growled at the sound of my wetness as he pushed his finger back in. This time when he removed his finger he replaced it with his dick. Using it to split my pussy lips down the middle. He rocked his hips, coating his hardened member in my essence.

His eyes never left the spot where my lower lips cradled him in their warmth. When he smacked his erection against my hardened nub, I came on a long moan and that was when he pushed into me as far as he could go. I cried out, the action caused my orgasm to fire back up. Jackson didn't wait, he pulled out just to sink back in me slow and deep. So fucking deep. My back arched off the bed and my hands flew down to his thighs resting between my legs. I tried to push him back from going so deep. Jackson knocked my hands away, I was not denying him tonight. He placed a palm to my right thigh pinning it back and down opening me up further. His hips rolled with each deep thrust. He was in no rush, but I was still clawing at the sheets.

"Fuck, Shit, Damn." Curse words flew from my mouth.

He knew how to work my body.

I reached for him, wanting to feel his body on mine. He came willingly, one hand by my head to prop him up and the other under my left thigh as he slide in and of me in an unrushed pace. He stared down at me. My mouth opened on a silent scream as he took my body slow and passionately.

I knew how to fuck, I could do it with my eyes closed, but this wasn't fucking. This wasn't smashing or banging, or having sex, this was something else. Something I'd never done before and something I never knew I would want until I was here sharing it with Jackson.

Jackson kept me on the edge of an orgasm. Speeding up with quick shallow thrust just to slow it back down with deep slow strokes. The moment my stomach would tighten and I would come to the brink of an epic orgasm, he would slow back down. I felt Jackson tense above me, his lips came crashing down to mine in a powerful kiss that had a tea slipping from the corner of my eye. He pushed in so deep, hitting that hidden spot inside me that caused me to erupt with an earth shattering orgasm. I ripped my lips from his and threw my head back with a gasping scream. My body shook from my orgasm. Jackson roared into my shoulder as I felt the heat from his semen filling the condom.

When we both came down from the greatest sex ever, Jackson pulled out and rolled onto this back. I tucked into his side like the dick whipped female that I was. For a moment our labored breathing was all that was heard in the silent house. I didn't even hear the dog.

"I want you to meet my parents." Jackson's voice broke the silence.

I tensed at his side. Ok, this was where I put my foot down. I didn't do family meetings. I drew the line at that. That's too much commitment and too fast for me. Besides, no man will meet my family. I didn't care how close I got to him, there would never come a time where he would be sitting down with Sadie Rose and Charlie Jefferies.

"OK!"

What the fuck, Duck? Where the hell did that come from and why am I not retracting it. What was going on with me?

Jackson planted a kiss on my forehead before climbing out of the bed and grabbing his boxers off the floor.

"I'll set something up with my mom and get back to you."

"Ummm, where are you going?" I asked sitting up watching him pull his boxers up.

"You thought I was going to sleep in the bed that a naked man just climbed out of? Hell no! We're about to have round two in the shower, and then we're burning these damn sheets."

"You are NOT burning these sheets. I paid $1100 dollars for these sheets."

He gave me a smirk that shoot right to my center.

"Come to the shower, I bet I can change your mind." He didn't even give me a chance to argue, not that I was going to argue. I calmly climbed my ass off that bed and headed towards the shower. Damn those sheets.

TWENTY

Three weeks to the day he announced he wanted me to meet his parents, we pulled up to the split level house.

"Are you nervous?" Jackson asked as we both stared back at the half brick and half vinyl house. Burgundy shutters made the exterior pop, and the manicured yard showed it was loved. It was a nice home in a suburb outside of Atlanta.

"No, I'm not nervous."

Despite it being my first time meeting someone's parents, I wasn't easily intimidated. I dealt with billion dollar business on a daily basis, his parents weren't going to shake me. Although I was as cool as a fan, Jackson seemed to be nervous enough for the both of us.

He turned the engine off to his truck and turned in his seat to face me. Lady whined in the back seat as she placed her head between the consoles. I stroked her head calming her.

"OK, Look!" He announced bringing my attention to him. "You know how I feel about you, right?"

"Yeah!"

He ran a hand over his mouth and tugged on his beard while his eyes looked back to the house.

"You're not going to run if shit is weird in here are you?"

I laughed. "Jackson, if you're freaking out so bad, why did you bring me here?"

"I'm not... freaking out. I just......" Another look towards the house.

A short woman with short gray hair was standing in the doorway with a huge smile on her face. When I turned back to Jackson, his head was down and he seemed to be rethinking this decision. I placed my hand on his jean clad thigh and he looked to me.

"I won't run, I promise. Not unless ya'll got some white hoods up in there or something."

Jackson threw his head back and laughed. I was glad I could make him laugh and calm down, I couldn't think of anything his parents would say that would make me run away from Jackson. I didn't need his parents' approval of me because I wasn't fucking them.

Jackson grabbed the back of my neck and pulled me into him for a passionate kiss. When he finally pulled away, that sweet smile was on his face.

"There are no white hoods hidden in any closets. I would never take you anywhere where you would have to worry about that."

I trusted him enough to believe him.

Jackson climbed out of his truck and came around to open my door. The woman at the door was on the porch now.

"Oh my! Bubba, she's so pretty." The woman said as soon as I stepped out of the truck.

"Bubba?" I questioned smiling up at a red faced Jackson.

"Don't start, Duck." He retorted and I laughed.

I had no room to tease anyone about a nickname.

Lady ran off around the back of the house while we walked hand in hand up to the front porch where the women waited. She was older than Nita, maybe in her early sixties. I could tell she was once a brunette, but the gray in her hair has taken away most of the old color. She was tiny, couldn't be taller than five feet even. Jackson's tall frame dwarfed her easily. Even I made her extra short in my red bottom 6 inch heels. Jackson bent down and planted a kiss on who I assumed was his mother's cheek.

"Mom," He said confirming my thoughts. "This is my girlfriend, Charlice Jefferies."

I didn't cringe at his title of girlfriend, but it did still make me slightly uncomfortable.

"Char, this is my mother, Sally Keller."

"Hello, Mrs. Keller." I said in my most professional voice.

I held out a hand for her to shake. She completely dodged my outstretched hand and went straight for a tight hug. I stood in my spot completely startled. Sally pulled back and looked me up and down.

"You are so beautiful. Jessica told me you were, that girl talks about you non-stop. Oh, and you can call me Sally, or mama if you want to practice." She gave me a conspiratorial wink then laughed.

"Mama." Jackson warned.

She waved him off and took my arm. "Come on in Charli. Can I call you Charli?" She asked as she led me away from Jackson.

"Yes, that's fine."

"Oh good. I've made some of Bubba's favorites for dinner. I can show you how to make them if you like. You know the fastest way to get to a man's heart is through his stomach, and if you can't tell, My Bubba is a big man." Sally was on a roll and I immediately liked her.

I could hear Jackson behind us grumbling, I gave him a smile over my shoulder right before his mother escorted me into the house.

Their home was quaint and clean. Immediately when you walked in the front door there were a set of stairs, one set going up and the other going down. Upstairs, there was a large open kitchen that reminded me of my Gram's kitchen. You could tell this kitchen was well used. It had that look to it. Before you reached the kitchen, was a small television area. A wall to wall television stand outlined a large flat screen TV. A floral printed couch and love seat sat in the middle of the floor in an L shape. A burgundy recliner that looked to have had many years of use was being occupied by a burly man that looked so much like Jackson it was scary.

"Look, Hank, they're here." Sally said, introducing us as if the man couldn't see us coming up the stairs.

Hank looked away from the television where he was watching a baseball game. Even the smile that broke across his face was like Jackson. Hank reminded me of the men you saw on those wilderness shows. He looked like a lumberjack all the way down to the flannel shirt.

"BUBBA!" Hank greeted Jackson joyfully, he was so happy to see him that even I smiled.

"Hey, Pop!"

Hank climbed out of the old recliner and it creaked as he got to his feet. He was just as tall as Jackson and just as wide. He and Jackson gave each other a one armed hard back pat hug.

"Hank, this is Charli. Isn't she pretty? Just look how pretty she is."

"Sally, she's not a damn sweater. You don't have to keep telling her she's pretty. She knows she's gorgeous. Our Bubba has great taste in women, just like his old man." Hank gave me a devilish wink that had me blushing.

I couldn't help it, I liked sexy men, and Jackson's dad was rocking that silver fox thing.

Jackson cut his eyes to me, he knew I was a flirt. I shrugged at him and he shook his head at me.

"Is that Jackson or Jefferson?" Another voice called out.

An elderly women came into view. She looked to be in her 80's maybe even closer to 90's. Her skin was paper thin, wrinkled and pale. She was slowly moving about on a walker, her back hunched over.

"No, mama, this is Jackson and his girlfriend." Sally said so loud my ears started to ring.

The older woman slowly walked over to us.

"Who is it?"

"IT'S JACKSON, MAMA!" This time I thought my ears actually bled.

"Damn it, Sally! You're going to have all of us deaf." Hank joked.

"Oh look, Sally! Jackson is here." The older woman said. "And he has a colored girl with him."

I felt Jackson tense beside me, he was as tight as a damn board. Sally mouth flew open and her eyes stared at me in complete horror. I could already see how many ways she was going to apologize for this. Hank frowned so deep he looked like he was ready to pop his mother in law.

"Hello, I'm Charlice, Jackson's girlfriend." I stated calmly to the old woman.

"Well aren't you pretty. And so well spoken." The older woman commented with a smile.

I cut my eyes to Jackson and he was the same color as the bottom of my shoes.

"Mama, how about you have a seat in the kitchen and I'll get your pills ready." Sally said steering the older woman away from me.

"Sally, I want to stay and talk to the colored girl. She's much prettier than that blonde haired witch he was married to."

What the hell? I turned to a wide eyed Jackson. He immediately started shaking his head trying to explain.

"Gladys, that's Jefferson." Hank explained. "Jackson's never been married."

I could feel Jackson's relief at his father's words.

"Well why not?" Gladys questioned turning back to us. "Jackson's a good boy. He's my favorite. You know they allow coloreds to marry whites now." She nodded towards me with an encouraging wink.

"Good to know." I replied with a smile.

At this point I didn't even think Jackson was breathing anymore. He was standing completely still and wide eyed.

"Mama, please stop saying that word. That's not what they want to be called."

"Really?" The woman looked genuinely surprised by this news. "Well, what should I call her?"

"Well Charli is just fine." Sally continued to explain as she escorted her mother in law out of the room.

"Sorry about that." Hank's deep voice drew my attention.

"It's ok. She's from a different era."

"Still doesn't make it ok." Hank says before following his wife and mother into the kitchen.

Jackson waited until they'd all left to turn to me.

"Baby, I'm so sorry. We can leave if you want."

I waved him off. "I'm ok. I'm not offended that your grandma called me colored. She's old, she gets a pass. But just so you know, if there are any other hidden racist in this house you need to give me a heads up."

Jackson smiled before wrapping his arms around me pulling me into a hug. I wrapped my arms around him burying my face into his chest. I couldn't get enough of his smell.

"Don't think I missed you calling my Memaw a racist."

I laughed so hard my body shook.

"Well if the racist shoe fits…"

This time Jackson laughed before giving me a kiss that had me forgetting we were in his parents' house while they were right in the other room with a clear view of us. It had been a long time since I fucked in someone's parents' house.

"Knock knock!"

A voice called out from the front door. Jackson cursed as he pulled away from me. We both turned to the front door to find, Jackson's brother, the blonde from the café and none other than mouse.

"Are you fucking kidding me?" Jackson growled out.

Oh yeah, dinner was about to get really interesting.

Jackson took a step towards his brother, but I grabbed his arm. He turned to me and I could read the rage on his face. If I didn't step in, dinner was definitely going to be ruined.

"Let it go."

Jackson shook his head. "He knew you were coming, and did this shit on purpose. He's disrespecting you."

"Sweetie, I'm a big girl. I'm not intimidated by your brother or your little Ex."

He bit his bottom lip the way that I liked, before pulling me in for another kiss on the lips.

"Say it again?" He whispered.

"Say what?"

"That was your first time calling me a pet name. I like it. Now you got my dick hard."

I smiled so hard my cheeks hurt. "Well, sweetie, lead me to the nearest bathroom and I'll help you with that problem."

"Excuse us."

We were interrupted by the sound of his sister in law's voice.

I turned to her, ready to tell her to walk her ass around, when Jackson's parents came out of the kitchen.

"Jefferson! What are you doing here?" Sally asked.

Obviously, from the shocked sound of her voice, she was not happy about Jefferson's appearance.

Jefferson walked between Jackson and I forcing us to take a step back or get trampled.

"Hey mama! I thought I'd come by and have some of your good home cooked food today. That's alright isn't it?"

A forced smile came to Sally's face. I'd known her for a full ten minutes and not once had her smile looked like this.

"Sure, Jeff! You're always welcomed."

Hank grunted beside his wife and I took it that he wasn't so happy to see his son either.

"Is that Jefferson?" Memaw called from the kitchen.

"Yes Mama." Sally shouted over her shoulder.

"He didn't bring that wife of his did he? You know i….."

"Mama take your medicine." Sally shouted cutting off Memaw.

She turned back to us. "Hey, Jackson! Why don't you show Charli around, dinner isn't quite ready yet."

"Good idea, Mama. I know she mentioned something about a bathroom earlier." Jackson gave me a devilish smile while placing a hand at my back.

He escorted me away, but before we were out of hearing range we could already hear the whispered argument of the others.

Jackson lead me down stairs where there was a laundry room, an extra bathroom, another large family room and open room used for arts and crafts. The moment we made it down the stairs, he pushed me up against the wall and started kissing me. His hands were all over me, grasping my aching breasts, wrapped around my neck, and squeezing my ass. If I knew this would happen, I would have worn a dress instead of these skinny jeans.

"Fuck, I want you so bad." Jackson gasped against my kiss wet lips.

He wasn't the only one turned on.

"Bathroom, Jackson." I demanded, slipping my hand between the waistbands of his jeans.

The head of his dick brushed against my fingers.

With a smile, he picked me up off my feet and carried me into the half bath. He shut the door with the back of his shoe, placing me down onto the sink. My legs opened and he placed his wide body in between them. Jackson ran his hand over my shoulder blade to the back of my neck giving it a massage before running his fingers in my hair to tug my head back. His lips covered mine and his tongue slipped into my mouth. He squeezed my breast on his journey down between my legs, then cupped my center and rubbed his palm in circles, giving my awakening nub a little attention.

I pushed at Jackson's chest and he released me, stepping back. The confused look on his face disappeared the moment I dropped down to my knees in front of him. It was time I showed Jackson another one of my special talents. I slowly unbuckled his belt and popped the button of his jeans, the entire time I kept my eyes on Jackson. When I slid his pants and boxers down, his heavy erection sprung out popping me on the nose. Jackson chuckled.

"He's anxious," I teased.

I wrapped my hand around him the best I could and licked the tip of him, taking away the drop of precum. Jackson hissed, and I wanted to laugh. He had no idea what I had instore for him. Without further ado, I opened my mouth, as wide as I could get it, and wrapped my lips around Jackson's member. I pushed all the way down, letting him hit the back of my throat. I tilted my head back and he went down further.

"Shiiiiiiittttt!" Jackson exhaled.

I slipped him out with a smile, my eyes watery from deep throating his shaft. I pumped my hand around him a few times distributing the saliva I left behind, then I placed him in my mouth again and bobbed my head up and down at a fast pace.

Jackson was cursing and breathing heavily over my head as I worked him. I swirled my tongue around the tip as I continued to bob up and down, moving my hand in the opposite direction. With my other hand, I grabbed his heavy balls and massaged them, giving him gentle squeezes.

"Gotdamn, Char." Jackson moaned, he moved his hips, pushing them forward.

I placed both my hands on his hips and allowed him to fuck my mouth. Jackson slid his hands in my hair and held me still as he guided himself in and out of my mouth at a fast pace. I relaxed my throat and tilted my head back so he could easily slide down my throat. When he picked up his pace and bit into his bottom lip, I knew he was close to his orgasm. I hollowed out my cheeks and sucked on his down stroke. Jackson growled like a grizzly bear as he filled my throat with his salty cum.

I swallowed it all down, not allowing any to slip out. When he finally pulled out of my mouth, he stumbled back like he was drunk, falling into the bathroom door. He was breathing heavy looking down at me with wide surprised eyes.

I smiled up at him and pushed up from the floor. Jackson immediately came over and offered his hand to help me up. Once I was back on my feet he slipped his dick back in his pants.

"Jesus! I feel like I need to buy you something after that."

I clutched my chest as I laughed. That was why I didn't show my head game to just any dude. Men get too attached when you can suck a dick well. Not having a gag reflex used to drive my Grams crazy when I was a baby, but I'd learned the benefits of it.

"You will pay me back when we get back to your place tonight."

He smiled. "Yes, ma'am."

After reapplying the lipstick that was now circling Jackson's dick, Jackson escorted me out of the bathroom. Giving me the tour his mother suggested.

I stared at a picture of Jackson on the mantle in the family room. He was wearing a Chicago Bulls jersey, his dark blonde hair in a bowl cut, those hazel eyes still just as stunning, and those dimples more pronounced without the facial hair. From the pictures I'd seen of him, he was always a chubby kid, and still just as handsome.

"I was fat." I heard his voice from behind me.

I looked over my shoulder to find his eyes glued to the picture I was just staring at. His words were light and joking, but I could tell his weight was a touchy subject for him.

"That kid would have never got your attention." He stated, wrapping his arms around me from behind.

I picked up the picture off the mantle and stared down at the little boy with the beautiful eyes and dimples.

"Are you kidding? With those dimples, I would have been riding his dick in the girl's bathroom during gym."

Jackson laughed out loud. I placed the picture back down on the mantle and turned in his arms.

"If I'd have known you back in middle school, it would have saved my parents a lot of sleepless nights when I was in high school."

I rubbed my hands up and down his back as I lifted on my tip toes and placed a kiss on his lips. "If you thought knowing me would have kept you out of trouble, you clearly don't know me."

Our laughter was interrupted by Hank's voice. "You two ready to eat?"

I tried to step away from Jackson, but he held on tighter.

"Yeah, Pop, we're on our way up."

Hank smiled and nodded before turning away from us and heading back out the room.

Jackson gave me another quick kiss. "Let's get this shit show over with." He joked before grabbing my hand and heading to the stairs.

TWENTY-ONE

Apparently while we were downstairs, something heavy happened upstairs. The mood at the dinner table was a lot different from earlier. I felt it the moment I walked upstairs. I still didn't let it ruin my time.

The only person that didn't get the notice of the mood change, was Gladys. She took up the majority of the conversation, and it was obvious that no one was paying attention to her. I was doing my best, but it was hard to concentrate when I had mouse sitting across from me looking like someone kicked her damn dog. Every now and again she would sniffle and Chelsea would rub her back affectionately while giving me the evil eye. And if that bitch touched her stomach one more time I was going to throw this meatloaf at her. When Sally offered beer and wine, Mouse declined with a bashful smile towards Jackson. I rolled my eyes and accepted my wine glass.

Jefferson wasn't making the situation any better. He was shooting daggers across the table at Jackson, who was glaring at him in return. Hank and Sally seemed to be barely keeping the room together.

"Hannibal Sampson." Gladys' dreamy voice brought my attention back to her. "He use to work the fields at my Daddy's farm."

She was telling yet another story of her involvement with colored people. This seemed to be where most of her stories were stemming from.

"I'll never forget him. Oh, he was amazing." Her voice took on a dreamy note. "He was a big strong colored man with large feet and big soft gentle hands that made a young inexperienced girl blush."

Sally choked on her wine and I froze with my fork midway to my mouth. It seemed Gladys' might have had her a taste of black dick in her past.

I ain't mad.

"Charli," Sally said clearing her throat. Her face was bright red. "How are you enjoying the meatloaf?"

"It's delicious, Sally."

Sally beamed proudly, that genuine smile coming back for the first time.

"Thank you, Charli. It's my grandmother's recipe, and one of Jackson's favorite foods when he was a kid."

"Everything was Jackson's favorite food as a kid." Jefferson mumbled loud enough for everyone to hear.

I had to bite my tongue. Even though I wasn't worried about impressing Jackson's parents, I also didn't want to tear up their house. And that was exactly what I was going to do if I got into it with his brother.

"Jefferson." Hank warned.

"So, Charli! How did you and Bubba meet?" Sally asked.

Jackson chuckled beside me. "She ran her car into the back of my truck."

Sally gasped and I hit Jackson on the shoulder.

"I did not." I corrected him. "I barely tapped the back of his bumper. He's being overdramatic."

Sally chuckled.

"Speaking of your truck." Hank started. "Have you had any more issues?"

Jackson swallowed the food he had just placed in his mouth. "Not since the brake thing."

"What brake thing?" I asked, taking a sip of my wine.

"It's nothing." Jackson replied.

"I wouldn't call having your brakes cut nothing." Hank explained.

I turned to Jackson. How was this the first time I'd heard anything about this? I hadn't had any more incidents with Cliff since Sean notified me that he left town, but what if Cliff was back and now fucking with Jackson.

"What else happened?" I asked Jackson.

He sighed. "It's nothing to worry about. I've had some issues with my truck being tampered with."

"Don't forget they smashed out the windows down at your office." Hank added.

"And you weren't going to tell me this."

I never wanted to be one of those couples that fought in public, but I was too pissed to worry about how I looked to others.

If someone was trying to hurt Jackson I wanted to know about it. In fact, I was going to call Sean as soon as we left here to let him know. They needed to know if Cliff was back in town.

I felt Jackson's hand on my thigh under the table. He was trying to calm me down. I hated that it was working.

"I was going to tell you if something else happened. I assumed it was unrelated."

"What do you mean unrelated?" Hank asked.

"Char, had a stalker about a month ago, but the police handled it."

"Oh you poor girl. I'm glad the police was able to catch the culprit. They haven't caught the one messing with Jackson yet." Sally said.

"They'll catch him, Mama."

"Maybe they should look into your past. I'm pretty sure some of your old associates are involved."

Jackson's body once again went ramrod straight. Jefferson must really hit a sore subject for Jackson. I'd never seen him look this way. I almost wanted to ask what past was Jefferson talking about, but I had a feeling that wasn't a conversation I should bring up right now.

I turned my head when I felt fingers playing in my hair. Before coming, I'd met up with Devin to get my hair done. Today I was sporting mid back length body waves with a side part. My hair slid through Gladys' gnarled fingers when I turned to her.

Now see, I gave Gladys a pass for the colored comment, but I'd whoop her ass for touching my hair.

"Your hair is so pretty, and it feels so real."

Sally started coughing and Chelsea laughed for the first time since she'd been here.

"Well it should," I said keeping my cool. "I pay enough for it."

I had no shame in admitting this wasn't my hair. I paid hundreds of dollars for this hair, I could give a shit if it was mine or not. I wore weave because I liked it, and I didn't like doing my own hair.

"I've always wanted to try extensions," Sally said, again trying to lighten the mood.

I noticed she was really good at that. Something I was starting to think she'd had years of practice with.

"But Hank doesn't want me to get them." She continued.

"That's cause those men down at that bingo already stare at you, no need to get those hair extensions tempting them. I'd hate to get you banned from that place."

I loved the blush that spread over Sally's face when Hank showed his jealous side. It reminded me of Grams and Papa. It seemed Sally had her an amazing man like my Papa.

"You don't need that mess in your hair anyway, Sally," Blondie said looking directly at me. "Only superficial people pay for things like that. Real people are confident with what god gave them naturally."

Really? Did she really want to do this with me?

"Funny, you speak of natural. Did god give you that naturally Blonde hair? I just asks, because it seems if he did, he would have given you the roots to match it."

This time Jackson and Hank chuckled. Chelsea's face turned bright red. That's right bitch, don't ever come for me.

"You of all people shouldn't mention god. I'm sure if he knew the type of person…"

"Don't fucking talk to her." Jackson warned, interrupting his brother.

"Boys." Hank tried to bring the tension back down.

"No Pop!" Jefferson said turning to his father. "This needs to be said. You guys are always defending him, that's his problem. Jackson needs to take care of his responsibilities and stop being such a fuck up."

"What responsibilities?" Sally asked confused.

"We agreed we wouldn't bring this up to your mother until we were sure." Hank tried again to bring the peace back.

Jefferson, completely ignoring his father, turned to his mother. "Jackson has a baby on the way. Congratulations, you're going to be a grandmother again."

Sally turned to me with a wide smile on her face. "I knew it. Mama I told you she was glowing."

Trust me, Sally, I'm glowing, but it has nothing to do with a baby. However, your son was the cause.

"Not by that woman," Jefferson explained with a disgusted look on his face as if babies by me would be the worst thing to happen to Jackson. "Vanessa is pregnant."

Sally's smile fell as she turned to a teary eyed Vanessa.

"Oh! Well that's nice. Congratulations you two."

"Mama, no need to congratulate me, Vanessa isn't having my child. She might be having a baby, but it's not mine."

"How dare you!" Chelsea shouted. "My friend is not like that and you know it. I should have never introduced you two. You are so immature, Jackson. You'd rather parade this gold digging tramp around than to be with a good wholesome woman."

"Gold digger?" I'd been called many things in my life, but never that.

"Yes, we know you're only after Jackson for his business. I'm sure you and your many baby daddies laugh about how gullible he is."

"Sweet heart, do a fucking google search before you slander someone. My bank account has more digits than your fucking phone number. Trust me, I don't need Jackson's money."

Chelsea scoffed. "You're nothing but a tramp."

"And you are on your last insult."

Chelsea opened her mouth, probably to say something that would cause me to drag her ass across this table, but Jackson spoke first.

"I've tried to keep my cool." Jackson explained calmly, but I could tell he was reaching his breaking point. "But you're pushing me. I'm still not even 100% sure she's pregnant. And even if she is, it isn't mine. This is just Vanessa's way of trying to get me to marry her."

"Please." Chelsea mocked. "My best friend can do so much better than some fat gardener."

"Now! See that was your last insult."

I tossed my fork in my plate and went to stand. Jackson placed a hand on my thigh to keep me in my seat. I wanted a piece of his sister in law so bad I was shaking. How dare she insult Jackson? First of all, he wasn't fat. Thick, yes. Husky, maybe. Sexy, very. There was nothing wrong with Jackson's body. Plus don't belittle what he does by calling him a gardener. He was much more than that.

I wanted to tell that bitch off, but Jackson spoke instead.

"Don't worry, Baby. It's not worth it. Eventually, the truth will come out and they will see Vanessa for the manipulative female she is."

"So now we are to believe that she's the manipulative one?" Jefferson said. "She's not the recovering drug addict with a murder charge."

A few things happened all at once. I gasped, Jackson soared to his feet and grabbed his brother across the table, Sally screamed, and Hank immediately climbed to his feet to grab Jackson. I looked around at the scene of Sally clutching her chest, Vanessa crying, Chelsea trying to pry Jackson's hands from pinning Jefferson to the table, and Hank still trying to pull Jackson back. It was then I realized, everybody's family had shit going on.

"Get off him!" Chelsea shouted.

"Bubba! Let him go. Let him go, son." Hank tried to calmly get Jackson to cool down, but it wasn't working and Jefferson was turning blue.

I hated Jackson's brother, and I was not ashamed to admit that I wouldn't be angry if Jackson choked the life out of him, but I couldn't let that happen. At least with not this many witnesses.

"Jackson," I called his name and the only sign I got that he heard me was the slight movement in his face. "Let's go home, Baby." I didn't care if it was his home or mine, I just wanted to get him out of here.

Jackson finally let go of Jefferson, who started gasping for air. He grabbed my hand, pulled me out of my seat, and without saying a word he started guiding me away from the table.

"He's unstable," Jefferson called out behind us. "I bet he's on that shit again."

"ENOUGH!!" Hank shouted cutting Jefferson off. "You've done enough, Jeff."

"Why did you break it up, Hank? You should have let Jackson kick his ass."

"Mama." Sally warned.

Ok, I like Memaw again.

I followed Jackson out the house and to his truck. He whistled once and Lady came running from the back yard. She hopped in the truck along with me, and we silently pulled away from the house.

***

The ride home was silent. I didn't know what had Jackson so quiet, but Jefferson's words were floating around my head. I wasn't angry or judging Jackson, I was more concerned with how he felt.

Why was he being so quiet? I was even more nervous when we pulled up to my place instead of his like we had planned earlier.

Jackson turned off the car, but he also didn't step out to open my door like he usually did. Instead he exhaled and leaned back in the seat.

"I was a fat kid." He started and I remained silent, allowing him to tell the story at his own pace. "I got bullied a lot about it. That isn't an excuse for the shit I did, I'm just telling you how it was. My parents weren't exactly poor, but we lived on a budget. Pops was so busy trying to make ends meet and mama was trying to stretch everything that came in the house from clothes to food. I guess that's kind of the reason Jessica started making her own clothes." He chuckled for a minute before getting serious again.

"I was struggling, and I felt like I couldn't talk to anyone. My parents were trying to keep us afloat, they didn't need to worry about my problems. I started off smoking cigarettes, then it was weed and alcohol. By the time I got to high school, it was coke and pills. I thought it was helping. It was numbing me. Now when some privileged jock would make fun of the fat kid, I would kick his ass because I was numb to the hurt. Yeah, I was angry all the time, but I wasn't depressed, at least I thought."

He was quiet again for a moment. Staring off into the distance. "The night started like most nights. I was hanging with some of the shitty friends I'd discovered. We were sitting around getting high and being stupid. I remember we ran out, and we decided to ride around to see if we could get some money to buy more. I'd already tapped out at home. I had started stealing from my parents. The little they had I thought it was ok to take." He shook his head in disgust. "My friend, Terry, said that he had a girl that worked at Subway and she would give him $15 dollars. I thought it was a brilliant plan at the time. Except we didn't go to subway, instead we went to an apartment complex. They told me to sit in the car. At the time I thought nothing of it when they always asked me to stay behind when they went to meet girls, but as I look back on it, it was their way of not including the fat kid.

That night I sat in the car as they went in to see Terry's girl. About thirty minutes later they came running back to the car. I'll admit, I knew something was wrong then, but I didn't say anything. Two days later I get pulled out of my house by the police. That night a sixteen year old kid was robbed and murdered.

We were all charged and went to trial, but I was spared because an eleven year old boy saw me sitting in the car. He told the police that he watched the fat boy sit in the car and eat donuts. That's the reason I'm not sitting behind bars right now, because I sat in the fucking car eating a donut while a kid was being killed."

He ran his hand over his face wiping away the tear that fell from his eyes.

"After the trial was over and I was cleared, Pop's packed my bags and sent me to the military. He said he was done. I didn't blame him. It was the greatest thing to ever happen to me." He finally turned to me and I saw the shame and disgust for himself written in his eyes. "I brought you home tonight, Charlice because I know you need time. And if you never want to see me again after this, I understand."

I remained silent taking it all in. The fact that Jackson was on drugs and the death of the young man. I allowed my mind to wrap around all of that before I made any decisions.

"When's the last time you used drugs?"

"Not since the night of the murder. I've never even smoked another cigarette."

I nodded my head. "Did you have any idea that they were going to that apartment for anything other than to get money from Terry's girl?"

"No! Even they admitted that it was why they were there, and the murder was spur of the moment. I was a fuck up, but I would have never stood for anything like that, Char. I swear it. Every day I wish that I could go back in time. That I would have gone with them, because I would have never let that shit go down. That kid would have still been here if only I would have got my fat ass out of the car."

"Don't do that to yourself. You had no control over those guys' actions that night. And you had no idea they were going to do what they did. You can't go back in time. You can only make sure that you don't make the same mistakes again."

"I want you so bad, Char." He turned to me with pain shining in his eyes. "I don't deserve you, but damn if I don't want you. If what you found out today is too much...."

"I never asked you to be perfect, Jackson. Remember, I got shit in my past too. I don't care about the guy you use to be. As long as you remain the guy you are now."

He smiled before pulling me in for a kiss. For a girl that once despised kissing, I damn sure seem to be doing a lot of it lately.

Jackson pulled back and smiled at me. "I'm sorry dinner with my family turned out to be horrible."

"I owed you one for the casserole anyway."

He laughed.

"Besides," I said. "It could have been worse."

He looked at me and lifted a thick eyebrow. "How the hell does it get worse than my Memaw calling you colored, my Ex showing up, and my brother and I fighting?"

"You could have had an entire family like your brother."

Jackson laughed again.

"So what's the deal with your brother? He seemed pretty damn spiteful."

He sighed and placed his head on the headrest.

"At some point while I was in middle school, I became the thorn in his side. I think he despised me for being the brother to the bullied fat kid." He grunted. "It's hard to be popular when everyone reminds you of your family's imperfection."

"Jackson, don't take this the wrong way, but your brother's an asshole."

He threw his head back and laughed.

"Come on, let's go in." He climbed out of the car and came around to my door to let me out. Lady hopped out right behind us.

"I still want to kick you sister in law's ass."

He smiled. "I was kind of turned on when you were about to fight her for dissing me."

"That bitch had it coming, even Memaw would agree,"

We entered the house and headed straight for my bedroom.

That night, Jackson and I fucked until we couldn't move. I think Jackson sharing his story with me seemed to bring us closer. We bonded on another level that night. However I knew that since Jackson opened up to me, he was going to push for me to open up to him. That could never happen. So instead of us talking, I fucked him. I fucked him for being the fat kid in school, I fucked him for the guilt he carried over that sixteen year old kid, and I fucked him for the messed up relationship between him and his brother. We both went to bed sweaty and tired.

TWENTY-TWO

The buzzing of my phone brought me out of a deep sleep. Jackson's arm was thrown over my body, and his leg covered mine. It took me a minute to locate my phone beside the bed.

"Hello?" I answered groggily.

"Aunt Duck?" Kylie's tearful voice had me fully awake and sitting up in bed.

"Kylie, what's wrong?"

The alarm in my voice must have woken Jackson up, because he's sitting up in bed too.

"Can…..can….. you come get me?"

I pulled the phone from my ear to see what time it was. 2:40 in the morning.

"Kylie, where is your mother?" As the question left my lips I heard my cousin scream in the background. I was out of the bed instantly with Jackson right behind me.

"Babe, what's going on?"

I couldn't take the time to reply to Jackson. My mind was on my cousin and my god children.

"Kylie, is Naya with you?"

"Yes, she's under the bed." Kylie whispered on the other end of the phone.

When I bought her the phone for her last birthday, her parents thought it was unnecessary. I was so fucking glad I convinced Devin to let her keep it.

"Alright, I want you and Naya to stay where you are. Stay out of sight. I'll be there soon."

"Hurry, Aunt Duck. I'm scared."

My heart dropped. I could imagine how scared my babies were.

"I'll hurry."

Her tearful goodbye prompted me to hang up the phone. I warned Miles once before that if he ever put his hands on my cousin I would kill him, I guess today he thought to test that theory.

Both Jackson and I were dressing.

"What's going on?" He asked again.

I realized he had no idea what was going on, but was still dressing for war with me.

"That asshole is drunk and he put his hands on my fucking cousin. I'm going to kill him." That was a promise.

Jackson drove us to the house, because I was clearly in no mood to obey traffic laws. The moment his truck pulled to a stop I was out. I didn't need Jackson to open my door this time.

Jackson told lady to stay put and she whined but didn't follow us. I used my phone to call Kylie.

She answered on the first ring.

"Aunt Duck?"

"Come open the door." I told her, then hung up.

The moment we stepped on the porch we could hear the cursing and screaming from the inside. Jackson placed a hand on my back rubbing it in circles.

"Breathe, baby. I need you to breathe for me."

Following his directions I exhaled. I hadn't even noticed I was so tensed.

"I could kill him." I mumbled to Jackson.

"Killing him won't help. We would end up on the run from the cops, because I'm not letting you go to jail."

That got a smile from me.

"When we get in here, let me handle it." I warned Jackson.

Devin was my family and I didn't want him mixed up with this bullshit. Besides, I owed Miles this ass whooping.

"You got it." He agreed easily.....a little too easily.

I didn't have time to question him further because the door opened and a red eyed Kyle stood behind it. She ran into my arms the moment I walked in.

"I want to leave." She begged.

"In a minute. Go get your sister." Kylie reluctantly ran back down the hall.

"Devin!" I yelled out over the noise.

Miles voiced immediately cut off.

"I know that bitch ain't in my house." His voice came towards me from down the hall.

He rounded the corner and paused when he saw me standing with Jackson. His white t- shirt was stretched out at the collar and a few drops of blood stained the fabric.

"Devin!" I called out to her again.

"Why are you in my house?" Miles said coming further into the living room.

I ignored his ass, I just needed to see that my cousin was ok. Once I saw her, I could whoop his ass accordingly.

Devin came around the corner. She was wearing a tank top that had been ripped and sleep pants. Her heavy belly was sticking out from under her shirt. However the most jarring thing was the blood on her nose and her red swollen jaw. Her hair was a tangled mess as if someone had been pulling on it.

"Duck, what are you doing here?" She looked away shamefully.

I had seen enough.

"You piece of shit!" I yelled at Miles, taking a step towards him before Jackson pulled me back.

He was right, I wasn't going to fight Miles. Fuck him.

"Get your shit and get out." I told Miles.

He chuckled, crossing his arms over his chest. "This is my muthafucking house. You can't put me out."

"Bitch, show me a receipt of a bill you paid in this house?" I argued. "In fact, I've paid the rent more than you have, so technically it's my house." My words accented by my hand claps.

"Don't matter. I've lived here more than thirty days and all my shit is here. You can't put me out. I know my rights."

Fucking dumbass.

"You know what, Miles, keep this piece of shit house. Come on, Devin, I'll get you another one."

Devin took a step towards me and Miles turned to her and yelled. "Sit your dumbass down."

Devin flinched at the shouted words and stood in her spot.

Miles turned back to me. "She ain't going nowhere. Especially not with your whore ass. You're the reason we in this shit now."

"It's not her fault, Miles."

"Didn't I tell you to shut the fuck up?" He turned and yelled at Devin.

By this time Kylie and Naya had walked into the room with their little book bags on their backs. They both walked up to Devin's side and hugged her legs.

Miles turned back to me. "You're one lonely, bitter bitch. You can't get a man to love you so you throw your used up pussy on them like free samples. And your family, they can't stand your ass." He chuckled at his joke as if he was telling me something I didn't know. "The only reason Devin fools with you, is because you always opening up your purse. All you do is buy her love, but you too stupid to see that."

"Duck that isn't...." I held up my hand to stop Devin from denying what Miles was saying.

"Unlike you." I told Miles calmly. "I'm not easily intimidated or insecure. I don't give a shit what you think about me. You thought because you put your hands on a pregnant women you became a man? You are still the bitch that I knew you always were. So quick to jump bad at me, but not the boys in the street. They have you hiding out at home like a pussy."

Miles' arms dropped from over his chest as his eyes widened. Yeah, I got that bit of info from Cliff's crazy ass. He was at least useful enough to tell me that.

"Get the fuck out of my house."

"Not without my family." I demanded.

"Fuck you! Have your own goddamn family, or is your pussy to warn out for that."

My retort died on my tongue. Jackson stepped forward. I guess he was done with letting me handle it.

"That's enough. You're drunk and you need to cool down."

"Who the fuck are you?" Miles asked. He looked Jackson up and down and then chuckled. "Oh that's right. You the new man." He shook his head in disgust. "You got you some discount black pussy and now you bad?"

"Out of respect for your daughters, I'm trying to give you a pass.

But if you disrespect Char one more time, we're going to have a problem." Jackson threatened in a tone that I'd never heard before. It was even more severe than when he spoke to his brother.

Miles stared at Jackson. I assumed he was seizing him up, wondering if Jackson would really follow up on his threat. I knew damn well he wasn't thinking he could take Jackson. Miles was 5'8", 190 pounds tops. He was barely the size of one of Jackson's thighs. He was no match.

After a long pause, Miles finally said. "Both of ya'll get the fuck out of my house."

"Gladly." I replied. "Come on girls."

Both girls started to walk towards me, but Miles turned to them and told them to stay.

"You're not taking my kids."

"Watch me."

I reached my hands out for Naya and she ran for me. Miles grabbed her arm and yanked her back.

"GET YOUR HANDS OFF OF HER!" I charged for Miles, but Jackson blocked me with his arm.

"Not when he's drunk." Jackson spoke the words in my ear.

"Let me go, Daddy." Naya yelled.

"Miles let her go, you're hurting her." Devin pleaded.

Miles pushed Naya behind him and she fell to the floor. Kylie ran for me, but this time, Miles didn't grab her, instead he swung his hand in an arch hitting Kylie in the face. She screamed and immediately crumpled to the floor. Like a raging bull, Jackson was on Miles. He slammed him into the wall so hard he put a hole in the plaster. With his hand wrapped around Miles' throat, Jackson pulled him away from the wall just to slam him in the wall again.

"Have you lost your fucking mind?" Jackson roared down at Miles.

Miles whimpered. "I…. I didn't mean to."

I went to Kylie and Naya, helping them off the floor. Naya wrapped her arms around me like a baby monkey and wouldn't let me go. I examined Kylie's face, a bruise was already forming on her cheek. That bastard.

"Devin, tell him to let me go." Miles pleaded.

I looked up at my cousin who was looking down at her daughters that were in my arms. I couldn't tell what she was thinking. I just hoped it wasn't about staying with Miles.

"Devin, you are greater than this." I told her truthfully. "I don't care what you think of yourself, for these two girls and the baby in your belly, you are better than this."

Her light brown eyes shimmered with tears as she looked me in my eyes.

Devin turned to Miles and squared her shoulders. "We're done."

Hell—Fucking—yeah!

Devin picked up the girls book bag that must have fallen in the shuffle and headed towards us.

"What the fuck? Get back here, you stupid bitch." Miles screamed at her. "You think you're going to be like Duck, but you won't. You're never going to be more than a dumbass baby momma."

Devin ignored him as she grabbed her girls' hands and headed out of the house.

"You'll be back." Miles continued to shout. "Nobody's going to want you."

I walked up to him while he was stilled pinned to the wall by Jackson.

"Poor little Miles," I gloated. "Can't get any respect in the streets and now you can't force it from home." I shrugged. "I told you that I would kill you if you ever put your hands on her, but I'm feeling generous. I won't kill you, but I am going to make your life hell. You have no idea what I am capable of. You thought I was a bitch before, you're really going to see one now. Enjoy your night, let's go Jackson." I smiled devilishly at Miles, while Jackson released his hold around Miles neck.

I meant what I said. I was going to make him pay for all this bullshit. I had friends in high places that would love to do me a favor. I was running down a list of people I could call in my head.

"Fucking Bitch!" As soon as the words left his mouth, I spun around so fast Jackson couldn't even catch me. Before Miles could guard himself, I kicked him in the balls as hard as I could. He screamed and dropped to his knees.

"Call me a bitch again!" I threatened.

Jackson came up behind me and gently turned me away from Miles.

"Come on, Baby! I think you've won." Jackson chuckled as he escorted me out of the house. The sound of Miles cries followed us onto the porch. I still wasn't done with him.

***

Despite Devin not wanting to go to the hospital, I made her. And she filed a police report. Something she would need to have when I took Miles to court to take his custody of his kids away. It wasn't like he ever did shit for them anyway. After making sure, Kylie was checked out, I headed back into the hospital room with Devin. Jackson was down stairs getting the girls something to eat while I waited with Devin.

"I'm going to ask you this question, and I want you to tell me the truth. Has he ever hit you or the girls before?"

Devin's light brown eyes stared up at the ceiling. The sound of the baby's heart beat floated around the room.

Devin sighed. "No! He use to grab me some times and he pushed me once, but he never hit me or the girls."

I still wasn't comforted by that information. I prided myself on knowing my family secrets, yet this one went right over my head. I knew I didn't like Miles, but at the end of the day, I thought his stupid ass loved my cousin. Which is why I tried to leave him alone. I should I have paid closer attention.

"Why would he, mental scars are easier to hide and just as harmful."

Devin turned to me and then cut her eyes away shamefully.

"How did you know?"

"I didn't, not until today." I answered before sighing. "I kind of suspected something at our brunch, but I thought I was just being paranoid. Why didn't you tell me?"

I knew it wasn't her fault. Most women being abused don't tell out of fear or other reasons. However, I had to ask the question.

"What would I say? He wasn't beating me, and Mama said that relationships are hard, but as long as he's not beating you, you should work it out."

See it's bullshit advice like that that kept people in toxic relationships. Yes, relationships require work, but there is a difference between working through problems, and ignoring danger signs.

"You can't go back to him, Devin. Not after…"

"I'm not." She answered. "What you said at brunch that day, it really stuck with me. I always had him and Mama telling me that I wasn't smart and I couldn't do what you wanted me to do. Daddy would try to tell me different, but I just kept listening to the wrong people. Seeing you finally find love and how it made you light up, I started to realize that I didn't have that. Miles didn't give me that light that Jackson gives you. And then when you told me how I was already running a business, and I didn't even realize it. It made me see that I deserved more. I showed him my class schedule today and he flipped. He demanded I drop out, when I refused, he got mad and left. I think it pissed him off when I didn't stop him or call for him to come home. When he finally came home he was drunk and well, you see what happened." Devin sat up in bed, causing the machine attached to her belly to make a loud rumbling noise.

"Seeing him hit Kylie was like a wakeup call. I don't ever want my kids to think that his behavior was ok. Not the mental stuff and definitely not the physical. It's time I showed my girls the type of woman I can be."

I smiled and nodded. I already knew the type of woman she could be. I'd just been waiting for her to see it too.

"Well, until we find you guys a place to stay, you can stay with me."

"Are you sure? I don't want to put you out."

I waved her off.

"Absolutely."

The door to Devin's hospital room opened and Jackson and the girls walked in. Naya was fast asleep on Jackson's shoulder, and Kylie was holding his hand. They hadn't let Jackson go from the moment we got here.

"Everyone has been fed." Jackson informed us.

"Good." Devin replied. "Hopefully we will be heading home soon."

Three hours later, we were finally back at my place.

TWENTY-THREE

Jackson: Can't wait to see you tonight.

I blushed, I couldn't help it. It's been a month since the night Kylie called my phone. It took that long to find a decent place for Devin and the girls. It also took that long to help Devin come to terms with the type of man her baby daddy was.

Two days after they left, Miles tried to get Devin to come back home. She only wavered a few times. Despite me continuously telling her she was crazy to even consider it, it took Kylie begging her to not go back. I'd spent the last month trying to erase the damage Miles had done to her. She spent seven years in a relationship being told she was worthless, lazy, dumb, and replaceable. She needed my attention.

Jackson had been by my side the entire time. He spent most of his time with the girls, I think seeing their father like that really scared them. Naya had nightmares for a week after the event. Jackson has made it his personal goal to make them feel safe again. He even went over to their old place with his crew and got the rest of Devin and the girls things. And since Miles remembered the last time he crossed paths with Jackson, he didn't fight him on taking anything.

Even though Miles had learned his lesson about crossing Jackson, apparently his brother did not feel the same way. He and his wife are still being a problem. Between the phone calls, the pop ups at his house and office, I was ready to strangle them both.

They were even able to drag Jackson's mother into it. I

overheard her telling Jackson that she really liked me, but if Vanessa was pregnant that he owed it to his child to give their relationship a try. Since that conversation, Jackson and I have been blocking them out.

Even with all the shit going on, we still found time for ourselves. We started taking a cooking class together. He didn't really need it, but he enjoyed going with me. The only thing I could really do without, other than Vanessa's ass, was the questions.

Jackson had started to ask me a lot of questions about my past and my childhood. He was trying to dig my truths out of me despite how vehemently I fought him. So far I was always able to change his mind by offering up sex. That works like a charm.

"Oh my, gosh, Duck! Can you put your phone down?" Keisha whined.

Tonight, I took my cousins to an upscale wine bar. Even though half of them couldn't actually drink, and one of them considered alcohol the devil. However, tonight we were celebrating Devin finally finding a place, and her last few weeks of freedom before the baby came. She was due in three weeks and I was more than excited. So excited that I let her talk me into bringing Keva, Keisha, and Chante with us. So even though she couldn't drink, I damn sure needed it.

I placed my phone back down on the table.

"I told y'all she's in love." Devin chuckled as she sipped her lemonade.

"And I told you, I'm not in love."

Devin rolled her eyes and shook her head at me.

"It might not be love, but you are definitely whipped." Keisha joked.

"Yeah, you're about as bad as Devin was." Keva added.

Devin and I opted out of telling the family what happened that night. All they know was that Devin left Miles. And it couldn't had come at a better time, it seemed Miles had had one bad day after the other. He was jumped by some guys in the street, ended up with a cracked rib and broken hand. The case worker did a pop up visit after an anonymous tip led her to the house. She easily evicted Miles, sending him back home to his mama. And to top it all off, he has a court date for domestic violence coming up, with a very good judge friend of mine. I still wasn't done with his ass.

"Hey," Devin frowned. "Don't bring up my Ex."

"Yes, Please! Let's leave his dumbass in the past where he belongs."

"Damn right!" Keisha agreed.

"That's right, " Devin giggled beside me dancing to the pop song coming through the speakers. "Because I'm single now, and in a few weeks this baby will be here, and I'll be ready to mingle."

I raised my glass to my cousin in cheer to her newfound happiness.

"Devin, don't let someone that just found a man, give you relationship advice. You need to work it out with Miles." Chante said sipping her margarita.

I rolled my eyes. She'd been baiting me all night, but I won't let her bother me. I was in a good mood.

We continued to enjoy the music, and nice vibe until something caught my eye.

"Oh, hell no!" I said out loud and grabbed my phone off the table.

"What is it?" Devin asked as the entire table followed where my phone was pointed.

"Who is that?" Keisha asked.

"Oh my god, that's her. That's his Ex isn't it?"

I ignored Devin's cousin question because I was too busy sending pictures to Jackson's phone.

Here, in a tiny pink dress, was mouse. She was sitting on a man's lap at a table full of females, and the most damning thing of all, was the bottle of Bud light she was sipping on. Well damn, Mouse was lying after all.

I placed my phone back in the pocket of my black Ted Baker skater dress. I slid out of the booth and pulled my dress down.

"Duck, what are you going to do?" Devin asked alarmed.

"I'm just going to say hi!" I said with a smile and winked to my table before I walked off.

"Hold up let me go with you." Keisha announced, and I could hear her sliding out of the booth.

I didn't pay any attention to my meddling cousins as I made my way over to Vanessa's table. I sat down at the open seat right across from her. Immediately conversation dies down. Mouse eyes went wide when she finally saw me.

"Hello, Vanessa." I said politely. "How's the pregnancy coming along?"

The guy she was sitting on looked just as shocked as the friends around her.

"I...uh....uh." Vanessa fought to find the words to say.

I waved her off, no need to lie to me. My phone chimed in my pocket, I pulled it out and glanced down at it.

JACKSON: I hope she chokes on that beer. I'm sending this to my mom.

"Jackson sends his love." I said holding the phone up for her to see.

For the first time since I saw her in Jackson's office, I saw the real Vanessa. That coy, sweet girl shit dropped away and the real bitch came out.

"This doesn't change anything. Jackson will always come back to me. He's been doing it for years. Your novelty will wear off and he will be back in my bed, just like with all the other girls."

I laughed. "It's funny, I think if I would have saw this side of you a little earlier, I might would have liked you. Nevertheless, let me school you on something, sweet heart. You see, I can't speak for those other women. I don't know them. But I do know this, even if Jackson and I don't last another day, I can guarantee, you will never have him. You see, chicken wings and beer is appeasing to men with basic pallets." I glanced to the dude sitting under her. "However, once a man dines on filet mignon and fine wine, his taste buds changes. He craves the finer things in life, so basic meals no longer appease him."

"Daaaammmmnnnn." Keisha said behind me.

One of the girls at Vanessa's table mumbled, "I think she's calling her basic."

"You are not a threat to me, Vanessa." I smirked. "Not even when you were supposedly pregnant."

Vanessa stared back at me, her mouth wide open. I gave her a wink and stood to my feet.

"It was nice meeting all of you. Take care, Mouse."

I turned around and walked away slowly with Keisha behind me.

"Oh My God, Duck! That was so fire. That bitch couldn't say anything. I was hoping she popped off because I was ready for her."

I shook my head at her. First off, I wasn't fighting anyone. I was too damn old for that, and I actually had a career. Secondly, I wasn't letting her pregnant ass fight either.

As soon as we got back to the table Keisha was ready to explain what happened.

"Y'all missed it. That shit was so good." Keisha started, but before she could finish, Devin grunted in pain and we all turned to her.

"Oh shit! Oh shit!"

"Devin what's wrong?"

She looked to me with wide eyes, "My water just broke. Ahhhhhhhhhh!"

We all jumped to our feet. I signaled the waitress and squared up the check, then ushered us all out of the restaurant and into my car. We had a baby to bring into the world.

At 10:11 pm my 8 pound 2 ounce god son was born. He was big and beautiful. Charlie Ross Davis, named after his Papa and God mother. I couldn't be prouder.

It was after 2 am when I finally pulled into my driveway.

"Alright, Jackson, I'm home." I said through the phone.

"Good, baby, stay on the phone until you get in the house." I turned off my car and climb out.

I was exhausted, and as bad as I wanted Jackson to be here, I didn't think I had enough energy for him.

"Seriously, I can't wait until you see him. Jackson, he's gorgeous." I said as I walked into my house.

"I can't wait to see him either."

I gasped and dropped the phone.

My hands shook at the sight of my house. Everything was destroyed. My furniture had been shredded, pictures were broken, glass was shattered, and large holes were in my walls.

I stood in the middle of my living room and stared at the disaster until I finally heard Jackson shouting through the phone. I picked the phone up off the floor.

"Char! Char! Baby, please answer me. Char, I'm on the way."

"Jackson." I didn't realize I was crying until my voice broke. "My house. He destroyed my house."

I heard him sigh through the other end of the phone. "Jesus Char! Are you ok?"

"He's back."

"Alright, I want you to get out of the house. Get in your car, drive

196

down the street and call the cops. Ok?"

"Ok!"

I headed back out to my car and climbed in. I did as Jackson said, but instead of calling the cops I called Sean.

"Hey, Charli. What's up?

"Sean," I said, rushing the words out. "I need you."

"Charli what's wrong? Talk to me."

"I think he's back."

"Fuck! Ok, don't go in the house. Stay right where you are, I'm on my way."

"Hurry Sean!"

"I'm coming."

I hung up the phone and a few minutes later Jackson pulled up behind me. He must have been driving like a madman. He jumped out of the truck followed by Lady.

"Are you alright?" He checked me over from head to toe.

I nodded my head.

"Ok! Stay here, I'm going to go inside and check." He headed towards the front door but I grabbed his arm.

"No! Don't go in there."

He faced me. "Baby, I have to go in to make sure he's gone."

He pulled away from me and I yanked him back. I didn't know why, but I didn't want Jackson inside that house. What if Cliff was still there? I kept getting visions of Cliff taking all the anger he took out on my house and using it to attack Jackson. I felt the first signs of my panic attack coming.

"No!" I shouted yanking at his arm.

I was thrashing against him trying to make him stay. I almost lost my footing, but Jackson caught me with his arms wrapped around me. Both of us missed Sean's car as he pulled up behind us. He was out of his car instantly.

"Get your fucking hands off of her." He shouted to Jackson with his gun raised.

Two police cars pulled up behind him with their red and blue lights flashing.

"Get your hands up." A cop yelled as soon as he got out of the car.

Lady, who had no problem with me fighting against Jackson, was now losing her shit. She was growling and snapping at Sean and the cops.

Jackson let me go and Sean ran to me immediately wrapping his arms around me, he scanned my body from head to toe.

"Are you ok?"

"Yeah, I'm fine." I looked up to find the two cops walking up on Jackson with his hands still raised in the air, their guns aimed at him.

Lady was still growling and snapping at Sean.

"Hey do something about that damn dog." Sean yelled when Lady snapped at him again.

One of the officers aimed their gun at her and I stepped towards her. I wasn't an animal person, but Lady had started to grow on me. No way was one of these trigger happy cops putting a bullet in her. Us bitches had to stick together.

Sean grabbed my arm and pulled me back. Lady really got worked up then, even taking a step toward Sean.

"Lady, down." Jackson said in a commanding tone.

Lady looked over to Jackson and whined, but sat down on her haunches.

The other two officers continued towards Jackson. One even went for his handcuffs.

"What are you doing? He didn't do anything." I said to the cops.

"That's not what it looked like when I pulled up. It looked like he was pushing you down." Sean pulled me into him for another hug.

"How did you get here so fast?" Jackson asked.

Sean watched him, before replying. "I was out not too far from here working on another case when I got Charli's call."

"You called him?" This time Jackson questioned me.

Before I could reply, the cop with the handcuffs grabbed one of Jackson's hands and yanked it behind his back.

"Hey! I said he didn't do anything. Why are you putting him in handcuffs?"

"It's just procedure, Babe. He was hostile when we pulled up." Sean explained.

He tried to wrap me in another hug, but I stepped away from him.

"Procedure my ass, let him go."

"Charli…"

"Let….Him… Go."

Sean stared at me for a minute. Then he turned to the other cops and nodded. The officer that was handcuffing Jackson sighed, but pulled out his keys and undid the cuffs. Jackson rubbed at his sore wrist.

"So what did you call me for?" Sean asked confused.

"He's back. Cliff is back and he trashed my house." I was getting worked up again.

"Ok! Calm down. We're going to go in and make sure he's not still inside." Another nod from Sean had the other two cops pulling out their guns and heading towards my house.

"Stay here." Sean ordered while following the other cops inside the house.

I watched Sean disappear behind my busted glass door that I didn't notice when I first pulled in. I turned to Jackson and the look on his face wasn't the same as the one he shared when he first arrived.

He was angry with me.

"Are you alright?" I grabbed his wrist to examine it.

An angry red line circled where the tight cuffs were.

"I'm good." He didn't sound good.

"Charli!" Sean called my name from the other side of my door. "We need you to come in and see if anything is missing."

I was already shaking my head no. I couldn't go back in there, I didn't want to see what he did in my home. I didn't think I could ever feel safe in there again. And I didn't like not feeling safe.

Jackson turned me to face him, he cupped my face in his warm hands. "Hey, don't worry. I got you."

Hearing him say it and being in his arms helped calm my nerves. I took a few calming breaths and nodded.

Jackson entwined my hand in his and led me into the house. I didn't get to see just how much damage was done the first time I came in. I only saw the mud room and part of my living room. The damage was so much worse throughout the rest of the house. He must have taken a hammer to all my walls. Small holes were randomly doted throughout the house. The word MINE was painted on over my bed in big black letters.

Only some one that was seriously sick and deranged could do something like this. They had to have been furious. And if they could do this much damage to inanimate objects, imagine what they would do to me.

"I need to go." I said, finally having enough.

"You have to see the rest of the house, make sure we aren't missing anything." Sean said.

I shook my head no. I couldn't stay in this house a second longer.

"Jackson, get me out of here."

Jackson instantly reacted, pulling me towards the door and back out into the cooling evening air. Sean met us outside.

"You can't leave yet. They need to ask you questions like your whereabouts tonight."

"I was at the...."

"I thought you told Char that this guy had moved out of town." Jackson asked cutting off my reply.

He helped me ease into the passenger seat of his truck where Lady was once again growling furiously. She was really worked up over those cops manhandling Jackson.

"That's what I was told. However, the family is the one that told the cops that."

"Yeah, well obviously they lied."

"Hey, don't catch an attitude with me. I'm just as pissed off as you are about this."

"Trust me, you couldn't possibly be angrier than I am right now. That asshole destroyed her house, what the hell do you think would have happened if she would have been home?"

Jackson's shouted words made the fear I was feeling real again. What if I had been home when Cliff came? I wasn't scared to put a bullet in his ass, but what if he would have snuck up on me in the middle of the night or while I was in the shower.

"Well, let's just be glad she wasn't home." Sean gritted out before turning to me. "Hey, I want you staying with someone for a while. And don't let it be the same person, I don't know if this guy has eyes on you or not."

"If he's watching me, could my family or Jackson be in danger?"

"I'm not sure about your family, but Jackson is definitely a possibility. This guy may see Jackson as a threat."

I faced Jackson, ready to tell him that maybe we should back off this for a while. He was already having issues with his truck and business. I didn't want Cliff to escalate. Obviously he was unstable, so it wasn't farfetched that he would go after Jackson.

"We are not breaking up." Jackson said before I could open my mouth.

I bit my tongue, I wouldn't argue with him now, but I was definitely going to bring this conversation back up when we got to his house.

"Breaking up?" Sean repeated.

He turned to me with a huge smile.

"Am I hearing this correctly? Is the unconquerable, the never settling down, Ms. Charlice Rose Jefferies in a relationship?"

I blushed. "Yes!" I felt more awkward admitting it to Sean than it did to my family.

Sean stared at me for a moment in shock, then said. "Congratulations, Char. I'm seriously happy for you."

The moment Sean wrapped his arms around me to give me a hug, Lady snapped at him nearly taking a chunk out of him.

"Goddamn it, Keller, do something about that fucking dog." Sean looked down at his arm.

I took his arm in my hand looking over it. Thankfully Sean's reflexes were so fast.

I looked up and found Jackson watching Lady closely. I'd never seen her act like this and I'd been around this dog for months. She didn't behave this way when she found Howard in my bed. She was pissed about something.

"Detective Myers!" one of the cops called out Sean's name.

"You guys should go. We can get statements later. And don't worry, Charli. We will board up the door for you." Sean said before walking away from us and towards the cops.

**

When I finally stepped out of Jackson's shower the clock on his nightstand read 4:25 am. I was beyond exhausted. His bed was calling my name. I didn't want to think about my house or Cliff. Today, Jackson was able to get Vanessa and her bullshit off our backs, and my godson was born. I wasn't going to let one fucked up individual ruin my day.

"I'm exhausted."

"I bet you are. Give me your foot."

I placed my feet in Jackson's lap at the foot of the bed and he used his thumb to massage the bottom of my foot.

I moaned so loud you'd thought I was getting my pussy ate.

"That feels so good." My head hits my pillow and I whimpered.

Jackson chuckled briefly.

"How long have you known Detective Myers?"

With my eyes still closed I answered. "Since he was a freshmen in high school."

Silence greeted me, I cracked open one eye to see Jackson staring down at my foot as if he was thinking.

"It's not what you're thinking. We aren't in love or anything. At the most we're friends. Plus, he's in love with his girlfriend of three years."

"Mmhhmm." He said looking up at me. "The girlfriend he brought to the table while he flirted with you?"

I laughed. "He was not flirting. Plus, they are getting married. I helped pick out the engagement ring. He is in love with her."

Jackson shrugged, but he didn't look convinced.

"Jackson Lee Keller, are you jealous?" I asked teasingly.

Another shrug from Jackson. "NO! I'm just saying, you've had a sexual relationship with this guy for at least sixteen years. Despite having him having a relationship or not, I know marriages that didn't last that long."

I removed my foot from Jackson's lap and sat up crawling closer to him. I placed my hand on his cheek turning his face towards me.

"It isn't like that. Sean and I were really good about keeping everything platonic. We care for each other's wellbeing, but we aren't in love. Besides, I never cooked for him."

I finally got that sexy grin on Jackson's face. He planted a kiss on my lips that turned steamy quick. I crawled into Jackson's lap straddling him.

"You're trying to distract me." He said pulling his lips away from mine just long enough to talk.

I smiled against his lips. "Is it working?"

He grunted. "Fuck Yes!"

Jackson stood to his feet and I wrapped my legs around his waist. He turned me towards the bed and laid me down while covering my body. This was how I wanted to end my day, with an orgasm.

Lady started barking and Jackson groaned. He placed his

forehead to mine.

"You have to go handle that." I teased Jackson as I spread my legs wider brushing my exposed pussy to his crotch.

"Fuck!" he moaned. "Lady can wait a few minutes." He placed kisses down my chin and to my neck.

That's when we heard it, the unmistakable sounds of gunshots. Jackson covered my body fully until the sound was gone. Three shots rang out.

"Are you ok?" he asked as he lifted up from me.

"I'm fine."

The silence after causing my heart beat to sound like drums.

Silence.

Jackson and I recognized it at the same time. Jackson jumped up and rushed towards the door. I was right on his heels.

"Stay in the house." He shouted as he ran barefoot into the back yard.

I followed his directions as I waited at the patio door for him to reappear. When he finally did, I cried out. Jackson was covered in blood, but I already knew it wasn't his blood. It belonged to the black dog that was in his arms.

I slid the door open for him as he carried her limp body into the house and into the living room. He didn't care about the blood he was dripping on his floors, all he cared about was the dog in his arms.

"Is she breathing? Do I need to get towels? Shouldn't we take her to the hospital?" I was firing off questions like a mad woman.

Jackson kneeled on the floor before his fireplace and placed Lady's body down on the ground before him.

"Jackson don't just stand there let's take her to the hospital." I was crying.

He shook his head, his shoulders slumped.

"It's too late." Those simple words stole my breath.

I fell to my knees at his side. We both stared down at Lady's still form. Jackson's body shook as he broke down beside me. I wrapped my arms around him and he dropped his head on my shoulder and cried.

After we called the police to report the incident, we buried Lady under a small tree in Jackson's backyard. She was wrapped in her favorite red blanket. By the time we went to sleep, it was eight am.

☐

TWENTY-FOUR

I stood in my bathrobe rocking little Charlie to sleep. He was three months old today. It was his first time getting to spend the night with me. I was supposed to get all three kids, but Devin wanted to keep the girls to spend alone time with them.

It took eight in a half weeks to fix my house. The holes were patched, the walls repainted and the furniture and front door was replaced. Jackson even saw to upgrading my security system along with adding cameras and motions lights around my house. I was finally home and I felt safe again.

I placed little Charlie into the crib I had redone for him. I always kept things at my house for my godchildren when they were babies so that Devin wouldn't have to haul their stuff over when I kept them.

I turned around and Jackson was leaning against the door frame of the bedroom watching me closely. A smile on his face.

I loved to see that smile. It was even better now since I didn't get to see it often. Not since Lady. Her death took a toll on Jackson, he tried to hide it from me, but I noticed it. For a moment I feared he was going to realize I was too much trouble and drop me. The police hadn't been able to prove Cliff was behind Lady's death but who else would do it. Thankfully, since Lady's death, Cliff has gone silent again. I prayed to whatever higher being there was, that Cliff had went back to whatever hell he came from.

Even Eli had said it's been harder than he planned it to be to get information on him. He said that Cliff's family wasn't talking to anyone.

I placed my finger to my lips and he smiled as I tip-toed out. I shut the door behind me.

"He's down like a light." I joked.

Jackson just stared at me with that amazed look on his face.

"What?"

"You're incredible." Jackson said as we headed into my bedroom.

I checked the camera on the baby monitor to make sure little man was still ok.

"You've cleaned up baby vomit, changed diapers, and even dodged a very close call with a trail of piss." I laugh at the reminder of little Charlie taking a shot at me earlier.

Jackson walked up behind me and wrapped his arms around me placing a kiss to the back of my neck. "You'll make an incredible mother one day."

My body tensed tighter than a guitar string. I slipped from Jackson's arms and headed into the bathroom.

"What do you want for dinner tonight?" I called back into the bedroom where I left him. "I could really go for Thai."

Jackson appeared in the doorway of my bathroom. He had that look in his eyes, the one he got when he was thinking over something.

"Char, why've you never had kids?"

I continued to dig through my bathroom drawers in search of nothing in particular. I was thankful my back was to him. I didn't want Jackson to see how his question affected me.

"I'm about my business, Jackson. I don't have time for kids." I said forcing a laugh.

"Come on, Char! You spend all your free time with your god children and little cousins. You have time. Plus, I know it had nothing to do with needing a man, because I've met at least two of them that seemed more than willing." He laughed behind me before continuing on with his line of questioning. "So what is it? Do you not want kids?"

I turned to face Jackson, my irritation growing. "Why all these damn questions?"

Jackson watched me closely. Those prying eyes reading me. I hated how he was looking at me, like he knew what I was hiding. This wasn't the first time Jackson had started to ask questions that I didn't want to answer. Every now and again he would pry into my past.

I placed a smile on my face and tilted my head to the side. I stepped up to him placing a hand on his chest.

"How about, we not worry about having kids, and instead we practice the act of making them? I haven't had your dick in my mouth since this morning before little Charlie woke up." I reached for the waist of Jackson's pajama bottoms. He stepped back dodging my touch, glaring down at me.

"Why is that every time I mention kids, you change the subject? What aren't you telling me, Charlice?"

I threw my hands up and walked around him to the bedroom. With my back to him, I said. "Nothing."

I lied down across my bed and spread my legs, allowing him to see the sexy red thongs I was wearing tonight.

He shook his head. "I'm not some high school kid that you can distract with pussy, Char. Answer my question."

I rolled my eyes, fully done with this conversation. "This is bullshit! Why are we even talking about kids…..Where are you going?" I asked when Jackson started grabbing his pants off the chair in my bedroom in a fury.

"I told you from day one I wasn't going to play your fuck boy."

"You're not."

"I want a relationship with you."

"What the fuck do you think we've been doing for seven months?"

Jackson stopped his rushed dressing to turn and glare at me.

"We!" He shouted, before bringing his voice back down. "What we've been doing? I've been sharing everything with you, from my fucked up past to all my time. I've been opening up to you so you could get to know me and hopefully fall in love with me. But you've been peddling out information like it's the last box of candy on Halloween. If your fucking life story was water and I was a plant I'd be dead from drought. Every time I try to get to know you, or take our relationship to the next level you pull back or throw your pussy at me. I've done everything to prove that I want to be with you. I love you, Char."

I was startled at the words. I never thought I would care to hear those words come out of anyone's mouth ever again, but here they were and I wasn't sure how I felt about them.

Jackson shook his head. "I can't do this anymore. This one step forward two steps back dance is tiring. After all the shit we've been through, you're still keeping secrets. If you can't answer one simple personal question then…" he threw his hands up and let them fall back at his side.

"Oh so you're going to leave?" I said climbing off the bed to stand in front of him. "All that bullshit about fighting for me and I'll wait for your heart, Char. That's all bullshit now?"

"I promised you I'd fight as long as the end goal was your heart, but I don't think you want that. I think you enjoy watching me pour my heart out to you while you give me nothing."

"Well fuck you, Jackson! Sorry I'm not moving fast enough for you now. You know what? Just get out. I should have never let your pasty white ass in my life in the first place."

Jackson stared at me. I could see the anger in his eyes, but it was what I didn't see that bothered me. There was no hurt or sign of relenting. My heart stuttered and started to beat faster. Jackson turned his back to me for a moment and I watched him, waiting for him to tell me to knock it off, or to get my ass back in the bed because he and I were not done, but instead he grabbed his shirt off the back of the chair and pulled it on.

"Fine! You win." He grabbed his shoes off the floor and walked out of my room.

My feet were glued to my bedroom floor for a second. Then it hit me. My anger built up.

"Fine!" I shouted following him out of the bedroom not thinking about my godson sleeping in the next room. "And don't even think of crawling your ass back to me." I followed him down the steps shouting at his back. "We both know you will never be able to stay away from this pussy. You will be right back at my door after you realize your homely little ex and her dry pussy can't do shit for you. So take your ass own, Jackson. I….don't…..need….you."

The more I shouted the less he reacted. When he got to the bottom step he stopped just long enough to put on his shoes. I continued to yell hurtful words at him.

"This is why I don't fuck with white men. As soon as you leave I'm going to call up a fine brother to come over here and…."

Jackson spun around so fast I had to take a step back. He marched over to me with a look of pure rage. I continued to keep my ground. I'd never show him or any damn man weakness. He stood in front of me, nostrils flaring, and that vein in his neck throbbing. For a moment he just stood there, then he held out his hands. When I looked down, my spare key was in his palm. I didn't take the key, I just stared at it, my heart beating rapidly in my chest as if it had sprouted wings and ready to fly off. Jackson flipped his hand over and the key fell to the ground at my feet with a clunk. When he turned and walked away, a feeling came over me. One I haven't experienced since I was sixteen. I started to breathe heavily, my heart raced. The feeling of someone pressing on my chest hit me, followed by that feeling of not being able to breathe. My eyes watered as I tried to fight to gain control.

"Please!" I gasped out. "Please don't leave me, Jackson. Please don't go."

Jackson pivoted around on his heels. I clutched a hand to my chest as my panic attack took full control over me. I felt his strong arms wrap around me and lift me off my feet.

"What's wrong, Char? Baby, tell me what's wrong."

The slow leak tears turned into whole body shaking sobs.

I buried my face in Jackson's neck.

"Please don't leave me. Please don't leave me." I kept repeating the sentence over and over.

Jackson held me close to his chest as he carried me back up the stairs to my bedroom. The closer we get to my room the easier my breathing became and the less my body shook. Jackson sat on the bed with me in his lap.

"You have to give me something, Char. I can't keep doing this with you."

"You won't want me when you find out the truth." I mumbled the words against his flesh, still burying my face into his neck.

"Look at me." He demanded.

I pulled away from him and slowly looked into those calming eyes.

"There is nothing you could tell me about you that will make me not want you."

He was lying. It's ok, he didn't realize he was lying. He believed that what he said was true, but I knew that he wouldn't stay once he heard my story.

I climb out of his lap and pace the floor in front of him. I've only admitted this truth to one person, and that was Sean. But even he didn't know everything. He didn't know all that I was about to tell Jackson.

"I don't have kids, because I can't have them."

Jackson climbed to his feet to reach for me, but I stepped away. I needed to tell him all of this before I changed my mind. Before I lost my courage.

"I can't have kids, because when I was sixteen, I had a partial hysterectomy. A uterine rupture caused by trauma. The doctor had to take my uterus in order to save my life. I still have my cervix and ovaries, but no place to carry a baby."

"Charli, I'm so sorry." He grabbed my arm and pulled me into him.

I went easily, allowing him to hold me tight. We stayed like that for a moment. Allowing my truth to penetrate. This was a turning point in our relationship. It could truly make or break us.

"What caused the trauma?"

This was the question I wished he didn't ask. The question that I dreaded, the one that was going to change how he felt about me. I stepped away from his arms and took a seat in the chair across from him.

"It was probably the wire hangers I had shoved up there a few times."

Jackson looked as confused as I figured he would be. "Why would someone do that to you?"

I sighed and rubbed my hands through my hair pushing it out of my face. "Because doctors ask a lot of questions when you bring your eleven year old in for an abortion." I kept my eyes on the wall as I explained to Jackson just how fucked up I was and why I would never get the opportunity to be a mother.

"I didn't know I was pregnant that first time. I just remember being sick one day at school. The nurse called my mother and explained that I wasn't feeling well. Nita had already figured it out. She didn't even panic. She picked me up from school around noon and by the time the school bus dropped off Eli, I wasn't pregnant anymore. She told me that she was helping me. She said that when she got pregnant with me, Grams and Papa wouldn't let her get an abortion, but she was going to help me. I remember lying in the back seat of her car thinking, why help me now. If she really wanted to help, she would make him stop. She wouldn't leave the house every time he came over. And when I cried and begged her to stay and help me, she wouldn't walk away.

When I turned fourteen, I got pregnant again. This time I discovered it first. I cried for days after I realized what was wrong. I was too afraid to tell Nita. I hurt for so long after that first abortion. I knew I didn't want to keep his baby, but I just didn't want to go through that pain. This time, after it was done, I remember him and her arguing in the living room. She told him that if he was going to keep getting me pregnant, he was going to have to pay her more because she couldn't afford all these abortions. Can you believe that? She didn't ask him to stop, she just didn't want to have to pay for his fuck ups."

I stopped for a minute allowing that to set. My mother didn't care that I was being raped and molested, she just didn't want to use her money to clean up the mess.

"I was sixteen the last time it happened. I had made up in my mind that I was done. I wasn't going back to that house and letting that woman torture me. If I was going to be a single mother living on the streets, then that's what I was going to do, but I refused to go through that procedure again. I was probably about five months pregnant before he discovered my secret. He was pissed, like he had any right to be. I remember he smacked me so hard that day my lip started bleeding. He blamed me for trying to ruin him, said that he loved me and would never give me up. He always talked about how much he loved me. That he did what he did because he was in love with me. He even told Nita that we were in love with each other. I was too young to know what love was, but I knew that wasn't what I felt for him.

That day, he called Nita and she dragged me to that woman again. I cried and screamed. I even promised them that I wouldn't tell anyone how I got pregnant if she let me keep it. I just didn't want to go through it again. But Nita wouldn't hear of it. I knew immediately afterwards something had gone terribly wrong. I was nearly doubled over in pain, I couldn't even stand up straight. Blood was everywhere, it just wouldn't stop. The pain had gotten so bad that I started vomiting and eventually I blacked out. I still don't know what made Nita take me to the hospital. I figured she would have let me died and finally been done with me. When I woke up, doctors told me that I almost died, and that the only way to save my life was to take my uterus.

Like a lot of little girls, I had dreamed of being a mommy, Jackson. I'd picked out names and features I'd hoped they would have. I was convinced that I would have three, all boys. At sixteen years old those childhood dreams were ripped away from me. When I finally left the hospital, I went to stay with my Grandparents. Nita and I have not spoken since the day she sat beside my hospital bed as the doctor told me that I would never be able to carry my own child."

The room was quiet after my confession. The warm tears continued to slide down my face. My awful secret was out. No one knew my secret, no one but the people involved. I wanted to take this dirty truth to the grave, but here I was, telling Jackson. I was allowing him into the darkest part of me. The part that I covered up with a fake smile and a tough exterior.

I turned to him and his eyes were bloodshot. His hands were fisted on his knees and he looked like he was about to explode.

"You told me on that first coffee date that your mother loved men."

I should be shocked he remembered that. We haven't talked about my mother since that coffee date six months ago. But this was Jackson, he pays attention to everything, especially when it's about me.

"Was it one her men that hurt you?"

"It was a long….."

"Don't." One simple word spoken with so much authority, gave me no option of denying him.

"No, it wasn't a boyfriend. Nita would never allow that. She was stingy and would never share her men. My story is a little more fucked up."

I took a deep breath, allowing a moment to build up enough strength to say a name that still haunts me. The mention of it still made me nervous and gave me nightmares.

"It was my uncle Martin."

I could almost hear the ticking in Jackson's jaw as he bit down so hard I was sure his teeth were cracking. The room was silent. I wasn't sure if Jackson was just processing this, or trying to come up with the best exit speech. I wouldn't blame him. This was a lot of shit to deal with. I was raped by my uncle from the age of six to sixteen. I had a crazy ex-lover stalking me and torturing Jackson, and to make matters worse, I couldn't even give him kids. Any normal man would run for the hills. He would pack up his shit and get the hell out of town. I wasn't worth a relationship.

This was why I stuck to short term sex agreements. No one asked you questions when it's only about sex. No one needed to know that you woke up in cold sweats screaming with nightmares about your childhood rapist, when they aren't allowed to sleep over. They didn't figure out you're a broken woman when they didn't have a chance to get to know you or plan a future with you. This was why I had rules, this was why I never wanted to have a relationship with Jackson.

After the silence in the room had gone on for far too long, I decided to give Jackson an easy exit.

"I know this is a lot to deal with. If you want to go, I won't hold it against you. You didn't sign up for all this."

His nostrils flared as he stared back at me. "If you, for a second, believe that about me, you have no idea who I am."

Relief.

That's the feeling that I felt. I had no idea how bad I wanted Jackson to accept my truth until he finally did. I felt as if the windows of my soul had finally been ripped open. They weren't nailed shut anymore. The doors weren't sealed tight, it was freeing.

"I can't give you kids, Jackson."

I needed him to understand that. He needed to know that that was never an option. "At least with your Ex, you had the possibility of one day becoming a dad, but I can't give you that."

Jackson was out of his seat and on his knees in front of me. He grabbed my hands in his.

"I never asked you to give me kids. All I want is you. I will take you any way I can get you, as long as you're mine."

"I'm yours." I honestly admitted.

And I was his. Despite my refusal to admit it, I've been his for a while.

"I love you, Jackson."

He smiled for the first time since I started talking. "I love you too, Char."

That night, Jackson and I didn't make love. We didn't do anything sexual at all, but we've never been more intimate. We laid in my bed and talked. We talked about everything from my childhood, to my family, to my hopes and dreams. I completely opened up to Jackson, and it was the most intimate I had ever been with a man.

    □

TWENTY-FIVE

I should have known things were too good. I was too happy, and I'd never been this happy before.

I was in New York on business when the call came through. I hopped on a flight and landed back in Atlanta at noon. I took an Uber straight to the hospital.

My entire family was there, including Uncle Walter, Aunt Vivica's husband. That was the first sign that things must be really bad.

"Gram's what happened? Is Papa ok?" I rushed into the room asking questions.

The forlorn faces in the room made me nervous. When Devin called me in tears about Papa having a heart attack, I was on pins and needles to get back. Papa was doing so well with taking his medicine and eating healthier. What happened?

"What is she doing here?" Aunt Jo yelled.

What was she talking about? Why wouldn't I be there?

"You and your whorish ways!" Aunt Vivica shouted. "Get out of here, you tramp. This is all your fault."

"What the hell are you talking about?"

"This came in the mail today." Devin stood, handing me a Manilla envelope. I looked around the room at the sad and hostile faces before opening the envelope to see what was hidden inside. I slid all the content out. A yellow paper with rushed scribbled handwriting greeted me.

It's time you saw the type of woman you raised.

I quickly flipped the note to the back of the pile to look at the stack of pictures in my hand. I gasped at what I saw. They were action shots from my bedroom of me in different sexual positions. So many different men ranging from dark to light skin. From business professionals, politicians, to blue collar workers. My taste was all across the board. After the first twenty photos, I stuck the pictures back in the package with shaking hands.

I looked up to my Grams and there were unshed tears in her eyes. I'd never been ashamed of what I did. After the situation with my uncle, I dealt with a lot of emotional scars. I felt unworthy and unclean for so long. At one time I wanted to die, but I refused to let them win that way. I fought to gain control of my life, but it wasn't just my life that I felt needed the control. My body needed it just as much.

I started out just trying to erase the taint of his touch. For so long after I moved back in with my grandparents, I constantly felt the ghost of him. It drove me crazy. So I started to sleep around, anything to erase the memory of my uncle. I always had my rules; no kissing, no pet names, no holding me down, and no I love you. Everything my uncle did to me, he said he did it out of love. I wanted nothing that would remind me of him. After a while I started to feel more in control. So I started demanding more control. I made sure that every man I was with was because I wanted it. They didn't get to call me, I called them. I asked for it. I told them what I wanted and how I wanted it, I was always in control. Soon I started to crave that power I got during sex.

Sex was my therapy. This was my body and I had a right to do with it as I pleased. That right was taken away from me for ten years. I was owed my sexual freedom.

However, as I saw the unshed tears in my Grandmother's eyes, and I watch the disgust written on her face, I started to feel regret.

"Daddy found these whorish pictures, and it gave him have a heart attack." Vivica yelled.

Everyone's hostility towards me was starting to make sense.

"If he dies, it's all your fault!" Aunt Jo added as she buried her face in Uncle Kenny's shoulder.

"I told you, Mama. I told you that girl was a problem."

"It's not like I sent the goddamn pictures." I said in my defense.

I understood everyone's anger. Hell, I was angry too, but they're acting like I gave Papa the pictures.

"There shouldn't even be pictures." Aunt Vivica stated throwing her hands up in the air.

"Calm down, Viv." Uncle Walter pleaded stepping up to my side and placing a hand on my shoulder. "Duck's a victim too."

I still didn't understand why Papa and Uncle Walter couldn't get along. This man had always been nice to me. Often times treating me like I was Devin or Chante.

"How dare you." Aunt Vivica screeched. She glared at Uncle Walter like he had committed the greatest sin ever. "Don't you dare defend her in front of me."

Uncle Walter slowly removed his hand from my shoulder and stepped away from me.

"Well, I'll defend her." Eli said coming to my side. "It's not her fault."

Aunt Vivica glared at me with her nose turned up. "She's just like her mother. It's never their fault no matter whose lives they destroy."

"Don't you ever compare me to her." My anger made my voice cold.

If Vivica knew how close she was to needing this damn hospital, she wouldn't open her mouth again.

I was nothing like Nita.

"Oh, but it's true! That bitch spread her legs to everything moving and you are no different."

I took a step towards my aunt and Eli held up a hand to block me.

"Fuck you, Vivica! You don't know shit about me or my mother."

"You little disrespectful…."

"Enough!" Grams finally spoke bringing the escalating fight back down.

She turned her eyes to me and glared. "I told you that your lifestyle would come back to bite you in the butt one day. Now I let you get by once without telling me what's going on, but not now. You tell me what's going on Charlice."

"Gram's I can handle it…"

"I SAID ENOUGH!"

I'd never heard Grams yell like that, especially not to me.

"You tell me what's going on, and you tell me right now, Bernita." She gasped the moment she realized the mistake she made.

She could have smacked me and it would have hurt less.

"I'm so sorry, Charlice. I didn't mean…."

"Mama don't apologize to that tramp."

"Hey! That's enough." Devin came to my defense. "Daddy is right, Duck didn't send the pictures. No need to all gang up on her. We need to come together for Papa."

"Exactly!" Eli stated in agreement.

"Typical." Keva said. "You two are always making excuses for her. This is her fault. We've told her many times about her ways."

"Facts." Keisha added.

That was what did it for me. I was so sick and tired of my family treating me like I was the only person with shit going on. Like I was the black sheep of the family. I took the credit for being a hoe. Yes, I liked the power I got when having sex. But that did not make me a bad person. That did not allow anyone to turn up their nose in judgement of me. If they wanted to point fingers, then it was time I started pointing some back.

"So I'm the only one here with issues I guess?"

As always, Keva was the first one to open her mouth. "Duck, no one is truly without sin. We all have come short of God's love, but our sins just aren't as big as yours. Your body is a temple, you should keep it undefiled."

"Like you, right Keva?"

Keva had the nerve to blush. "Yes! I took my virginity seriously. I gave my husband the gift of my pureness on our marriage night."

I laughed at that. "You know what's sad, I think you've told that lie so much even you believe it."

Aunt Jo looked over to Keva. "What is she talking about?"

Keva was watching me hard, she's hoping I didn't know what I did.

"It's alright, mama Jo." Roy said getting to his fat ass feet. "Now I can attest to what Keva says. Duck is just lying to save herself."

"You're right Roy. I guess she would have still been a virgin when you had her, it's not like your first actually had a dick, right Keva? How is Tracey now a days? Do you still keep in touch after you two munched each other's carpets all through High school?"

The entire room gasped.

"OOOOOOHHHH!" Keisha sung covering her mouth.

Keva's eyes got so wide I was shocked they didn't fall out of her head.

"How.....Who..."

"Tracey." I answered the question she couldn't get out. "She told me all about it. She was heartbroken when you called it off, she wanted me to talk to you."

"Wait a minute, are you talking about that little white girl that use to come over to the house all the time? I know that's not what ya'll was up in that room doing? Not in my house!" Aunt Joe's face was scrunched up in disgust.

"Definitely in your house." I confirmed. "Tell me, Keva, did you guys reconnect when she was here a few months ago?"

Keva covered her mouth with her hands.

I'd always been really good with making friends when I needed to be. Especially when the person I'm being friends with had a secret on my family. I never knew when I'd need to step in on my family's behalf. That's why Tracey couldn't wait to contact me to tell me how she was coming to town and had planned to see Keva.

"That's disgusting." Aunt Jo shouted. "What do you think those people are going to say down at the church when they find out about this?"

Keva buried her face in her hands and started sobbing.

"Oh stop, Aunt Jo! Don't act like you're innocent. Did you ever tell the people at the church that you aborted your fourth child because you didn't know if it was Uncle Kenny's?"

Apparently Aunt Jo and I went to the same lady. I heard the woman telling mama all about it at one of my god awful visits.

"What the fuck!" Uncle Kenny yelled.

"Please," I rolled my eyes at him. "Wasn't like you could afford another kid anyway. Not with those two side children you got out in Augusta."

Aunt Jo gasped and turned to Uncle Kenny.

"Daddy is that true?" Keisha squealed.

Uncle Kenny opened his mouth and reclosed it like a fish.

Keisha turned to me and narrowed her eyes. "You're a bitch."

I chuckled. "Absolutely. And since we're on the subjects of bitches, do you even know who this baby's daddy is?"

Her current boyfriend shot to his feet and stared down at her.

"Shut up, Duck!" Keisha screamed.

"Why? Are you afraid I'll tell your sister that you're fucking her husband and that this new addition may be his?"

Roy opened his mouth, ready to deny it when everyone turned to him.

"Don't even," I said shutting him up. "I've kept your secrets all these years, never judging either of you. Yet all you did was turn your noses up at me like I'm the dirty one."

"Just because you know a few secrets doesn't mean you're still not a whore."

"What the fuck did you just call my cousin?" Eli took a step towards Quincy, but this time I held him back.

I caught Chante's eyes. I wasn't doing this to hurt anyone, I just wanted them to see what I'd done for them. The measures I'd taken for them.

I was the one that talked Tracey out of crashing Keva's wedding. I made sure that Nita didn't tell Grams about Aunt Jo's abortion. I stopped Kenny Sr.'s side chick from putting him up for child support. I knew a guy that worked in the court house that told me when she filed the papers. That's how I found out about them. I'd done more for my family than they will ever know. So when I watch Chante's eyes, I watch for any sign that she might not be able to handle the truth I was about to drop on her.

When her eyes narrowed at me, I realized, maybe she was ready.

I turned back to Quincy. "I think everyone knows I'm not the only whore in this room, Quincy. How many times have I had to delete your unsolicited dick pics from my phone?"

"What the fuck?" Eli roared.

"Are you sleeping with Chante's husband?" Aunt Vivica accused.

I laughed. "Hell no! But I'm probably one of the only females in the state that isn't. Not that Chante would care anyway, she's too doped up on pain pills to feel anything."

This time the entire room gasped. Even Quincy seemed surprised at that information.

"That's enough, Duck!" Grams said drawing my attention back to her. If I thought she was disappointed in me before, she looked completely disgusted in me now. "You have done enough for today."

"Have I really?" I sneered. "Because I can keep going."

Grams shook her head at me. "There is no pride in hurting your family."

"I hurt them?" I gawked at her words.

Could she really stand here and tell me that I'm wrong?

"Look at them, Charlice! You humiliated them for your own gain."

I actually stopped to look around the small hospital waiting room. It was mostly filled with my family, but there were four other people here with us. Everyone in my family was either in tears or angry. Maybe I went about it wrong, maybe I shouldn't have blew up on them like this, but where was all this concern when I was the one being attacked.

"My apologies, Grams. I know how you like your secrets. Buried and forgotten, right?" I said to her.

Grams looked at me confused.

"I'll do you all a favor, from here on out, just forget I existed."

"Duck!" Devin called after me as I stormed out of the hospital. I climbed on the elevator and closed the doors before Devin and Eli could get to me. The moment the doors closed the tears fell, and they didn't stop.

**

"Babe!" I heard Jackson's voice call me as he climbed the stairs.

My brain was so muddled I could barely make out anything. The cold floor and white ceiling stared back at me in a blurry haze.

"Char! Oh my god!" Jackson was in the bathroom with me now. He came into view and I blinked my watery eyes up at him.

"Hey, Jackson." I smiled.

"Baby, don't move. Are you hurt?"

Funny he asked that question. I didn't hurt anymore. I did feel pain earlier, ugly searing pain in my chest, but I felt wonderful now.

"I feel better." I laughed.

I didn't really know why I was laughing.

Jackson moved away from me and disappeared. I heard water running from somewhere. I tried to sit up, but the room spun. I grabbed for the toilet and emptied my stomach.

"Damn it!" Jackson shouted. He grabbed my hair and held it back. "Fuck, Char! It's all in your hair."

What was in my hair? Once I finished throwing up I leaned my head on my toilet seat. Jackson must had flushed the toilet, because I could hear the water swishing around the bowl.

"I'm going to put you in the tub and then clean up this mess."

I finally got my eyes to focus on the room, it wasn't an easy task. I was in my bathroom and it was a mess. Red splotches rained down my all white surfaces. What the hell? I looked down and found a shattered bottle of Merlot on the ground. That explained the red stuff on the walls. Also on the floor, was an empty bottle of tequila. I got a glimpse of a memory. I grabbed the bottle of Tequila when I realized the bottle of wine wouldn't help me forget what happened today. I didn't remember much after that. Also amongst the mess was a pile of vomit near the trash can and another at my feet by the toilet. That pile was smeared, and I was pretty sure it's what I was smelling and feeling all over me.

I burst into tears.

"Aw, Baby, don't cry. I got you."

Jackson lifted me up, sitting on the side of the tub, he placed me in his lap. He helped me undress before lifting me in the warm bubble bath. I sunk down into the warm water allowing the heat to help clear my head. Jackson busies himself around my bathroom cleaning up my mess. When he came back upstairs after sweeping all the glass off the floor and mopping up my vomit he was on the phone.

"Yeah, I'm here, Devin. No, she's not doing well." He paused. "I'm going to take care of her, no need to worry about her." Another pause. "No, I'm glad you called. You can call me anytime. I do have one question. She's made a mess of her hair. A real mess. How do I take it out?"

He walked out of the bathroom after that. When he came back he had a pair of scissors in his hands and a grocery bag. He was no longer on the phone.

Jackson pulled up a chair behind me in the tub and started to part my hair.

"Talk to me, Char. What happened?"

His fingers in my hair was so relaxing. I pulled my knees to my chest and closed my eyes.

"Did you know that my mama didn't want me?" I asked, but I didn't expect to get a response and he didn't give it. "She was only fifteen when I was born and she wanted to abort me, but Grams and

Papa wouldn't let her. Can you imagine that? She hated me so much that she wanted to get rid of me before she even met me. She didn't even name me. She had nine months to come up with a name and she didn't even care enough to do that. Papa had to name me. When the nurse put me in his arms he came up with the name Charlice Rose. Charlice after him and Rose for my Grams." I fought the sob that tried to come up. I was tired of crying. "There aren't any pictures of her holding me. All the pictures I have of my childhood was either Grams or Papa holding me. Bernita told me often how much she didn't want me. I still tried to be the perfect daughter. I thought if I was good enough, she would love me, but it didn't work.

I asked her one time, why she let him hurt me? I asked her why she couldn't love me enough to make him stop. You know what she said?" Another question I didn't expect him to answer. "She told me that she was molested when she was eleven by my grandfather's best friend and when she finally built up enough strength to tell, Grams told her to never mention it again. Nita said nobody cared about her, so why should she care about me. And it was my fault anyway, I was seducing him." At this I gave a dry laugh.

I could feel Jackson's nimble fingers removing the braids Devin placed in under my weave. It felt so good that I kept talking.

"I've always thought that maybe, some way, she was right. Somehow I was seducing him. I mean, half of my family hated me and I didn't even know why. I had to obviously be doing something to make my aunts dislike me, and my mother not want me. So maybe I was doing something to turn him on. Do you know what it's like to grow up in a family where you felt unwanted? I always had my grandparents and Eli, but when you're young, you don't focus on those that do care, all you see are the ones that don't. That's why I've always kept their secrets. I just wanted to fit in with them. I'd do anything for my family. I've cleaned up their messes without ever bringing it up or throwing it in their faces. When Aunt Jo and Uncle Kenny was about to lose their house, I'm the one that paid the back taxes so they could keep it. When Uncle Walter was diagnosed with prostate Cancer two years ago, I paid to get him in the early medical trial that saved his life. I pay medical bills, school tuition, I provide jobs, homes, and anything they need, all they've ever had to do was ask. And I've done it all without any notion of ever being paid back, because all I wanted from them was to not feel unwanted."

I hated the tears that fell down my face. I hated that at thirty-three I was still feeling the pains of that six year old little girl lying in her own blood wondering why her uncle made her hurt. Why no one took the time to look at me and tell I was hurting, or that I needed help.

I let the sobs shake my body as I continued to cry. Jackson never spoke a word. He bathed my body and washed my hair. Devin must have given him some really great advice because he even separated it in four uneven parts and plaited it. I was looking extremely unattractive at the moment. My eyes were puffy and dark from alcohol and crying. My hair had me looking like an extra in The Color Purple, and my skin was dry from sitting in the bathtub too long.

Jackson pulled back the covers to help me climb into my bed. Once he got me settled, he slid in bed beside me and wrapped me in his arms. My head laid on his chest as I curled my body into his side, my leg thrown across his thigh.

"Your grandfather is doing fine. The doctors said it wasn't a heart attack, that it was most likely an anxiety attack."

I sighed. "God, I'm the worse granddaughter ever. I didn't even think to check on him."

Jackson chuckled. "A lot happened today. Besides, Devin has been keeping me informed."

"Devin?" I said looking up at him. "How did she get your number anyway?"

"From Kylie." Jackson laughed. "When they were staying here, Kylie was watching YouTube on my phone and apparently sent Devin a text."

I laughed, that sneaky little girl. Once the laughter died down I could tell Jackson wanted to say something else. It was crazy how much I could read him now. I could tell by the way he was aimlessly rubbing my back that he had something on his mind.

I finally asked, "What?"

"I want to see the pictures."

"No!" I said rolling away from him.

He grabbed me and pulled me back down, before climbing on top of me sinking between my legs.

"I know you have a past. It does not intimidate me, I just want to check something."

"Check what?"

"Let me see them, Char?"

I stared into his eyes for a moment, trying to see if this was a good idea or not. I was pretty sure it wasn't, but the day couldn't get any worse.

"Nightstand, top drawer. Brown envelope."

Jackson placed a kiss on my lips and lifted from the bed. He sat on the side of the bed and fetched the pictures out of the drawer. I lied on my back and covered my face with the pillow, he was not going to like them.

"Damn, you weren't kidding when you said you didn't date white guys."

I groaned. "Can we not talk about my lack of variety....."

"Hold on!" Jackson said climbing from the bed.

I lifted the pillow and stared up at him, that tone in his voice startled me.

"What's wrong?" Jackson stared down at the pictures and then over the bed. He moved around the bed and faced me.

"These pictures are all from your bedroom."

"Yeah, I know."

"Did you take them?"

"What? No, why the hell would I take these pictures?"

Jackson walked to my wall where my sorority wall art was hanging. He turned to look at the bed and down at the pictures in his hand again, then he turned back to the framed picture on the wall. He took the picture down and flipped it over.

"Jackson, what are you…"

When Jackson pulled up the small black device from the back of my picture I was shocked. A muthafuckin camera. Ok, this shit was out of control.

"Grab your stuff." Jackson said stuffing the camera in his pocket.

I didn't argue, I jumped off the bed and grabbed a Louis travel bag out of my closet and started tossing things in the bag. I loved my house, but I was at the point where I was ready to sell this goddamn house and call it a day. I thought when Cliff wrecked my house, I would never feel comfortable here again. But this took the cake. I was shaking while I packed my bag. When I finally had enough stuff to last me, Jackson grabbed my hands and ushered me out of the room.

"I have a friend from the military that specializes in this type of stuff. I'll get him here to sweep the house before you can come back."

When we made it to the front door he turned to look at me cupping my face in his hands. My body was still shaking.

"I'm done waiting on the police to fix this shit, Char. I'm not taking any more risk with you. You don't stay anywhere without me, do you understand?"

I nodded my head vigorously. He led me out to his truck and we sped away from my house.

TWENTY-SIX

This was the longest I'd ever gone without seeing my family. It's been two weeks since that incident in the hospital. Despite my phone ringing off the hook, I refused to speak to anyone. I really was done.

Eli sent me one text since that day that simply said, "I'm here when you're ready." That had me crying again because it was Eli, and he has always known what I needed. Devin has not got the memo, and she has resorted to calling Jackson. He informed her that I was alright and that I just needed time.

In the meantime, I'd been spending all my time with him.

"Woman, why the hell are you cleaning again?" He asked the question as I walked in front of his television with my broom and dustpan.

"I think I'm going to bake a cake." I replied instead of answering his question.

I haven't been back to my house since we found the cameras. Jackson's friend came three days ago and did a sweep of the house but found nothing. He told Jackson that Cliff most likely knew that we had one of the cameras and came back to collect the others. They took the camera we found to get information off of it, but Cliff wiped the information. Only thing they could tell us was that it was working, and someone had been servicing it. I was given the ok to go back home, but I didn't want to. I liked being here with Jackson. I didn't know I would enjoy it so much. I'd never really shared space with anyone since I got my own place in college.

Lately, I'd been constantly moving, trying to stay busy. Grams use to say idle hands were the devil's workshop. So I figured, if I stayed busy, I didn't have time to think about all the shit I had going on.

Jackson looked up at me from his position on the couch. I was wearing nothing but one of his shirts and some rubber gloves. My hair was still in its natural form because I obviously hadn't been to Devin's to get it done, so right now it was in a large afro puff at the top of my head.

"You." Jackson paused to make a point. "The person that almost burnt the house down three days ago while boiling an egg, is going to bake a cake?"

I place my hands on my hips. "Hey, you are the one that wanted to fuck me against the kitchen counter, it's your fault the water boiled out."

Jackson laughed and climbed to his feet placing his beer bottle down on the table in front of him. He stepped in front of me, took the broom and dustpan out of my hands and leaned it on the wall behind me. He then pulled me into his lips for a kiss.

"You know I love you right?" He said as I wrapped my arms around his neck and pushed up on my tiptoes to get another kiss.

"Yes, I know, Mr. Keller."

He chuckled. "So you know it's from love that I say, please don't make me eat your cake."

I laughed and smacked his chest.

"Shut up! I have been doing a lot better with cooking."

We'd continued the cooking classes and I could officially make a full breakfast without anything burning, with the exception of the boiled egg situation. However, in my defense, when you're getting the dick as good as Jackson was giving it, you didn't mind a little house fire.

"Yeah baby, you're doing better, but not bake a cake better."

I tossed my head back and laughed, when I'm done Jackson was smiling at me.

"What?" I asked.

"I love your laugh."

"You love everything about me."

He smiled showing me those dimples. "I do. I especially love your tasty pussy, and the face you make when I sink my dick inside those tight wet walls." He said the words like a stroke against my nipples.

"Is that all you love about me, Mr. Keller? Just my pussy?"

Another flash of dimples. "No! I love the faces you make in the morning while you're putting on your make-up. I love that you sing every song that comes on the radio. I love the way your nose scrunches up when you're angry and the way you curl into a ball when you sleep. I even love your little snore."

I rolled my eyes and laughed.

Jackson kept going. "I love how you ask me a million questions while we watch something for the first time, as if I'll have the answer. I even love your inability to correctly place a roll of toilet paper on the holder." I burst out laughing and he did too.

We finally calmed down and Jackson just stared in my eyes. "Charlice Rose, I love so many things about you. Things I find new every day. Your strength, your heart, your giving nature, and your ability to keep going. I love you, Char."

"Awww, I love you too!"

"Then marry me!"

If this were a movie or a tv show, this was where the record would scratch. It's where the sappy love music would stop and reality would step in. However, this isn't a movie. There wasn't going to be a cut scene where we left the audience with the unanswered question. No, in this reality, hazel eyes were watching me with so much intensity I couldn't look away from him.

"Jackson. Whoa!" I said stepping away from him. "We've only known each other for a few months."

"So," He said with a shrug. "I've dated girls for years, and I've never felt the way I feel about you. From the moment you stepped out of your car that day I knew you were meant to be mine. I thought about you all day long. I won't say it was love at first sight, but I will say I knew there was something about you. After that robbery, I promised myself to never sit by and let life run over me. I realized as I sat in that court house waiting for them to either give me prison or send me on my way, that I would never allow life to go by without living it to its fullest. That's why I chased you, that's why I fought so hard for your heart, because I knew you were always meant to be mine. I don't need a certain amount of time to tell me you are it for me. I just want to marry you."

Damn it, now I was on the verge of crying again. Jackson didn't need beautiful sonnets or poems to make me melt for him. It was the realness it his voice, the truth in his eyes that made whatever he said so much more.

I'd never wanted to get married. Not even when I was a little girl before my life was ruined and love became a nightmare. I knew I wanted kids, but never did those fantasies include a husband. Then after that started, I didn't think any of this was possible. Not for me. It really did feel good to know what love felt like. Jackson was able to take something so tainted for me, and turn it into something beautiful. He was able to love me so good, it erased the pain in my past. I no longer feared love or thought I didn't deserve it. He rescued me from myself and taught me that I deserved him.

"OK." I find myself saying the word.

Jackson's eyes widen. "Ok as in?" he asked again as if he needed to make sure I said it.

I laughed through my tears. "Yes!"

He picked me up and spun me around.

This wasn't one of those romantic proposals that are recorded and liked on YouTube. No dance number with surprised guest or singers. It was just us, but it was perfect. Two broken and damaged people finding love where love was once lost for them.

Jackson finally planted me on my feet. I raised up on my toes and kiss him with all my heart. I poured into Jackson everything he had made me feel over the last seven months. Safe, happy, sexy, special, adored, and loved, I wrapped it all in this one kiss and gave it back to him. His heavy hands slid up the side of my thighs, pushing up my shirt. He pulled away from the kiss just enough to yank the shirt over my head, my rubber gloves came off with it. Jackson took a second to stare down at me. My dark brown skin on full display for him. He shook his head in awe as he backed me up to the side of the couch, sitting me down on the arm. He got to his knees and opened my thighs placing them on his shoulder. Jackson was never slow when it came to eating my pussy, he dived in as if he was afraid someone would snatch it from him. He sucked my folds into his mouth and slid his tongue inside me.

"Jackson!" I moaned his name as I buried my fingers in his short hair.

His tongue worked my clit and I rode his face. He ate me out until my legs quivered and I was screaming his name. After planting wet kisses on my thighs, he stood to his feet. His hardened dick was standing at full mast in his baller shorts. He pushed his shorts and boxers down kicking out of them and yanked his shirt up. I got to my knees in front of him and wrapped my lips around his dick. I loved giving Jackson head. I enjoyed it so much because he loved it. He was so verbal when I was sucking his dick to the back of my throat.

"Fuck, Char! That shits so fucking good." He groaned and threw his head back as I took him to the back of my throat.

I moaned around him when I tasted his salty precum on my tongue. The vibrations caused Jackson to curse under his breath, his fisted hands lifted to his head. I used my hands to pump him a few times as I slurped on his dick. Jackson, grunted and slid out of my mouth with a pop.

"Fuck that, I need to be in your pussy, baby."

I laughed as he pulled me to my feet then leaned me back against the arm of the couch, spreading my legs in a wide V. He bent his knees slightly and surged into me.

"Ahhhhhh!" I yelled at his abrupt entrance. He stretched my walls so good every time.

"No Condom?" I breathlessly asked. He was riding me hard and fast, I sounded like I had been running a marathon and we had just started.

He shook his head. "Nothing between us anymore. This shit is mine. I want to feel your walls wrapped around my dick from here on out."

Shit that made me wetter.

Jackson must had realized it too, because he sped up. Pushing into me like he was on a mission. My back was on the seat cushion of the couch and my ass was on the arm, at this angle he was diving straight to the back of my pussy and it felt so amazing. I screamed for Jackson to keep going, to fuck me harder.

He was up for the challenge. Jackson placed an arm under my back lifting me up. With my thighs over his forearms, he stood straight up. I wrapped my arms around his neck while he bounced me up and down on his dick. His large work hardened hands gripped my ass cheeks as he powered into me from below. My moans and wet pussy serenaded the room.

Damn, I didn't think he could get any deeper inside me. And to think, he was going to be my husband. The man I would get to do this with for the rest of my life. Just the thought had me coming. I tossed my head back and cried out as my orgasm rocked me. My pussy squirted my essence all down Jackson's shaft.

"Gotdamn, Baby, your shit is so fucking good." Jackson growled as my wet walls clenched around his bare dick.

I was spent. My body went limp against his chest, and this point Jackson was doing all the work. He placed a kiss against my sweaty forehead as he carried me back over to the couch, still inside my contracting walls. He took a seat and allowed me to straddle him. I placed my forehead to his and he lifted my ass and rocked into me.

"I love you, so fucking much." He admitted in a whisper.

"I love you too." I whimpered as my orgasm started to build back up.

I was finally able to move again on my own accord, grinding my hot pussy down onto his lap, moving my hips like I was hula hooping.

"That's it, Char. Ride this dick, baby." His head hit the back of the couch as I took over.

I planted my hands by his head on the couch and started to lift my hips and drop down with a swirl.

He smacked my ass and I purred for him, kissing his lips and sucking his tongue like I would his dick. I felt his body tense underneath me, signaling his release. The sweat was beading on his forehead. Jackson could hold off an orgasm for forever. He usually would only allow himself to come if I'd had at least four orgasms first. Which I loved, but that's not what I wanted right now.

I moved faster on him, grinding my hips. "Let go, Jackson. Give me what I want. Come inside your fiancée."

That did it! He roared his release, his hot semen bathed my walls as he folded in on himself wrapping his arms around me. He held me tight to his chest as he continued to pump into me from beneath.

When his orgasm finally faded, he continued to hold me to him. Our heartbeats were synched as we caught our breaths. Jackson stroked my sweaty back.

"Anytime I've ever gotten good news, I always called my Grams first. When I got accepted into Emory and Harvard. When I pledged my sorority. Even when I got my first client. I've always called Sadie Rose to share my excitement. On the day I have the best news to share, I can't call her."

"Yes you can." He said as his hands made slow circles on my

back. "Just call her."

I looked up into Jackson's hazel eyes as he stared down at me.

"You didn't see the look on her face." I explained. "She saw those pictures, and she took their side. They don't want me around, Jackson. You're the only one that wants me." I closed my eyes and listened to his steady breathing.

Jackson didn't say anything else. He just held me in his arms, exactly where I wanted to stay forever.

***

"Ms. Jefferies, your two o'clock is here." My secretary Patricia said through the speaker phone.

I pushed the intercom button. "Thank you, Patricia. Send him in."

"I'll get that information back to you before the end of the day." Paula, one of my employees said as they all stood to head out of my office.

"Make sure that you do." I scolded her lightly as I escorted her out of my office.

Troy gave me a silent nod. He knew I was pissed about this meeting. Thankfully, I was still on a high from Jackson proposing.

I smiled as my two o'clock appointment walked into my office.

"Detective Myers, how are you!" I greeted Sean with a kiss on the cheek.

I was dying to tell someone about my engagement. It had only been a day since Jackson popped the big question. He hadn't exactly given me a ring yet, but I didn't care. We had talked about what we wanted in a wedding. The only preference Jackson had was that we did it as soon as possible. I believe he thought I would change my mind, I wouldn't.

Since I'd never really dreamed of getting married in the first place, I didn't really have any ideas either. I didn't care for a big wedding, especially since I wasn't talking to my family. I would even go to the court house, but Jackson didn't want that. He said since we were only doing it once, we might as well make it special.

I grabbed Sean's hand and lead him to the small sitting area.

"Damn, girl! What's got you so excited!" he took a seat and I sat down beside him.

"Well, I have some very exciting news and you're pretty much my only friend, so I wanted to share it with you first."

Other than Devin, Sean was my only other friend. Despite our sexual relationship, we had a close bond.

"So what's this big news?"

I grinned as I took a moment to build up the momentum.

"I'm getting married!"

Sean blinked a few times as if his mind had completely blacked out. I waited for him to say something.

"Umm, Sean you ok?"

He shook his head. "Sorry, I blinked out." He said with a laugh. "So, you're serious? You're actually considering marrying this guy?"

"Yeah! I mean I never thought I would get married, but Jackson is different. I love him."

Another stare down from Sean.

"And he still wants to marry you without you being able to have kids?"

I was a little thrown off by his question. Sean knew I couldn't have kids, he of course didn't know why, but he made it sound like me not having kids should have been a deal breaker.

"Yeah, he understands and is ok with it."

He shook his head and stood to his feet.

"You haven't even known him long? What if he's crazy? What if he's using you?"

I shot to my feet. "I've known him long enough, and I would know if he's crazy."

"Like you knew with Cliff?"

My head snapped back like I'd been slapped. I expected Sean to be happy for me. Maybe a little disappointed that he and I could no longer hook up, but I didn't expect him to be like this.

"I'll admit, Cliff was a surprise, but Jackson is nothing like Cliff."

"Are you so sure? Do you know he was on trial for murder? A sixteen year old black kid was stabbed to death because of him."

I was already shaking my head. "He was not involved. In fact he was acquitted and all charges were dropped."

"Is that what he told you?" Sean laughed and threw his hands up.

"That's what I know." I stated folding my arms over my chest.

My good mood was gone and now I was pissed. First of all, how dare he ask me all these goddamn questions about my life decisions? What I decided to do had shit to do with him. Secondly, why the fuck was he looking into Jackson's background.

I asked him that last question.

"Because someone has to look out for you, Charli." Sean said stepping towards me. "You are my best friend, I'll do anything for you. I don't think marrying this guy is a good idea."

I stepped away from Sean and headed to the door. "As I've said before, I don't need anyone to look out for me. And I definitely don't need you to tell me what I should do." I grabbed my door and held it open for him. "I told you this news because I thought you were my friend. Clearly, some lines has crossed. You need to leave."

Sean stood in his spot for a moment too long, like he had no plans of leaving, but then he walked over and stood in front of me.

"I'm sorry. And you're right. If he makes you happy, Charli, then...... I just want you happy."

He planted a kiss on my cheek and headed out of the door. I closed it behind him.

Although it didn't go as planned, I was still happy about my decision to marry Jackson.

***

That afternoon I hung my keys on the hook as I walked into Jackson's kitchen from the garage.

"Babe! Let's do Thai tonight for dinner." I said heading towards the living room looking down at my phone. "I'm in the mood for Pho...." My words died down when I looked up from my phone to find my grandparents sitting on the couch where just yesterday I fucked Jackson.

Jackson stood to his feet and walked over to me.

"What's going on?" I asked him. "What are they doing here?"

"I called them, Baby!" I rolled my eyes and turned away from Jackson, but he grabbed my arm and turned me back to face him. "I couldn't ask you to marry me without asking your grandfather too, and we can't plan a wedding without the most important people in your life there. I'm sorry if I upset you, but you need to work this out with your family."

"You had no right, Jackson." I yanked away from him. "I told you I wasn't ready."

"Char…"

"No!" I said interrupting him. "You are out of……"

"That's enough, Duck!" Grams scolded cutting me off. "Now you stop carrying on like that. This man cared enough about you to reach out to us in order to fix this mess between us. Now you are going to sit your tail down in that seat, and talk to us."

I crossed my hands over my chest defiantly, but I sat down in the chair.

"I should go…." Jackson announced.

"No, son!" My Papa said towards Jackson. "You're family now. You need to stay here and hear this."

Jackson nodded his head and sat down in the chair across from me. I avoided his eyes. Despite what Grams said, I was still pissed at him.

"Now I heard what happened at the hospital." Papa started. "And I don't like none of it." He cut his eyes to Grams and then back to me. "And if you would have been around when I heard of it, you would have heard me putting everyone in their place. I don't fault you for what happened. Even if I would have took my last breath that day I would not have blamed you. Look at me." Papa demanded and my watery eyes finally looked at him.

The disappointment and disgust I planned to see on his face was absent. He didn't look at me like the others or Grams that day. He looked at me like he always had. Like I was the little girl that waddled behind him like a little duck every day.

"Don't hold your head down or hide your eyes from me. You could never disappoint me, Duck. I know that's what you thought. The family made you feel that way, and that's not right. Family isn't perfect. We are flawed, problematic, and we don't always agree. Sometimes we hold grudges against people that don't deserve it. People that have no fault in the hurtful act that was done. And honestly, I am going to take blame for that. I let secrets stay buried too long and ignored the rot that started to fester. I couldn't see how it was infecting the family. My pride wouldn't let me fix it. But, I've since done the right thing."

"What are you talking about, Papa? What secret?"

Papa shook his head. "I plan on telling you all about it at family dinner Sunday."

I was already shaking my head. I was not going to family dinner.

"NO!"

"No?" Papa repeated.

"Charles, how about you let Jackson show you that back yard you been talking about. Let me have a minute with Duck."

Papa looked over to Grams for a moment, but then nodded his head. Jackson and Papa stood to their feet.

"Right this way, Mr. Jefferies." Jackson said showing my Papa to the sliding glass door.

"Call me Charles or Pop." Papa smiled at Jackson.

Jackson nodded his head as they both disappeared out of the door.

"He's nice." Grams voice brought my attention back to her. "And fiiinnee." She sung the last part.

I smiled briefly, but turned away from her.

She continued. "But most importantly, he loves you. That boy wear his heart outside his chest for you. He looks at you the way Papa use to look at me."

I didn't comment that Papa still looked at her that way. The room remained quiet. I didn't know what Grams thought was going to come out of this, but I was sure it wasn't this.

Finally Grams sighed. "You're not your mother, Duck."

"I know that." I retorted angrily.

Grams held up her hands in surrender.

"Ok!" she said with a smile. "Well, I'm still going to say sorry."

The room fell back quiet again.

"I knew you had secrets, Duck. I didn't know you had quite that many." She chuckled. "I always assumed that one about your aunt Jo. I remember telling her she looked pregnant one time, and then all of a sudden she didn't. And Kiesha and Roy," She shook her head. "That is just a mess. But that Keva one nearly took me out."

I didn't fight the smile that spread across my face.

"Eli and I laughed about that one for a while."

We were silent again.

"How is everyone doing after...all that? Bet they're still blaming me?"

I knew they were. That's why I hadn't answered any of their calls or messages. I could imagine they thought it was my fault everything came out.

Grams shrugged her shoulders. "Not really. Everyone knows that what's done in the dark eventually comes to the light. It was never your job to be the family secret keeper, in the first place."

"I know." I admitted.

"Duck, you have to learn that family will fuss and fall out. We will disagree and judge and be ugly towards one another, but at the end of the day, we have each other's backs. You know why?"

"Why?"

"Because life is too short, and there is nothing worth falling out with your family forever over."

For the first time I looked my grandmother in the eye.

"I don't know about that Grams. There are somethings that just can't be forgiven."

Grams did that thing she always did when she was reading me deep beneath the surface. This time, I didn't hide it. I didn't cover up my truth with an easy smile or a subject change, I displayed my pain directly in my eyes where she could read it. If she would only ask the right question, say the right thing I would tell her everything.

"Well to those things, I would say let the Lord handle it."

Just like that, I shut down. I wrapped my pain back up in my perfectly erected façade and smiled.

"Alright, Sadie! Let's give these young folks back their house." Papa announced walking back into the living room followed by Jackson.

Grams and I both got to our feet. I stepped into Jackson's open arms and wrapped my hands around his middle. He dropped a kiss on my forehead.

"I'm sorry! I just wanted you to be happy." Jackson whispered.

I looked up at him with a small smile. He tilted his head to the side and narrowed his eyes. He knew something was bothering me.

"It's ok. Thank you!"

"Well now!" Papa said interrupting our moment. "I gave Jackson my approval for this marriage. And he told me he promises to have you at the house for Sunday dinner."

"Did he really?" I asked cutting my eyes to Jackson.

"It's going to be a big deal this Sunday. We need you to be there. We're getting the family together to hash out the mess I've made." Papa smiled over at Grams. "Now come here little Duck and give me a hug. I've gone too long without one."

I obliged with the biggest smile on my face. Just like when I was a little girl, Papa's hugs had the ability to cure anything.

Papa wrapped me in his arms and kissed the top of my head.

"I like him." He whispered in my ear. "You did well."

That night I slept fitfully. My nightmares were back. That should have been a sign of what was to come.

TWENTY-SEVEN

"You look like you're going to vomit." Jackson mentioned as we pulled up to my grandparents' house.

The driveway was already full with my family's cars. Looks like everyone was already here. A new Cadillac was parked behind Papa's truck. Probably the Pastor again.

"I have a bad feeling about this." I turned back to find Jackson smiling at me. "What?"

He chuckled. "I'm sorry, but remember that day at my parent's house? You laughed at my nerves."

"I shouldn't have." I grunted. "You see how that turned out right?"

Since I sent the picture of Mouse at the bar to Jackson, a lot of the pressure from his family died down. His mom even called me to apologize about the whole thing and wanted me to come back for dinner. I told her I would, but we had yet to go back.

Jackson's brother and sister in law was a different story. Both still equally disliked me, and I equally didn't give a shit. Jackson's brother even tried to show up at my job to tell my boss what a disgusting person I was, he nearly shit his pants when they announced he had a meeting with the President of the company and I walked in. His dumbass left my office so fast, you would have thought Satan had walked in instead of me. Since then, he and his annoying ass wife had stayed out of our face.

"This isn't going to be good, Jackson." I pronounced in a somber voice.

He grabbed my hand out of my lap and brought it to his lips to kiss.

"You know there is nothing they can say or do that will change my mind about you. But I really think you need this. Your family is close and they're a big part of you."

I rolled my eyes and he laughed again.

"Ok, how about this, because I made your grandfather a promise, and I am trying to get on his good side so I can marry his granddaughter, we go inside for just a second. If things get uncomfortable, you let me know and we can leave. Deal?"

He gave me a smile and those dimples flashed. I swear his ass could get away with anything as long as he showed me those dimples.

"Fine!" I sighed in surrender. "But you're fucking me all night long as a reward. And none of that let me recuperate shit."

Jackson tossed his head back and let out a hearty laugh.

"You know damn well I don't need to recuperate. I'm going to make you pay for that comment later."

Just the mention of it made me excited.

Jackson opened the door to his truck, but stopped before climbing out. He closed the door and turned back to me. I knew this look. He was nervous about something.

"What's wrong?"

He tugged at his beard, cutting his eyes towards the house and then back to me.

"I want to give you something before we go in, but I don't know how you will feel about it."

This brightened my mood. I liked gifts.

"What is it? Give it to me."

He laughed at my excitement.

"Alright, but if you don't like it, we can look for another one." He reached into his back pocket and pulled out a small red velvet box.

My eyes widened when he opened the box. Sitting on a white cushion, was a rose gold heirloom style diamond ring. Filigree scroll work was carved on the band. One princess cut diamond was in the center and two smaller ones were on the side.

"It was Memaw's. I went by my parents' house to tell them the news, and Memaw wanted me to give you this. She said that the man that gave her this ring, also gave her sixty wonderful years of marriage. She only hopes it gives us the same fortune. I know it's probably smaller than what you can afford, and if you want…."

"I love it!" And I did.

This ring was nothing like the one I helped Sean pick. The diamonds were much smaller on this one, but this ring had more character and meant so much more.

"Are you sure, because I have money saved…."

"Shut up and put my ring on." I teased as I wiggled my fingers at him.

He chuckled as he removed the precious ring out of the box and slid it on my left hand.

It was more beautiful on my finger.

I was so busy starring at my ring, I didn't realize Jackson had climbed out of the car until he opened my door. He helped me down then grabbed my hand and walked me to the porch. He let go of my hand once we reached the door, and cupped my face before bringing his lips to mine giving me a sweet kiss. Just a gentle press of his lips to mine. My body melted into his like it always did when we kiss.

He pulled away and those hazel eyes searched mine.

"What was that for?"

"Because you're incredible, and plus you know I can't go too long without kissing you."

I did in fact know that. I reached up on my tiptoes bringing my lips close to his for another one of his kisses. We got lost in the taste of each other until the front door suddenly swung open.

"Ooooooh, Grams, Duck out here kissing." Keisha yelled back through the house.

Jackson and I pulled away from each other, and I turned to her with a glare. Keisha crossed her arms over protruding belly and stuck her tongue out at me before turning to Jackson with a smile.

"Hey, Jacks!"

How was this bitch going to give my man a damn nickname?

"Come on in and meet the rest of the family." Keisha grabbed Jackson's hand and pulled him into the house.

He gave me a wink before following her in. I shut the front door behind me and exhaled before I followed them.

Keisha led Jackson into the living room where most of the menfolk were sitting. Papa in his favorite chair, Roy and Uncle Kenny were sitting on the short couch. Uncle Kenny looked up at me then cut his eyes to the floor in shame.

Ok! Odd.

Kenny Jr and Uncle Walter were sitting on the long couch next to a man I didn't know.

"Everybody, this is Duck's boyfriend." Keisha introduced Jackson as if she had an inside joke that no one else knew.

Papa climbed out of his chair to greet Jackson and shake his hand. "This isn't Duck's boyfriend." Papa announced with a proud smile. "This is her fiancé."

I smiled and held up my new ring proudly.

Keisha gasped and turned to me with wide eyes. Uncle Walter came over to Jackson and patted him on the back.

"Nice to meet you young man, I'm Walter Perkins, I'm Charlice's fa......." He looked over to me and smiled. "I'm her Uncle."

"Nice to meet you." Jackson greeted, holding out his hand for Uncle Walter to shake.

"Come on and sit down with the men, Jackson."

"Not yet, Papa." Keisha said abruptly. "He has to say hello to Grams first."

Keisha looked toward me and I saw a flash of warning in her eyes. What was she warning me about? I didn't get a chance to ask, because the guy that I'd never seen before walked over to me with a practiced smile. He was dressed like what I'd imagine a modern day pimp would look. He wore a long sleeved powder blue walking suit with matching square toed alligator dress shoes. He looked me up and down, then smiled, showing off a gold tooth.

"Well look at you." He stated. "You look just as good as your mother."

My heart picked up pace. No way. There was no way in hell she was here.

"Well look at my baby!" Bernita's bedroom voice purred.

My mother always had a practiced sexy voice for whenever she was around men. Even if she wasn't using that damn voice, I would still know a man was near. Nita never called me her baby. Probably not even when I was a damn baby.

"Come here, Duck. Let me get a good look at you."

Bernita Lynn Jefferies stood before me in a red silk wrap dress. Her body was still that perfect hourglass shape that she was when she was younger. She was a prime example of how black don't crack.

Flawless golden bronze skin, high cheek bones, upturned eyes, narrow nose, and her hair was cut in beautiful shoulder length curls. I'd always thought Nita resembled the actress Vivica Fox. Nita was gorgeous, which was why she was never short of men's attention. It wasn't her beauty that turned men away from her, her outside just didn't match her insides.

By now most of the family had come out of the kitchen to see the happy reunion between mother and daughter. Aunt Vivica, Grams, Aunt Jo, Keva and Devin are all standing in the door of the living room. Only people missing was Chante. And Quincy, but who the fuck cared about him. I also noticed Eli wasn't here either.

After taking Nita all in, I turned my attention towards Gram's. She had the right mind to look guilty.

"Are you kidding me?" I dragged out the words to show my frustration.

Grams knew how I felt about Nita, hell everyone did. Yet, she set me up to come here for this bullshit reunion.

Grams' opened her mouth to say something, but Papa cut her off.

"It's not your grandmother's fault, Duck. I wanted you all here. It's some truths that need to be told, and I'm ready to tell it."

"What truth?"

He kept talking about truths, but I've told all the truths. Well, all that I was ever going to tell.

"Daddy?" Aunt Vivica stepped forward, both hands planted on her hips. "I know you aren't talking about what I think you're talking about."

Papa held his hands up, palms facing out. "Now, Viv…."

"No, Daddy! You promised me we could forget it. You said that if I let her keep it, we would never mention it again."

"I know, but that was before I knew it would cause problems."

"Problems for who? Her?" Aunt Vivica pointed towards me.

"Daddy I agree with Vivica. Let's not bring up the past." Nita said stepping up beside her new man.

She wrapped her arms around his and looked up at him lovingly. If I wasn't so pissed I would have laughed at the show she was putting on.

"Besides, I've been delivered of my old ways." Nita continued.

I scoffed, and Nita cut her eyes to me. The only thing that bitch knew about delivering was pizza.

"Well I agree with Mr. Jefferies." Uncle Walter said standing on the other side of me. "It's time."

Aunt Vivica stormed up to Uncle Walter and slapped him across the face so hard his head turned.

"Mama!" Devin shouted.

I gasped. I would have knocked her ass out, but luckily Uncle Walter was more of a gentlemen. He just rubbed his sore cheek and stared back at her like a scolded puppy.

"I told you your shit would come back and bite me in the ass." Aunt Vivica yelled at him.

"Vivica, that's enough." Gram's finally said stepping forward.

"Can someone please tell me what's going on?" I demanded.

We had just stepped in the house and already this shit show had stared. I felt Jackson's hand stroking my back soothingly. Thank God for his presence.

All eyes turned back to me.

"Sit down, Duck." Papa offered.

"She don't need to sit down." Aunt Vivica yelled and the arguing ensued.

Everyone was shouting to be heard and I was standing here in the middle of the floor trying to figure out why the hell I let them talk me into coming here. It was definitely too soon. I was two seconds away from grabbing my man, saying fuck it, and just leaving, until Uncle Walter's voice called out over all the noise.

"I'm your father."

The room went silent. Uncle Walter turned to me and smiled. A smile that I realized was familiar, just like a few other things. Walter was a lot lighter than me, resembling Grams color, but his smile was similar to mine. Even the few curls that surrounded his bald spot was a match to the mass of black curls that draped my shoulders. He and I weren't twins, I had too much Nita and Papa for that, but we definitely resembled.

"I been wanting to tell you that a long time, Charlice. But your grandparents thought it would be too confusing for you to grow up with an Uncle that is also your father, and I respected their opinion."

I stood in stunned silence. A flurry of emotions rushed through me. Happiness initially.

All my life I've wondered about who my father was. Many times during my childhood I wished my father would've came and taken me away from my mother. I prayed that he would stop my Uncle from hurting me and he would show me the love that I craved. The love every little girl needs from her daddy.

Sadness came next. Sadness because I finally understood why my aunt hated me. She'd had to look at me every day of my life and be reminded that my mother slept with her man. And since Chante and I were only a few months apart, it was obvious they were sleeping with him at the same time. I was also sad, because I knew that this revelation came at a cost to Devin. She had always been a daddy's girl and thought highly of her father. From the look on her face now, I knew she was heartbroken.

Thinking of Devin's ruined relationship fed into my bitterness. Bitterness because I missed out on Thirty three years of having my father in my life. Thirty three years of missed hugs and I love you's. Thirty-three years of a relationship that I needed.

That's when anger hit. The third emotion, and the one that stuck the longest. Who gave them the right to take my father away from me? Who told them that they could make decisions over my life? Maybe when I was younger, I might have been confused, but at some point I would have been old enough to understand. Hell, I had gone through more shit by the age of eleven than most people experienced in their lifetime. I would have been able to come to terms with knowing who my fucking father was.

"Charlice, do you have something to say?" Uncle Walter, or I guess I should call him my dad, asked.

He was staring at me cautiously like I might pass out. From the swooshing sound in my ears I just might. Actually, everyone was looking at me like I might pass out.

I found Nita's eyes in the crowd of faces. She had the audacity to look at me like she hadn't kept a huge secret from her only child. Like a person that didn't nearly ruin a family because she couldn't keep her fucking legs close.

"You are such bitch." I said to Nita.

The shocked look on her face didn't surprise me, she never knew how to own up to her shit.

"Your entire life has been spent fucking up everyone else's." I continued.

"Now hold up." That sweet flirty voice was gone and the real Nita was here. "Don't act like it was all my fault. I told Walter I was pregnant, and he didn't want you. Too busy running behind my bitch of a sister."

Vivica took a step towards Nita, but Uncle Kenny held her back.

"That's not true." Uncle Walter turned to me, his light brown eyes pleading for me to believe him. "I never said I didn't want you Charlice. I told your mama that I didn't want her. She wanted me to leave Vivica and be with her. I admit that I messed up by sleeping with your mama, but I was in love with Viv. Nita got mad and told the entire church on our wedding day that she was pregnant by me. That's why your grandfather banned me from coming to the house."

"Love?" Nita laughed. "How much did you love my sister when you was fucking me in your car after dropping her off? Huh, Walter? You would have been still picking me up from school if I hadn't got pregnant. You wanted me, you just didn't want a damn baby. Don't lie to Charlice now because you're trying to play the victim. Soon as Viv had your little light skinned baby, you didn't give a shit about my black ass daughter. Don't pretend like you cared about Duck."

The room grew silent again. I realized, right then that knowing my father didn't change anything. I was still the bastard unwanted child of Bernita Jefferies. My father had been seven minutes away from me all my life, and not once had he tried to reach out to me. Yes, Uncle Walter had always been nice to me. He had a smile and a hug every time he saw me, but where was he the other times. Where was he when I needed him? He could have been more involved in my life, I wouldn't have suspected anything other than he was being a good uncle. But I guess Nita was right, he already had the daughters he wanted.

"Jackson let's go." I didn't wait for him to follow me, I turned on my heels to get the hell out of that house.

I kept my secrets because I wanted to help my family and because deep down I loved them all. But this secret wasn't to help me. It wasn't in my best interest. This secret was for everyone else but me.

As soon as I got to the front door it swung open and Eli was standing on the other side. I walked right into him before I could stop myself.

"Duck, what's wrong?" My cousin immediately knew something was off with me.

I shook my head. "I have to go." My eyes were already burning from the tears that were threatening to fall.

Eli's eyes scanned my body like he was looking for physical harm.

"Ok," He said after he realized I wasn't hurt. "But I need to talk to you. It's about that Cliff guy."

I heard nothing else Eli said after ok, because walking up behind him, was my biggest fear.

My heart took off in my chest, my pulse was racing and I could feel my lungs closing up.

"Hey, Baby Girl! How you been?"

"Martin is that you!" I could hear Grams' footsteps as she came closer to the foyer.

I didn't turn around to see her because I was too afraid to take my eyes off of him.

He was still the same man I remembered from all those years. Penetrating brown eyes, light brown skin the same color as Grams'. His wide nose and thick black eye brows over sleepy looking eyes. To many woman, Uncle Martin was an attractive man, but to me, he was the boogeyman. And although it had been seventeen years since the last time he hurt me, he still had the ability to scare the hell out of me.

The entire family came out of the living room to greet the long lost son. They surrounded him in hugs and cheerful greetings. I used the distraction to slip away into the upstairs bathroom. I shut the door and flopped down on the toilet trying to fight my ragged breathing. I could barely get enough air through my lungs. The room spun and I felt close to passing out.

The knock on the door startled me.

"Hey Duck! You alright?" Eli called out from the other side of the door. "Your fiancé, the one I'm just hearing about by the way, is looking for you."

"Tell…" my voice cracked and I had to stop and start over. "Tell him I'll be out in a minute."

As I knew he would, Eli picked up on my tone. When he asked if I was alright again, the playfulness in his voice was absent.

"Please, just give me a minute." I pleaded to Eli.

He stood at the door for a few seconds before leaving. I listened as the sound of his footsteps lead him back down the stairs. I couldn't stay here. I may have been able to stay in the same room as Nita, but I couldn't stay in the same general area as Uncle Martin. However, I had to get myself under control before I could even go back down the stairs.

It felt like forever, but it was really only twenty minutes. My breathing was finally slightly manageable. I just needed to make it down the stairs long enough to walk out the door. I didn't need an excuse to leave. I was already heading out.

As soon as I opened the door he was standing there.

"You alright, Baby Girl?"

That fucking smile on his face. The same one he wore.... No! You're not that little girl any more.

I tried to walk past him and he grabbed my arm.

"Don't fucking touch me." I seethed.

Uncle Martin held his hands up in surrender, but the smirk remained.

"Why you acting like this, Baby girl. I came all this way to see you. You looking so good, you miss me?"

I was transported back in time. That fucking pet name, his voice and that grin on his face. My childhood nightmares came back to me all at once leaving me shaking and paralyzed in fear. I didn't even realize he had walked up on me until Jackson's voice spoke from the steps. From the way the bathroom was located, you had to be almost fully up the stairs in order to see it. Jackson couldn't actually see us, but I guess he heard our voices and knew we were close by.

Thank God for Jackson, he pulled me out of those horrible memories that were trying to swallow me whole. I yanked away from the hand Martin had placed on my shoulder. I didn't even realize I had allowed him to get that close to me. Never again. I rushed down the stairs pass Jackson like the pits of hell were on my heels.

"Duck, what's wrong with you?" Grams asked before I could make it to the door.

Everyone seemed to have calmed down from earlier. Papa was back in his chair. Grams and Eli were standing together whispering. Aunt Viv was on one side of the room staring daggers at Nita and her new man. Uncle Walter seemed to be consoling Devin, while Keisha, Keva and Aunt Jo stood together near the kitchen door. They all turned to look at me when I appeared.

I opened my mouth to tell Grams I was leaving, but the only sound that came out was a strangled cry.

I was in the midst of a full blown panic attack now. My lungs were constricting, the room was spinning and my heart was racing.

I could hear everyone talking around me, but it sounded like they were miles away. I knew someone was calling my name and someone was touching me, but I couldn't make out anything. It wasn't until I felt his arms wrap around me that I was able to get any semblance of control. Jackson spun me around in his arms. His hands cupped my face, while those hazel eyes flashed back and forth between my brown ones.

"Talk to me, Char. What's going on?"

I just needed to go. That's all I wanted to do. I couldn't stand breathing the same air as Uncle Martin.

"I.....I..... I." I couldn't get a reasonable sentence out.

I wasn't making any sense.

Martin walked down the stairs at that moment, that fucking grin still on his face.

"What's going on?" He asked.

The moment I heard his voice my body started to shake uncontrollable.

"Duck is having an episode."

"Is baby girl going to be alright?"

"It will pass. She use to have them when she was younger. You can go on and eat Martin. I know you had a long flight." Grams said as her hand continued to stroke my back the same way it did when I was younger.

I knew the exact moment it all clicked for Jackson. I saw the realization dawn in his eyes. I also knew that nothing I could have did would have stopped him from doing what he did next. Faster than he'd ever moved before, Jackson nudged me to my Grams arms, rushed over to Martin and nailed him in the face so hard he might have broken his jaw. The cracking sound echoed around the room.

The first blow took everyone by surprise. The second one landed Martin on his ass and had everyone running to Martin and Jackson. It took Kenny Jr, Royce, and Uncle Kenny to pull Jackson off of Martin. I'd never seen Jackson that out of control. I thought he was bad that night he slammed Miles into the wall, but he beat Martin like a demon possessed him. Once they were able to break Jackson and Martin apart, Papa stood in between them with his hands out. Aunt Vivica and Uncle Walter attended to Martin.

"What's going on?" Grams shouted.

"You need to get that crazy man out of this house?" Vivica yelled.

Everyone was yelling, either threatening Jackson or trying to figure out what would make him attack Martin.

Uncle Walter helped a bloody face Martin get to his feet. He looked bad. One eye was swollen shut and the other was blood shot. Blood ran from his nose and split lip. Aunt Vivica tried to look at his face, but he snatched away from her.

"What is wrong with him?" Martin yelled at Jackson. "He's insane! Get him out of here. He shouldn't even be allowed around, Baby girl."

Jackson broke away from the hold Kenny Jr, Royce, and Uncle Kenny had on him and charged at Martin. Martin ran behind Aunt Vivica. That was the only thing that kept Jackson back. The shouting started back. Jackson was being called a trouble maker, a racist, and a loose cannon. Someone even threatened to call the police.

"SHUT UP!" this time it was Eli's voice that cut through the room.

When I turned to Eli he was watching me in that uncomfortable way that let me know he was seeing more than what was going on in front of us.

"What's going on, Duck?" Eli demanded.

I had this sinking feeling that Eli already knew the truth, he just wanted me to admit it. I could tell by the way those light brown eyes stared back at me. I also knew that Eli was a loose cannon and that telling him the truth could set him off. If I thought Jackson was bad, Eli would be worse.

I shook my head no, ready to tell him that it was nothing. The glare in his eye cuts my lie off.

"Not this time."

He wasn't going to let me get out of this.

I looked away from Eli to find Jackson's eyes on me. It was then, as I fought to breathe, that I realized how much I loved him, and how much of an impact that he'd had on me. I also realized how strong he had made me. I had my shit together on the outside, but on the inside I was a mess before Jackson. Too afraid to admit out loud what I endured as a child, because part of me really feared that I might actually had been at fault. That maybe Nita was right and I was leading him on. I feared that my family would blame me too.

But, finding the kind of love Jackson had for me, assured me that despite the outcome of the truth, I would be ok. I knew what real love was, and because of that, I didn't need to be loved by my family. I was no longer desperate for their acceptance. I also knew that I was a child and I did nothing to encouraged him hurt me the way he did. It was not my fault.

Jackson nodded at me, giving me the encouragement I needed.

"He raped me." The words came out without any further thought.

"Who raped you?" Devin asked the question that I knew everyone was wondering.

Instead of answering her, I turned to Eli. I noticed his eyes were watering, despite the angry flames I saw dancing in them.

I continued to speak, looking only at Eli. "From the time I was six years old to the day I moved back in with Grams. The nightmares were all about him. The panic attacks, the horrible stomach pain, they were all caused by him." I turn to a wide eyed Grams. "Sorry you won't get any great-grands from me Grams. They made sure of that. Nita cleaned up after his mess every time. So, no, Grams. I don't want a relationship with her. I don't even want to be in the same room with her, and I damn sure won't pray for either of them."

It happened so fast that I barely had time to register it. Eli reached in the back of his pants, and pulled out a gun. In four steps the barrel of the gun was held directly in the middle of Martin's head. Everyone in the room screamed.

"Ellis Jr, put the gun down." Papa demanded taking a step towards Eli and Martin.

Jackson stepped in front of me, blocking me from a stray bullet or the sight I feared could come next.

Eli cocked the hammer of his gun back making a clicking sound.

"Tell me why I shouldn't put a fucking bullet in your head."

"Wait a minute! Just wait!" Uncle Martin cried out. "She's lying. Mama, you know I wouldn't do that. Tell them, Nita."

Nita's mouth dropped open, I was pretty sure to collaborate with his lie in order to save herself.

Grams held up her hand and turned to me. "I told you once before, Duck. A mother knows her children. She knows when they are hurting, when they are lying, and when they are telling the truth."

My heart dropped. She believed him. I knew there was a chance that this could be the outcome, I even prepared for it, but standing here watching her take his side breaks my heart.

Jackson wrapped his arms around me and I borrowed his

strength.

Grams turned to Uncle Martin. "The only reason I won't let Eli put that bullet in your head, is because you aren't worth him going back to jail for."

I was shocked at her words. Wait! She believed me?

"I knew Duck was going through something, but I never would have thought....." Grams paused and a sob ripped from her lips. She shook her head unable to finish her sentence. "Get him out of my house."

"Mama wait! Let me explain. She loved me. She wanted..." Before he could finish the disgusting lie he was about to tell, Eli cocked his gun back and brought it down on the side of Martin's face knocking him out cold.

"Eli, you and Kenny Jr. load him up and drop him right back off at the airport." Papa said looking down at Martin like he was trash. "That is the only bit of kindness I will ever offer him."

Kenny Jr grabbed Martin's feet and started to drag him towards the front door. When Eli went to follow, Papa held out his hand.

"You're angry, and so am I, but give me the gun, son."

Eli paused for only a second before handing the gun over to Papa. He then followed Kenny Jr back outside with Martin.

"Duck! I'm sorry you went through that." Papa said. He ran a hand under his eyes wiping away the tears that were trapped in his eyelid. "And if you are up to the legal battle, I think you should press charges."

"Hold on!" Aunt Vivica said coming towards me. "Martin isn't the only one that should go down." Vivica turned to Nita with a sneer. "You are the lowest of the low. What kind of mother would allow a man to take advantage of her daughter?"

"Oh fuck you, Vivica! You don't even like Charlice." Nita said in her defense.

Vivica looked disgusted at the accusation. "I admit that I took my anger and hurt that you and Walter caused me out on Duck." Vivica turned to me and for the first time ever her face softened toward me. "For that, Charlice, I am sorry." She looked back to Nita. "But even with all the built up hatred I had, I'd never let what he did to her go down. She is your child, how could you not care?"

"BECAUSE I NEVER WANTED HER!" Nita screamed. "She was just mama and daddy's way of punishing me for what happened.

At least I helped her get rid of her unwanted bastards."

"You took her to that woman?" Aunt Jo asked once it dawned on her. "The one you sent me to that nearly killed me? Nita, she was a drunk with a clothes hanger and rubbing alcohol."

"She did the job didn't she, Jo? You aren't out here trying to pass off some kid as Kenny's. I did Duck a favor."

"You robbed me of being a mother." I argued.

"Even better." Nita shrugged. "Trust me it's overrated."

The living room was silent. The only sound heard were the kids in the backyard playing and cars riding through the neighborhood. I think everyone was coming to the realization that there was no help for Nita. She didn't see that what she allowed to happen was a problem. In her selfish mind, I was a burden that she never wanted.

"Nita, I can't even look at you." Tears tracked down Grams' face. "I always prayed that you would grow to be more of a mother to Duck. I knew you didn't want her, but I never thought you would have allowed something like this to go on."

"So now we're pointing fingers at me, Mama? I'm not the only bad parent in this room."

"What are you talking about?" Grams shouted.

"Never mention it again." Nita said. "Isn't that what you said to me after I told you about Mr. Hurley?"

Grams stared at Nita in horror.

"Why should I have cared about what he did to her, when no one card when it happened to me."

"So you let your brother abuse your child, because mama didn't handle your situation the way you wanted her too?" Aunt Vivica asked the question in disbelief. "That's not an excuse, Nita."

"Mama didn't believe me." Nita said glaring at Grams. "I told you what that man did and you told me never to mention it again."

Grams sighed. "I told you not to mention it, because your father was going over to Mr. Hurley's house with his gun. He had planned to kill that man, and if he was going to be able to get away with it, we couldn't mention what happened to you. That is why I told you that, Nita."

The room grew silent again.

"He what?" It was obvious Nita had never been told this part before.

"I had the gun to his head the same way Eli had his pointed at

Martin. Except when I fired that first shot, the gun jammed. Your brother Ellis was with me. He told me that the gun jamming was a sign. So, I left Robert Hurley's house that day and told him that if I ever saw him again, I wouldn't care if the gun jammed a hundred times I would kill him dead."

"I didn't know that." Nita whispered.

"Good thing he didn't kill him, right?" Grams said with her eyes narrowed at Nita. "Especially since you were lying."

Nita gasped placing her hand over her mouth.

"How did you find out she lied?" Papa asked.

Grams placed a hand on her hip and stared at Papa like he should already know the answer to that question. "Same way I knew Duck wasn't. I know my kids. I knew it the moment Nita told me what happened that she was lying, I just didn't know exactly what she was lying about."

"All of it." Papa said towards Nita. "On his death bed, Robert Hurley begged me to finally hear him out and listen to the truth. He even showed me the letters you had written to him begging him to be with you." Papa narrowed his eyes at Nita. "A Forty-Seven year friendship was ruined, because he turned down your childhood crush on him. Since that day I've had nothing else to do with you Nita. I kept that secret from your mother, but I was done. I only invited you here because I wanted you to do right by Duck." Papa sighed and rubbed his head. "But some people just don't deserve second chances. I'm going to tell you the same way your mother told your brother, get out of my house and never come back."

Nita stood in the middle of the floor completely shocked, like she had the right to be.

"So you're just going to toss me out like that? Fine, I don't need any of you. The only reason I came is because mama promised me some money. Come on, Robert."

Robert looked put off. "Bernita, I think you need to find your own way back to Florida. Mr. and Mrs. Jefferies, it was nice meeting y'all. I'm just sorry it had to be on these terms."

He grabbed his matching hat off the couch and headed towards the front door. We watched him in silence as he left the house. I was shocked he stayed around that long.

"You see what you did!" Nita turned and yelled at me. "I hate you. You should have died...." The last of her words were cut off when

Aunt Vivica socked her in the mouth.

"Get out of this house, and don't you ever speak to her again." Vivica yelled.

Nita was so stunned that she stood in one place for a second holding her swelling lip.

"Get out Nita." Aunt Jo demanded, coming up to stand beside Aunt Viv.

Nita glared at me one last time before storming out of the door.

It felt like everyone took a collective breath. To me, it felt like a heavy weight had been lifted off my shoulders, but it left my body weak. I knew a break down was coming. I felt exposed and raw. My legs were seconds away from giving out. I turned into Jackson's chest and buried my face in his shirt. His familiar scent and warmth comforted me.

"Jackson, I think its best you take Duck on home. I think she's had enough for today"

"I agree, Charles." Jackson bent over and lifted me off my feet carrying me like a bride.

"You take her own to the car. Keisha, Keva, and Devin, ya'll come on in here and help me make Duck and Jackson a to-go plate." Gram's voice directed.

I never lifted my head from buried in Jackson's neck as he carried me out to his truck. He sat me in the passenger seat and buckled me in. He lifted my head with his finger to bring my eyes to his. He didn't acknowledge the tears or the lost fragile look I imagine that was looking back at him.

"I'm so fucking proud of you." He stated, then placed a kiss on my lips.

He stepped back before shutting my door. I watched him walk back up the stairs to talk to Uncle Walter, or my father—I guess. I'm not sure what I should call him now.

"Duck!" Papa appeared at the passenger window and I turned to him. His eyes were still red.

"I'm going to give you time to register everything that has happened today. I think we all need time to come to terms with it. But I want you to know, it wasn't your fault. None of it was your fault. Unfortunately you got stuck with a lot of adults that made a lot of really bad decisions. I will never be able to take away what you went through, and well, that's something I will have to deal with for the rest of my life. But that's ok, because it's nothing compared to what you've dealt with. Get some rest, Duck." He planted a kiss on my forehead and then turned away from me.

I couldn't stop the tears from falling from eyes. Jackson climbed back into the truck placing a grocery bag full of aluminum foiled cover plates between us. He placed a hand on my thigh and squeezed gently before starting the truck and pulling out of the yard.

□

TWENTY-EIGHT

I was running low on clothes at Jackson's place. I was going to stop by my house and grab a few things before heading back to his home. Jackson parked in front of the house and turned the truck off. He turned in his seat to look at me.

"Stay here. I'm going to grab you some things, and then we'll head back to the house. Are you ok?"

I shook my head no. "I think I always knew my mother hated me, but to hear her say it like that, in front of every one."

"Hey," Jackson said directing my attention towards him. "Forget her. You know what I saw today?" He didn't give me time to answer. "I saw your family come together to stand by you. I know you and your family had a rocky relationship, Char. But some of it was explained today, and I think that was a start to some changes. And even if it isn't, you got me, baby. You will always have me." He gave me that dimpled smile, and I couldn't help but to laugh. It was the first one I'd had since getting out of his truck at my grandparents' house.

Jackson leaned forward and placed a kiss on the tip of my nose, he then climbed out of the truck.

"I'll be right back."

Jackson always found ways to keep me from going back into my house. That camera he found really spooked him.

My phone started to ring in my bag the second Jackson slipped into my dark house. I reached down between my feet to fish it out.

"Hello?"

"Duck, where are you?" Eli sounded out of breath like he'd been running.

"At home. Look, Eli, let me call you--"

"Don't go in your house, Duck!" Eli shouted cutting me off.

"What, why?"

"They found his body!"

"Whose body?"

For some reason, I was getting this odd feeling in the pit of my stomach. Something was off.

"I was trying to tell you at Grams' house before shit got crazy. They found Cliff's body in Yellow River early this morning."

"What?"

"I told you something wasn't adding up. His family said they hadn't seen or heard from him in a while, right around the time the cops told you he went up north. They even filed a missing person's report on him. I knew something was off, so I had one of my guys dig a little deeper. Right before your boy Cliff went missing, a kid on the block said some guy was asking around about him. Guess who he described?"

I wasn't going to guess. I was already out of Jackson's truck making my way into my still dark house. My heart was racing because I was wondering why Jackson didn't turn the lights on. That was something Jackson always did. A little quirk of his. As soon as he walked into the house, he turned on the lights.

"DUCK!" Eli shouted getting my attention. "Are you listening?"

"I'm trying to find Jackson. He went inside the house, but he didn't turn the lights on." I knew I wasn't making sense, but my heart was beating too fast, and my head was spinning.

"Don't go in the house," Eli demanded.

I fumbled over a large object in the middle of my foyer, nearly falling to the floor. The lights cut on, and I screamed dropping my phone to the ground. Lying in a pool of blood was Jackson.

"Jackson! Baby, please wake up. Please!" I cried trying to turn him over.

"It's too late for him, Charli," the familiar voice pulled my attention away from Jackson.

Standing at the doorway leading into my living room with the gun still in his hands, was the last person I expected.

"Sean, what are you doing here?"

Sean gave me his signature smile, broadcasting his all white teeth.

"What do you mean, I'm here to help you."

"Then help me with Jackson."

The smile disappeared from his face.

"WHY THE FUCK ARE YOU WORRIED ABOUT HIM!" Sean pushed off the wall he was leaning on and pointed his gun directly at Jackson's head.

I slowly climbed to my feet. My heart was racing, but I was still thinking clear. It looked like Jackson had a gunshot wound in his chest when I flipped him over, but I could feel his chest rise and fall with his breathing. He was barely alive, but if Sean realized it, he may put another bullet in Jackson ending his life. Even still, if I didn't get Jackson help soon, the amount of blood he was losing will kill him. I just needed to get to my secret stash of guns. I still had a few hidden around the house. My job was to keep Sean calm so he didn't shoot Jackson again.

"Ok! Ok! You're right. I shouldn't be worried about him."

Sean shook his head at me. "You're damn right. He doesn't love you like I love you, Charli. No one will ever love you like I love you. You can't see that?" He stepped in front of me, and for the first time, I could see that glimmer of madness dancing in his eyes. Something I had missed all these years.

"What about your girlfriend? What about Rochelle?"

Sean laughed and took my hand escorting me towards the stairs.

"You don't have to worry about her anymore, Charli. Rochelle knew that I would never let you go, but she purposefully got pregnant." He shook his head. "She thought I was going to let a baby get between get between what you and I have. She was always just a decoy. I only used her to make you jealous." He chuckled. "You used to get so jealous of Rochelle." He held my hand all the way up the stairs towards my bedroom.

I allowed him to lead me, because most of my guns were in my room.

"Plus, having girlfriends use to also helped me keep up your time frame. I knew you had your limits. You only liked to be in relationships with short term goals. That's why I always went back to my girlfriends. I knew if I didn't have a girlfriend to go back to, you never would have let me keep coming back."

He was right about that. That was part of the thrill when it came to Sean. He would always call it off with me about every four to five months, right when it was starting to feel too clingy. It's like he knew every time just when to go back to his girlfriend.

"What about the wedding ring?" I asked.

There was no way he dropped that amount of money for someone he didn't want to be with.

He smiled over at me. "It's yours. You picked out your own wedding band." He laughed like it was the funniest fucking thing ever. "Don't worry, I'll give it to you tonight. Tonight we don't have to worry about anyone else."

This truly bothered me. It's the second time he mentioned not having to worry about Rochelle.

"Sean, what happened to Rochelle?"

Sean shook his head as he turned to me. "I told her to get rid of the baby, but she wouldn't. So I got rid of both of them. I did it for you." He says the last part when the tears started to fall down my eyes.

I never really liked Rochelle, but I damn sure didn't want this to happen to her. I wouldn't wish this on my enemies. I mourned for the beautiful girl and her unborn child.

Sean stopped in front of my bedroom door and directed me to walk in in front of him. The moment I walked into my room I paused.

This muthafucker had clearly been staying in my house. His clothes were thrown across my room haphazardly. There was takeout food and boxes thrown everywhere and on the television, was a recorded video of Sean and I having sex.

"This is my favorite part," he said, stepping up behind me, wrapping his hands around my waist.

At that moment in the video, I opened my eyes and looked right at the camera while biting my lip. It was so natural, it was almost like I knew the camera was there.

"It always amazed me at how perfect we were together," he whispered in my ear. "You never knew the cameras were there, but you would always make eye contact with it. It's like you could feel my eyes on you."

Just then, Charli on the screen came on a load moan that made the real Charli want to vomit. I turned away from the screen. Seeing this monster use my body was too much. I noticed that lying on the bed was one of my Louis Vutton suitcases.

"Why are my bags packed?"

Sean pulled me to the side of the bed where my suitcase was sitting open. My clothes were crammed inside.

"We're going to go away for a little while." Sean explained. "I took care of Cliff for you, baby. I made sure he would never hurt you again. That muthafucker didn't get to live after he put his hands on you. It took me longer than I wanted to track him down. He figured out I was after him. And he had the audacity to try to call you and ask for help."

My stomach sinks. That day he showed up at my house, he was asking me for help to save his life. He even called me a few times after and I ignored him because I assumed he was the problem. Oh my god!

Sean placed a kiss on the side of my neck.

I dug my nails into the palm of my hand to keep from flinching away from him. Now was not the time to make him angry. I was closer to one of guns, but I still didn't have it in my hand.

"They found his body today." He went on to say as his gun-free hand slipped under my shirt to stroke my skin. "I got desperate when I was searching for him, so I asked around to find him. Now there might be someone that can point me out as a suspect. And if they start looking they may find Rochelle's body. Which means you and I have to go away for a while. But I don't want you to worry. I have it all taken care of."

The fact that he had a gun in one hand and telling me how he murdered two people—one being his pregnant girlfriend—but still had his hard dick pressed into my ass told me he was fucking insane.

"It's been so long since I've been inside your pussy, Charli," Sean moaned as he continued to ground his dick into my ass and squeezed my breast through my bra.

I took a deep breath, I was a fucking fighter. Even when I was a little girl I proved that I was a fighter. No matter the situation I would never lie down and take shit. I made the promise to myself at sixteen that no other man would make me afraid, well that goes for this one. I didn't have time to be weak and scared. I needed to handle Sean so that I could save Jackson.

Jackson!

Just thinking about him lying down stairs, possible bleeding to death gave me all the added strength I needed.

I spun around in Sean's arms. That practiced smile I'd perfected over the years in place. I placed my palm on his chest.

"You need me, Sean?"

He gave me that smile that I once thought was charming, but now I saw the evil in it.

"I need you so fucking bad." He gripped my hair with the gun hand yanking my head back to devour my lips with a kiss.

I didn't focus on how different his kisses were compared to Jackson's. I didn't even think about how much his tongue in my mouth made me want to puke. I just kept myself focused on the end goal. Get him to the bed, get my gun, and save Jackson.

I pulled away from his kiss. "Lie down, Sean."

Sean knocked the suitcases and the boxes of leftover pizza onto the floor and then climbed on the bed, the gun still in his hand. He placed his hands behind his head.

I steadied myself as I kicked off my shoes and climbed up on top of him. I straddled his waist.

"This is how we were supposed to be, Charli. I know you got distracted by that dude," Sean said as he peered up at me with half-mast eyes. "You thought I was really going to get married and leave you. That's why you wanted to be with him. Right?"

I placed my finger to his lips. I was barely keeping myself together, I didn't want to hear the sound of his fucked up voice.

"Stop talking." I purred as I placed kisses from his jaw to his neck, the entire time, my hand was down between the headboard and my bed searching for my gun.

As soon as my hand wrapped around the gun, I sprung up and aimed it at his head. I popped the safety off and cocked the gun.

Sean only smiled at me.

"You won't really kill me, Charli. You're angry because I lied to you, but you won't kill me."

Clearly, he didn't know me.

I pulled the trigger to my gun, and it clicked. I pulled it a few more times and the same thing happened.

Sean laughed, and that's when I remembered showing him all the hidden guns in my house for him to check. I didn't see his hand move from under his head, but I felt his fist strike the side of my face. I fell from on top of him hitting the bed before bouncing to the floor. It felt like my entire face was on fire.

"HOW COULD YOU!" he yelled down at me.

He grabbed me by my hair and pulled me to my feet.

"After everything I've done for you. That asshole down stairs would have never killed for you. I did!"

Sean slammed me face down onto the bed before picking up my suit case and tossing my belongings back into it

"All I've tried to do is love you, Charlice. And this is how you treat me. From the first day I paid Chris to grab your ass, I've been watching out for you."

He truly was insane. He paid that kid in high school to grab my ass, and he still beat him unconscious, and here I thought our first meeting was by chance, but he'd plotted and orchestrated that.

"You put me through hell these last seven months. Breaking into my house, trashing the place, sending those pictures to my family, and killing Lady. That isn't love."

"I DID IT FOR US!" he shouted down at me sprawled across the bed.

He ran the gun hand over his head. "I tried to get you to see that you were making a mistake with him. I never bothered the others. Just a little warning to the ones that you seemed to favor. I allowed you to have your fun because I knew they meant nothing to you, sharing you was just a part of our relationship. But that guy..." Sean pointed at the door indicating Jackson down stairs. "You took him out on dates, let him spend the night, and even called him your fucking boyfriend to my face. Everything I did, I did because you were making a mistake. I even tried to give you a break. I left you alone for a while, thinking you would grow tired of him. But then you accepted his marriage proposal." Sean shook his head. "I can never let you marry anyone else, now that I know that you're ready to get married, we can do it before we leave."

"I'm not marrying you. You have to understand that, Sean."

Sean started hitting the side of his head like he was battling voices. He was pacing my bedroom floor and I slowly climbed to my feet, despite the headache pounding in my head.

"Sean," I called his name and his brown confused eyes turned to me. "You need help. And if you let me call an ambulance for Jackson, I'll go with you to get help. It will be the both of us working through our issues together."

I was lying. If he let me call Jackson some help I wasn't going anywhere with him. However, I would say anything he wanted to hear to get out of this.

"Do you love me, Charli?"

His question was simple. And maybe if he had of asked me this about an hour ago before this shit went down I would answered honestly yes. I did love Sean, but only as a friend. At the time that was a big deal for me. Before Jackson, even loving a friend was a huge step.

However, none of that matters, because when I answered his question now, I have to answer it with a lie.

"Yeah, I love you."

Sean's smile wasn't as bright as it usually was. This smile was sad and defeated.

"I've been watching you since I was fourteen-years-old. You were sitting across from me at a basketball game. That was an entire year before I came to your rescue in that hallway. From the moment I saw you in that crowded gym, I knew you were the woman for me. I used to follow you home and stare at your bedroom window. You and I were made for each other, Charli." He raised his gun and pointed it at me. "So if I can't have you, no one can."

"Sean!" I screamed his name when the gun went off.

Wet blood coated my skin. My body must had been numb because I didn't feel any pain.

"Char! Char! Baby, open your eyes."

I must be dead and finally meeting Jackson in heaven. I opened my eyes and came face to face with his hazel eyes. He was a little paler than usual, but he was alive. I looked down to the ground and found Sean's crumpled body. Blood poured from a hole in the back of his head.

A gun was in Jackson's hand. Jackson stammered a little and I remembered that I wasn't the one with a bullet in my shoulder. I helped him sit down on the side of my bed.

"Are you ok?"

Jackson grunted. "Not exactly feeling like a million bucks, but I'm not dead."

I closed my eyes and allowed a relieved laugh to fall from my lips. In the distance I could hear the sound of sirens.

"I love you," I said as I wrapped my arms around his middle and buried my face in his shoulder. "I'm sorry you got shot."

Jackson let off a short chuckle. "I'm starting to rethink this whole relationship thing. I should have known you were trouble when you rammed into the back of my car."

I lifted my head and laughed. I could now hear the police outside my front door. I even heard Eli screaming my name while the cops tried to keep him out the house.

"Well, it's too late now. You're stuck with me," I teased, showing off my ring finger. I would do anything to keep his mind off the pain he must be feeling.

Jackson turned to me, eyes shining with what I assumed was exhaustion and love.

"From now until forever." He declared before placing a kiss on my lips.

The cops swarmed the room shining their lights into our eyes. The rest of the night was filled with police statements, doctor visits, and crazy family members surrounding us. But as long as Jackson was still here with me, I didn't care.

☐

EPILOGUE

THREE YEARS LATER

"Oooh, baby, this pussy is so good."

I opened my mouth to tell him I already knew, but my second orgasm hit me, and my body locked up. I moaned so loud and long I sounded like a zombie coming back to life.

Nobody could eat pussy like my husband.

Jackson chuckled between my legs. "I thought I told you to be quiet, you're going to wake the boys."

Right on time. I heard the sound of tiny footsteps at my door and then a soft knock.

Jackson groaned before climbing up my body, placing wet kisses on my stomach then collapsing down beside me.

"Your sons are little cock blockers." Jackson huffed.

I laughed beside him.

Six months after Jackson asked me to marry him, we said I do in front of our family. It was a small outside ceremony where we said our vows looking out at the Atlanta skyline at dusk. My cousins and Jackson's sister were my bridesmaids and my Papa walked me down the aisle. Jackson's parents and Memaw were also in attendance. His brother and sister-in-law weren't, and their absence wasn't missed.

Since the blow up at my grandparents' house, things had certainly changed. The atmosphere in the family was better, no more secrets haunted us.

Uncle Walter was allowed to family dinners again. He and I had a slow growing relationship. We were starting to get to know each other on a deeper level. It wasn't that father and daughter bond like he had with Devin and Chante, but I was ok with that. I was glad I knew who my father was, but in reality, I didn't really miss out on anything, because I was raised by a strong man that I loved as if he were my father.

Aunt Vivica and I have definitely come a long way. She had turned into my self-assigned stand in mother. She called me a hundred times a day just to check on me and always offered advice on marriage and parenting. I imagined that if I'd had a real relationship with Nita that it would had been like that. Aunt Vivica and I still had our moments where we bumped heads, but neither of us felt the cold finger of hate towards the other.

Keisha had her baby, and it wasn't Royce's. Thank God! She admitted to fooling around with Roy a few times, but she said they'd never slept together because she didn't want to hurt Keva. However, the accusation was enough to spook her, and she and Royce stopped messing around. Not long after the new baby came along, Keisha found a new man. He was a truck driver that doted on her and the kids. He looked at her like Jackson looked at me. They'd been together for a year and a half now. That's a record for her.

Keva had a remarkable change. Once her secret came out, she realized that she had been stressing herself all these years by hiding it and even overcompensating with the bible thumping. She admitted that she was in love with Tracey, but that she didn't want to be with her. Apparently, Tracey had been a onetime fling. She and Royce agreed to do marriage counseling, and it helped. Keva was a lot more fun. She still loved her God, but she didn't remind you of it every five seconds.

Unfortunately, Chante's battle was not an easy one. For months, she kept her distance from the family. Despite everyone trying to reach out to her. Her addiction got so bad, Quincy threatened to leave her and take their son with him. The family called me in as a last resort. I took off the kids' gloves everyone was trying to handle her with. I showed up at her house one day ready for battle. We screamed, we accused, we fought like cats and dogs, and then she cried. In the end, she agreed to go to rehab. It wasn't an easy journey, but she pulled through. She has been sober ever sense.

Devin probably had the biggest success story so far. She never did go back to Miles, and after finishing cosmetology school, she realized that she actually enjoyed college and decided to enroll in a four-year business program. Now my cousin was working at a salon part time, raising her kids full time, and a full time college student. I couldn't be any prouder of her. I knew she was capable of great things.

No one had heard from Nita since the day she walked out of my grandparents' house. Grams wasn't playing when she said she was done with her. I wasn't too worried about her though, Nita would always find some unsuspecting man to take care of her.

As for Martin, he did make it back to California, but only to find his wife and kids had left him. Apparently he was a shitty husband and father. Go figure. I opted out of pressing charges. I knew I probably should have sought justice, but I was tired of letting that past dwell over me. After finally telling my family, I released it. I didn't want to relive it for a jury. One day, Martin would get his, his battle with karma wasn't over.

I opened the door to my bedroom and our one year old son, Jackson Junior, or JJ as we call him, walked into the room followed by King, our puppy German Shepherd.

"Mama, duise," he ordered.

I scooped him up and placed a kiss on his forehead. After Jackson and I married, we had planned to live a childless life. That was until my cousins came to me with an offer I couldn't refuse. Apparently, Devin, Keva, and Keisha had done research on my condition and found out that even though I couldn't carry a baby, I could still have one by surrogacy. All three cousins volunteered their wombs to carry Jackson and my baby. However, it was Devin that won the coin toss. She gave me the greatest gift I could have asked for--the chance to be a mother to my boys.

JJ had his father's eyes and nose, but he had my smile. Ellison, named after my favorite cousin, had my brown eyes, but still favored his twin.

"Mommy will get you juice," I told him. "Where is your brother?"

"The good child is probably still sleep," Jackson said as he got up from the bed. "El knows that Daddy is trying to get some."

I hit Jackson in the arm when he walked up to me to plant a kiss on my cheek.

"Come on, JJ, Daddy will get you juice and breakfast." Jackson took his son out my arms and kissed his head full of dark brown curls.

"I'll grab El and join you," I said, following them out of the room.

After the situation with Sean, I never went back to my house. I sold it and moved in with Jackson. However, once we found out that the procedure worked and Devin was pregnant, we sold Jackson's house and bought a bigger one. The new home was a mix of both our style. Clean and modern for me, with a little rustic for him, and most importantly, it didn't remind me of the ordeal I went through with Sean. The case was pretty open and shut. Even if they didn't have all the evidence of him living in my house, shooting me, and the kid that pointed out Sean as a suspect in Cliff's death, what they found in his house sealed the deal. Hours of video footage of me in my house. A room dedicated to me with pictures and stolen objects from me. And the most damning thing, the body of Rochelle locked in his deep freezer. That still brought tears to my eyes.

El was sitting up in his crib when I walked in. We had long ago stopped trying to figure out how JJ broke out of his crib. The moment El saw me, he reached up for me.

"Hey, my man," I said, lifting him from the bed.

I changed his diaper and headed down the stairs. My phone chimed in my pocket, and I pulled it out to see who it could be.

KEISHA: It's positive.

I smiled at the notification. Jackson had been dying to have another baby. For most people, it would be too soon, the twins were only one. However, I still had three viable eggs left, and I wasn't getting any younger. I couldn't wait to be a mother again.

ME: Thank you! I'm going to announce it at Sunday dinner tomorrow.

KEISHA: Good! Bring some cheesecake, y'all baby greedy.

I rolled my eyes at that last part.

I walked into the kitchen to find my husband at the stove and my son in his high chair at the island, I placed El beside his brother in his high chair and went to join Jackson.

"Need some help?" I said, wrapping my arms around his waist from behind.

"Nope, I got this. You relax and get ready because I'm going to finish what I started this morning."

I laughed and kissed his shoulder. I loved this man. Who would have ever thought that a girl as scarred as me, could find love?

TIYA RAYNE

ABOUT TIYA RAYNE

Tiya Rayne is an avid reader and writer. She has an unhealthy relationship with coffee and is known to hide numerous bags of jelly beans around the house.

When she is not reading or writing—which is rare—she's trying to master this thing called parenting. She is married to her high school sweetheart and they live in Arkansas with their three— subjectively wonderful—children.

Although very pretty, Tiya Rayne is not her real name. It is a pen name that she chose to represent the two most important girls in her life, her daughters. She does, however, write Young Adult books under her real name, K.C. Connor.

Despite what you choose to call her, she still enjoys reading feedback on her work. So, please leave a review or send her an email.

But wait, there's more! Stay updated with the author's latest releases, learn more about her, and have some fun by subscribing to her newsletter at www.tiyarayne.com

And if you enjoy social media, follow her on facebook : https://m.facebook.com/AuthorTiyaRayne/ or send an email to kcconnorbooks@hotmail.com.

Other Books By Tiya Rayne
(Fantasy)
Lilly I
Lilly II
Lilly III
Lilly IV
Lilly V
(Contemporary Romance)
First Love
(Sci-fi)
Alpha

And, if you enjoy YA paranormal, check out the Keeper Series by KC Connor.
The Return
The Dagger
The Originals (Coming Soon)